"C'N YOU SHOW BELLE HOW TO DANCE?" SARAH ASKED. "I WAS TRYIN' TO, BUT I CAN'T."

Rand sighed, "Little Bit—"

"Please!"

"All right, but just for a minute." He reached down, grabbing Sarah's hands. "Step up on my shoes—"

The little girl tugged away. "Not *me*," she said impatiently. "I know how. Show Belle."

"Rand," Belle said, "this isn't—"

He glanced at Sarah. "We need some music," he said.

"I c'n sing," she said brightly. She stepped back, plopped down on an upended bushel, and began clapping her hands. "All right. Ready, set, go!"

"All right," he whispered, his voice hoarse and raw. "Ready? One-two-three, one-two-three . . ."

Belle couldn't look at him. Every inch of her was aware of him as he led her into the first steps of the dance. She felt the brush of her skirts against his legs, the press of his hips against hers.

Rand's hand tightened around hers. "You're shaking," he said in a low voice.

"I'm not." Belle swallowed.

"Yes, you are."

Belle tried to draw away, but he held her fast. She felt overwhelmed and strange . . . it was as if all the dreams she'd had in her life had come down to this moment. . . .

HIGH PRAISE FOR

MEGAN CHANCE

*"Extraordinary!"**

*"Bravo!"**

AND HER DEBUT NOVEL

A CANDLE IN THE DARK

"It takes extraordinary skill to unveil these characters in a manner that makes them not only admirable but respectable, attractive, and appealing—everything two romance characters must be. Cain is sexy and desirable. Ana is brave and tender at the same time. Their story is sprinkled with brilliant sparkles of history, adventure, and sensuality . . . truly touching. In short *A CANDLE IN THE DARK* is a romance in every sense of the word. Bravo, Ms. Chance, for bringing us what we want in such an unusual and distinctive way." —*Affaire de Coeur**

"Megan Chance's debut novel is an emotionally intense, absorbing story that immediately grips the reader. The passion and power of the story lie in her ability to craft believable, vulnerable characters whose pain and rebirth will capture your attention. The unusual backdrop lends an exotic aura to a wonderful read." —*Romantic Times*

"This is truly *A CANDLE IN THE DARK*! Bittersweet love come to two cruelly hurt people under the pen of a very compassionate author. Tugging relentlessly at the emotions of the reader, Ms. Chance proves her skills are more than adequate to move a reader to tears."

—*Heartland Critiques*

"*A CANDLE IN THE DARK* is as heartwarming as it is unconventional. It is my kind of book, and I loved it."

—Karen Robards

Also by Megan Chance

A CANDLE IN THE DARK

MEGAN CHANCE

A Dell Book

Published by
Dell Publishing
a division of
Bantam Doubleday Dell Publishing Group, Inc.
1540 Broadway
New York, New York 10036

ISBN: 0-440-21488-2

Printed in the United States of America

Published simultaneously in Canada

October 1994

10 9 8 7 6 5 4 3 2 1

OPM

To my grandparents, Kenneth and Ernestine Solt,
for giving me a history.
To my mother, Anita, for making it come alive,
And to my sister, Amy, for giving me Belle—
and putting up with me after.

Suddenly, as rare things will, it vanished.

—Robert Browning,
"One Last Word"

Chapter 1

LANCASTER, OHIO
EARLY OCTOBER 1855

The house was just as she remembered it. Yellow walls, pristine white pillars and trim, windows that rippled with reflections. The edges—the wrap-around porch, the steps swept clean of falling leaves, the gables of the kitchen—peeked out from between the circle of oaks surrounding it, protecting it, making it look safe and secure and well kept. It was the perfect house for a farmer, clean and serene. The kind of house that appeared to be a perfect home.

But Isabelle Sault knew better.

She stepped away from the buckboard and pushed back the brim of the floppy man's hat she wore. The muggy afternoon breeze touched her face, along with the smell of dirt and manure and corn. Familiar scents, all of them, bringing back a score of memories she thought she'd forgotten, wished she'd forgotten.

Home. She made a soft sound of disgust at the thought. Someone's home, not hers. Not anymore and not for a very long time. Now the house seemed almost malevolent in its serenity, the distorted windows hiding secrets, the new paint covering cracks that burrowed deep into the foundation.

Belle took a deep breath and started across the yard. The nervous knot that had settled in her stomach during the long train ride from Cincinnati climbed into her throat. She tried to ignore it as she hurried up the stairs. "Well, ready or not, here I come," she whispered under her breath, raising her hand to rap sharply on the door. The rapid patter of feet from inside stopped her, and Belle surged back just as the door flew open. A sleek streak of gray shot out, flying past her legs. She turned just in time for another, larger blur to slam into her.

The impact sent Belle stumbling. It was a child, she realized at the same moment she grasped the little girl's shoulders, catching herself before she hit the railing. "Whoa there," she said. "Slow down before you hurt somebody."

The little girl pulled away, rushing to the railing and leaning over it. "Scout!" she called. "Scout! Come on back here. I love ya, Scout!" Then, without pausing, she turned to look at Belle, her brown eyes wide beneath a shock of bright blond hair. "Did you see my cat go by here?"

Blond hair. Blond hair and a face that was hauntingly familiar.

Sarah.

Oh, good God . . . Belle froze, unable to tear her eyes away from the little girl. She had the look of Rand all over her. The shape of the face, the chin, the nose—all familiar and yet not familiar. The face of a stranger. Belle realized suddenly that she hadn't seen Sarah since the child was born, and she had held tightly to her first image, to the vision of a small, mewling face and closed eyes. But the little girl who stood before her now, warm and vibrant and alive, was no longer that little newborn baby, no longer just a vague and formless imagining.

No longer anyone she knew at all.

She felt an instant, overwhelming flash of fear, a stab of regret that made her throat tighten and her mouth go suddenly dry.

The child stepped back from the railing. "Who're you?"

Belle swallowed. It was too late to back away now, and she didn't want to anyway. "I—uh—you must be Sarah."

Sarah frowned, looking instantly wary. "D'you know my grandma?"

"Uh—yeah. Yeah, I do."

"You come to visit her?"

"Well, I don't know." Belle hesitated. "Is she—"

"Who's that you're talking to, Sarah?" The voice came from the hallway inside the house, disembodied, sharp, and too loud. It silenced both of them. Belle's head snapped up. She felt the nerves again, fluttering in her stomach. Sarah spun on her heel and ran back into the house, leaving the door wide open behind her as she hurried down the hall.

"Grandma, there's someone here!"

Belle stiffened. She glanced over her shoulder, back to the road. The wagon was still waiting there. That simple reassurance gave her strength. She turned back to face the door again just as she heard the sharp rap of heels on the hardwood floor. *Clack, clack, clack.* Precise, efficient. The sound brought back a rash of memories.

"Dorothy, is that you? I'm sorry, I didn't hear—" Lillian Sault reached the doorway and stopped short. She made a small, garbled sound in her throat, put her hand to her heart as if the motion steadied her. Shock and an emotion Belle couldn't name flashed over her face—affection maybe, or relief, or maybe it was only surprise. But it was soon gone, replaced by a chill so strong, Belle shivered in the warm air.

"Good Lord. Isabelle." Lillian's voice was as icy as her face.

Belle didn't move. "Hey, Mama."

"I don't believe it. Oh, my Lord." Her mother stepped forward—just as she was supposed to—and held out her hand in a reluctant greeting.

Belle stepped back. "Well, it's really me. And I don't guess you should be takin' the Lord's name in vain that way, Mama. God knows you never let me get away with it."

Lillian's hand dropped to her side. She glanced over her shoulder to where Sarah stood in the shadows of the hallway. "Sarah, go on and find your papa, please. Tell him we've a visitor." Then, when Sarah didn't move, "Sarah, go."

The tone of her voice, unbending and stern, stabbed into Belle, along with the sound of Sarah's pattering footsteps as she ran through the house to the back door. Belle remembered that voice—oh, how she remembered it. And hated it. She felt as if she'd stepped into a memory—she heard the same punishing voice, saw the same elegant, snow-queen control that matched Lillian's icy blond looks. Her mother's hair was perfectly smoothed back, there wasn't a wrinkle on the clean white apron or a line on her perfect skin.

Belle immediately felt ten years old again.

She straightened her shoulders in silent rebellion, smiling slightly. "Well, it's good to see some things haven't changed anyway."

Lillian turned to face her. "Why are you here?"

Belle snorted. "You must not be goin' to church lately, Mama. I never did care much for preachin', but even I seem to remember somethin' 'bout a fatted calf."

Lillian's expression tightened. "Don't you sass me, Isabelle. I asked you a question."

"What if I said I just came back to pay you a little visit? Just to say hey?"

Lillian's expression didn't change. "Did you?"

Belle laughed shortly. "No. Believe me, there's only one thing on this earth that could bring me back here."

"And that is?"

"Give her back to me," Belle said without hesitation. "Give her back and I'll turn around and leave quietly, just like you want me to. No one will ever know I was here."

"Give her back?" Lillian's voice rose. "Give her back?"

Belle leaned forward, raised her own voice. "That's right, Mama. Give her back. After all, Rand *stole* her—"

"Quiet." Lillian said sharply. She glanced at the driver in the road, then at the Alspaughs' house just beyond the narrow field. She backed away from the door, slipping into the shadows of the hallway. "Come inside."

"Where the neighbors can't hear." The words weren't said, but Belle heard them loud and clear. Appearances were everything to her mother. It made Belle want to stay right there on the porch, to yell the reasons she'd returned so loudly, they'd be able to hear her clear into Canal Winchester.

But she didn't. She followed Lillian into the house, wincing at the harsh sound of her mother's heels on the worn floorboards. The hallway was cool and dark after the bright mugginess of outside, and it smelled of bees-wax and pears and sugar.

It was familiar—too much so. Like the outside of the house, the inside hadn't changed. The parlor door was still tightly closed; the same framed sketches hung on the roughly plastered walls, faded from the years they'd hung there. Even the rust-colored mums in the vase by the door looked the same.

Belle felt a needling sense of foreboding, and she ignored it, following the trailing fragrance of her mother's lavender water to the bright kitchen. Where the hall had been cool, the kitchen was sweltering, and the air from the open back door did little to ease it. Lillian was already inside, standing beside the huge black Oberlin stove, and Belle saw immediately where the aroma of pears had come from. Jars of the newly canned fruit filled the kitchen table; steam still lingered near the ceiling.

Lillian crossed her arms over her chest. Her face was overly calm and composed. "So, you came here to take her back, just like that." She shook her head as if to say, *"Shame on you."* "She's been here for two years, Isabelle. Don't you think you're a little late?"

Two years. Belle's breath caught in her throat. Two years. She hadn't known—hadn't realized it had been so long. One year maybe—she would have believed one year. After all, it had taken nearly that long for her to discover Rand had taken Sarah from the couple Belle had left her with in Cincinnati, and several months more before she could save enough money to make the trip from New York City. But Bill Mason had led her to believe Sarah had only been gone a short time, and Belle realized suddenly that he had only told her what she wanted to hear. *Damn him. Two years.*

But Lillian was watching her carefully, avidly, and so Belle struggled to maintain her own composure, to bury her surprise. "Don't fight me on this, Mama, I'm warnin' you."

"Your threats don't worry me. We agreed—"

The commotion at the back door interrupted Lillian. Belle followed her mother's gaze to the man coming up the stairs, the man who saw her suddenly and jerked to a halt. His form filled the doorway, just a silhouette against the sun, shadowed so that Belle couldn't see his features, couldn't see anything to identify him at all. But she knew who he was, knew his stance and the way he raked his hand through his tawny hair.

"Jesus. Belle."

She stared at him in shock. The sight of him rocked her for a moment, and memories came rushing back. Memories that made her feel cold and helpless. Memories that filled her with anger. She struggled to control it.

"One and the same," she said, deliberately flippant. "Hey, Rand."

He stepped into the room and immediately seemed to overpower it. She had forgotten how tall he was, how small and insignificant his broad shoulders and narrow hips made her feel. Had forgotten the square, chiseled look of his features and that damned implacable set of his full mouth.

But she hadn't forgotten the way his hazel eyes turned cloudy and narrow when he was angry, and she refused to let him intimidate her. *She* was the one who had been wronged, dammit. She met his gaze full on.

"What the hell are you doing here?" he asked.

Belle gave him an insolent smile. "Well, now. This is a reg'lar welcomin' party. I—" She stopped, seeing Sarah push past Rand into the kitchen.

"See, Papa? Here she is, just like I tole you."

"I see, Sarah." Rand didn't take his gaze from Belle. "Now, go on out front and see if you can't find Scout."

"I can't. She went under the porch."

"Then see if you can make her come out."

"But, Papa, I *can't—*"

"Sarah." Rand and Lillian spoke at the same time, a unanimous authority that made Belle stiffen mutinously. But Sarah only frowned for a moment before she sighed and turned around again, stomping out of the kitchen.

Within seconds the sound of light, childish humming floated back to them from outside.

Rand was looking at Belle as if he'd already forgotten about Sarah. "I can't believe you'd dare to come back here."

"Oh, no?" she asked. "Then you shouldn't have taken my daughter."

That surprised him, she noted with satisfaction. She saw confusion flit across his face, the quick glance to Lillian before he caught himself and looked back at Belle. "So that's it."

"Yes, Rand, 'that's it.' I've come to take her back."

"No."

Belle raised a brow. "No? Wait a minute—I guess you didn't understand. I'm not askin' your permission, Rand. I'm tellin' you."

"And you think I'm going to let you just walk out of here with her? Jesus, Belle, she's been here two years! Where the hell were you? Playing cards? Drinking? You sure as hell weren't with Sarah. What'd you do, forget about her?"

His words hit her like a blow—worse, because she hadn't expected it. Sharp and stunningly hard, they made her feel lacking somehow, brought back the guilt and regret she'd kept buried since she'd walked away from the Masons' boardinghouse six years ago, alone and scared. It filled her throat until she felt as if she couldn't breathe, couldn't think.

She looked away, trying not to wince, fighting to gain hold of her emotions. But still her voice sounded thin and forced. "Go ahead and think what you want."

"You're damn right I'll think what I want. Hell, you left her with strangers—"

"Randall." Lillian's quiet voice cut through his anger.

"Isabelle, perhaps there's a better time to talk about this—"

"There's no better time." Rand bit off the words, crossed his arms over his chest, and stared at Belle. "Get off my land."

She shrugged deliberately, fixed him with an innocent smile. "I'll be happy to. I'll just get Sarah and—"

"Take her and I'll kill you."

"Randall," Lillian said.

Belle laughed—a quick sound, devoid of humor. "I'm just terrified, Rand. Quick, tell me how you'll do it: pistols at dawn? Or will you take after me with Henry's shotgun? If you're lucky, you can shoot me in the back before I get too far."

"Isabelle." Lillian's voice was stern. "Please."

"Please what, Mama? Please go? Please don't cause trouble?" Belle shook her head. "Too late for that, I'm afraid." She smiled. "What you've got is trouble starin' you right in the face. Unless you let me walk out of here with her."

"And take her where?" Rand demanded. "Back to that hellhole I found her in? Or have you even thought that far?"

"Anywhere but here."

"She's happy here." He motioned to the back door, where the sounds of Sarah calling for the cat could be heard in the distance. "Goddammit, she's happy."

Belle choked a sound of disbelief. "I remember what bein' happy here meant, Rand. I'm surprised you don't. Look at you—stuck here on this farm, workin' in the fields. Why, you remind me of your daddy." She raised a brow. "Are you happy, Rand? Is this where you want to be?"

"Yes," he said stiffly.

"I don't believe you."

He tensed. "Get out." Rand's voice was white-hot anger, fiercely controlled, so softly spoken, she wasn't sure she'd heard it.

"I do think it's best if you leave for now, Isabelle," Lillian said with a quick warning glance at Rand. Her voice was calm. "We need some time to think. We'll talk about this later."

Belle laughed softly, skeptically. "How much later, Mama? Next week? Next year?"

Rand stepped forward. "Damn you, Belle. Get out."

She stood her ground. "Go to hell."

"Enough." Lillian stepped between them. Her lips were tightly pursed in displeasure. "Please, Isabelle. This is ridiculous. Once we all calm down, we can talk about this like civilized people."

Ever the diplomat, Belle thought sarcastically, but she looked away from Rand and retreated like the obedient child she had never been. Though she hated to admit it, her mother was right. Belle felt shaky, barely on the edge of control. She had not handled this well. It would be better to leave, to come back when she'd had time to think, to plan.

"All right," she said. She lifted her chin, yanked the brim of her hat back down, and gave them both a defiant smile. "I'm leavin'. But I won't leave this town without her. I never meant for her to be with either of you."

Rand only stared at her, his fist clenching sporadically at his side.

She walked across the kitchen, past Rand, who moved aside as if she were poison and paused at the back door. "See you later."

Then, stinging from the echo of their silence, she walked across the yard to the waiting wagon.

Chapter 2

Rand stood there, unable to move or think or even breathe. The kitchen seemed suddenly stifling; he could still smell the remnants of her scent—harsh soap and dust—floating in the air, suffocating him, mixing with the sweet, spicy aroma of pears.

She was back. Sweet Jesus, she was back.

Lillian took a deep breath; her slender fingers smoothed imaginary wrinkles in her apron. "Well, that was—"

He spun angrily on his heel, knocking his shoulder on the doorframe in his haste to leave before she could finish her sentence. Whatever his stepmother wanted to say, he couldn't stand to hear it. He heard her startled gasp and then "Rand! Randall, please!" as he ran across the yard and into the fields, but he didn't slow his step. He searched for Sarah and saw her playing peacefully at the side of the house. He felt a moment's relief, but it wasn't enough to calm him, and he didn't stop, just rushed past her into the fields. He needed to get back to the corn, to be in the center of the fields, where the heavy smell and the clacking rustle of the stalks in the breeze were all around him; where he could think about nothing but the corn and when it should be cut or when the next thunderstorm would hit.

God, yes, to think of nothing but those routine, day-to-day things. The things he'd hated thinking about until just this moment, the things he'd spent his whole life avoiding.

The drying corn sawed at his face and hands as he pushed through it; he felt the spidery tassels in his face and the corn dust shiver into his collar. The warm, milky smell was all around him, soothing him.

"Are you happy? Is this where you want to be?" Belle's words mocked him, tormented him, just as she must have known they would.

"Are you happy?"

Rand pushed his way through the heavy stalks, moving single-mindedly until he was in the center of the corn, until the house was gone, until there was nothing but brown leaves and dusty tassels.

Are you happy?

"Dammit!" He shoved his hands against his ears, trying to block the sound. "Dammit, why the hell did you come back?" But his words taunted him and did nothing to banish the image of her face. He almost laughed at the irony of it. There had been a time when he would have given his life to see her again, and now all he wanted was to exile her forever.

Why had she come back? Why now?

The question was meaningless; Rand already knew the answer. It made sense that she had returned now. Perfect sense, because he had finally managed to stop thinking about her, to stop feeling guilty about the past, to concentrate on anger instead. He laughed softly, bitterly. He'd been feeling contented, or if not that, then almost complacent. He should have known she'd show up now.

Someplace in the back of his mind he *had* expected it, he knew. The truth was, he'd waited for it, in some strange way even wanted it. But not this minute. Not today.

He thought of her standing in the kitchen. She was still small, still delicate. He thought of her slender neck and the fine bones of her face, dwarfed by the huge man's hat, the thick hair that hung in a heavy braid down the middle of her back—a hundred colors of gold all twisted together. All so much the same, just as he remembered.

Rand stared at the tall stalks without really seeing them. He'd told himself that the next time he saw her—if he ever did—he'd be in control. Cool, calm, self-possessed. He told himself she didn't matter, had never mattered, that he'd outgrown the madness that had overtaken him when she was fifteen and he was . . . old enough to know better.

But then he'd walked into that kitchen and seen her standing there, facing him with that familiar, defiant lift of her chin. *Hey, Rand.* He heard her greeting again in his mind, challenging, wary. She'd lowered her voice to say his name, had almost whispered it, and it felt as if he'd been hit in the stomach—as if, for some strange reason, he hadn't expected her to remember it. And with her voice had come his guilt, barreling back as if it had never truly gone.

What the hell was he going to do now?

"Papa?" Sarah's voice came through the corn, cutting through his thoughts. "Papa?"

Rand shoved a hand through his hair. Sarah. The thought of his daughter brought instant, blessed relief. If anything good had come from that brief, turbulent madness six years ago, Sarah was it. She had kept him sane the last two years—since the detective he'd hired had found her in a boardinghouse in Cincinnati, abandoned by her mother at birth. If Belle thought she was going to take his daughter from him again . . .

She wouldn't, he told himself fiercely. She would have to kill him first.

"Papa!"

Rand took a deep breath. "Stay where you are, Sarah. I'll be right there." He knew exactly where she'd be—perched on a weed-covered stump at the edge of the field, hugging her knees tightly to her chest, waiting for him the way she waited for him every night.

He made his way back through the corn. She was there. Her golden hair shone in the sunlight, and the smile she gave him through the dirt on her face was brighter than any summer day.

"Papa," she said, climbing to her feet and flinging herself into his arms, "you ain't goin' to work no more today, are you?"

He buried his nose in her hair. It smelled of dust and sun and little girl. "No, Little Bit, I'm done."

"Good." She leaned back to look at him, her eyes serious. "Who was that lady who was here?"

He hesitated, not knowing what to tell her. Neither he nor Lillian had ever told Sarah about her mother, and to his knowledge she'd never asked a single question. It had seemed best, when they'd first brought her back—a wary and frightened three-year-old—to wait until she was older, and now he supposed they'd just fallen into the habit. God knew he and Lillian never discussed Belle, at least they hadn't for a very long time.

There might be no need to tell her now. The thought jabbed into his brain, hopefully, fleetingly. It was possible that Belle would just go away. Not likely, but certainly possible. His lips tightened. God knew he'd do everything in his power to make sure she did.

"Who is she?" he repeated. "She's Grandma's daughter. Your . . . aunt. Belle."

"You didn't seem very happy to see her."

He smiled grimly. "No, I guess not. I was surprised, that's all."

"Oh." Sarah looked pensive, and Rand realized with a pang that the expression was a copy of Belle's.

He tightened his arms around her. "How's Grandma doing, anyway? Is she finished with the pears?"

Sarah leaned her head back, ignoring his question, staring up at the sky. "Belle could play with me since Janey's dead."

He closed his eyes. "I thought you told me Janey might be better tomorrow," he said wearily.

"Well, I lost her *head,* Papa. She won't get better."

"Maybe you can find it and Grandma can sew it back on."

"Maybe." She stared at him thoughtfully, her large brown eyes focused on his. "Belle's comin' back, ain't she, Papa?" Then, when he was silent: "Ain't she?"

He wanted to say no, she wasn't. But the words wouldn't come, not to his mind or to his throat, and Rand just stared helplessly at his daughter, unable to think of a single thing to say.

She watched him for a moment, waiting, and then she nodded and squeezed his neck with her plump little arms. "Grandma's makin' pancakes for supper," she said. "With jam. I like that best."

Rand felt the desperation inside him unwind, drifting away, and he gave Sarah a squeeze of relief and joy and fear. "Me, too, Little Bit," he said softly, walking back to the house. "Me too."

From the hotel window Belle watched the street below. She saw the men striding down the planked sidewalk, rounding the corner on their way to the Black Horse Tavern, heard the sound of the Cincinnati, Wilmington, and Zanesville train moving out at the edge of town. From here she could just see the curve of the canal as it followed the bend of the Hocking River. There was a packet boat moving on it now, slowly, leisurely, the people sitting on the upper deck tiny little shadows against the sunset. For a moment she wished she were one of them, wished she had nothing to wait for, nothing to keep her from leaving this town—leaving Ohio.

Though she'd done that already, and she knew that running away didn't change things—not really. Memories had a way of festering in a person's mind, always there, never really disappearing. Oh, there were times when they seemed to be gone, when the day stretched before her open and inviting, full of promise, without regret. But those days were few and far between.

Belle sighed, leaning her forehead against the cool glass, closing her eyes. New York was already like that now—just a memory, a place she didn't have to go back to. She thought of her tiny room in the boardinghouse, the narrow bed and the plain, unadorned walls. Thought of the fact that when she'd left, she never intended to return, had packed everything she owned into the small carpetbag sitting on the bed.

"And take her where? Or have you even thought that far?"

No, she hadn't thought. Hadn't thought of anything but the need to get to Lancaster, hadn't even bothered to expect anything on her return.

Belle squeezed her eyes more tightly shut. What an idiot she'd been. Had she really thought she could just walk into the house and demand they give Sarah back? Had she really believed it would be so easy? She should have realized the moment Bill Mason told her Rand had come for Sarah that Rand wasn't waiting for her to come back, didn't want her to.

Not that she ever really believed he did. Bitterly she remembered the last day she'd seen him. It was six years ago, and there had been no fond farewell then, no gentle words. He'd avoided her the two weeks before he was to return to his uncle's in Cleveland to help with the grain shipment, and she knew by the way he averted his gaze whenever she was near that he couldn't stand to look at her. But until that last day she hadn't really believed he hated her. She didn't believe it until he'd already left, until she realized he'd waited for her to go visiting before he sneaked away to board the train.

He'd gone without leaving a single message. Not even a good-bye.

She'd known then that her memory of his cold gaze two weeks before was no illusion, that it had truly been loathing on his face as he watched her flee the barn that clear November night, her hands shaking as she tried frantically to straighten her skirts, still feeling the ache of his body between her legs and the roughness of his touch. He hated her—the certainty of it had stunned her, the white-hot pain of his rejection left her feeling lost and confused. She had not known where to turn or what to do.

He'd been gone a week when she discovered she was pregnant. He was still in Cleveland when, in desperation, she finally turned to her mother for help.

"He will not marry you, and you will not have this baby here, do you understand me? What were you thinking, Isabelle? You're a disgrace to this family, a disgrace, do you understand me?"

"But when Rand comes back—"

"Rand? Do you expect him to defend you after what

you've done? I want you out of this house, Isabelle. My God, looking at you makes me sick. . . .

The voice from the past came swirling back to her, even though she'd spent the last six years trying to forget it. But her mother's words didn't hurt anymore, not really. Her mother had never taken her side in anything, and the pain of that was long gone and mostly forgotten—as was the pain she'd felt over Rand's betrayal.

Once, she'd thought she could bear anything as long as he was her friend.

Now she knew she could bear anything without him.

Belle backed away from the glass, straightening her shoulders. The lesson had been hard learned, but she wouldn't forget it. And she wouldn't leave Sarah with the two people who had taught her so well. She had left her daughter in the Masons' care deliberately. They had been her first friends in Cincinnati, had taken her in when she was lost and afraid and destitute. They had given her a job in their boardinghouse and cared for her through the first hard months of her pregnancy, and when Belle decided to go to New York to make a living for herself and her daughter, she had trusted Gem and Bill to care for Sarah—to give the child laughter and love until Belle could return.

But before today that resolution had little impact on Belle's life. Before today Sarah had barely been a person in her mind. Her daughter had been more of an elusive thought, a vague memory of pain and sorrow, of regret. Certainly not a chubby little girl with her father's face and hair and deliberate manner.

Now Sarah was real, and Belle had seen something of herself in her daughter. Not just the long blond hair, but something else, something in the little girl's eyes, in the resentment that had crossed Sarah's face when she stomped out of the kitchen. That was the legacy Belle had given her daughter, and she knew the misery that legacy would cause Sarah, what it was like growing up in that house, smothered by Lillian's rules. For a child with any longing for freedom at all, it was pure hell. Sarah would never be happy here. Safe, maybe—too safe—but never happy.

Belle had no choice but to take her away.

She sank onto the bed, feeling the creak of the bedframe ropes clear up into her spine. There was only one small problem. She didn't have time to wait them out, to somehow convince Rand she should have Sarah. Belle glanced at the small leather bag on the scarred table. She had money for only one or two days. It wasn't enough, especially since she had to decide where to go from here. She couldn't return to Cincinnati. It would be the first place Rand would look, and there was nothing there for her anyway. Gem had died, and Bill . . . Bill was so drunk with grief, he hardly knew the days were passing.

Belle felt a swift surge of anger at the thought, a quick resentment that the man she'd trusted had shuffled Sarah off to his sister, who hadn't known to contact Belle until long after Rand had taken Sarah away. Belle wasn't sure she could ever forgive Bill for that. And she knew she never wanted to see Cincinnati again.

No, she would somehow have to find the money to get herself and Sarah someplace else. Maybe back to New York. She didn't want to return, but she had a few friends there, and she could find a place for the two of them to stay—at least for a while—until she could find something else. Belle bit her lip. There was no other choice really. She couldn't leave Sarah behind, and she sure as hell couldn't stay.

Or could she?

Belle frowned as the idea took hold. Why not move

in? Just until she had the money to leave. Only a few days. She wouldn't be leaving Sarah alone with them then; she could keep a watchful eye,. make sure her daughter was all right. *Why not?*

She was no longer a child. She'd learned not to care about Lillian or Rand. She could survive living with them now; the last six years had made her strong. They could no longer hurt her. The only problem was how to do it. She couldn't simply walk in and announce she was staying.

No, moving in had to be by invitation, and that would be a hell of a long time coming. Rand had inherited the farm when his father died, but Lillian still obviously ruled it. And Lillian—Belle nearly choked on the thought—Lillian would never ask for a daughter who only caused trouble, a daughter who would destroy the untarnished appearances she worked so hard to maintain.

Appearances. Belle laughed softly to herself. There was a time when she hated that word. Hell, she still did. Appearances had run her mother's life—and hers—since before she was born. Appearances were what made Belle leave Lancaster, what had sent her running—

What were going to help her stay now.

Belle remembered how Lillian had told her to come in from the porch yesterday, away from the prying eyes of the neighbors. God knew, if there was one thing Lillian couldn't stand, it was looking bad to her friends.

And turning a long-lost daughter away—no matter what kind of daughter—would certainly look bad.

Very, very bad.

A small smile crossed Belle's face. It was Saturday night. Tomorrow was Sunday, and Sunday meant church. Her mother would be sitting in the front row, head held high, radiating goodness and purity so bright, it would be painful to watch. And if her very contrite, very downtrodden daughter were to ask to move back home—in front of four or five very curious neighbors—then what answer could a devout woman make—except yes?

Belle took a deep breath. It would work. It had to.

The thought brought a surge of relief, a quiet contentment that surprised Belle, and she pushed it away, determined not to look at it too closely.

Because in spite of everything, in spite of Rand and her mother, there was something that drew Belle back here, and she knew it. Because for the last six years she had walked down the muddy streets of New York, past the taverns and the businesses, had dodged pickpockets and grasping hands and smelled the rotting, salty scent of the sea and the smoke in the air—and had thought of cornfields and rivers, of canals running straight and even through the rolling hills and the smell of ripe tomatoes and musty barnyards.

She had missed Lancaster.

It frightened her how much.

Chapter 3

"Hold still, Little Bit," Rand cautioned, pausing as Sarah wiggled on the edge of the table.

"I am sittin' still." She moved again, sending bits of blond hair sifting to the floor.

Rand glanced down at his feet. Hair sprinkled his shoes, lay in soft, scattered piles on the worn boards of the kitchen floor. He sighed.

"Don't stop! Why're you stoppin'?" She twisted back to look up at him, frowning fiercely. "Papa!"

"All right, all right." Carefully Rand brought the rusted scissors closer, snipping off the strands around her ears, trying the best he could to trim it. Lillian should be the one doing this, he thought, glancing at his stepmother. She sat quietly by the still-warm stove, flipping through the "Ladies' Department" pages of *The Ohio Cultivator* in the dim lamplight, seemingly ignoring both of them, though he knew she heard every word. He looked back at the floor, at his daughter's shorn braids lying there, still plaited because he'd cut them off without bothering to loosen them. They looked strange, disconcerting somehow, but not as disconcerting as Sarah's newly shortened tresses. Her hair still looked a bit ragged, but he was afraid to take any more off. Lillian would have done this better. Too bad Sarah had asked—insisted—that he do it.

Rand stepped back, critically examining his handiwork. "All right, Sarah," he said, putting the scissors on the table. "You're all done."

She looked at him with wide brown eyes, put a tentative hand to her head. "I think I still feel a braid there."

He smiled and shook his head. "Look down at the floor. How many do you see lying there?"

"Two."

"That's right. How many were on your head?"

"Two." The word was drawn out, hesitantly, thoughtfully, as if she wasn't sure whether to believe him or not. "But I think you should do it some more, Papa. It doesn't feel right."

"It feels fine." He reached for the towel he'd put around her neck and whisked it away, shaking the tiny clippings of hair to the floor. Then he lifted her down from the table. She barely spared him a glance. Instead she raced across the kitchen floor to Lillian.

"How's it look, Grandma?"

Lillian glanced up from the journal. She frowned, weaving her fingers through Sarah's short locks. "Don't you think it's a bit short, Rand?"

He shrugged. "That's how she wanted it."

"Well, then." Lillian smiled and sat back. "You look pretty as a picture, Sarah. Be careful, now. You've got hair all over your shoulders."

Sarah stepped away. "Where's Janey?"

"Upstairs, I think." Lillian picked up the farming journal again.

"I wish she had a head so Papa could cut her hair too."

Rand reached for the broom in the corner. "I think your grandma could cut Janey's hair better."

"I'm gonna go get her." Without waiting for either of them to answer, Sarah rushed out of the room. In moments Rand heard her footsteps on the stairs. He finished sweeping up the hair and put the broom away, pausing at the small window overlooking the backyard.

It was a beautiful night. The sky was deep blue, the trees black shadows against it, their limbs raggedly dressed with leaves that fluttered loosely, ready to fall. There were no stars; the same clouds that had kept the day muggy were hiding the moon. It meant there would probably be no frost tonight either, and the thought disappointed him. He was ready for autumn. Ready for the trees to be bare and the cold nights and colder mornings. Ready for the thick hoarfrost crunching beneath his feet, coating the corn. It was harder to work in the autumn, harder to face the cold mornings, but he loved it anyway.

Even though the season held all his worst memories.

He turned away from the window. "Looks like there won't be a frost tonight," he said, moving to the stove and pouring himself a cup of coffee.

Lillian glanced up. "I've still got potatoes to get up."

"Well, you'll have time." He took a sip of the steaming brew, grimacing at the strong, bitter taste. "The apples look good."

"Yes. We're lucky. Dorothy's trees look terrible this year." She flipped pages. "I think I'll wait until after the fair to pick."

"Hmmm." He pulled out a chair. It groaned as he dragged it across the floor and sank into it. The coffee cup in his hand clanked on the table, spilling a little pool of the hot liquid onto the wood. He looked at it idly and then glanced back to Lillian, who was still immersed in the journal.

But she only looked as if she were concentrating on it, he realized. And her chair was moving quickly, erratically back and forth, not with her usual slow and gentle motion.

She was restless, he thought. Like he was. Restless and jumpy and irritable. And it was all because of one person—the one person he and Lillian had been careful not to mention all day.

Belle.

He suddenly felt warm. Rand shoved his hand through his hair and pulled at the collar of his shirt. He grabbed at the coffee, bringing the cup so roughly to his mouth, he scalded his lips.

"Damn!" He slammed the cup on the table again. Coffee splashed out, burning his skin, and Rand jerked away, swearing beneath his breath.

Lillian looked up, raised a slender blond brow. "Randall?"

"I'm fine." He bit off the words.

"I see. Good thing you weren't that fine when you were holding those scissors."

He tensed instantly at the slight reprimand. They were both edgy, and her chastising only made him want to blurt out the words he'd been struggling to keep at bay. He felt he might explode if he didn't.

Rand clenched his jaw, vowed to keep quiet. There was no point in mentioning it, in making them both upset. And, too, he was afraid to say the words, afraid that voicing his worries might somehow make them real. But before he knew it, the words on the tip of his tongue slipped out anyway. "She'll be back, you know she will."

Lillian sighed. "Of course." No *"who are you talking about,"* or *"what did you say?"* Belle was there in the room with them even though she'd been gone for an entire day. "She's always been willful."

"Willful." Rand laughed shortly. "That's diplomatic."

"What would you have me say?" Lillian was achingly calm as she rose from the rocker and put aside the periodical. She went to the stove as if she had a purpose, as if there was something for her to do, but she just stood there, her callused fingers playing over the jars of pears still resting on the sideboard, her hand casting shadows over the glass glinting in the lamplight. She didn't look at him. "I didn't expect to see her again."

There was something in her voice, something he didn't recognize, but it didn't sound like the sorrow or distress he expected. It was more like—fear. Rand frowned. "Neither did I."

"What will you do?"

He took a deep breath, buried his face in his hands. He had no idea what to do. The last hours it was all he'd thought about, even through the distraction of dinner and cutting Sarah's hair. Belle never left his mind, as much as he tried to force her out. Jesus, he wished he could just tell her to stay away and trust her to do it, wished he could put physical space between them—so much of it, and so hard to cross, that she wouldn't even attempt getting near him or Sarah. God, how he wished.

But he couldn't do those things, and he knew it.

"I don't know," he said wearily, looking up. Lillian was watching him impassively, and he wondered what she was thinking. "I can tell her to get off the farm, but I don't guess that will work for long."

"No." The word came out on a whoosh of breath. Lillian picked up the coffeepot, made to pour herself a cup, and then set the heavy tin pot back on the stove without taking any. "Belle does what she wants."

The fear was in her voice again. It surprised him. Not because she struggled to hide it but because it was there at all. He tried to remember if he'd heard it from her before, but he couldn't. They'd made it a point never to talk about Belle. He'd assumed it was because Lillian knew how much the subject pained him.

But now he wondered if she had other reasons as well, reasons that had nothing to do with him.

He had never bothered to wonder how Lillian felt after Belle left. The truth was he'd been too twisted up by his own emotions to care. Now when he thought about that time, his memories were clouded by fear and guilt. He could no longer see it clearly, and there were days when he wondered if he ever had. In his memories Lillian was only a formless blur. He remembered coming home from Cleveland and her telling him Belle was gone, remembered her saying Belle was pregnant but that was all. If she had been angry or condemning then, he had forgotten. He'd never even had a hint that she might be afraid.

Now Rand thought about asking her about it, but he thought better of it. The two of them had a courteous, careful relationship. He'd been almost grown—nearly eighteen—when she married his father, and Lillian had never been a mother to him. But after Henry died, she just kept on taking care of the farmhouse—and Rand—as if nothing had changed.

And he liked it that way, liked the way the days had led one into the other, always the same, sunrise to sunset; requiring no thought, nothing more than daily routines that only changed with the seasons.

Damn Belle for coming back, for trying to change things. Damn her for making him have to decide on a course of action when all he really wanted to do was go on, day after day, without having to think or act or do anything more than grow corn and oats and hogs.

Rand closed his eyes, feeling anger well up inside him,

struggling to force it away. From upstairs came the sound of footsteps. Rand glanced at the ceiling. "She'll try to take Sarah. We'll have to watch her," he said finally, slowly. "Every moment."

"You think watching her will be enough?"

"There's no other choice," he said, hearing the faint edge of desperation in his voice. "What else can we do? We can't—"

The sound of Sarah's footsteps pounding down the stairs stopped him, and Rand swiveled in his chair, looking toward the doorway to see his daughter burst into the kitchen, clutching Janey, the headless doll. She skidded to a stop just in front of him, and it was as if she brought sunshine into the room.

"I'm gonna be a monster now," she declared, shaking back her head and baring her teeth. "An' everyone has to do what I say, or I will—eat them."

"You will, huh?" He smiled. "Well, I'll show you what we do to monsters here—" and before she could move, Rand lunged forward, grabbing her and pulling her to him, burying his face in her neck and feeling her warm, wiggly vibrance clear into his bones.

Sarah giggled in his arms, a pure, happy sound that made her whole body squirm. "Papa!" she said. "You're s'posed to be scared of me!"

"Oh, I am scared." He pulled away, making a face. "See? I'm shaking."

Sarah roared, curling her fingers in pretend claws and launching herself forward to bite his neck. "I've got you forever!" she declared. "You can't escape!"

He threw a glance at Lillian over Sarah's head, saw her watching them with a small, satisfied smile, and Rand closed his eyes.

"Papa!" Sarah protested. "You're s'posed to be screamin'. I've got you!"

"You sure do, Little Bit," he said slowly, feeling desperation and fear and longing sink inside him. He buried his face in her hair, held her tight. "You've got me."

Chapter 4

Organ music was swelling from the open doors of the Salem Church by the time Rand finally maneuvered the buckboard into the yard. They were late. The morning had been filled with little frustrations —not the least of which was Sarah's sulking about her new haircut—and he was exhausted. Too exhausted even to look up when Lillian grabbed her woolen shawl and climbed from the seat. She gripped the splintery gray wagonside and leaned over Sarah, who was a ball of blue gingham in the corner. Her voice held the sharp edge of impatience. "Sarah, come along, now, you'll miss Sunday school."

"I don't wanna go. I look like a boy."

"I've had about enough of this, young lady." Lillian's voice brittled with exasperation. "Come along."

"No." Sarah stamped her foot against the floor. The wagon shook. "I look like a boy!"

His daughter's voice shrieked in his ears, making Rand's head pound, and he looked up wearily. "No, you don't, Sarah. Do as your grandma says. Please."

Sarah didn't budge. Her sunbonnet was hanging uselessly around her neck, her fingers clenched Janey. Her face was set in a look he knew well—too well. She was prepared to sit there all morning.

Not today, he prayed silently, uselessly. *Please, God, not today.*

Rand rubbed his eyes. The prayer didn't help, just as he'd known it wouldn't. Sarah's expression didn't change. Damn, he was too tired to deal with this today. He tried to ignore the pain in his head as he climbed down from the seat and went to her. "Come on, Little Bit," he cajoled impatiently. "You're the one who wanted your braids cut off. You liked it last night. Remember?"

Her lower lip protruded farther. "I thought it would come back. You said it would."

"It will," he said wearily. "It just takes awhile to grow."

"I want it back now!"

"Sarah—"

Rand silenced Lillian with a look and turned back to his daughter. He held out his hand. "Come on."

Sarah threw him a tentative glance, and then she shook her head. "I don't want to."

Christ, what he wouldn't give for a few hours of sleep. For a moment Rand toyed with the idea of climbing back in the wagon and going home, but a quick glance at Lillian put an end to that idea. She and Sarah were in a test of wills—again. His stepmother was prepared to stand there until dark if she had to. Once again she was expecting him to be on her side.

And once again he was somewhere in the middle.

Rand sighed. "You look just fine, Sarah," he said, forcing a weak smile. "No one's going to make fun of you. Why, with that new dress, you're the prettiest girl here."

She looked at him doubtfully. The organ music grew louder, there was a commotion on the steps behind him, and Rand turned to see the Sunday-school students gathering beneath the huge maple tree to take their lessons in the warm morning air.

"Look, you see? They're already starting. Why don't you go on over and say hello?"

She tried not to look over, though he could tell she wanted to. "No."

Rand looked over his shoulder. "I guess you don't want to see Mary Helen, then, do you? Or Lizzy—why, it looks like she's brought her doll too."

Sarah's pout disappeared. She got to her knees, hesitating as she looked at the crowd of children. "Where?"

"Maybe it's even a new doll," he said as casually as he could. "I can't tell from here—"

"All right." She stood up. "I'll go see 'em for just a minute."

Rand lifted her out of the wagon, careful not to meet his stepmother's chastising gaze as he set Sarah on her feet and watched her run off to join the other children.

"You spoil her, Rand," Lillian said as they started across the lawn. "You need to tell her what to do, not cajole her. If you don't watch it—"

"Don't say it." He held up a warning hand.

Lillian frowned. "We should talk about this, Randall. She has too much of Belle in her as it is."

"Don't say her name to me today. I don't want to hear it. We can talk about this tomorrow." *Or the next day, or the day after that. Or never.* He pushed back his broad-brimmed hat, already feeling sweat gather on his forehead. "It's Sunday, she won't be coming around. Let's not ruin the day."

It was the only good thing about this morning, the one thing he counted on. The entire goddamned night he laid awake in bed, staring at the planked ceiling and torturing himself by wondering when she was coming back. And the one thing—the only thing—that had comforted him was the knowledge that today was Sunday. Belle hadn't been in a church since she was old enough to say no, and he doubted that aversion to religion had gone away. At least he hoped it hadn't.

It was possibly the only time in his life he actually *wanted* to go to church.

They approached the steps of the small brick building just as the congregation burst into hymn. The singing streamed from the doors to float on the air, and Lillian quickened her step. "Good heavens," she murmured. "We're already late."

"No one will even notice," he reassured her in a low voice as they went through the doors and into the tiny vestibule. The chorus was painfully loud, the voices only increased the hammering in his head, and he swept off his hat and ran a hand through his hair, wishing he could turn around and head back home. But it was too late now. They were here. They paused at the entryway, and his gaze ran over the congregation, searching for an empty space in the pews. He'd just have to make sure they went directly home afterward. No going to dinner at someone's house, no visiting—

He stopped short.

She was here.

She was here, in church, and she was dressed all in yellow, with an old straw hat perched on her braided blond hair. She was standing alone at the end of one pew, turned toward the aisle, and she held a hymnal in her hand. But it was closed, and she wasn't singing.

She caught sight of him, and her head jerked up as if she were waiting for him. And then she smiled—a defiant, challenging, "try to do something about it" smile that sent a familiar ache deep into his stomach. An ache followed by anger so intense that for a moment he couldn't breathe.

The music stopped. The hymn was over. He heard the thud of closing hymnbooks, the rustle of clothing as people turned to stare.

"Rand." Lillian's voice was low and urgent in his ear, her face flushed. "Rand, for heaven's sake, let's sit down."

He barely heard her. Anger made him hot and stiff, and he struggled to control it. He felt Lillian's fingers on his elbow. Mechanically he walked with her to the nearest pew and slid onto the smooth wooden seat. He took the Bible she placed into his hands and let it fall open. Belle wasn't looking at them any longer. She had taken her seat with the others. But he knew people were looking at her—and him. He heard the whispers, quiet little daggers piercing his skin, and the warm air suddenly seemed muggy and suffocating. He felt dizzy with the pain in his temples.

"Welcome, neighbors." Reverend Snopes walked to the pulpit, his dark robes billowing around his corpulent knees. "Please open to Luke ten-thirty, and let us begin . . ."

What the hell was she doing here? It was *Sunday,* for Christ's sake.

" 'A certain man went down from Jerusalem to Jericho, and fell among thieves . . .' "

She wouldn't even go to church for funerals, much less a Sunday service.

" '. . . stripped him of his raiment, and wounded him, and departed, leaving him half dead . . .' "

Rand felt as if the world had turned upside down. He was more stunned by this than by her unexpected visit the day before yesterday, because this was more puzzling, more unexpected. He stared at her, seeing every detail: the way the rapid fanning of the woman beside her stirred the tendrils of hair escaping from her braid, the way her shoulders shifted beneath the yellow muslin delaine, and he had the sudden urge to yank her outside and demand to know why the hell she had come to church this morning.

Then he felt Lillian's hand on his wrist. Her fingers tightened on his skin, both a warning and a comfort, and Rand forced himself to take a deep breath, to close his eyes for a moment. Gradually the pain in his head receded slightly; the preacher's words became a meaningless murmur in the back of his mind. He knew what he would see if he opened his eyes—Lillian's tight expression, the curious glances of their neighbors—and so he kept them closed. He knew it all, had lived it all before. God, he'd thought—he'd hoped—he would never have to bear it again, but here it was, and incredibly it felt just the same. Six years later, and it felt just the same.

Belle's sudden disappearance had spawned a hundred different stories, enough to fuel months of gossip. Even now sometimes in a bar or at a social, he heard low voices speculating about what had happened to Belle Sault, heard the half-admiring, half-disapproving "She was a character, all right," and saw the slow shaking of heads. As though there'd been a goddamned tragedy, he thought angrily.

Rand swallowed, trying to calm himself, to banish the guilt washing over him in heady, nauseating waves. No one knew the truth anyway. It was just another example of how skillfully Lillian had smoothed over the whole thing. He couldn't remember now the story she'd told—something about Belle living with a cousin in Philadelphia, maybe—but whatever it was, Lillian had done her best to create a seamless fiction.

Now he felt his stepmother's tension in the grip of her fingers, knew she was trying to think of how to explain the sudden reappearance of her daughter, and he wondered, a little meanly, what palatable lie she would come up with. Perhaps some tale that Belle had been held captive by Indians in the West, or maybe a story about how Belle had lost her memory. He could hear his stepmother's smiling words now: *"We thought she was lost, but then—oh, it was such a miracle—she regained her memory and came back to us!"*

The image nearly brought a sarcastic smile, and Rand forced it away, chastening himself mentally. He owed Lillian too much to be disrespectful—even in his mind. Without her he wouldn't even know he had a child, much less have Sarah with him. If nothing else, Lillian had been there for him the last six years. Without her he never would have survived.

Rand squeezed his eyes shut, blocking from sight the yellow dress a few rows in front of him. Yes, he had Lillian to thank for Sarah, if nothing else, and because of that he would go along with the story she invented. For her sake he would pretend. For her sake he would help however he could.

Whatever it meant.

By the time Reverend Snopes wound through an hour and a half of Bible thumping, delivered the community bulletin board, and read the sick list, Belle was bored stiff. The reverend was still as dull as ever. He should be thanking God she had arrived, she thought irreverently, because at least while she was here, the congregation had a reason to stay awake.

It was the only joke she could bring herself to make. The gossipy whispers were all around her. It was all she could do to hold her head up and pretend to listen to the preacher. She heard bits and pieces, words said just loudly enough for her to hear, hastily muttered questions. "Where has she been?" "—she was in Cleveland last," "stepbrother's death—scandal—" "I heard she was a—well, you *know.*"

She tried to close her ears, not to hear, but it was impossible. She told herself she should be used to it. They had always talked about her. Even when she lived here, she knew the things they said about her. She was too wild, too strange, too everything. It had always been like that.

Though until today it had never been mean. It was a shock to hear what they'd been saying, the lies that had been passed as truth. Suddenly in their minds she was little better than a whore.

She laughed shortly, softly. Well, maybe they'd stone her when she walked out. God knew it wouldn't be the first time someone had wanted to punish her for her sins. They could all just stand in line.

"God bless you, my friends. Keep God in your hearts this week, and I will see you next Sunday." Reverend Snopes spread his hands to encompass the entire congregation, his sleeves flapping like the wings of a fat raven. On cue, the crowd rose, the organ swelled.

Belle inhaled deeply. It was time to put her plan in action. *"Keep God in your hearts,"* the reverend had said. She hoped the crowd here remembered it.

Pasting a smile on her face, she rose and turned to face the aisle, searching for Rand and her mother.

The congregation filed by.

Not one good Christian spoke to her.

But she heard their talk, their hateful gossip, as they moved past, and she met their curious looks. Belle felt her face redden, and she raised her chin, fighting to keep her expression even. Their lack of charity surprised her, even though she knew it shouldn't. After all, she was the first to say what hypocrites churchgoing people were. Still . . .

It didn't matter. She was here only for one reason, and it wasn't to hear the sermon or make friends with the neighbors.

Then she saw Rand and Lillian hurrying out the front door, and she forgot all about gossip and godliness. Belle pushed into the crowd, ignoring the shocked gasps as she made her way up the aisle toward the back of the church. By the time she got to the front porch, groups of people were already gathered on the knoll, and she spotted Lillian among them. Rand had disappeared, and Belle felt a quick surge of relief. She only wanted to deal with one of them at a time, and Lillian was more than enough.

She took a deep breath, running down the steps and hurrying through the grass. She slowed just before she reached her mother, pushing back loose tendrils of hair and trying to look as composed as possible.

"Why, hello there, Mama," she said, smiling the broadest smile she could muster. "Miz Dumont, Miz Miller, how nice to see you both again."

The talk died. An uncomfortable silence swept the group. Ernestine Dumont and Stella Miller stared at her as if she'd just risen from the dead.

Lillian swept into action, just as Belle knew she would, but her mother's expression was stiff, her smile frozen in place. She clutched the folds of her black silk dress convulsively. "Hello, Belle. I didn't expect to see you at church today."

"Well now, I couldn't stay away." Belle smiled brightly at the two women standing beside her mother. "It's been so long since I saw everyone, I just had to pay a visit."

"It has been a long time," Ernestine Dumont's blue

eyes sparkled with malice. "What has it been? Five years? Six?"

"Six years," Belle said. She looked at her mother. "Wouldn't you say so, Mama?"

Stella Miller broke in before Lillian could answer. "You never told us Belle was comin' in, Lillian," she said, her tone faintly accusing. "Why, it's such a surprise."

"For me too," Lillian said hastily. "I didn't know myself until yesterday."

"I wanted it to be a surprise," Belle said. "Mama had just been naggin' me for months to come on home, but you know how it is."

Stella and Ernestine murmured their assent.

"But I finally managed to get away—and here I am."

"Get away?" Ernestine said sharply. "From what, dear? We haven't heard from you in so long—we were concerned you might have fallen into trouble."

Lillian broke in before Belle could answer. "It hasn't been that long, Teen, really. Why, it's not as if we haven't kept in touch."

"Oh?" Stella frowned. "Lily, you never mentioned—"

"Well, of course we did," Belle lied. "I'm surprised you thought otherwise. What kind of a daughter would I be if I didn't write my mama once in a while?"

Both women looked discomfited. Lillian reddened.

"I've had several letters," she said. "Belle wrote me from—"

"New York," Belle supplied.

"Yes." Lillian's glance was begrudgingly grateful. "From New York."

Stella Miller looked thoughtful as she fanned herself with a small, gloved hand. "New York City? Why, Lily, I thought you told me Belle was with a cousin somewhere. I don't think you said New York, but of course that was a while ago—"

Lillian stiffened.

"You must mean Cousin Sally," Belle said, seeing her mother's surprise as she embellished Lillian's lie. "I was there for a while."

"Yes," Lillian said reluctantly. "Sally—in Philadelphia."

"Sally and I just didn't get on," Belle continued, ignoring her mother's warning glance. "You know how it is. And her husband—well, he's not much for family." She shook her head sadly, feeling a surge of amusement at their quick murmurs of understanding.

"That's such a pity," Ernestine said, her concern as false as her sympathy. "But you know, Belle, we were talking about you the other day, weren't we, Stella? We were wondering what you were up to these days. Claudia Akers thought you must have a passel of little ones running around by now."

I'll just bet that's what they were thinking. Belle forced her smile wider. "Not a passel, no," she said cheerfully.

"How long are you plannin' to visit?"

"I don't know." She plunged ahead. "In fact I was thinkin' I might just stay." She smiled at Lillian's appalled expression. "That is, if you don't mind, Mama."

"No, no of course not." Lillian recovered quickly. She smiled weakly, sweeping the other two women with her glance. "We're just delighted you could come back."

"I imagine you are," Stella said drily. Her gaze was shrewd and measuring. "Belle, your mama and Rand are comin' over for dinner this afternoon. You'll join us, won't you? I mean, I assume you're stayin' at the house?"

Now. Do it now. Belle threw a quick glance at Lillian.

Her mother's face was so stiff, it looked like it might crack. The expression sent such a strong stab of satisfaction through Belle that her own smile was genuine. "Well, actually I'm stayin' in town for now. It just seemed easiest when I got in the other night. But now that I'm thinkin' I might stay awhile, I was hopin' Mama wouldn't mind if I came on home."

Lillian's brown eyes widened in shock and surprise, and Belle saw the instant protest begin on her lips. Protest that died away the moment her mother saw the avid stares of the other women. Stella Miller looked ready to pounce at the slightest word. And Ernestine Dumont wore a wicked smile on her heavy face, as if she was enjoying Lillian's obvious discomfort.

"Goodness, I can't imagine why she wouldn't," Ernestine drawled. "Why, a hotel's not only dangerous, it's unseemly."

"Absolutely," Stella put in. "I'm sure your mama would love to have you home again after so long."

The coldness in her mother's gaze went clear into Belle's bones. "I'm surprised you thought you had to ask, Belle," Lillian said slowly. "You're always welcome, you know that."

Belle suppressed a shiver. Even if no one else did, she heard the anger in her mother's carefully modulated voice. She'd heard it too many times to mistake it. There would be hell to pay later when they were alone, but now she felt a rush of triumph. She had won. Lillian could not back out now—Stella and Ernestine would not only tell everyone, they would be watching for the slightest hint that things were not as they seemed.

Belle smiled at the thought. "Thank you, Mama. I thought that might be your answer."

Chapter 5

She had trapped them neatly, Rand thought angrily, watching her from across the Millers' dining-room table. Like rabbits caught in a snare, they'd stumbled in without hesitation and now were too dumb and surprised to struggle.

He would have told her no if she'd asked him. He knew just how he would have said it—solidly, so that there was no room for misinterpretation or pleading. A quiet, forceful no. But she had not asked him, and he knew why.

She leaned back in her chair and laughed, pulling meat from a piece of chicken with strong, tanned fingers. Her eyes sparkled as she responded to something Paul Miller had said. For just a moment, deep inside him, Rand felt a spark of admiration—just a spark, and barely there, but he felt it nonetheless. If he'd been less angry, he almost could have congratulated her on the success of her plan. He was sure even this dinner was part of it—a way to charm the neighbors and lull him and Lillian into complacency. There was no doubt in his mind that what Belle really wanted was to get inside the house, to wait until they were unsuspecting and then run off with Sarah.

They'd been blithely, easily manipulated.

Or Lillian had anyway, so he was caught as well, because he would not publicly embarrass his stepmother. If he refused to let Belle stay, if he kicked her out of the house or made things so bad for her, she left, it would be gossiped about for years. It would be humiliating for Lillian, and as for him, well, he had lived through that once. He did not want to again.

Belle laughed again, throwing her head back to bare her slender throat. The motion accentuated her slight overbite, the teeth that seemed a bit too big for her mouth, a feature he'd once found charming. Now the realization that he still did—that he noticed it at all—brought back his guilt, and that made him furious. Damn her. He clenched his fist beneath the table. At the very first opportunity he would confront her, let her know in no uncertain terms that she wasn't fooling him with her charming laughter and seemingly innocent words. He knew what she was up to, and he'd be damned if he'd let her get away with it—

"More green beans, Rand?" Stella Miller was leaning over him, pushing a nearly empty serving bowl at him, and Rand blinked in surprise.

He shook his head. "No thanks, Stella. I've had plenty."

"Why, you've hardly had any at all," she admonished him. "If I didn't know you better, I'd think you didn't like my cookin'." She sat down again beside him, a swoosh of blue-striped silk and cotton. "I guess I prefer to think you're only excited at havin' your sister back."

"Stepsister," he corrected softly.

Across the table Belle paused, a bite of chicken halfway to her mouth. She grinned. "You should have seen the welcome he gave me yesterday, Miz Miller. Why, I wanted to leave just so I could come back again."

"I imagine." Stella smiled. She reached for the platter of fried chicken and handed it around the table. "We're all so happy to see you. I guess Lily's the happiest of all, isn't that true, Lil? It's not every day your own daughter comes back." She looked pointedly at Lillian, who smiled woodenly.

"No, it's not."

Rand took a bite of mashed potatoes. It was all he could do to swallow them.

"Try these pickles, Rand." Stella handed him a small dish. "They're this year's."

He took one politely, plopping it onto his plate. It glistened sickeningly beside his half-eaten chicken.

Stella leaned forward, her beady eyes flashing. "So what kept you away so long, Belle? You were in New York, you say?"

"New York's a big city." Paul Miller, Stella's husband, spoke from the end of the table. He wiped his heavy mustache with a napkin and sat back in his chair. "I hear it's full o' pickpockets and such."

Stella flashed her husband an irritated glance.

Rand's stomach tightened. He didn't want to look at Belle, told himself he didn't give a damn where she'd been or what she had done there. But he couldn't take his eyes from her. He felt the tension in his body as he waited for her answer.

"Well," she said slowly, still picking at her chicken. "I guess you could—"

"Mama, we're all done." Abby Miller took her last sip of milk and looked at her mother. She squirmed impatiently in her chair. "Can Sarah 'n me go out to play?"

Stella nodded distractedly. "Yes, go on—but come on back if you want pie."

"Don't get dirty, Sarah," Lillian said.

No one was watching Belle—no one but Rand—and he saw the slight tightening of her jaw, the way she took a deep breath as if to hold in her temper. The chicken fell from her fingers, and she wiped them on the napkin in her lap. He wondered if her hands were clenched beneath the table, wondered what the hell she was thinking.

There was a clamor as the two girls pushed back their chairs and rushed outside. The front door slammed shut in their wake.

Stella swiveled back to Belle, her sharp features taut with curiosity. "I'm sorry, Belle. You were sayin'?"

"Dangerous place, New York is," Paul said. "Ain't that so?"

Belle looked at him and smiled, the kind of charming smile Rand had seen so many times before, knew intimately. "I s'pose it's dangerous enough," she said slowly. "There are lots of people there. It's a big city."

"And you all alone." Stella tsked. "How did you bear it?"

"I wasn't alone, Miz Miller," Belle said. "A friend of mine lives in a boardin' house there. I worked for her."

Stella looked scandalized. "In a boardin' house?"

"A very respectable house, Stella," Lillian broke in.

"I see."

"Didn't you say you cooked for them, dear?"

Belle laughed, a snicker that set Rand's nerves on edge and stiffened his spine. "No, Mama. I couldn't cook to save my life."

Lillian's eyes clouded. Rand saw the subtle thinning of her lips. Her voice was steel-edged. "But when you wrote me, you said—"

"When I wrote you?" Belle's eyes opened wide in surprise. "Why, there were so many letters, Mama, I hardly remember that one. Are you sure I said cookin'?"

Stella looked avidly from Belle to Lillian. Rand could almost see the woman sniffing for blood.

He scooted back his chair. It screeched on the floor. "How about some coffee, Stella?"

"Oh, of course." Stella jerked to her feet. "Goodness, I was so interested in Belle's stories, I nearly forgot."

Rand felt Lillian's eyes on him, but he leaned forward, focusing his gaze on Paul, determined to change the subject. "So, Paul, are you still planning to show that ram at the fair?"

"You bet I am." Paul nodded. "Spent the last two weeks workin' on that damn sheep's weight. You know old John Stillwell's got a Merino ram himself. Bought it at auction over in Clinton County last week . . ."

Paul went on talking, a slow, heavy cadence that hummed in Rand's ears even though he no longer really listened. He nodded at the appropriate times, made noises of agreement, but he didn't hear what Paul was saying. He was too aware of Belle sitting silently across from him, and of Lillian's cold, stiff silence. Too aware of the fact that they had to spend at least another hour with the Millers before they could gracefully leave.

"Oh, Paul, stop talkin' about that silly ram." Stella bustled back into the room, a steaming pot of coffee in her hands. "Not when Belle was just tellin' us what she's been doin'."

God, the woman was relentless. Rand sat up, opened his mouth to say something, anything to head her off, but Belle beat him to it.

"There's really nothin' to tell." She smiled. She waited while Stella poured coffee and then she reached for the sugar bowl. "I'm just glad to be back."

Paul chuckled. "You can't ever get home outta your blood, I guess. You know, I remember when you and Cort and Rand here used to run wild on the Hocking." He poured a heavy stream of yellow cream into his coffee. "Used to scare old Henry to death."

Rand felt a chill clear into his bones. He grabbed for his coffee, stunned to see that his fingers were shaking.

"Yep." Paul took a sip from his cup. "You know, Stella used to say that if Rand jumped in the river and drowned hisself, Belle'd be right behind him. Ain't that right, honey?"

Stella nodded. She pulled two pies toward her and sliced a knife into one of them. "I surely did say that. Custard or gooseberry, Rand?"

His voice felt forced from his throat. "Gooseberry."

"You two were never apart, that's for sure. We used to laugh at it—why, I remember Belle just sittin' on the cracker barrel at the store, waitin' for Rand to be done workin'. 'Course, that was before you went to Cleveland, Rand. For a while after that it was mostly Cort gettin' Belle outta all those scrapes." Paul shook his head. "That brother of yours was a wild one. Sad thing, the way he died."

Rand's stomach tightened painfully. Stella handed him a piece of pie, and he could only stare helplessly at his plate, at the sticky, amber-colored filling leaking from the crust. "That was a long time ago."

"Ummm, not so long," Stella said. "But then, I guess it seems longer, it bein' so many years since Belle was home. It must seem like ages to you, Belle—especially when you see how much your niece has grown."

Rand's head jerked up just in time to see the surprise in Belle's face.

"Niece?"

"Why, yes. Sarah's just sproutin' up like a weed." Stella kept cutting the pie.

"Sarah." Belle spoke the word on a breath of air, and her brown eyes sparkled dangerously. Rand felt her gaze on him, felt a surge of discomfort at the quick, sarcastic lift of her brow. She was going to say something, he knew it, something to tear apart the careful lie he and Lillian had spent years building and nurturing. One careless word would undo it all, and he felt helpless to stop it, felt the wave crashing over him even as she opened her mouth to speak—

He was on his feet before he knew it, so fast, the table jiggled at his movement. Dead silence fell. They all looked at him curiously.

"I just remembered—something—I—uh—think I left it in the wagon," he muttered. He motioned abruptly to the door. "Belle, come on out and help me."

"I'll help you, Rand." Paul started to his feet. "Just let me get my boots on—"

"No, Paul, I need Belle for this." Rand tried to smile, but the effort was a dismal failure. "We'll be right back."

She sat there, staring at him, and he saw the stubborn light come into her eyes. She was going to refuse and embarrass him in the bargain, he knew it, and Rand felt the urge to go over and pull her bodily from the chair. But that would mean touching her, and he already knew he wouldn't do that, knew it even before she changed her mind and got slowly to her feet, watching him warily as she came around the corner of the table.

"We'll be just a minute," Rand said. He waited while she preceded him out the front door, her yellow dress swinging about her ankles, the long braid still and heavy between her shoulder blades.

The door shut heavily behind them, separating them from the others. In the distance, near the barnyard, he heard the sounds of Abby and Sarah playing some game, but before he could figure out what it was, Belle turned to face him.

She was inches away. So close, he could see the small scar across her upper lip, the mole just below her mouth. So close, he could smell the sun and the dust on her skin, feel her warmth. Rand backed away, his anger disappearing in sudden fear. Jesus, this had been a mistake, asking her to come out here. A horrible mistake.

"What's wrong, Rand?" she asked softly, sarcastically, the whisper of her voice accentuating her slight lisp. "Afraid I might tell on you?"

"Something like that." He was embarrassed by the hoarseness in his own voice. He jerked his head at the door. "You don't know what's been going on here since you left. I didn't want you to embarrass your mama."

"My mama?" The scorn in her words was unmistakable. "My *mama* is a liar. And so are you."

"Maybe. But I won't have you embarrassing her, do you understand?"

"Do I understand?" She stared at him defiantly. "What are you, Rand, her knight in shinin' armor? Come to make sure the nasty dragon doesn't kill the princess?"

The words stung. "Go to hell."

She laughed then. "She doesn't need protectin', haven't you figured that out yet? She can take care of herself better than either of us."

The bitterness in her voice stunned him. "Look, you don't understand—"

"I understand," she said. She didn't take her eyes from his face. "Tell me, who came up with the lie, Rand? You or her?"

Her unrelenting stare was uncomfortable, reminded him of too many things. "It doesn't matter."

"Like hell it doesn't." She crossed her arms over her chest and looked away, out toward the fields. "Does the whole damn town think the same thing? That Sarah's my niece? What'd you tell them?"

The condemnation in her tone stabbed into him, making him feel embarrassed for a lie he'd learned to accept long ago. Rand fought to keep his voice flat. "They think I got a woman pregnant when I was in Cleveland working for Uncle Charles that spring. She died, so I got Sarah."

Belle made a sound—a snort, a half laugh, he didn't know what to call it, but it carried everything she felt in it—bitterness, disbelief, sarcasm, even a vague, self-deprecating amusement. She used to make that sound, he remembered, but it hadn't been so hurtful then, hadn't felt as if it held a world of disappointment in its syllables.

She didn't look at him, stared down at her feet as if she were afraid to look at him, though somehow he doubted that was true. "You were that ashamed of the truth, then?"

"Yes."

"Well, that's good to know." He thought he heard a quaver in her voice, a soft shake that sounded like pain, but when she turned to him and he saw the pure, blazing anger in her eyes, he knew it wasn't pain she was feeling at all.

For some reason, that disappointed him.

But her next words surprised him. "Why did Mama cut Sarah's hair?"

He frowned. "She didn't. I did."

"You did?" Her lips pursed. She looked confused and then, inexplicably, more angry than ever. "Tell me, Rand," she said, "how're you gonna explain it when I take her and leave?"

"I'm not going to have to explain anything," he said. "You aren't taking her anywhere."

"Oh, no?" She raised a brow again, quirked her mouth in a bitter half smile. "You might want to start comin' up with some good stories, Rand."

Her words made his heart pound in his chest. Rand felt suddenly afraid. The thought made him want to laugh at himself. Rand Sault afraid of small, delicate Belle. Belle with the ready laugh and charming ways. Everyone in town would laugh if they knew.

Except he *was* afraid. Small, delicate Belle had a will of steel, and he hadn't forgotten how that ready laugh and those charming ways had torn him up inside and twisted him around so that he didn't know where he was or what to do.

Yes, he was very afraid.

But he couldn't let her see it, didn't even want to face it himself, so Rand stepped away from her, clenched his fist. "I'm just going to say this one time, Belle," he said softly, forcing emotion from his voice. "Just once, so you don't mistake it. I know what you're up to, don't think I don't. You may have trapped your mama, but you can't trap me. You stay away from Sarah. I don't want you near her. Not now, not ever—and I'll do whatever I have to to make sure you stay away. Cross me and I'll make you regret you ever set foot in this state again."

And then, because he was shaking so hard, he couldn't stay another moment, he turned and vaulted down the steps toward the field, where Sarah and Abby played.

The ride back to the farm was silent, the Indian summer sun still hot. The dusty air blew against Belle's skin, bringing with it grit that clung to her lips, and the heavy scent of drying corn and manure from the farms they passed. Sarah lay curled up on a pile of burlap bags in the back of the wagon, asleep. Her strange doll had fallen from her fingers to bounce erratically on the weathered boards. Lillian had insisted on sitting in back with her—as though she was afraid any contact with Belle might hurt the child.

Belle pulled down the brim of the rough straw hat to hide her eyes. She was so angry, her face felt tight, and her head ached with the tense clenching of her jaw.

They had lied about Sarah. The realization stunned her. The Rand she'd known had always been brutally truthful. He had never cared about what people said or thought.

But things had changed in six years.

Belle swallowed painfully and looked out at the passing fields. She had not expected much from Rand, but she'd at least believed he would fight Lillian when it came to telling the truth about Sarah. The fact that he hadn't shocked Belle as much as the sight of Sarah's shorn tresses—and infuriated her. He had taken away any claim Belle had to Sarah as neatly as he'd cut their daughter's hair.

Yes, Rand had changed.

His dreams had somehow died; he was locked inside his own world, a world of cornfields and hogs, a small-town world where Lillian's lie seemed better than the truth simply because it protected him from gossip.

"You were that ashamed of the truth, then?" The question she'd asked him drifted through her mind. She'd expected him to deny it, expected him to be surprised she had asked such a thing. She'd asked the question only to hurt him and not because she truly believed they were ashamed of her, not really.

So his answer, his simple, quick yes, had startled her.

And hurt. Surprisingly it hurt. She had not thought he could affect her anymore, but when it came to this, anyway, she was wrong. It had hurt, and it was that more than anything else that reaffirmed her feeling that she could not leave Sarah here. He was ashamed of her—so be it. If that was true, then it had to color how he felt about their daughter. It meant Rand would try harder to stifle anything of her in Sarah. He would smother Sarah's dreams, her freedom. Belle could not let that happen. She would not allow her child to grow up with nothing to see but Rand's crushed dreams and Lillian's restrictions.

No, her daughter would learn to have dreams of her own.

The resolution made Belle feel stronger. She lifted her chin to steal a glance at Rand, who sat implacable and expressionless beside her on the seat. His large hands held the reins expertly; his broad shoulders shifted beneath the heavy brown coat he wore. They sat as far apart as they could on the narrow seat, careful not to touch each other, and his movements were stiff. In fact everything about him was stiff: his perfectly formed, full lips were pressed together in a hard line, his square jaw clenched. Those deep-set eyes, shadowed by the brim of his hat, stared straight ahead, barely blinking. Even his thick, dark blond hair was stiff where it brushed his collar—too stiff even to curl.

He had changed, but at least she knew how to handle Rand now. He was just like Lillian. And like her mother he had a lot to learn about giving her orders.

They turned into the narrow dirt road that wound past the house to the barn, and Rand pulled up beside the porch and jumped down. Sarah jerked awake at the sudden stop.

"Where are we?" she asked sleepily. "Are we home?"

"Yeah, we're home." Roughly Rand grabbed Belle's carpetbag and tossed it on the porch. It landed with a heavy thud, and he threw her an inscrutable glance. "Anything else?"

"No." She shook her head. "No, that's it."

"Good." He turned to help Lillian and Sarah out of the wagon, and Belle jumped from the hard seat, landing so hard, pain shot up into her ankles. She winced, grabbing the side of the wagon for support, and when she turned around again, Lillian and Sarah were already on the porch.

Rand paused before climbing back onto the seat. "What's wrong?"

Immediately she let go of the buckboard and backed away. "Nothin'."

He nodded stiffly toward the satchel. "If you leave it there, I'll bring it in after I unharness the horses." He spoke as if it was a task just slightly more appealing than beheading chickens.

"It's fine," Belle said sharply. "I can get it."

"All right, then." He clicked to the horses, and the wagon moved off, heading down the road to the barn.

Belle took a deep breath. Lillian and Sarah had already disappeared inside the big house, and she stood there, staring at it, feeling unexpectedly uncomfortable. It seemed sinister again, vaguely threatening, neatly wiping away any good memories she had of it, the things she'd thought about—was it only last night? The dark curtains at the parlor windows were drawn together, closed eyes against the world. Beyond the open front door the hallway was dark and somehow menacing.

She didn't want to be here suddenly, had forgotten what moving back into this house would be like. *Leave now.* The threatening words whispered in her mind like those from a familiar ghost story. Her mouth went dry.

Then, from inside the house she heard Sarah's voice, and Belle's fears lessened. This was why she'd returned.

For Sarah. And because of Sarah, Belle wouldn't let memories stop her.

She picked up the satchel, moving purposefully through the front door.

She stood there for a moment. The scent of pears was gone, but the beeswax was still strong, and there was the faint aroma of yeast and the musty smell of the dying mums on the hallway table. The smells were comforting, but the darkness of the hall held a coolness that belied the warmth of outside.

Lillian came out from the kitchen, her face expressionless. "You can use your old room," she said in that chillingly flat voice.

Belle glanced at the stairs. She waited for something more, some other instruction, but Lillian only nodded shortly and turned on her heel, disappearing into the kitchen. Belle heard the murmur of her mother's voice, a soft counterpoint to Sarah's chatter. She was already forgotten. Belle felt a surge of relief and turned to the stairs.

The stairs creaked beneath her weight—they always had—and she hurried up the rest of them, down the long, scarred floor of the hallway and past the half-open doors of the bedrooms until she got to the one at the opposite end of the hall, overlooking the front yard.

The door was firmly closed; there was a key in the lock.

Belle paused and let her satchel fall from her hand. It banged on the floor, startling her with the noise. She licked her lips, feeling like an intruder. It was just a room, she reminded herself, nothing but a place to sleep. Probably it looked completely different from when it had been hers.

But in some small way she hoped it didn't.

Slowly, holding her breath, she turned the key and pushed open the door.

The light blinded her for a moment. The setting sun streamed in through the windows, past the closed, thin muslin curtains, slanting across the floor and the bed shoved against the wall. The room was boiling hot. And empty.

Not completely empty, she amended. The bed was hers. She recognized the fine lathed maple of the headboard, the notches on the bedpost where she'd tied her escape rope so many nights. Beside it was her bedstand, holding a single lamp. But the bedspread was a many-colored, wedding-ring quilt where before it had been just a blue-and-white weaver's blanket, and the tin lard lamp on the table was new. There was no dent in the base, no soot-stained metal.

A rag rug lay on the floor, and she couldn't remember if it was the same rug that had always been there—surely it was? The big maple armoire took up the far wall. It was the same too—her initials were scratched into the fine wood at the base, the same initials she'd been spanked for carving when she was twelve years old.

But other than that the room was without character, and despite the fact that she'd known it would be that way, Belle felt a pang of disappointment. It was her room, but it wasn't, and she felt as much a stranger as she did standing in the hallway downstairs.

She took hold of her carpetbag, walking slowly into the room and throwing it on the bed. Then she went to the window, pushing aside the curtains to open it. It stuck as if it hadn't been opened for a long time, and she smacked the sill with the base of her hand, trying to loosen it.

She was sweating by the time she managed to get it

open and the cooling air of evening swept over her, drying the sweat on her face. Belle sank onto the bed and reached for her hat.

Her hand stopped in midair, her breath caught in her throat. On the wall next to the door was the portrait. It was huge—three feet wide and three and a half tall, with a heavy, dark frame, and it showed a portly man with thinning brown hair and a neatly trimmed mustache. The artist had been one of the best—he had captured the stern light in the man's blue eyes, the humorless set of the mouth and the heavy jaw. The fabric of his dark blue coat looked fine and thick, and the patterns in his multicolored waistcoat glowed richly.

The picture was of her real father, John Calhoun, and like the rest of the room the portrait was the same but it wasn't. The feathers and dried flowers she'd pasted over his sanctimonious face were gone, leaving only a wispy frond of feather, a glue stain by his eye and another on his pristine white cravat. But *he* was unchanged, a whole presence now that the guise was gone, unadorned and glowering, just as he'd been for years and years and years.

"Well, well," Belle muttered finally. "Damn me to hell if it isn't Jesus John." And then she started to laugh uncontrollably, until it seemed the walls were shaking with the sound.

Chapter 6

Belle woke early. For a moment she couldn't remember where she was, and she blinked groggily at the armoire, confused and disoriented. But then she remembered, and the realization that she was home again brought her wide awake in seconds. The spicy, thyme-heavy scent of sausage drifted from downstairs, along with the aroma of coffee. Murmurs of voices—Rand's deep baritone, her mother's measured tones—came muffled from the kitchen along with the heavy tread of footsteps.

It felt familiar—too much so. Belle pushed back the blankets and swung her feet over the floor. The morning was chilly—she could feel the cold from the boards before her feet even touched them—and she hesitated for a moment, debating whether or not to huddle back under the covers and wait for Rand to go out to the fields and Lillian to the garden.

Yes, now that she was safely in the house, maybe it would be better to wait and face them on her own terms. Later this afternoon perhaps.

She frowned at the door, inadvertently glancing at the portrait sitting in judgment nearby. Belle stiffened. She had almost forgotten about him, had forgotten how much she hated him. Her father had died when she was two, and the painting had hung in her room since, a constant reminder. Not that she stood a chance of forgetting him, Belle thought resentfully. His spirit had been a living, breathing presence in her aunt Clara's house in Columbus—the small home where she and her mother had lived until Lillian married Henry Sault. And even if it hadn't been, Lillian would never have let Belle forget her father or what a paragon of virtue he'd been.

"Your father would be so ashamed of you . . ." "Oh, Belle, what would your father say?" Her mother's words rang in her mind. Even after all these years the painted face of John Calhoun still filled Belle with the urge to get down on her knees and atone for her sins. It was that more than anything else that made her push aside the blankets and get out of bed. If nothing else, she didn't want to have to look at him all morning, didn't want to hear the imaginary sermons coming from a mouth permanently painted closed.

Hurriedly Belle combed out her hair, braiding it again before she slipped into an old brown calico work dress, and shoved her feet into a worn pair of boots. Then, steeling herself, she started down the stairs. The old wood creaked and groaned under her footsteps.

"There you are." Lillian stepped from the kitchen into the hallway, wiping her hands on the heavy twill of her apron. "So you haven't decided to lie abed all day. Good. There's work to be done."

Belle paused on the bottom stair and gave her mother a sarcastic smile. "Good mornin' to you, too, Mama. You didn't have to wait around just to tell me that."

"I didn't." Lillian turned, walking back into the kitchen. "I want to talk to you."

Belle's smile faded. She felt the telltale tightening in her neck, her jaw. Still, after all this time, the anticipation of talking with her mother made her edgy. Her steps were wooden as she went down the hallway into the kitchen, and the bright morning sun and the cool air from the open back door only increased her tension. The room was cheerful, though she felt anything but. The familiar scents of sour milk and yeast nearly choked her.

Lillian began scrubbing the dishes. Breakfast was over; the only thing left was the coffee steaming on the stove and part of a buttermilk pie.

Belle forced herself to relax. "Nice of you to leave me some breakfast," she said, pulling out a chair. "Pie looks good."

Lillian didn't spare her a glance. "If you want to eat, be up when the rest of us are."

"I'll remember that." Belle went to the stove, easing past her mother without touching her, and poured coffee into a thick yellowware cup. The pottery was hot, nearly burning her hands as she hurried back to the table and set it down, taking a seat herself. At least there was a place setting there for her, she noted, grabbing a spoon and pulling the cream and the sugar bowl toward her. That was something, anyway.

She shoveled three spoonfuls of the coarse brown sugar into her coffee and a healthy pour of yellow cream and stirred it, clanking the spoon noisily against the cup. "Where's Sarah?"

"With Rand." Lillian plopped a dish into the tub with such violence, it sent water splashing up her arms. "Doing chores."

"Isn't she a little young for that? Hell, I didn't have to feed the chickens at Aunt Clara's till I was seven."

This time Lillian did look over her shoulder, though her eyes were expressionless. "Don't sass me, Isabelle. If you think I've forgotten about yesterday, let me assure you I haven't."

"Why, Mama, I don't think you've forgotten a thing."

Belle took a sip of her coffee and pulled the pie tin toward her. The buttermilk custard wiggled gently as she sliced into it with her coffee spoon and took a bite. The taste of it melded with the lingering coffee on her tongue, sweet and milky. "Ummm—good pie."

Lillian slapped another plate into the tub. "Jimmy Dumont came by this morning on his way out to Alspaughs'. He said his mama asked how you were doing."

Belle took another bite of pie. "You can tell her I'm doin' just fine."

"That is *not* what I meant."

The anger in her mother's voice made Belle smile. Deliberately she exaggerated the country accent she knew Lillian despised. "Well, now, Mama, s'pose you tell me just what you do mean. I can't read your mind, y'know."

Lillian spun around so quickly, warm water flew from her hands, spattering on the hot stove and sprinkling Belle's face. "Don't you play these games with me, Isabelle. I cannot believe the things you said to Ernestine and Stella yesterday. You deliberately—"

"Deliberately what, Mama?" Belle worked to keep her tone even. "Deliberately told lies? Seems I'm not alone anyway."

"Just what is that supposed to mean?" Lillian frowned.

"Don't tell me you forgot." Belle laughed shortly. "Maybe I'll just bring my pretty little *niece* on in here, and she can remind you."

Lillian's face tightened. "We had to tell them something."

"And the truth wasn't good enough?"

"The truth was unthinkable." Lillian's voice was condemning, so soft, it squeezed Belle's heart. "I will not tell the world that my daughter—" Lillian choked on the word as if she couldn't bear to say the rest. She stopped, and her delicate nostrils flared as she seemed to marshal her strength. She looked away. "You knew how I felt then, Isabelle. That has not changed."

Belle squeezed the spoon in her hand so tightly, it imprinted her skin. *"You knew how I felt then, Isabelle."* Yes, oh yes, she knew how her mother felt. Had always known and had tried to forget it, even though it still haunted her sometimes in the quiet of darkness. In her nightmares she remembered the night she'd told her mother about herself and Rand; she still saw the wild way Lillian's hair had come loose from her chignon and the paleness of her skin, the red dots of color on her cheeks. Still heard the sharp, spitting words: *"You're a disgrace to this family . . ."*

Belle swallowed, forcing her fingers to relax on the spoon. "I haven't changed either, Mama," she said quickly, because she was afraid she wouldn't be able to say the words. "I wanted Sarah then and I still do. I had plans for her. You and Rand were wrong to take her from the Masons'. You were wrong to lie."

"You don't know what you're talking about, Isabelle. Things have changed in the time you were away. It's best if you would remember that."

"Best for who, Mama? What were you plannin' on tellin' everyone when I came back?"

"When you came back?" Lillian raised a brow. "Had you planned to come back, Belle?"

The words fell between them like stones. Belle wished she could deny it, wished she could say yes, she'd always intended to come back, to bring Sarah back, but she couldn't. The truth was she'd never meant to set foot in this town again, wouldn't have now if not for Sarah.

Though it wouldn't have mattered even if she had

wanted to return. She'd always known she wouldn't be welcome—and she'd been right. She wasn't.

She raised her chin defiantly. "You told me to stay away," she said. "I thought that's what you wanted. Or was I wrong, Mama? Tell me, did I get it all wrong?"

Her mother stared at her silently, and Belle saw the thinning of Lillian's lips, the way the blood drained from her face. No, Belle thought, she hadn't been wrong.

She pushed back her chair and got to her feet, working to keep the emotion from her voice. "I didn't think so. Now, if you don't mind, I'm goin' to find my daughter."

Her mother didn't make a sound as Belle went out the back door into the morning sunshine. She felt oddly drained as she leaned back against the wall of the house. The clapboards were warm and rough against her back, and the air smelled like dry leaves and dust and hay. She took a deep, relaxing breath, willing herself to calm down, closing her eyes. She heard the chickens clucking in the barnyard, the hogs grunting, and for a moment she could almost see herself—twelve years old and chasing the chickens back to the barn, bare feet raising clouds of dust as she ran.

Once, she had loved it here. The day her mother had married Henry Sault was the happiest day of Belle's life. Then she had reveled in the barnyard and the forest and the canal, had loved the loft in the barn where she could see the whole world, had cherished the nooks and crannies where a young girl could hide.

For a moment the high, childish voice coming from near the barn sounded like her own. Belle straightened, blinking away her thoughts. She pushed away from the wall and shielded her eyes with her hand to see into the sun. She thought she saw a movement by the pigpens.

Sarah. Belle's heartbeat sped. Nervously she licked her lips, feeling strangely reluctant to hunt Sarah down. It was stupid, she knew. Sarah was the whole reason she was here. But now that the opportunity had come, she felt—afraid.

She licked her lips, gathering her courage. To hell with it. It couldn't be that damn hard to talk to a five-year-old. She'd faced far tougher things than a little girl.

She kept telling herself that as she walked across the yard, following the dirt road past the spring and smoke-houses to the barn. The huge gray building sat on a hill a short distance from the house, and the road led directly to the second story, where hay and the wagons were kept. Sarah was below, where the big doors swung open into the cluttered barnyard. She was looking at the pigs, her bare toes curled precariously around the second slat of the fence so that she could lean farther over the pens. A group of chickens pecked at the ground around her feet, and Belle saw that the burlap chicken-feed bag clutched in Sarah's hand was leaking a steady stream of cracked corn.

Belle bit back her smile, almost sliding down the steep, narrow path leading to the barnyard below. The deep, heady smell of animals and hay was heavier here, making her nostrils tingle. The chickens scattered as she approached, but Sarah was too involved with the two huge black hogs to pay any attention.

"Hey there," Belle called out. "You s'posed to be feedin' the chickens?"

Sarah looked over her shoulder, then down at the bag at her waist. Her small mouth opened in an O of surprise. "It's leakin'!"

"Yeah, it is." Deftly Belle snatched the bag, folding it so that the hole was at the top. She motioned to the birds. "They liked it, anyway."

Sarah tilted her head back, and the loose sunbonnet slipped off her head, revealing her short locks. Without that long blond hair, Sarah looked even more like Rand. Like him, those brown eyes were too serious, too thoughtful, the small mouth set too firmly. And the wary expression on her face was a copy of Rand's.

Sarah stared for a moment and then she turned back to the pigs. Belle licked her lips, thinking suddenly of Rand's orders yesterday to stay away.

She forced them from her mind and leaned against the fence, watching the big animals snort their way through their meal. "What're you doin'?" she asked.

Sarah shrugged. She didn't bother to look up. "Watchin' the pigs."

"Oh, I see."

Silence. Belle felt uncomfortable and ill at ease, and she guessed Sarah felt the same. The little girl was staring at the pigs as if she expected one of them to talk at any second.

"Which one do you like better?" Belle tried.

Sarah gave her an exasperated glance. "You don't *like* pigs," she admonished.

"Oh. Sorry."

Silence again. She searched inanely for something to say. Hell, what did one say to a child? Something equally brilliant, like "Which chicken do you think is prettier?" With adults, at least, it was easy. Most people were interested in the same things, even if it was nothing more exciting than the weather.

She bent over, resting her elbows on the fence and leaning out as far as Sarah.

"She's a nice-lookin' hog." Belle pointed to the bigger of the two, pure black except for the spot of white just beneath her chin.

"That's Bertha."

"Bertha, huh?"

"Papa's takin' her to the fair. He thinks she's pretty."

Belle lifted her brows in surprise. She couldn't imagine Rand thinking such a thing, much less saying it. "He does?"

"Uh-huh. Ain't she?"

"Uh—yeah. I guess another pig might think she's pretty."

They were quiet for a moment, both watching the two hogs root around in the dirt.

"Papa said we could have baby pigs next spring." Sarah spoke suddenly. She slanted Belle a tentative glance. "Is it almost spring yet?"

"We've still got a little while."

"Oh." Sarah looked thoughtful. "I wish it was spring now." She wiggled a little, tightening her chubby hands on the splintery fence. " 'Cause I'll be ten then, and I'm gonna take me a baby pig and run away."

Belle stared at Sarah in surprise. "You're goin' to what?"

"I'll be able to ride a horse then. Papa said I could when I was ten."

"Is that so?"

"Sarah." His voice came from behind them, low and melodic, startling them both with its quiet intensity. Sarah jumped down from the fence guiltily, and Belle twisted around.

Rand stood there, a wicked-looking ax hanging loosely from his hand. Dirt and chaff spotted his bleached linsey-woolsey shirt and clung to the heavy brown workpants, and a few bits of hay threaded through his thick hair. He looked sweaty and tired, and his mouth was set in a familiar grim line.

"Papa, I was just showin' her Bertha." Even Sarah

seemed to sense his volatile mood. Her voice was softly pleading.

"I see that." Rand jerked his head toward the house. "Why don't you go on in and see if you can't help your grandma?"

"But I was feedin' the chickens."

"You were?" Rand's gaze slid to the feedbag, still in Belle's hands.

Belle shifted it uncomfortably. "She was. There was a hole in it," she explained lamely.

"Well, you can feed them later. Go on in, now."

Sarah looked stubborn. Belle stepped forward. "It's all right. We can feed them to—"

"No." There was no anger, no threat in his words. Just a solid, implacable order. "Sarah, I said go inside. *Now.*"

This time Sarah went. Belle watched as the child walked slowly and deliberately across the yard, both hands behind her back, her feet dragging.

Belle turned back to him. "How—"

"Is there something wrong with your memory?" he asked, his eyes narrowed, his tone coldly furious. "I told you I didn't want you around her."

She shrugged. "I know what you told me. I don't give a damn."

"You don't, huh?" He leaned forward, took a step that brought him close enough so Belle could see the dust coating the lines at the corners of his eyes, staining his shirt. Close enough to smell the tang of sweat.

She lifted her chin and faced him. "No, I don't. What're you goin' to do about that, Rand? Scare me away?" She stepped toward him.

He jerked back so sharply the ax he held scraped along the ground. "I won't let you take her," he said, his voice a hoarse whisper. "Never."

Anger surged through her. "Oh, no? We'll see about that."

"I'll fight you every inch."

"I never expected anythin' different from you."

He swung the ax slightly in his hand, glancing down at it as if he wanted to use it on her. "Make it easy on yourself, Belle. Leave."

She glared at him, hostility made her voice tight. "I'm only goin' to say this one time, Rand," she said evenly. "You can threaten me all you want, you can even run me off this farm, but I won't leave without her. I'll keep comin' back and comin' back until Sarah and I go together. That's a promise."

And then she turned and walked away.

Chapter 7

"Twenty-eight, twenty-nine, twenty-eleven, twenty-three—" Sarah's singsong counting rang in the air over the sound of the boiling kettle and the clinking of utensils on pottery. She scraped her two-tined fork along her plate, through a mound of mashed potatoes and into a puddle of applesauce. "Twenty-six, twenty-one, twenty-two . . ."

"Sarah, please," Lillian said.

"But I'm countin' to a hundred."

"Count quietly."

Rand didn't look up. He concentrated on the potatoes and the cold boiled beef on his plate, forcing himself to chew and swallow—anything to keep from looking at Belle. He couldn't stand to see her defensive expression—it was all he could do to ignore the anger already hovering between them. He didn't need to see the proof of it in her face. He slashed into his meat, drowning the bite in horseradish before he put it in his mouth.

"Thirty-ten, thirty-eleven—" Sarah said, her voice a low murmur.

Rand reached for the sugar and put two heaping spoonfuls into his buttermilk. The clank of the spoon hitting the cup seemed obscenely loud. He caught Lillian's nervous gaze across the table, and involuntarily he followed it to Belle, who was slowly, deliberately, opening a biscuit. She spooned apple butter on it thickly, then followed it with a lacing of maple syrup.

"Thirty-six, thirty-seven . . ."

Rand's eyes narrowed, and he looked away and took a gulp of the sweetened buttermilk. But the sight of her pouring that syrup wouldn't leave him. She used to do that, he remembered. Before or since, he'd never seen anyone else eat a biscuit quite that way.

It bothered him that he remembered.

"Thirty-eleven . . . Papa, what comes after thirty-eleven?"

"There is no thirty-eleven," he said gruffly. "It goes thirty-eight, thirty-nine, forty, forty-one."

"And then what?"

"Pass the applesauce, please." Belle looked at him pointedly.

Rand grabbed the bowl and shoved it toward her.

"And then what, Papa?"

"Thank you." Belle made a show of dipping the spoon in, plopping the sauce onto her plate so that it pooled next to those smothered biscuits.

"And *then* what?"

"Sarah," Lillian admonished.

"Papa—"

"What?" Rand turned to his daughter almost violently, feeling a surge of impatient exasperation. He inhaled deeply, forcing calm into his tone. "What do you want to know, Sarah?"

"What comes after forty-one?"

"Forty-two."

"And then what?"

"Sarah, that's quite enough." Lillian said. "If you want to count to a hundred, count quietly—and not until after supper."

"Forty-three comes next," Belle said. Abrupt silence

followed—so abrupt, her words seemed to echo. She looked up from cutting her meat. "Doesn't it?"

Sarah sat up straighter in her chair. She looked at Belle with big, round eyes and then at Rand.

His stomach tightened and rolled over. He nodded to Sarah. "Yeah. But listen to your grandma, all right?"

She smiled and banged her fork into her potatoes. "Forty-three, forty-four, forty-eight . . ."

Rand sighed and pushed aside his plate, no longer hungry. "I have some things to do in the barn," he said. He rose, grabbing the latest issue of *The Ohio Cultivator* from the sideboard where he'd left it earlier.

It was a lie. There were always things to do, that was true enough, but tonight he'd planned to settle himself in a chair and read—read long enough and hard enough so that he couldn't think about today or yesterday or years ago. He wanted to lose himself in farming techniques and stories—hell, even the ladies' section sounded good.

But he couldn't do that with her sitting there all night. Not with that damnably uncomfortable silence that filled every room she was in.

He went out the door quickly and crossed the yard, was up the road and to the barn in minutes. The building was big and dark, the sounds of the animals and the smell of hay and oil was comforting. There was no silence here, uneasy or otherwise. The dusty, musky scents were all around him, the darkness and the constant movement soothed him, just as it had hundreds of times before.

Rand threw *The Cultivator* aside and went to work, feeding the animals and tightening down for the night. It was easy work now, while it was still warm, with the cows and the horses pastured. Only the pigs and the chickens needed any care at all, and when he finished, the sky was just turning a dusky shade of gray.

There was an old rocker by the toolroom, kept there just for nights like these. It was roughly made of maple, but the arms were smoothed and dark with oil from men's palms, and over the years the seat had seemed to form to his body. It had belonged to his grandfather first, and his father after that, and there was a time when he'd thought Cort would own it next. But it hadn't happened like that, and in spite of the bitterness and guilt Rand felt over being the brother who inherited, he was glad the rocker was his.

He remembered the days when his father, Henry, sat in it, creaking back and forth over the crackling straw, rubbing his thick beard as he worked over a piece of leather harness, talking in time with the rocking. *"It wasn't so long ago—" creak, creak, "that a man—" creak, "never had to use credit for a thing—"*

Rand smiled. It was nearly seven years ago now that his father had died, but he still couldn't look at the rocker without seeing Henry there, without hearing the steady rocking of the chair. Rand sat down, sliding back over the smooth seat, fitting his hands around the arms, letting his body melt into the shape. He never felt so close to his father as he did in that chair—even walking the lands his father walked and sitting at his father's place at table. But then he guessed it wasn't that strange. He and his father had never been close. Henry was too tied to the land, too bound to its rhythms, and Rand had been anything but.

He felt a moment of sadness that Henry Sault had never raised a son who loved the land that way. God knew Cort never had. And Rand, even though he worked it every day, even though he felt its grit on his fingers and its dust in his hair, only felt like an intruder, not like he belonged. Not ever like he belonged. There had always been too many other things.

Rand closed his eyes, leaned his head back. The dreams still hovered at the back of his mind, multicolored images that beckoned and pleaded. He heard their music, the laughter. He smelled the smells and tasted the air. They were hazy now, where once they had been bright and vividly real, but even at their dimmest, they were more compelling than the corn he'd grown with his own hands and the rich smell of freshly turned earth.

No, he was nothing like his father. Not even now.

But he was no longer like himself either.

Rand sighed. He picked up *The Ohio Cultivator,* banishing thoughts of his father and dreams, and flipped through the pages, hoping something—anything—would catch his eye. The words were dim on the page, too hard to read, and it took him a minute to realize that he'd been out in the barn longer than he'd thought. The light was dying; he either needed to light a lamp or go to bed.

Neither idea was compelling. He was tired, he felt it all the way to his bones, but his mind was wide awake and he wouldn't be able to sleep. Usually he didn't need much sleep—three or four hours at best—but tonight he didn't even know if he would get that.

He felt restless. As though something were reaching inside him, searching for his soul. It was calling him, tempting and inescapable, and Rand put aside the journal and went to the doors of the barn. He heard the chickens clucking and scraping and the heavy breathing of the hogs, smelled the cool dampness of the night air tinged with the scent of apples and hay.

It was growing dark. The stars were beginning to twinkle. He saw one, then two, and then he saw the edge of the moon rising through the trees on the horizon, big and bright like late-summer moons always were. The katydids' chirping was raspy and strident by the pond, and in the distance he heard the howling of the Alspaughs' dog.

Something called him then. He didn't know what, didn't know anything except that he wanted to see the road again, wanted to imagine how far it went, even though he already knew, knew that road like the back of his hand.

Still, he followed the call, hurried down the drive, slipping and sliding on the gravel beneath his feet, feeling the breeze in his hair and on his face as he went to the front of the house. In the yard the oaks were sighing, their leaves dancing shadows, and he leaned against one of them and stared out at the road, feeling his heart swell and his head ache with wanting—something—he didn't know, had never known.

It was almost as if he heard a noise, though there couldn't have been one. Rand turned, saw the lamp flicker to life in the upstairs window, saw the shadow against the fine muslin curtains.

Belle.

He knew suddenly why he was there, what had called him, and he felt desperate and afraid, tasted again the harshness of shame in his mouth. The darkness he thought he'd banished threatened him again, the memories of six years ago shifted in front of him.

He wanted to leave, to turn around and walk into the house and search out his daughter. Sarah, whose silly stories would lull him into sleep. Sarah, whose presence comforted him even when his yearning for a different life made him desperate for peace. He knew if he sat on the porch and waited, she would somehow know he was there. Would sneak out of her room and patter silently down the stairs, just as she had a hundred times before.

He should discourage it, he knew. But he had always drawn so much comfort from her presence; her chatter made his demons disappear, gave him a sense of belonging, of future, that nothing else could. He knew he would feel her little body cuddle up against his as she sat beside him on the porch, would hear the soft whisper of her voice as she talked and told stories until they were both limp with weariness.

He sighed and looked up at the window, seeing the shadow cross the curtains and the flickering light, feeling the sharp edge of need well up inside him again. Rand's mouth went dry. He squeezed his eyes shut, working to push it away, to forget. Christ, he was afraid of it, afraid of the way that obsession had ruled him once, afraid of becoming like his mother, who had killed herself rather than face her madness.

It's not in you anymore. You fought it. You destroyed it. He told himself that and he wanted to believe it. But then he looked up and saw Belle's silhouette, and the longing lodged in him, along with the harsh touch of fear.

And he knew that even Sarah couldn't help him tonight.

Belle's dreams were disjointed—disturbing fragments touched with anger and tension—and when she opened her eyes finally to stare into the darkness, she felt as if she hadn't slept a wink.

It was very late, and the moonlight shining through the thin curtains was faint, appearing and disappearing as clouds swept over the moon. She heard the breeze outside, rattling the giant oaks and sending a single branch creaking against her window.

The sound would have comforted her once, but tonight it only increased her tension. Her whole body felt tight; her jaw was sore as if she'd been clenching it for hours. There was no point in trying to relax. She already knew she wouldn't be able to, just as she hadn't been able to the entire, miserable day. Belle felt a tightness in her chest as she remembered the way her mother had whisked Sarah from the table and set her to playing with a bunch of shelled corncobs. When Belle started to join her, Lillian had asked her—sharply—to help with the dishes. Then, before she had even finished, Sarah had been sent to bed—early, Belle was sure.

Between her mother and Rand, Belle hadn't spent more than a few minutes alone with her daughter.

She sighed again, turning onto her side, watching the play of shadows cast by the fluttering curtains. That would change soon enough. Tomorrow or the next day she'd go into town, see if maybe they'd hire her on at the Black Horse Tavern. Or maybe Cly and Son's grocery had a position. Anything to get some money so that she and Sarah could get the hell out. She couldn't stay here much longer without going crazy. Even if she hadn't known it before, tonight had made it very clear.

The porch swing creaked outside, cutting into her thoughts, a startling, steady rhythm in the night, too steady to be caused by a breeze. Belle froze, listening.

". . . then he ate all the ones standin' by the pond, and he called his friend the troll . . ."

Belle frowned. A child's voice. Slowly she sat up in bed. It had to be nearly three in the morning. What was a child doing up at this hour?

It was her imagination. Frowning, she started to lie back.

". . . and then they went lookin' for monsters."

It wasn't her imagination. The voice was tiny and soft.

Sarah.

Belle jerked upright. She stared at the window in surprise. Sarah? What was she doing up so late? Frowning, Belle pushed back the covers and slid out of bed. She was nearly to the window when she heard a low voice rumbling through the darkness.

She stopped, confused. There was someone else out there with Sarah. Someone—a man—

"Hmmm. Did the monsters let them in?"

Belle knew that voice, would recognize it anywhere. Rand. Rand was out there too.

"No. They were very, very selfish, 'n they wanted all the food for themselfs."

As quietly as she could, Belle went to the window. Slowly she raised the sash and leaned out until her stomach rested against the sill. She wished she could see them, but the roof blocked her view. She could picture them, though, sitting on the creaking porch swing, rocking it back and forth with their feet, and she knew they were sitting close together, because their voices were so low.

". . . they cut the heads off all the bunnies."

"Not the bunnies."

"Well, not *all* of them. Just the mean ones."

"Oh."

"They ate the good ones."

"Hmmm." Pause. "Sleepy yet?"

Another pause, as if Sarah was trying to decide the best answer. "No. Are you?"

Rand laughed shortly in reply. Then they were silent again, for so long, Belle wondered if they had gone in. She strained to hear, leaned farther out. The splintery sill dug into her skin, her nightgown caught and ripped. Belle bit off a curse and stopped, hoping they hadn't heard. Rand had already given her a lecture today; she didn't need another one.

"What was that?" Sarah's voice floated up to her. Belle closed her eyes, held her breath.

"Hmmm?"

Rand's lazy answer brought a sigh of relief. They hadn't heard. Thank God. This was all so strange. It didn't fit at all. The Rand she had seen these last days would not let a five-year-old child up at three in the morning. That Rand would be in bed himself, waiting for the first touch of dawn on the fields. Certainly he wouldn't be sitting on the porch with Sarah, telling stories in the middle of the night. Hell, in the time she'd been here, Belle hadn't heard him do more than order Sarah around or scold her.

She frowned, listening to his soft chuckles in response to Sarah's story, trying to reconcile this man with the one with the stern face and sterner lectures. She would not have expected this from him. Not anymore.

This—this was more like the old Rand.

Belle felt suddenly cold, oddly disturbed, and she drew back from the window, lowering the sash and closing the curtains against the night and the voices. Something nudged at her mind, something she didn't want to hear, didn't want to consider.

Stiffly she crawled back into bed. *It doesn't matter,* she told herself. *It was just one story. Just one.* Just one story against a hundred don't-do-thises, a hundred don't-do-thats. It couldn't make up for years of scolding, days of meaningless noes and silly rules. She knew that better than anyone.

The niggling doubt disappeared, replaced by a reassuring certainty. She wasn't wrong. Rand was no longer the boy she'd run with so many years ago. He had changed, and one story couldn't take away the harsh, unsmiling look in his eyes.

Even though it had taken only one night to put it there.

Belle banished the thought, refusing to remember, to think about it at all. She was doing the right thing. The only thing she could do. She had no choice but to take Sarah away from here, from the same strictures that once made Belle long for freedom. That still did.

No other choice.

She felt more certain of that than anything else in her life. In her mind Belle saw Sarah running free, her long blond hair trailing behind. The image made Belle smile. Yes, this was the best idea; she could hardly wait to make it happen.

Still it was a long time before she forgot Rand's soft laughter.

Chapter 8

"Delia Johnson made bread-and-butter pickles last year," Dorothy Alspaugh said, holding a jar of pickles up to the light. Her soft gray eyes narrowed as she surveyed them critically. "But these look good, Lily. My, look at how pretty they lie. It looks almost as if you packed them that way."

"I did." Lillian smiled, and wiped her wet hands on her apron. "Those are my fair jars. I did a dozen."

"Well, they are pretty." Dorothy set the jar carefully on the table. "I guess Delia has some competition this year, don't you think so, Belle?"

Belle glanced up from the table, her fingers trailing idly over the jars. "I don't know," she drawled. "Miz Johnson makes pretty good pickles, if I recall."

"Usually," Dorothy agreed. She pulled out a chair and eased her thin body into it. "But she was complaining that some blight got the cukes this summer, so we'll see." She took a sip of coffee and smiled at Belle. "I'm so glad you decided to help us today. We could use an extra hand with the sauerkraut."

"Yeah, well it's been a while since I did any preservin'."

"It'll come right back to you, you'll see."

"Maybe." Belle took a deep breath and smiled at Mrs. Alspaugh. Then she glanced up at Lillian and wished—

again—that she hadn't agreed to help. It had seemed like a good idea at first, when she'd thought Sarah would be in the kitchen as well, but as soon as Belle walked into the room, she knew Lillian had deliberately tricked her. Sarah was outside helping Rand with the chores.

Belle felt a quick surge of resentment. Just one more day, she told herself. One more day of feeling trapped. She hadn't had the chance to go into town yet, but tomorrow . . . Tomorrow she'd visit the tavern and get a job. After that it would only be a few weeks before she and Sarah could leave. She could bear anything that long.

"I think I'll do my spice cake for the fair," Dorothy said.

"The one that got second place last year?" Lillian turned from the ten-gallon earthenware jars she was readying.

"I think it would have got first prize if John Abrams didn't have such a fondness for coconut cake—and rum." Dorothy snorted. "I just wish I could get my hands on whoever told Bernice Goslin he was judging. Imagine, a coconut cake with rum icing. Whoever would have thought of such a thing?"

"I don't s'pose you know who's judgin' this year, Miz Alspaugh?" Belle teased.

"Well—no—but I did hear Robert Leith might be."

"Robert Leith?" Lillian asked. She turned back to the crocks, a small smile playing at her lips. "That's certainly lucky. He ate three pieces of spice cake at Peter Benson's funeral a few weeks ago."

"Did he?" Dorothy looked appropriately innocent. "I didn't notice."

"Three pieces." Belle shook her head in mock amazement. "That's somethin'."

"Yes, well." Dorothy got to her feet, fussing at her apron. An attractive blush stained her cheeks. "Where is the cabbage, Lily? I'll get to trimming it."

"It's in the cellar." Lillian stepped back. "I'll run and—"

"I'll get it, Mama." Belle got to her feet.

Lillian hesitated. She flashed a glance at the back door. "No—"

"Even I can find a cabbage." Belle picked up the bushel basket sitting by the table. "How many?"

Lillian looked oddly perplexed. "Really, Belle—"

"How many?"

"Just bring what you can carry. And hurry back."

Belle frowned, feeling suddenly strangled. "It's not like it's miles away, Mama," she said, moving to the door. "I'll be right back."

Quickly, she went down the back steps, the slatted basket banging gently against her legs. The air today was cooler, touched with the dusty smells of autumn: dead leaves and apples and drying hay. There would be a frost soon, Belle thought idly, moving to where the huge doors of the cellar were angled against the house. She noticed the potato plants lying in a browning, tangled heap in the garden. Time to get those up and into the cellar—

Belle stopped, frowning, surprised at the turn of her thoughts. In the six years she'd been gone, she'd never once thought about gardens or frosts or even the weather. The seasons had come and gone in New York, meaning nothing more than sweltering summer days and icy winter streets. She had forgotten that they ever brought anything else.

And yet here she was, knowing instinctively that it was time for a frost.

It made her uncomfortable suddenly, for no reason

she could say, and Belle hurried into the dark, shallow pit of the cellar, past the last few crocks of wax-sealed apple butter and the jars dark with fruits and vegetables to the bins that held the pale green cabbages. She grabbed as many as she could and tumbled them into the bushel until it was full.

It was heavy, and Belle lugged it awkwardly around the corner of the house, toward the backstairs, feeling every step grow heavier and heavier the closer she came to that kitchen. The cellar had been a relief, an escape, and now the thought of spending the rest of the afternoon with Lillian and Dorothy, trimming cabbage and listening to their mindless gossip, made her taut with tension.

Belle hesitated at the steps. She heard them bustling around inside, heard the murmur of their voices and their soft laughter. Her stomach tightened.

She took a deep breath, took one step up.

And heard Rand swearing at the hogs in the barnyard.

Belle stepped back. She turned around, seeing Rand and Sarah hovering around the pigpens in the near distance. Carefully, quietly, Belle set the bushel of cabbages on the bottom step. Suddenly she knew why Lillian had hesitated at the idea of sending her for the cabbage. Her mother had been afraid of this very thing, afraid that Belle would see them out there and take the first opportunity she could to escape the mindless chore.

Belle smiled. Her mother was right.

"Mama!" she called up. "The cabbages are right here! I'm goin' on out to the barn for a minute." Then, before Lillian could answer, Belle lifted her skirt and ran across the yard. Rand was bent over the hog, and Sarah was perched on the fence, watching. Neither one even noticed her coming. By the time she reached the barn, Belle was breathless.

"Hey there, Sarah!" she called as soon as she was close enough. "What're you doin'?"

Sarah twisted around, her sunbonnet whipped off her head at the motion. In the pen Rand glanced up. He was struggling with one of the hogs, the one Sarah had called Bertha, and he looked sweaty and irate. He shook back his hair from his eyes and frowned.

"What the hell are you doing out here? I thought you were helping Lil." He glanced at Sarah. "Put your sunbonnet back on."

Sarah didn't budge. She regarded Belle somberly. "Did you come to help us with the pigs?"

"I sure did." Belle gave Rand her biggest, most insincere smile. "Since your papa looks like he's havin' some trouble."

Rand straightened. "Go on back to the house and help Lillian. We're fine here."

"She's got Miz Alspaugh to help." Belle stepped onto the fence, carefully balancing on the top rung beside Sarah. "I think I'll just stay here for a while and watch. That all right with you?"

Rand's eyes narrowed, he looked ready to say something, but then he glanced at Sarah. "Fine," he said tightly.

"Good." Belle looked at Sarah, ignoring Rand. "So what are you doin'?"

"Helpin'." Sarah watched her shyly. She put a careful, tentative hand to her hair. "My hairs is all cut off."

Belle nodded. "I see that."

"I look like a boy."

In the pen Rand exhaled in exasperation. "You do not look like a boy, Sarah. Jesus."

Belle lifted a brow. "Well, it's pretty short."

"Papa said he wanted me to be a boy," Sarah said.

"Oh?" Belle felt a surge of pure anger. She looked at

Rand, not even trying to fight it back, and her voice was raw with it. "Is that what you told her?"

He looked surprised, she thought. Surprised and disconcerted, but then he stepped away from the pig and wiped his sleeve across his dust-streaked face, and his expression became stony. "Don't tell stories, Sarah," he said tersely. "I didn't say that at all." He looked at Belle. "She wanted it cut that way. She didn't know it wouldn't grow back right away."

Belle faltered for a moment. He was so matter-of-fact, so damned calm, that she almost believed him. Almost. But she had learned long ago not to trust Rand, not to believe him. Learned that Rand's truth was often just what he wanted it to be.

And she knew what the truth was here. Maybe he hadn't wanted Sarah to look like a boy, but he damned sure wanted to make sure she didn't look like Belle.

She smiled bitterly, reached out to touch Sarah's soft, silky hair. The shortened tresses slid through her fingers, glinted golden in the sunlight. "You don't look like a boy," she said. "You still look just like a little girl."

Sarah gave her a hopeful smile. "Janey needs a haircut too. Only she don't have no head now."

Belle frowned. "Who's Janey?"

"My doll."

"Oh." Belle nodded. "I see. Where's her head?"

"I lost it. Papa says it's in my room, but I think a 'coon got her."

"Really?"

"Uh-huh. On account o' her neck's all chewed up."

" 'Coon's don't eat dolls, Sarah," Rand said distractedly.

She didn't even glance at him. "One ate Janey."

"Maybe you left her in the pigpen," Belle offered.

Sarah considered for a moment, her round face

screwed up in thought. "Maybe I did," she said finally. "Them pigs'll eat anythin'." She turned to Rand. "Did I leave her here, Papa?"

Rand was examining Bertha's hoof. He didn't look up. "I don't know, Little Bit. Maybe."

"I'll show her to you," Sarah said. The fence shook as she climbed down. "I'm goin' to show Janey to her, Papa."

Rand's head jerked up. "No, Sarah, don't . . ." His words trailed off. Sarah was already racing from the barnyard to the house, her chubby legs pumping.

They were alone.

Alone. Belle took a deep breath. She had not come out here to talk to Rand. She wanted to avoid him. She pursed her lips, focusing on Sarah until the little girl disappeared into the house, trying to remain calm and in control.

"It won't work, you know," he said quietly.

Belle turned to look at him. He had released Bertha, and now he stood, hands on hips, a resigned look on his square, handsome features. Belle feigned confusion. "What won't work?"

"Trying to be her friend. Making me think you care about her."

"Maybe it's not you I'm tryin' to convince."

"No?" He raised a heavy brow. "Who, then?"

"Sarah."

"Ah. Sarah." He looked away for a moment. "Do me a favor, Belle. Leave her out of your little games. She's just a child."

It was amazing how he knew just what to say. She tried not to wince. "It's not a game, Rand."

"Oh?" His eyes searched her face, darkened when he met her gaze. "Tell me something, Belle. Did you think of her at all when you were in New York?"

The accusation floated between them, condemning, wounding. The implication in his words infuriated her. As if he expected she wouldn't think of Sarah, as if the decisions she'd made had been impulsive and selfish.

As if he expected nothing else from her.

Anger rushed through her, hot and uncontrollable. Belle jumped from the fence, yanking the brown wool of her skirt back when it grabbed onto a rough board. She glared at him. "You'd like it if I said no, wouldn't you?" she asked hotly. "It would make it all so easy, wouldn't it? Then you could go ahead and believe what you did was right. That it was all my fault and you weren't to blame for any of it."

He flinched. "That's not what I meant."

"Isn't it?" Belle laughed shortly, disbelievingly. "I don't think I've ever even heard you say you were sorry, Rand. So I guess that means you never were." She picked up her skirts, half turned, meaning to walk away, feeling the burn of his words in the sudden ache behind her eyes. Damn, this was stupid. Stupid that he could still affect her at all after all this time. . . .

"Belle. Dammit, don't—" Rand lunged forward, reached to grab her arm through the fence.

Belle's breath caught in her throat. Fear, so potent she felt paralyzed, rushed through her. She jerked back at the same moment he stopped short, his hand outstretched, inches from her. For a second she saw that hand in all its intimate detail, creases and dirt, rough fingernails, calluses, and then slowly he curled his fingers into his palm, dropped his hand back to his side.

She looked up at him. He was white beneath his tanned skin. His breath shuddered from his chest. She heard it as loudly as her own, and it sounded just the same—harsh and rattling, sharp with fear.

Carefully she took a step backward. She wondered

what to do, whether to run away or stand there and pretend it hadn't happened. He had almost touched her. Had almost laid his hand on her and yanked her back, and the realization brought with it flashes of memory. Almost as strongly as if he had touched her, she felt his hand. Flesh on flesh. Dry and warm—almost hot. At her throat, at her waist, at her breasts . . .

Belle swallowed, fought the urge to close her eyes. She couldn't let him know, wouldn't let him see that she remembered, that she cared at all. Much better that he should think she didn't remember anything.

She raised her chin, even though she was shaking inside, and tried—unsuccessfully—to look him in the eye. "I'll just go on inside," she said weakly. "Mama prob'ly needs me now."

"Yeah." He sounded as shaken as she felt. "I saw her at the door a minute ago, looking for you."

"Oh. Then I guess I'll—"

"Here's Sarah," he whispered.

Belle heard it then, the pounding of footsteps on the hard ground as Sarah ran toward them, cutting off escape, relief. Belle turned slowly, watching as Sarah skidded to a stop in front of her.

"Look! Look, here she is!" Sarah held the headless doll out to Belle solemnly, brown eyes wide. "This is Janey."

"Janey." Belle forced a shaky smile. She was incredibly aware of Rand behind her, of the fact that he was watching them as she knelt in front of Sarah and reached for the doll. Her hands were trembling, and she took the lumpy rag body quickly into her lap. It lay there limply, grossly reminiscent of a broken human being, bits of stuffing leaking from the torn neck. Belle poked at it with her fingers. "You'd better have Grandma sew this up, or she'll lose all her insides."

"It's her guts," Sarah informed her.

Belle nodded. "I know."

"I'm gonna bury her tomorrow if I can't find her head."

Belle looked at her somberly, wishing she could think of what to say, knowing with some far part of her mind that she had wanted this opportunity to make friends with Sarah, had wished for it. And once again Rand had ruined things. It was the first time Sarah had said more than a few words to her, yet Belle was too shaken to think of a single thing to say back.

She got to her feet. "Well, then," she said inanely. "Why don't we go see if we can find it first?"

Sarah looked at her, hesitating for a moment, still cautious. "If we can't, will you come to her fun'ral tomorrow?"

"Sure," Belle nodded distractedly. "I'll come."

"Good." Sarah smiled. "You c'n bring the flow'rs."

The acidic tang of cabbage was heavy in the kitchen. It, along with the anisy scent of caraway seed, nearly knocked Rand back when he came into the room. He grimaced as he grabbed a cup of coffee and slumped into the rocker by the stove. They'd been making sauerkraut; the thought depressed him. God, he hated sauerkraut, the smell of it, the slimy feel, the sour taste. It reminded him of when he was young. It had been his mother's favorite food, the thing she ate whenever she was depressed or lonely, the dinner she served whenever she was begging for his father's forgiveness.

Which was always, he thought angrily. The house had always held the odor of sauerkraut. Always. He couldn't smell it now without thinking of her, of the way she'd been, sad and too penitent, throwing herself in Henry's lap while his father flushed with embarrassment, her voice sharp with fear. *"I'm sorry, love—oh, I'm so sorry. I didn't mean to act so jealous. You were just askin' Dorothy if she needed anythin', I know that now. It's just that . . . I'm so afraid you'll leave me. Please say you won't leave me. . . ."*

Rand winced and pushed the memory away.

"I kept some dinner warm for you," Lillian said as she walked into the room. "Are you hungry?"

Rand scowled. "This whole damn place smells like cabbage."

"We made sauerkraut today," she answered lightly. She moved past him to the stove, her calico skirt brushing against his arm, and spooned some stew into a big yellow bowl. "I know you hate it, Rand, but I don't, and I'm not letting all that cabbage go to waste just because you don't like the smell."

He felt instantly rebuked; the feeling annoyed him. Rand took the bowl she offered him, but the scent of cabbage was strong in it as well, and he set it back on the stove with a clank. "I'm not hungry. Where's Sarah?"

"In bed. She seemed tired today, so I put her down early."

He felt a twinge of guilt, and he took another sip of coffee, letting the steam warm his face.

"Belle's on the front porch."

He didn't look up. "I didn't ask where she was."

Lillian sighed, sitting in the chair at the other side of the huge fireplace that housed the stove. He heard her rustling in her sewing box before she settled back. "What did the two of you talk about today?"

He looked up in surprise. Lillian had a sock formed around her darning ball, and she was busily threading a needle, squinting at it to focus.

"I tried to keep her here in the kitchen," she said

when he didn't answer, "but the first chance she had, she was gone. I assumed she wanted to talk to you about something."

"No." Rand stared at her, at her tight, economical movements, and struggled to keep his feelings at bay. All evening he'd tried to keep from thinking about this afternoon. He'd buried himself in chores, working until he could no longer see, unable to bear the thought of coming in to supper and sitting at this table, watching her and remembering how he'd almost lost control today.

Hell, he'd almost touched her. Almost wrapped his fingers around Belle's wrist and pulled her back. Because he couldn't bear that damned vulnerability, the tough shell she put up around it. Because he wanted to see that shell crack, wanted to see her cry, even—hell, just wanted to see *anything.* She made him feel guilty and afraid, and when she'd said the words, when she'd said, *"You never said you were sorry, Rand. I guess that means you never were,"* he had wanted to touch her so badly he couldn't stop himself, wanted to spin her around and look into her eyes and tell her it wasn't true. Tell her he'd spent every damn waking moment since she'd gone hating himself, hating her, being sorry.

But he couldn't say that, because then she might forgive him. Because then she would let him close enough to touch her again, and that was the most dangerous thing of all. Touching her meant the darkness would come to bury him again. And he couldn't let it, had to fight it before it overtook him the way it had his mother, before it controlled him for good. It almost had once—he remembered that much too well.

His hands shook when he remembered.

He gripped his cup forcefully. Lillian was looking at him, questioning him with her silent gaze, and he wished he knew what to tell her. But there was nothing to tell, nothing that didn't shame him. What should he say? *"Belle said I'd never told her I was sorry—is that true? Didn't I? Couldn't she tell how sorry I was? Didn't she see? Didn't you?"*

No, he couldn't say those things. He couldn't even think about that time anymore; the thought of it brought a deep, dark bleakness that filled him up inside. He remembered how it was before, how the obsession for her had started with such a little thing—nothing more than her smile of welcome, the light he saw in her eyes when he came home from Cleveland that spring. A smile that was for him alone, he knew, because even though Cort had watched over her in Rand's absence, she never smiled at his older brother that way.

Rand had been intrigued and pleased, and it had changed the way he looked at her. Suddenly he found himself watching her, wondering what it would be like to touch her, to kiss her. But that easy emotion had grown out of control so damned quickly, had grown demanding and insatiable before he knew what happened, and he could not forget how pervasive it was, how hard to fight. Jesus, he was afraid of it. So damned afraid.

He swallowed. "She came out to talk to Sarah, not me."

Lillian frowned. "Do you think that's wise?"

"No, I don't think it's wise. But you tell me how the hell to stop it. I don't know."

"Hmmm."

That was all, just "hmmm," but there was a wealth of meaning in that sound, and Rand had the sudden notion that his stepmother already knew exactly what had happened in the barnyard, knew what he and Belle had talked about, knew he'd lost control. It wouldn't matter what he said, she already knew and had already made up her mind what it all meant and what to do.

"You haven't seen Marie lately, have you?" she asked suddenly.

Rand choked on the coffee. "Marie Scholl?" he asked in surprise.

"Um-hmmm."

"God, no. Not for weeks."

"Perhaps you should." Her voice was calm, without inflection, and Rand stared at her for a moment, trying to figure out just what she meant.

"You want me to see Marie."

Lillian shrugged. "Only if you want to, Rand. I thought you liked the girl."

Rand frowned. He hadn't thought of Marie Scholl since before Belle had returned. Not since the church dance in August. There, in the balmy summer night, with lightning bugs glowing in the wheat fields, he'd thought idly that maybe Marie would be a good wife if he ever decided he needed one. She was pretty in a soft brown way—brown hair, brown eyes, brown dress. Slender, gentle, smelling of . . . of roses, he remembered.

"I liked her well enough," he said. "I heard Charlie Boston's seeing her now."

"She's a fine girl."

"Yeah." He nodded. "She is."

Lillian dropped her darning into her lap, straightened slightly in the chair. When she looked at him, her gaze was probing. "Have you given any thought to marriage, Randall?"

He nearly dropped his cup. "Marriage?"

"I know we haven't talked about it," she said, picking up the darning again, whipping her needle in and out with swift, efficient strokes. "But I had hoped by now you might have found someone you cared for. After all, you're nearly twenty-eight."

He paused, uncertain what to say. "I don't—"

"Why not Marie Scholl?"

Rand stared at her in confusion. "What's this all about? I didn't know you were so anxious for me to get married."

"Well, it's not my decision," she said, taking a deep breath. "But I do think it's time. Sometimes I'm afraid you . . . Because I'm here . . . Well, I didn't want you to feel you couldn't get married for my sake."

"No, I—"

"People are beginning to talk. Most of your friends are either married or gone." She paused. "You've never said how you felt about it, Rand. You *do* want to get married, don't you? It would be good for Sarah to have a mother."

She already has a mother, he thought, but he didn't say it; in fact he banished the thought as soon as he had it.

Lillian was looking at him avidly, as if the answer was important to her. "Do you want to get married?"

He didn't know how to answer her. Once, yes, once he had wanted that more than anything. Wanted more than that even, a marriage that made him whole, that filled up the empty spaces inside of him. Had wanted to look at brown eyes staring up at him in the morning, and golden hair slipping through his fingers. Once, Christ, once, he had longed for that with every part of his soul, even though he knew it was wrong, even though he fought it with everything he had.

It made him sick now to think of it. Sick and afraid.

He swallowed; his mouth felt dry, his tongue thick. "Yeah," he croaked. "Someday."

"I did think you liked Marie."

"I do like her."

Lillian smiled, a little smugly. "Perhaps you'll see her at the fair."

"Yeah." His voice was quiet; he heard the shake in it and wished it wasn't there. "Maybe."

He felt overwhelmed suddenly. The smile on his stepmother's face twisted him up inside. He couldn't believe it, couldn't believe the sudden revelation that she wanted him to get married. Jesus, that she wanted him to marry Marie Scholl. The thought made him cringe, reminded him of today, of what he'd almost done.

Hell, if Lillian had known, if she even guessed at how powerful his emotions had been only hours before, when he'd almost touched Belle, she would never be telling him to find a wife. She would be warning the girls in town away from him instead of trying to match him up. She would be—

He stopped, gripping the cup in his hands, stunned.

Because he suddenly realized that Lillian knew that, too, and it was why she was encouraging him to see Marie. The thought nauseated him. Nauseated and—somehow—tempted him. Rand clenched his fist around the cup, staring down at it, at his hand, at the long fingers still creased—always creased—with dirt. He remembered what that hand was capable of, what he was capable of, with a shudder.

What if you can't control it?

But you can. It's only Belle who makes you feel this way. Only Belle.

He closed his eyes, forcibly loosened his grip on the cup, and then looked up again at his stepmother, who was watching him with steady, assessing eyes.

"I wonder what Marie is up to these days," he said.

Chapter 9

Belle sat on the back-porch stoop listening to her mother and Dorothy and Kenny Alspaugh chattering away inside. Their voices rang with excitement, every word focused on the Fairfield County Fair as if it were the most important thing to come along in years.

But it wasn't important to Belle. The fair had started after she left Lancaster, so she'd never been, and the thought of spending days talking about cows and pigs didn't excite her at all. No, right now the only thing that brought any enthusiasm was the thought of going into town, finding a job.

She sighed, resting her chin in her hands and looking out at the yard beyond. She wished she hadn't decided to wait until the Alspaughs came over to go, wished she had just saddled Duke and gone to Lancaster herself. But Lillian told her Kenny was going into town today anyway, and it seemed easier to go in with him—especially because she wasn't certain Rand would even let her take Duke, and the last thing she felt like doing was fighting him over a damn horse.

Rand. The thought of him sent a shiver coursing through her, made her feel suddenly anxious and ill at ease, and Belle crossed her arms over her chest and hugged herself tightly. She threw a glance out at the fields. She couldn't see him, just as she hadn't seen him all day.

She was grateful for that at least. The memory of yesterday left her even more determined to get the hell away from here. He had almost touched her. Even in her dreams she'd seen his hand, his fingers outstretched to grab her, to yank her back. And her dreams had taken it further, too, had spun out the memory of that long-ago night when everything crashed around her, had brought back every detail: the heated feel of his skin against her hands, the press of his body, the desperate, hungry way he'd kissed her—as if she were his salvation. Then she had believed she was. In the beginning she'd trusted his words and his touch and his need because she wanted to so badly, because she wanted him so much.

But with only a look he had taught her how foolish that trust was. Belle closed her eyes, remembering again the harsher memory of that night—hard, impatient hands pushing her away, fumbling with his clothes. Angry words that mistook her confusion for hesitation. *"Get away from me, goddammit. Jesus—get the hell out of here! I don't want you, don't you understand? Don't you understand?"*

That was the memory Belle had struggled to forget. But now it was back with a vengeance.

Because there had been that same look in his eyes yesterday.

She didn't understand why it was there, and that terrified her. She didn't understand the sudden paling of his face and his hoarse voice.

He'd been afraid.

Afraid.

Of what?

That was the most puzzling thing of all. Rand had never been afraid of anything—especially not of her. It was so odd that last night she had finally decided she hadn't really seen it, that the look in his eyes had been something else, something that wasn't fear at all.

But in the bright light of day she didn't believe it. Once, she'd known him almost better than herself, knew his every gesture and expression. Belle frowned in confusion. Yes, he had been afraid. She would bet anything on it. She had not imagined the shaking in his voice or his harsh breathing.

But *why*? *Why?*

It made her uncomfortable not to know, somehow vulnerable. She had the sense that it was important to understand Rand's fear, that not knowing could be . . . dangerous.

She shook away the feeling. It was probably nothing, she told herself again. Probably she was only imagining that it had something to do with her. Maybe he'd simply seen Lillian in the doorway.

Belle smiled. That would be enough to scare anyone.

A noise at the side of the house broke into her thoughts. Sarah scampered around the corner, skidding to a stop when she caught sight of Belle.

"Hey there," Belle said.

"Hey." Sarah twined her hands nervously in her yellow gingham skirt. "I'm gonna have the fun'ral today," she blurted suddenly. "I got Janey in a box, only I—I need a little shovel."

"I see," Belle said. "You want some help?"

"C'n you find it?"

Belle nodded. She looked out at the fields. "Where's your papa?"

"He's in the corn for a minute."

A minute? Or an hour? Belle took a deep breath and got to her feet. "I guess there's prob'ly a trowel in the barn, then." She glanced over her shoulder. Lillian and the others were still deep in conversation. They wouldn't even notice she was gone. Without hesitation she went down the stairs, motioning for Sarah to follow as she started across the yard toward the barn. If she was very lucky, she could grab the shovel and get out before Rand came marching back from the fields. That didn't give her much time. He never took his eyes off Sarah for longer than a few minutes. He was probably on his way back even now. Involuntarily she looked back at the rows of corn, relieved when she saw no sign of him.

They walked for a moment in silence. Then Sarah said, "We're goin' to the fair day after tomorra."

"I know."

"Are you gonna come too?"

Belle shrugged. "I don't know. Maybe."

"Last year we had a pic-a-nic."

"You did?"

Sarah nodded. " 'Cept I was little then, 'n I got all messy. I ain't gonna this year, 'cause I'm bigger now."

Belle smiled. "I 'spect that's true enough."

Silence. Only the sound of the drying grass crunching beneath their feet. Then, "Papa says you ain't comin'."

Belle glanced down. Sarah was pulling nervously on the strings of her sunbonnet, and her brown eyes were large and questioning. Until that moment Belle hadn't decided whether or not she would go to the fair. Until that moment she hadn't really known if she wanted to face the speculative glances of town or the veiled insinuations that had assailed her that first day at church. Besides, with any luck at all she might be busy working at the Black Horse.

But Sarah's words made all her rational reasons for staying fly away. If Rand didn't want her to go, there was only one thing she could do.

"Of course I'm goin'," she said. "You didn't think I would miss all the fun, did you?"

"Are you comin' with us?"

"I sure am."

Sarah smiled. "I wanna see the races, but Grandma says I'll get stomped on."

"Well, you can go see them with me," Belle assured her. "I'll make sure no one stomps on you."

They were at the barn. Sarah was quiet beside her as Belle wound past the hog pens and the scattered chickens, through the open doors. Even though the barn was full of hay and tools, it seemed empty somehow, every sound echoing eerily off the rafters.

Belle paused. She hadn't been inside the barn since she'd returned, and she wasn't surprised to see that it was just the same as when her stepfather was alive. Nothing ever changed in Lancaster, and this barn was proof of that. The harnesses in the tack stall were the same ones that had hung on the same hooks forever, the broken stool Henry had mended with a rough piece of fencing still stood by the milking stall—she would have sworn it hadn't been touched in six years—and the old rocker hadn't budged from its place by the toolroom. The piece of broken leather harness abandoned on the seat looked to be the same piece that had always been there.

It was strange, as if the barn had somehow been lost in time, and Belle stood there for a moment feeling puzzled and oddly unsettled.

Sarah ran across the straw-strewn floor to the toolroom, breaking the spell. "It's in here!"

Belle shook off her discomfort. She was imagining things. After all, how much did barns really change? Still, when she followed Sarah into the small room, Belle felt a surge of relief. It was cluttered, disordered as it had never been when she lived here as a girl. Henry had always lined his tools neatly along the walls, but now, though everything was well oiled and cared for, tools were piled on shelves and mounded in corners. Rand obviously didn't share his father's obsession with neatness.

"How do you s'pose we'll find a trowel in this mess?" she murmured, surveying the jumbled collection.

"There, maybe?" Sarah pointed hopefully to a darkened shelf.

It was as good a place to start as any. Belle searched hastily through the cluttered items—an awl, a broken hammer, and some odds and ends she couldn't identify.

"Not here," she said distractedly, bending to search lower. She reached back, pawing through the scattered tools, trying to feel for an old wooden trowel. "Maybe he's usin' it, Sarah. I don't see—"

"You don't see what?"

Rand's voice boomed in the small room. Belle jerked up, banging her head on the shelf above. "Damn!" She backed away, wincing. "Quit sneakin' up on me like that, Rand. Hell, you'd think you were an Indian or somethin'."

He glared at her from the doorway. "It's not me who's sneaking around. What are you doing in here?"

"We're lookin' for a shovel," Sarah said. "I'm gonna bury Janey today."

"I see." He went to one of the piles leaning in a corner and pulled a long-handled shovel from the chaos. "Here you go."

"That's too big," Sarah protested. "I just want a little one."

"This'll do," he said. "You show me where, and I'll dig the hole."

Sarah's face broke into a smile. "You're comin' to the fun'ral?"

"I wouldn't miss it."

Belle made a sound of exasperation. "No, I don't guess you would." Especially since she was going to be there. God forbid he should leave Sarah alone with her for more than thirty seconds. She crossed her arms over her chest, giving him her best sarcastic glance. "I s'pose you're plannin' to lead the singin'."

His mouth quirked. "Better me than you."

"Sure the farm can get along without you for a while?"

"Even if it couldn't, I'd find the time."

"Come on!" Sarah tugged at Rand's hand. "Let's go, Papa." She sent a pleading look in Belle's direction. "Are you comin'?"

"Oh, yeah." She nodded. "I'm comin'."

"Hurry 'fore Grandma calls us."

She glanced at Rand. He stepped back from the door, pulling Sarah with him, and nodded at the opening.

"After you," he said.

She widened her eyes in mock surprise. "Manners. How nice."

"I don't imagine you've seen many of them where you've been," he said. He jerked his head toward the door. "Come on."

The shock of his words broke over her like ice water. His implication was clear—that she'd been in unsavory, unacceptable places—and what was equally clear was that he felt she deserved to be there. She felt her cheeks redden, and Belle lifted her chin, moving past him quickly, determined not to respond. Not that she could. The surprise of his comment had robbed her of words, even though she knew he would never have said it if she hadn't goaded him.

You asked for it, a small voice chastised her. She bit her lip, knowing it was true, but the realization didn't make her feel any better. Damn him anyway. Damn him for knowing just what to say to irritate her.

Had he always known her this well? Had he always been able to wound her with a word, always known exactly what was in her mind? Belle couldn't remember; she had deliberately tried to forget, and now she wished she knew something—anything—of what he was thinking. Once, she would have known. But now those deep-set hazel eyes revealed nothing.

Except fear.

The thought reassured her, reminded her that she could get to him, too, that she had the power to disconcert him even though she didn't know why.

She slanted him a glance, watching his slow, swivel-hipped walk, his smiling nod at something Sarah said. What would it take to put that fear in his eyes again? A word? Something else? Maybe a touch? Belle shuddered at the thought. She swallowed, pushing away the images, concentrating on the ground beneath her feet. It didn't matter. She had no interest in making Rand angry, or fearful, or anything. It would be better if he didn't notice her at all, if he just left her alone until she could get herself and Sarah out of here.

"I ain't decided where to bury her yet," Sarah was saying as they entered the yard and started around to the front. "Janey liked tulips."

"I don't think your grandma would take kindly to us digging up her tulip beds," Rand said. "How 'bout if we put her over by the lilac tree?"

"That's where Scout lies."

"Well, do you think Janey would mind a cat lying on top of her?"

Sarah looked thoughtful. "I don't know."

"I don't think she would," he said.

"No, I guess not." Sarah looked at Belle. "Do you think she'd mind?"

"I don't think so," Belle said. "Scout might even keep her warm in the wintertime."

Sarah smiled. "That's what I think too."

"Good, then that's where we'll dig," Rand said. They rounded the corner of the house, and he eased the shovel from over his shoulder and went to the huge, spreading lilac tree beside the porch. "Where's Janey?"

"Over there," Sarah said. She grabbed a weathered wooden fruit box from the porch and hurried back to them. "She's in here."

Rand nodded briefly and began to dig. Belle stood back, watching as Sarah set the box on the ground and fumbled with the red flannel rag she'd wrapped the doll in. "I wisht we had some flow'rs," she said wistfully. "I couldn't find any."

Rand paused in his digging. "We'll just pretend we have flowers, Little Bit."

"I don't wanna pretend."

"We don't have much of a choice."

"But Mister Benson had flow'rs at his fun'ral."

"Mr. Benson was in a funeral parlor."

Sarah tugged at her sunbonnet. "Then I wanna take Janey to a fun'ral parlor."

Rand sighed in exasperation. He ran a hand through his hair. "Sarah, we can't—"

"What about leaves?" Belle asked.

"Leaves?" Sarah frowned. "What d'you mean?"

"Leaves are awfully pretty now," Belle said. "All those colors—seems to me they're even better than flowers. Why, it'd be like puttin' gold on Janey's grave, don't you think?"

Sarah's brow wrinkled in consternation. "Like gold?"

"Uh-huh. Not many people are lucky enough to have pretty gold leaves on their graves."

"That's right, Sarah," Rand agreed—surprisingly. "I think Janey would like it."

"Really?"

"Really."

Sarah nodded. "I think Janey would like leaves too." She ran off to gather them, her sunbonnet bouncing over her shoulders. Belle watched her go, dimly aware that Rand stood there, too, motionless for a moment before he began digging again.

She waited for him to say something to her, but he didn't. Just kept digging. The *thud-scrape* of the shovel against the dirt—rhythmic, steady—was the only sound between them. Goose bumps rushed over Belle's skin. Rand was digging with concentrated effort. Almost as if there was someone he wanted to put in that hole.

Me maybe. Belle forced a smile at the thought. She cleared her throat. "You only have to dig deep enough for a doll, you know," she said.

Rand glanced up at her, a look that sent shivers through her again. One cold, angry look. "I know." He didn't stop digging.

Belle took a deep breath and turned away. So much for conversation. She didn't even know why she tried. It wasn't as if she gave a damn whether he liked her or not.

"Papa!"

Sarah's screech of excitement cut through Belle's thoughts. Her head jerked up, she saw Sarah standing by one of the huge oaks, near a pile of leaves, gesturing wildly. "Papa, come see!"

Rand straightened. "What is it?"

"I got me a baby snake! Hurry!"

The shovel handle thudded to the ground. Rand raced

across the yard. He was almost there by the time Belle realized what Sarah had said. A baby snake. There were copperheads in these woods, and she knew a baby one was no less dangerous than a full-grown one. To a child like Sarah it could be lethal.

Quickly Belle followed, but by the time she got to Sarah, Rand was already pulling the little girl back from the pile of leaves.

"Where is it?" he was asking.

"In there." Sarah pulled away from him, pointing into the leaves. "You prob'ly scared it away, Papa."

"Stay back." He grabbed her hand and turned to Belle. "Watch her," he demanded.

Belle nodded. Slowly, carefully, Rand kicked at the leaves with his foot.

"Oh, that's smart," she said sarcastically. "Keep doin' that and I'll have to call Dr. Stewart."

"Quiet." He didn't even look at her. Warily he squatted down, leaned closer. Then incredibly he smiled. "Shhh," he whispered. "Little Bit, come here."

Belle put a hand out to stop Sarah. "Wait a minute—"

"It's all right." He gestured for Sarah to move closer. "Sarah, look at this."

Sarah pushed past Belle's skirt to stand beside Rand. "I don't see anythin'," she said.

"Right there." He pointed into the leaves.

Sarah frowned. "I can't see."

"All right. Just a minute." Rand reached into the leaves, poking around with his fingers. Belle leaned forward, trying to see over Sarah as Rand drew back, this time with something cupped in his hand. When he turned to Sarah, there was a broad smile on his face. "Ready?"

She nodded.

Slowly Rand opened his hand.

Sarah gasped. "It *is* a baby snake!"

Coiled in his palm was a tiny garter snake. How he had seen it, Belle had no idea. It was the color of the leaves, brown and gold, and it was still as death, its beady eyes watching them warily.

"Quiet," he warned. "It's just a little garter snake."

Sarah's eyes were round. "Can I touch it?"

He nodded. "Be careful, you don't want to hurt it."

Tentatively she reached out, touching the snake with the tip of her finger. The reptile moved, curling into a tighter ball, and Sarah jerked back. "It tried to bite me!"

"No, it didn't," Rand assured her. "You scared it, that's all. It's just a baby, Sarah."

"Can I—can I hold it?" she asked.

Rand's eyes were fastened on her face. "Promise to be careful?"

She nodded solemnly. "Uh-huh."

"All right, then. Hold out your hand." When she did, Rand straightened her fingers so that they laid flat. Then, with his hand still steadying hers, he slid the tiny snake into her palm.

The garter snake shivered. Its tongue flicked out.

Sarah jerked, but Rand held her hand in place. "Careful, Little Bit."

She stood there for a moment staring down at the snake, watching it carefully. Then suddenly she looked up, her large brown eyes alight with pleasure, and giggled.

It was a warm, sincere, heartfelt sound, and it went right through Belle. She wanted to laugh, too, from the sheer joy of seeing Sarah's screwed-up face, but somehow she couldn't.

You don't belong here. The words rushed through

Belle's mind, slicing into her heart, and she stood there watching Rand and Sarah smile together, watching the little snake twist in Sarah's palm. Belle felt suddenly confused, lost and abandoned—as if she were intruding on an intensely private moment between two people she didn't know. She saw the way Rand squatted in front of Sarah, a six-foot-tall man suddenly the height of a five-year-old, saw the way his tanned fingers curled around Sarah's, his eyes reflecting her pleasure—and Belle saw it all as if she were watching strangers in a park.

You don't belong here.

Her mouth went dry. Belle stepped back, wishing that she could disappear and hating herself for wishing it. Only minutes ago she'd been annoyed with Rand for intruding on her time with Sarah, but now the tables were neatly turned, and it reminded her suddenly, uncomfortably, of the other night. Everything was the same. She'd felt as out of place listening to their stories, seeing their quiet companionship, as she felt right now.

She would never have that kind of relationship with Sarah. Belle knew it with a sudden, blinding flash of understanding so painful, it left her breathless. Coming back here had been a stupid, reckless waste of time. What had she been thinking? That she could just walk into their lives and take over? That it would be a simple matter to wrest Sarah away from Rand—that Sarah wanted to be rescued?

The silly fantasy came racing back. The fantasy where Belle took Sarah's hand, led her to the train, and told her she was safe, that she would never have to go back again. The fantasy where Sarah looked up at her with loving, thankful eyes and smiled.

The same smile Sarah was turning on Rand now.

The same loving, thankful look.

Belle swallowed the lump in her throat, confused and

embarrassed. Because the look Sarah reserved for her was nothing like that. Because in her daughter's eyes Belle had never seen anything but uncertainty or common politeness.

"She's happy here," Rand had said not so many days ago. And she hadn't believed him. Had seen the rebellion in Sarah's eyes, the resentment, and believed that instead. But now, for the first time, Belle wondered if maybe Rand had been right.

"She's happy here. Goddammit, she's happy."

Maybe.

Belle's hands were shaking, she twined them in her skirt, trying desperately to steady them. Rand looked up at the movement. She saw the surprise in his eyes and she knew he had forgotten she was there. For only a moment, but he'd forgotten nonetheless.

The knowledge made her feel more invisible than ever. Belle swallowed again, tried to smile. "I—think—uh—I'll just go on upstairs for a minute," she said, trying to keep her voice even. "I'll be back—"

"You ain't gonna miss the fun'ral?" Sarah asked.

"No. No, I won't miss it."

But she would, and Belle knew it—and knew they wouldn't miss her at all.

She turned and walked back to the house.

Chapter 10

At first Belle didn't know where to go. She stepped inside the hall and closed the door quietly behind her. The darkened hallway was rich and warm with the scents of beeswax and spice, and she heard the steady murmur of voices, the ringing laughter from the kitchen. It made her feel more alone than ever.

She didn't know what to do. What the hell should she do? She hadn't expected any of this, hadn't expected Rand to love Sarah or for Sarah to love Rand back. Hadn't expected Sarah to be happy. But she was, and it was obvious Belle's plans to rescue her daughter were stupid and pointless. There was nothing to rescue her from. Nothing except Lillian's stifling control, and now Belle realized Rand would keep Sarah safe from that, just as he had protected Belle from it long ago.

You were wrong about him. Wrong about everything. Wrong, wrong, wrong.

No, that was not strictly true. She hadn't been wrong about everything. Rand *wasn't* the same man she'd run away from six years before. He was nothing but a farmer now, a man whose big dreams had somehow disappeared. A man she no longer trusted with her heart.

But those were the only things that were different, really. In other ways, important ways, he hadn't changed. The last few days crowded in around Belle, smothering her with images: Rand talking to Sarah on the porch, listening to her outrageous stories; Rand digging a hole for a doll's grave; Rand carefully putting a coiled baby snake into his daughter's hand. Belle had forgotten the kindness in him. It had been wrong to think he wouldn't know how to give Sarah the kind of life she deserved. Belle took a deep breath. Rand would do anything for Sarah, she knew that now. Because he truly loved his daughter.

Belle couldn't take Sarah away from that. In spite of the fact that she would never forgive Rand for what he'd done to her, she couldn't—wouldn't—take revenge on him by taking Sarah.

Hell, she didn't want revenge anyway.

She didn't know what she wanted.

Belle put a shaking hand on the banister and slowly went up the stairs, barely hearing the telltale creak of the third step. In her mind she heard laughter, Sarah's high-pitched giggle and Rand's deep, throaty tones. They went well together, belonged together. Rand and Sarah, Sarah and Rand—the names singsonged in her brain like an old game. *By all the laws of every land, I give Sarah unto Rand. By all the rafters of the house, I marry the cat unto the mouse. . . .*

She had played that game with Rand once, Belle remembered. One afternoon when she was barely thirteen, in the empty Salem church, she had laughed and married him to a rat, a dog, and a chicken before he'd chased her from the altar.

Back then it had been the two of them against the world—or against her mother anyway. Belle and Rand. Rand and Belle. There had been a time when Cort had been part of that too. Though older than Rand by two years, and busy with his own life, Cort had been their guardian angel—the one who covered their truancy with excuses, the one who defended her reputation that spring Rand was gone. She remembered a story Cort told her once, about a group of swordsmen who banded together against the enemies of a queen. She and Cort and Rand had been like that. The Three Musketeers, Cort had called them.

The Three Musketeers. The thought saddened her. The three of them had been a family once, just as Sarah and Rand were a family now—a family that didn't include her, even though without her it could never have existed.

You don't belong here. Not anymore.

Belle swallowed. She didn't belong anywhere. Not here in this house nor in New York City nor in Cincinnati. She had spent the last six years making sure of it, living a day at a time, never knowing where her next meal would come from or whether she would have a job tomorrow or the day after.

The only thing she had known for sure in those years was that one day she would come back for Sarah.

And now that she finally had, Sarah didn't need her.

Belle stopped at the top of the stairs, staring at the row of closed doors before her, and before she had time to think, before she even knew what she was doing, she moved toward Sarah's room. It was Cort's old room, at the other end of the hall from hers, and as she got closer, Belle could still see the lines drawn on the door, growth markings, scribbled in the cramped, tiny writing of Cort and Rand's mother: *Cort: 2 years, 5 years, 6 years . . .*

Belle frowned. Paralleling the marks were others, dark black lines she didn't recognize. She bent closer to trace one with her finger. Growth marks, like Cort's, but scrawled in a different hand, one that was darker, bolder. She squinted, trying to make out the round, uneven handwriting. *Sarah: 3 years, 4 years, 5 years.*

Belle's heart pounded in her chest; for a moment the ache was so strong, she couldn't breathe, couldn't even move. It was Rand's handwriting, she recognized it now. *Sarah: 3 years, 4 . . .* Belle squeezed her eyes shut, but she couldn't block the images. Sarah at three, at four. Sarah growing, inch by inch, into the child Belle had just left in the front yard with Rand.

God, it was incredible that it should hurt this much. But then she remembered how she'd felt the day she left Sarah at the Masons' boardinghouse, and Belle realized it had hurt this badly then, too, and she had only forgotten. In the years that followed, the pain had faded, leaving regret, yes, but relief more than anything else, relief that Sarah was safe and Belle was free—at least for now.

But she hadn't really been free, and Belle knew it. Freedom was not backbreaking work in boardinghouses and restaurants, scraping by for everything. Freedom was not living hand-to-mouth, working just to eke out a living for herself. No, she had never been free. Especially because the vision of Sarah was always there, always in the back of her mind. Sarah red-faced and mewling, just as she'd been when Belle put her in Gem Mason's arms and walked out the door. And always in the back of Belle's mind was the promise she'd made to return.

She had always intended to go back once she'd made a good life for them, to show up on Gem's doorstep one day and take her baby back into her arms.

But there had never been enough money, enough time, enough of the "good life," and though the vision of that baby had stayed with her, it grew fainter and fainter with each passing day, each year. She had not gone back until it was too late and that baby had grown into a little girl she didn't know at all.

Belle glanced again at the door, trying hard to imagine the way Sarah had looked through the years. Sarah at three had been that tall. Sarah at three had stood in front of this door, gazing up at Rand while he measured her height. Belle could see the way Sarah would have looked up at him, the way she laughed and held out her arms for a hug.

Belle could imagine all that. But only as a vague vision. She didn't know how Sarah had really looked or what she'd been wearing or what that day had been like. Those memories were Rand's, not hers.

She had missed it all.

Regret washed over her, so powerful it left her shaking and the black marks on the door wavered in front of her eyes, melted into a wash of tears. She had not wanted this, had never intended it. When she'd left Sarah with the Masons, she meant to be back in a few months, maybe even a year. No longer. But that time had slipped away from her, and now there was no way to get it back. No way, and yet she wanted it, suddenly wanted it so badly, she ached. Six years, and she had nothing. Nothing but memories of regret and sadness. Nothing but bitterness.

Rand had it all. He had seen Sarah every morning, had put her to bed every night. Had nursed her fevers and taught her words and shown her the night sky.

Belle squeezed her eyes shut. *It could've been you, and you gave it away. It could've been you.* Ah, God, how stupid she'd been. How stupid she still was, thinking she could take Sarah away from that and that things would be fine, thinking that Sarah would love her, trust her, even though they'd only known each other a week.

Believing she could just step in and be the mother she'd never bothered to be before.

Belle made a sound of disgust. She was Sarah's mother, yes, at least physically. But she knew that when it came right down to it, Rand was more a mother than she was. The thought made her sick inside.

What the hell did a person do to fight that?

She couldn't fight it, couldn't make Sarah love her. Today had shown her that, even if the last week hadn't. No, much as Belle wanted things to be different, those years had gone. She couldn't bring them back, and she couldn't deny that living in New York had made her a stranger to her daughter. It didn't matter that she was Sarah's mother. Being a mother didn't guarantee a child would trust you or love you. Trust was something that had to be earned, and love sometimes never came at all—Belle knew that better than most.

Suddenly she saw her plan to take Sarah and run for what it was—hasty and selfish. Sarah would hate her for taking her away from Rand, and God—*God*—Belle didn't want to see that hatred in her daughter's eyes. Didn't want a mother-daughter relationship like the one she had with Lillian.

But she couldn't leave either. Before, maybe, it had been possible. Before she'd learned that Sarah was a person and not just the vague, mindless child Belle had imagined. Now it was too late.

What she wanted was to be Sarah's mother.

Belle swallowed. She wanted to be a real mother, wanted to see trust and love shining from Sarah's eyes, wanted to hear laughter meant for her ears alone. There was only one way to have that.

She would have to stay.

* * *

Rand rubbed his forehead to ease the pain behind his eyes. God, he was tired. Tired and tense from the effort of being around Belle, even though he'd only spent minutes with her. It was more than enough. The strain of yesterday was between them, the memory of how he'd almost touched her tormented him, and he wondered again why the hell he'd done it, what had possessed him to reach out to grab her through the railing. After today, after seeing again that damned shield shuttering her eyes and hearing her brittle sarcasm, he wondered why he'd even wanted to explain anything to her yesterday, wondered what had seemed so important.

He did not like being around her. He hated the hungry way she watched Sarah. It was why he'd taken time away from the fields to dig Janey's grave today. He couldn't stand the thought of Belle being alone with Sarah, was terrified that one day he would return to find the two of them gone.

The thought sent a chill running through him, and Rand forced it away and glanced hastily back to where Sarah played near the newly dug grave. Her voice drifted back to him, high and singsongy as she sang to the buried Janey. He should keep the shovel handy, he thought. He wouldn't be surprised if tomorrow Sarah demanded that the doll be dug up again. Rand took a deep breath and walked across the porch, opening the front door and going inside the cool, dark hallway. It would be Sarah's version of the resurrection, no doubt.

"I need to talk to you a minute."

Belle's voice seemed to come from nowhere. He jumped, startled, before he realized she was above him on the stairs. His stomach knotted instantly. Reluctantly Rand looked up. He could have predicted how she would look just from her tone. Arms crossed, chin raised, and mouth set. That defiant, challenging look was in her eyes again, along with something else. Rand frowned. Something like—like tears. In fact if he didn't know better, he would have sworn she'd been crying.

He told himself he was imagining things. He'd never seen Belle cry. *Except once,* he amended. *Just the one time . . .* He shoved the memory away.

"I need to talk to you," she said again.

The words didn't bode well, and he didn't want to talk to her, didn't even want to look at her. Rand eased back toward the door. "Can't it wait?"

"No." She stepped down. One step, another, and Rand felt like a condemned man waiting for sentencing. But the feeling died abruptly when she stopped and uncrossed her arms, placing one slender hand on the banister. She looked away as if she were uncomfortable. "I —I've been thinkin'."

"Good news."

She didn't react to his sarcasm. "About Sarah."

Rand's blood froze. "What about her?"

"I want to tell her the truth about me."

He stared at her dumbly for a moment, unsure what she was talking about, and then it dawned on him. The truth. About Belle. Sweet Jesus.

The realization stunned him. "Jesus, Belle, you can't be serious."

"Why not? I'm back now, there's no need to keep lyin'. How am I s'posed to be a mother when everyone thinks Sarah's my niece?"

"Be a mother?" His voice was a whisper. God, he couldn't make it more than a whisper. "Oh, Jesus—"

She inhaled sharply. "Hell, Rand, you act like it was some kind of crime. All I want to do is tell her the truth. I would've thought you'd want that too. Or—wait—I s'pose you've come to like livin' a lie."

Her sarcasm banished his shock. Rand found his

voice again, and with it his anger. He stepped forward, curling his fingers around the banister, blocking her from coming down the stairs. "You don't know anything about the truth. And if you think I'm going to let you walk out there and tell that little girl anything, you're crazy. Do you understand me?"

"No, dammit, I don't—"

"Well, let me make it clear," he spoke carefully, watching anger tighten her face and not caring. "You don't give a damn about her or anyone else. You can't just walk in here after six years and announce you're ready to be a mother. It doesn't work like that."

"No? How does it work?" She stepped down until she was only inches away from him. Her brown gaze practically burned his skin. "Since when do you decide how the world works, Rand? Since when do you decide what's right and what's wrong?"

"Since it involves my daughter, goddammit!"

"*Your* daughter?"

She yelled the words. They fell into silence. Sudden, expectant silence where there was no sound but harsh breathing, nothing but the echo of words. The two of them stood there, glaring at each other. He felt the warmth of her breath on his face, saw the rapid rise and fall of her chest. And then from the kitchen came the sound of a chair leg scraping on the wood floor, a harsh creak that seemed abnormally loud in the stillness, and the quick, hushed chatter of voices.

Rand winced. He'd forgotten Lillian and the Alspaughs were in the kitchen. They'd no doubt heard the yelling, if not the words, and he knew Lillian would have his head for it later. But right now he didn't give a damn.

He stepped back, gripping the banister with white-knuckled tightness, struggling to gain control of himself.

"Belle," he said carefully, quietly. "Listen to me for a minute, will you?"

She let out a breath and backed away, crossing her arms again over her chest. Like armor, he thought without amusement. He recognized the look. She wouldn't back down. Unfortunately this time he had no choice but to make her. The thought of her telling Sarah the truth filled him with cold terror. Belle would never know, couldn't guess how hard it had been to live that lie the last two years. But he had done it, and not just for Lillian's sake but for Sarah's. God, she was just a child. She would never understand.

He swallowed and kept his voice low, too low for the people in the kitchen to hear. "There's a reason for the lie."

She lifted a brow. "There is?"

He nodded, took a deep breath. "There was a lot of gossip when you left. Not just about you, but because of Cort too—God, it was a mess. There were already rumors about us—"

"There were rumors before I left."

"Yeah, well, they got worse." Rand looked away, trying to keep the memory of that time away from his thoughts, trying just to tell her the truth as plainly as he could. "Your mama decided—" He saw the sudden fire in her eyes, and he rushed on —"your mama thought it would be better for everyone. There was so much talk, and we wanted to protect Sarah. There was—enough to bear without adding the scandal to it."

"And you were ashamed."

There was a note in her voice that Rand didn't understand. A note that made him vaguely uneasy. Guilt swept over him again, leaving his skin hot, his throat dry, and he looked down at the floor. "Yeah," he said slowly. "I was ashamed."

"I see." She stepped back farther away from him. "Well, I guess you'd better get used to it, then, because I've changed my mind about things. I'm not leavin' and I'm not takin' Sarah away. I'm stayin' here, with her."

"Staying?" he asked bitterly. "What does that mean? When have you ever stayed anywhere?"

"You don't know me anymore, Rand," she said quietly. That was all, just those simple words, and though her face was expressionless, he felt her condemnation with every part of him. He deserved it, he knew. Deserved her condemnation and more. Much more.

But she was not without blame herself, and he told himself that, hardened his voice to tell her he didn't give a damn what she wanted, that he didn't believe a word she said. He opened his mouth to say the words.

And stopped.

Because there was suddenly something in her expression he hadn't seen before. Something besides condemnation, something besides hurt. He saw it in her eyes, saw a vulnerability shining from them, a heaviness of spirit he didn't understand. It disheartened him somehow, and then Rand remembered how she'd looked when he first walked in, how he would have sworn she'd been crying.

Belle crying.

The image left him cold, left a hole in his heart, and Rand found he couldn't say the words. She was right, he didn't know her anymore. Especially today. In only a few hours something about her had changed. Unexpectedly. Quickly. Something—he didn't know what.

But he did know he was afraid of it, so afraid, he wanted to turn and walk out the door, away from her, to leave before that heaviness wrapped him up, before her vulnerability made him weak. But she was waiting, and he knew he had to make sure she wouldn't tell Sarah the truth. He had to protect his daughter from that until she was old enough to understand. Until he could explain himself. Because if Belle told Sarah now and then left when the impulsive notion of raising a child lost its appeal, if she ran away the way she had before, she would only hurt Sarah.

And in spite of what Belle said, he didn't trust her to stay.

But, Jesus, he wished he understood what it was he saw in her eyes.

Rand licked his lips. "I'm asking you not to tell her. I'm asking," he said. "Please don't tell her, Belle. Please. Not now. Not yet. I don't want to hurt her."

He looked up at her and was relieved to see there was no anger in her eyes, no shield. She was just watching him thoughtfully, and somewhere in that thoughtful look was a Belle he recognized. One he remembered.

She frowned, and he saw she was trying to think, to understand. "You think it would hurt her? Tellin' her the truth?"

He nodded slowly.

She took a deep breath. "All right," she said softly. "I won't tell her." She looked straight at him, and he saw the resignation in her eyes, the uncertainty. "But I won't wait forever, Rand."

"I'm not asking you to," he said, though he was. He was. "Thank you."

Chapter 11

The kitchen was so quiet, every little noise seemed too loud: the clanging of the skillet, the hiss of frying ham, the swish of Lillian's skirt. Rand took a sip of coffee, hoping it would help ease his headache—or at the very least his tension. The liquid burned its way over his tongue, down his throat. He drew in his breath sharply.

Lillian glanced over her shoulder. "Are you all right?" He nodded, and she turned away, silent again. It didn't surprise him. She had hardly spoken since he'd come into the kitchen, and he knew she was angry. He didn't blame her. He still found it hard to believe he'd lost control enough to shout at Belle while their neighbors were eating dinner only a room away. It embarrassed him to think of it, not because he cared what they'd heard but because he knew how much it humiliated Lillian. All too well he could imagine how she'd reacted, could see her sitting frozen at the table, working to keep a smile on her face.

He should have taken Belle someplace else. Upstairs, or even into the dark parlor, where they would disturb no one.

But he hadn't, and he knew why. Belle had disconcerted him with her words, with her eyes. He'd been too surprised to think, too busy trying to figure out what was going on. The Alspaughs, Lillian, dinner—they ceased to exist in those few moments. There had been nothing but Belle.

Rand winced at the memory of it. He wished he could take back the last hours, wished they hadn't happened, and it was because of more than just Lillian's embarrassment. Something had happened, something was different, and he needed time to sort it out in his mind. But, God, his head was pounding, and it was hard to think about anything at all.

"The wagon still has to be packed tonight," Lillian said without turning around.

The sound of her voice jarred Rand from his thoughts, and he stared at her in confusion before he finally realized she was talking about the fair. "Oh—yeah, I know. Is everything ready?"

"It's all in there." She pointed to a crate by the door.

He took another sip of coffee. "Is Belle coming?" he asked carefully, though he told himself he didn't want to know, didn't care.

For a moment Rand wasn't sure Lillian heard, but then he noticed how still she went, how stiffly she stood, and he cursed himself inwardly. Damn, he should never have brought up Belle's name. It gave Lillian the perfect opportunity to berate him for this afternoon, and he wasn't in the mood to hear it, would rather bear her uncomfortable silence than her tirade. But it was too late to take back the words, and any hope he had that she would let it pass disappeared when she turned from the stove. Her face was a polite mask, but her eyes glittered with anger.

"I don't know if Belle's coming or not," she said. Her voice was clipped and sharp. "You're the one who talked to her today. Though I heard you yelling, I regret to say I didn't hear what she had to say about the fair."

Her words hit him like shards of ice. Rand took a deep breath. "I'm sorry."

"Sorry? I should hope so. The whole neighborhood heard you fighting. Dorothy and Kenny certainly did. Couldn't you have had the decency at least to remember we had company?"

Rand clenched the cup in his hand. "Dorothy and Kenny are hardly company."

"It is still not"—she struggled for the word—"appropriate to fight so—so openly—in front of them."

She glared at him until Rand looked away uncomfortably. "What did they hear?" he asked.

"I doubt they heard anything but loud voices. I know that's all I heard. Thankfully I couldn't make out the words." Lillian wiped her hands on her apron as if just the thought was distasteful. "But I was just so—so stunned. Really, Rand—" She shook her head. "I don't understand. I don't understand why you didn't go into another room. The *stairs,* Rand—good heavens, anyone could have heard."

"I wasn't thinking," he said wryly.

"That is not an excuse."

No, it wasn't, but it was the truth anyway, and Rand couldn't think of what else to say, how to explain it to her. What could he say? *"I'm sorry, Lil, but she was crying, and I lost my head"? "I didn't mean to, but I saw something in her face I still don't understand"?* Lillian would understand that even less than he did.

Rand looked down into his coffee and ran a hand through his hair. "I don't know what to tell you," he said softly. "I'm sorry."

She was quiet. The only sound was the spattering ham, the soft percolation of coffee. The silence seemed to last forever.

Rand looked up. Lillian was staring at him measuringly, and he saw resignation in her gaze, along with concern. It surprised him, made him feel her disappointment even more keenly, and he pushed back his chair, wanting suddenly to be away from her. The legs screeched on the floor, screaming in his head, and he saw her wince.

"Please call Sarah for supper," she said, turning back to the stove.

Supper. Sitting here at this table, pretending everything was fine, was the last thing he wanted to do. He wished he could go out to the barn and sit in the rocking chair until he heard the soft chirping of the katydids at sunset. He wanted quiet. Peace. But he wouldn't get that tonight, he knew, hadn't had it since Belle returned.

The only respite he was likely to get was if Belle didn't come to the fair, and that wasn't likely. He couldn't imagine that she would sit meekly at home while the rest of them went off together. Especially because Sarah was coming, too, and he didn't believe Belle would give up the chance to perhaps take Sarah and run—despite her words.

He swallowed the last dregs of his coffee and rose stiffly, nearly turning into Belle as she came through the doorway.

"Hey," she said. She glanced at him and then she shrank by him without touching. She went to the stove and reached past Lillian for the coffeepot. "So when do we go tomorrow?"

Rand's chest constricted; what was left of his brief, ridiculous hope crumbled away. "Go?" he asked, wondering if it was at all possible to dissuade her. "Go where?"

"To the fair." She didn't look at him, but spooned sugar and cream into her coffee as though she hadn't a care in the world, as if they hadn't been screaming at each other in the stairway only a few hours ago. "It starts tomorrow, doesn't it?"

He ignored the glance Lillian threw him. "I didn't know you were planning to come along."

"Oh?" Belle looked at him then. Her eyes widened slightly, innocently, and she raised a brow. "Why wouldn't I?"

"There will be so many people there, Isabelle," Lillian interjected.

"I hope so. It's a fair, after all."

"They'll be talking—"

"They've talked before." Belle shrugged. "I'm not afraid of a little scandal. Besides, I've never been to a fair."

"But Isabelle—"

"But Mama." Belle's voice was hard with sarcasm. "I know you're worried about what's best for me, and I can't tell you how much I appreciate it, but I'm goin', and that's that." She glanced at Rand. "What time do we leave?"

"In the morning." His voice sounded hoarse; it was all he could do to get it out at all. "Early."

"Good." She pulled out a chair and sat down, but her eyes never left his, and Rand saw the challenge in them, the *stop me if you can* defiance. "The sooner the better. I'm lookin' forward to it, aren't you?"

He nodded reluctantly. "I wouldn't miss it."

She smiled. "Neither would I."

The morning was cold. Rand huddled in his bulky wool coat and wished he'd worn thicker gloves to handle the reins. There had been a thin layer of frost on the windows when he'd awakened, and the cold cut into his bones while he washed Bertha in preparation for the fair. Now, even after two cups of coffee and a huge breakfast, he couldn't get warm.

Though that may have been due to Lillian as much as anything. He stole a glance at her. She sat beside him on the wagon seat. Her spine was stiffly erect, her arms like bars around Sarah, who was sound asleep in her lap. Lillian was still angry with him for yesterday, he knew. She'd barely spared him a good morning.

He sighed, his breath clouded on the cold air. His stepmother had made it clear she expected him to order Belle to stay home. The fact that he hadn't no doubt added to her anger. But he didn't care. The last thing he wanted to do was antagonize Belle. He was already too worried she'd go back on her promise. He could not take the risk that she would tell Sarah the truth.

He felt Belle now behind him, sitting in the wagon bed. He knew she was nestled in the corner, practically drowning in that too-big, too-worn old coat. Like Lillian, Belle had been quiet this morning, but she didn't have to say anything to make him aware of her. He knew where she was every moment; he was aware of her everywhere, heard her muffled breathing, felt the way her body shifted with the movement of the wagon.

Jesus, he wished he could get her out of his mind.

Not that he'd ever been able to, he thought dryly, but he would give just about anything if she would fade into the background so he could easily ignore her. The thought nearly made him laugh. Ignore Belle? He didn't know if he could. His whole life had been full of her. He'd loved her, wanted her, hated her, but he'd never been able to ignore her.

Though he was willing to try. He wanted to enjoy the fair the way he always had, wanted to think about nothing but livestock and farming equipment, to laugh and gossip and eat.

He knew it was odd for a man who hated farming as much as he did to love the fair. He should care about which seed was better or what kind of hog gave up the most lard, but he didn't give a damn about any of it, and it wasn't why he went. It was the excitement of the fair that tugged at him. The salesmen, the hawkers, the auctions . . . All those things reminded him that there were other places in the world, places he would never see. The fair was the only way to experience them, and so he drank it up and wished for more, was sorry when the three days were over and he went back to being Randall Sault, farmer.

He clenched his jaw. Now even that respite was lost to him. He'd be spending these three days guarding Sarah. The fair was the perfect place for Belle to steal his daughter and run; it would be easy for her to get lost in the crowds. And even if she didn't do that, there was still the other threat hovering in the air between them, the knowledge that only her whim kept her from telling Sarah the truth. The thought of her doing so left him weak. She'd said she wanted to be a real mother to Sarah, but he didn't believe her. Belle was, had always been, impulsive. She lost interest in anything that took too long. It would be the same with this, he knew. She would get tired of waiting and move on, and as much as he hoped that would happen, he feared for Sarah if it did. She was already growing attached to Belle. If Sarah knew Belle was her mother . . .

The image of his daughter's hurt confusion wavered before him, made him stiff with tension, and he knew that his only choice was to hope Belle would stick to her promise. She had said she would wait, but not forever, and he had no idea what that meant to her, whether she would wait two hours or two years.

The turnoff for Lundy's Lane was ahead of him, and

Rand buried his thoughts and concentrated on the horses. There was a line of wagons behind and in front of him, all loaded with pens holding livestock and crates of baked goods, all on their way to John Reber's field. Gradually the murmur of hellos and quiet jokes blended with the shouts from the fairgrounds ahead. By the time they reached the field, excitement filled the air. Even Lillian seemed to relax. Rand turned the wagon off the road and onto the grounds, stopping beneath one of the huge shade trees at the perimeter.

"Are we here?" Sarah asked sleepily, lifting her head from Lillian's lap.

"We sure are, Little Bit." Rand climbed from the seat and reached for her, planting her firmly on the ground before he helped Lillian down. "Don't go running off by yourself, Sarah."

In the wagon bed Belle got to her feet. "I didn't expect anythin' this big," she said. "Why don't you come on with me, Sarah? You can show me around."

"No!" Rand and Lillian spoke at once.

Lillian stepped forward and took Sarah's hand firmly. "I need Sarah's help up at the grange exhibits this morning."

Belle didn't look at her mother. Instead her gaze fastened on Rand. The mix of anger and hurt in her eyes made him uncomfortable. Her words of yesterday came circling back, a low whisper in his ear: *"Since when do you decide how the world works, Rand? Since when do you decide what's right and what's wrong?"*

He cleared his throat and turned away, moving quickly to the horses.

"You're goin' to the grange?" Belle's voice carried in the clear, cold air, following her mother. "Maybe I'll come with you."

"Why don't you stay here?" Lillian said. "I'm sure Rand could use your help, couldn't you, Randall?"

"Couldn't you, Randall?" Rand struggled to restrain the urge to throttle his stepmother. His fingers were suddenly stiff and awkward as he fumbled with the harness. But he knew what Lillian was doing, knew she was trying to keep Sarah away from Belle, and so he heard his voice, low, barely audible. "Yeah. Yeah, I could use your help."

Behind him he heard Lillian grapple with the crate, and he let her struggle alone, feeling too angry to help. "Good," she said a little breathlessly. "Then we'll go on up."

Rand nodded briefly. He heard Belle mumble something, but he wasn't sure what it was. Then he heard only the sounds of the people around them and Lillian and Sarah's footsteps as they started off across the brown grass.

He didn't bother to turn around, just kept working with the horses, setting out feed and water, wishing—hoping—that when he went back to the wagon, Belle would be miraculously gone.

"So what can I do?"

He winced at the sound of her voice. It was close. Too close. She had left the wagon to come up behind him, and he hadn't even heard her approach. Rand closed his eyes briefly, took a deep breath, and straightened. "Nothing," he said slowly. "You don't have to help me, Belle. Go on off and find your friends."

She laughed, a short, oddly shaky sound. "What friends?"

"Lydia Boston's still around."

"Is she? I thought Lydia would've found a husband by now."

He unfastened the harness, moved back to lower the tongue of the wagon. "No."

She stepped out of his way. "Oh. Lydia was always such a flirt, I thought sure she'd be married."

"She's too much of a flirt," he said tersely.

"No worse than her brother." Belle paused. "Charlie's the biggest ladies' man I ever saw. I s'pose he's married."

Rand had a fleeting image of Charlie Boston and Marie Scholl at the last church social, laughing together. The tongue of the wagon slipped from his fingers, the chain pinched him. Rand cursed and yanked his hand away. "Dammit! No, he's not married."

"Oh." He heard her fidget. "Are you sure you don't need any help?"

He threw the chain to the ground and swiveled to face her. She was standing even closer than he'd thought, close enough so that she backed away at his movement. Her arms were crossed over her chest, hands tucked beneath for warmth, and in the moment of her surprise she looked heartbreakingly young. Young, innocent, wary. *Familiar. Jesus, too familiar.*

Rand cursed again and ran a hand through his hair. "I don't need any help, Belle."

"I see." She licked her lips, looked away thoughtfully. He waited for a sarcastic comment, but all she did was nod and motion toward the wagon. "Where are we takin' the pig?"

It surprised him. He'd expected her to say something to disarm him, some honest, if cynical statement meant only to confuse him. He had not expected her to pretend they didn't both know exactly why she was here. Her unpredictability bothered him, threw him off as well as a comment might have done. Rand frowned irritably. "Look, Belle, I said I don't need—"

"I know what you said." She looked straight at him, and those brown eyes were guileless, shockingly so. "But I imagine if I go on up to the grange, Mama will somehow find somethin' for me to do—somethin' on the other side of the fair from Sarah, no doubt. And . . ." She took a deep breath, her voice softened. "And I have no place else to go."

This was it, the honesty he'd been waiting for, only there was no sarcasm, and that disarmed him even more. Rand looked at her standing there, arms locked, her face pinched and tight from the cold, and he thought again of her words yesterday, felt the hot touch of guilt, the ache of fear.

"All right," he said abruptly. "Come on."

He strode to the wagon, to the narrow pen he'd set up in the back. Bertha paced and snorted inside, rubbing her snout against the wooden slats anxiously when she saw him, trying to rid herself of the rope around her upper jaw. "It's all right, girl," he murmured reassuringly. He gestured for Belle to come around to the back of the wagon. "She'll want to run," he said. "But she won't run over you. So just stand there until I get hold of the rope."

Belle nodded.

He reached for the latch on the pen. "Easy, girl," he coaxed, slipping the pin slowly from the loop. "Easy, now . . ."

Everything seemed to happen at once. Bertha pressed against the door. The latch sprung open so hard, it clipped Rand's hand. He jumped away, cursing as the door on the pen sprang open and out crashed two hundred and ten pounds of prime Poland China hog. She scrambled off the wagon bed, and the rest happened in a flash. He saw Bertha streak by, saw Belle take off after her, skirts flying.

Rand pushed away from the wagon and hit the grass at a flying run. People dodged and yelled around him, but all he saw was Belle a few steps ahead, and beyond her Bertha, trailing her lead rope. Desperately Rand ran harder. The breeding for the next year depended on that goddamned hog—

He surged past Belle just as Bertha headed for the road. *Christ, the road . . .*

He had barely finished thinking the words when he saw the wagons. They were moving smartly up Lundy's Lane, heading straight for Bertha.

"Stop her!" Belle yelled behind him. "Runaway pig! Stop her!"

The man on the lead wagon looked up. He waved his arm and urged his horses forward—right into Bertha's path. She hesitated, looked this way, that, and then she set her forelegs, trying desperately to stop when she saw there was no escape.

It was all the time he needed. Rand lunged. He landed hard, knocking away his breath, sending Bertha squealing to the ground. His fist closed on the rope around her upper jaw.

Belle crashed on top of him, slamming him and Bertha into the ground. Skirts, legs, feet tangled with his, and he heard her hoarse rasping, felt the uneven rise and fall of her chest.

"It's all right." He breathed. "We've got her. We've got her."

The man on the wagon jumped down and hurried over. "You two all right? That was some run there."

Rand looked up and nodded. "We're—fine," he managed. "Thanks. That was quick thinking."

"No problem." The man pushed back the brim of his hat and looked them over thoughtfully. "You need some help gettin' that pig back?"

"No—no." Rand glanced at Bertha, who was heaving beneath him, but quiet. "She's not going anywhere soon."

"Okay, then. Good luck." The man nodded and walked away.

Rand heard Belle's quiet laughter at his ear. "No, she's not goin' anywhere," she said. She scrambled back, pulling away from him. Her thick braid slid across his face and then fell away. He was suddenly cold.

"You plannin' on lyin' on that pig forever?" she asked.

He sat up, keeping a firm grip on the rope, and twisted to look at Belle. She knelt beside him, one hand still on the hog's heaving side. She caught his gaze and raised an eyebrow. There was the thin trace of a smile on her lips. "Well, Rand, guess you needed my help after all."

The teasing struck a chord, pierced through him with the sharp sweetness of the past. Rand swallowed. "Yeah, I guess I did."

"You're welcome."

"Thanks."

She scrutinized Bertha and then looked back to him. "She'll need a bath again, though. Guess that'll teach you to get up before dawn to wash a pig." She took a deep breath, shook her head slowly. "I have to say you surprised me. Damn, I didn't know you could run that fast."

Then she smiled.

Jesus, that smile. Rand lost his breath. He saw the teasing laughter glowing from her brown eyes, illuminating her face. Laughter he hadn't seen for a long time —God, it seemed like forever.

He didn't want to smile back. Tried to hold it off, but he couldn't, and finally he gave in and grinned at her, unable to help himself, in that moment wanting only to laugh with her, to tease her while her hair glowed golden and shining in the morning sun.

He had missed this. Sweet Jesus, how he had missed it.

Chapter 12

Belle leaned back against the rough clapboards of the grange building, pressing her palms hard against the sun-warmed wood. It had been two hours since she'd left Rand at the livestock ring, but she couldn't keep from thinking about him, couldn't stop reliving the morning over and over again in her mind. The images were so clear: the frozen sunlight, the smell of grass and dirt, the way the wind grabbed her hair as she chased that damned hog. Belle didn't know if she would ever forget the sight of Rand sprawled atop that pig, his hair in his face and mud stains on his cheek. There had been nothing dignified about him in that moment, nothing stiff or strained as he struggled with a squealing Bertha. No, in that moment he had been the Rand that Belle remembered, the friend she'd missed all these years.

And in the blink of an eye she had forgotten he was anything else.

It had all been so easy. Too easy. The last six years fell away as if they'd never existed. She hadn't known it was possible—could it be possible?—to forget so easily. She'd thought all her feelings for him were dead, that she had nothing but contempt and anger left now. But this morning feelings she'd spent years nurturing had disappeared, and she'd been left only with the ones she told herself she didn't remember, the ones she didn't want to feel.

It began yesterday, she knew. With the snake, and the marks on the door, and the way he'd stood at the bottom of the stairs, his eyes dark with desperation and fear.

That image haunted her all through the night and all this morning. She wanted to take comfort from it, wanted to enjoy the feeling of having some kind of power over him, of being able to make him afraid.

But she couldn't. Because he wasn't afraid of her, and she knew it. He was afraid *for* Sarah, and it made all the difference in the world.

He was afraid Belle would hurt her own daughter.

It made her heart ache to think about it. Yesterday it hurt so badly that she had wanted nothing more than for him to trust her—as if his trust would make her own suffering go away.

It was why she'd promised not to tell Sarah the truth. His concern for their daughter made Belle feel small and inadequate, and she remembered the black marks on the bedroom door with a suffocating sense of desperation. She wanted Sarah to know who her real mother was, but the concern in Rand's eyes held Belle back. There was something about that concern she didn't understand, and she was afraid of telling Sarah until she understood it. She knew so damn little about being a mother.

So she promised, even though the words meant nothing. She said them to comfort him, and instead she'd been comforted. The relief in his eyes made her feel as if she'd done the right thing.

She didn't like that feeling. She did not want to care what he thought of her. She'd spent years learning not to care. She'd thought she was strong, thought nothing

Rand could do would matter to her again, but she was wrong. How was it she'd been so defenseless?

Belle closed her eyes, forced herself to remember a harsh, raw voice. *"I don't want you, don't you understand? Don't you understand?"*

Humiliation surged through her again, and Belle opened her eyes, staring into the bright sunshine and seeing the shadows of a dark November night, feeling the harshness of memory as vividly as if it had been yesterday.

No, she would not forget again. Not ever again. And she would never forgive him.

She took strength from the knowledge, grabbed onto it like a shield. As long as she didn't forgive him, he couldn't hurt her, he couldn't get close enough. She could protect herself against the little hurts, could even bear them. She could be civil to Rand, could even be friendly for Sarah's sake, but she would never care for him again. As long as she remembered that, she would be fine.

Belle took a deep breath and moved away from the wall. She'd come to the fair to be with Sarah, and she wanted to do just that. The crowds around the exhibit hall were dwindling, and she glanced at the sun, trying to gauge the time. The trotting races were in less than an hour. It was what she'd spent this whole miserable day waiting for. At last the chance to be with her daughter. Belle went through the entryway leading to the exhibits. She would lock her mother in the horse barn if she had to in order to get to Sarah.

The judge's booming voice echoed in the rafters. Women gathered before the makeshift podium, anxiously awaiting the results of the judging. She saw Dorothy Alspaugh straining near the front. Belle stood on her toes, craning her neck to spot her mother. It didn't take long. Lillian was near Dorothy, and unlike the other ladies there, she was silent and still. Not even the slightest excitement showed on her face, and she certainly wasn't twittering like the others. Belle smiled dryly. She doubted her mother even knew how to twitter.

"Third place, with a prize of twenty-five cents, goes to Mrs. Emily Groves, for her outstanding corn relish."

There was a flurry of clapping. Belle pushed her way through the crowd, barely sparing a glance for the podium, where Mrs. Groves was graciously accepting her ribbon.

"Second place, with a prize of fifty cents, goes to Miss Margaret Browning, for a simply wonderful pickle relish."

Her mother was just in front. Belle uttered a hasty "excuse me" to the woman beside her and squeezed through. As she'd thought, Sarah stood beside Lillian, looking bored and restless while Lillian watched the judge with rapt attention.

"Hey there, Sarah," Belle said in a loud whisper. "Ready to go to the races?"

Sarah whipped around, and Lillian turned, looking startled. "Isabelle!" she said, frowning. "What are you doing here? I thought Rand—"

"I lost Rand about three hours ago, Mama," Belle said impatiently. "I came lookin' for Sarah. The races start—"

"Shhh!" The woman next to her glared. "They're announcin' first prize!"

Lillian jerked back to the front. The judge smiled broadly, holding up a blue ribbon.

"And now, at long last, it's time for the first prize in the relish class." He paused for effect. "First prize, with an award of one dollar and fifty cents, goes to Mrs. Dorothy Alspaugh, for her delicious pepper relish!"

Dorothy gave a little scream of delight and hurried up to the podium to accept her award. Lillian set her mouth, took Sarah's hand, and started to move away.

Belle followed. "You look upset, Mama," she noted. "I didn't know you even entered a relish."

"I didn't."

"Well, don't feel so bad. I expect your applesauce cake'll win plenty of prizes."

Lillian waited until they were just beyond the crowd, and then she whirled around with a sharp sound of exasperation. "What do you want, Isabelle?"

Belle widened her eyes innocently. "Why, I told you already, Mama. I just want to take Sarah to the races."

"The races?" Sarah's face brightened. "Oh, Grandma, the races!"

Lillian gave Belle an annoyed look. "Sarah's too young."

"I don't know why. I'll hold her on my shoulders so she can see."

"Isabelle, I really don't think—"

"She won't get lost if she's with me." Belle ignored her mother's protest, bending until she was even with Sarah. "What d'you say, Sarah? Want to go watch the horses with me?"

Sarah looked hopefully up at Lillian. "Please, Grandma? Please, can I?"

"Your father and I decided you could go when you were ten," Lillian said.

"I'll be ten when the piggies are born!"

Belle lifted a brow and looked at her mother. "Did you hear that, Mama? She says she'll be ten in no time."

"I said no."

Belle straightened, working to keep her resentment from surfacing. "Mama, I think you'd better let Sarah go with me," she said softly.

Lillian gave her a sharp look. "I don't think . . ." she said, abruptly trailing off.

Belle saw the spark of uncertainty in her mother's eyes, and she knew suddenly that Rand had told Lillian about her threat to tell Sarah the truth—and that Lillian was afraid she would. Belle's throat tightened. God, even her own mother didn't trust her. Her own mother.

She told herself she shouldn't be surprised. Lillian had never trusted her with anything, and Belle didn't know why she expected it now. But still, the thought brought a stab of pain that Belle forced away. It didn't matter. She wanted Sarah, and she would do whatever it took to get her. If that meant letting her mother believe she would go back on her word, then so be it.

Belle took a deep breath. She could almost see Lillian's mind churning, could almost hear her thoughts: *"Will she tell Sarah the truth? Or won't she? Should I take the risk?"*

Deliberately Belle smiled.

Lillian looked startled, and then she stepped back. "Very well," she said stiffly. "But we'll *all* go to the races. Together."

Belle felt her smile waver. She hadn't thought Lillian would decide to come with them, but she guessed it wasn't that important anyway. There was no way her mother would put Sarah on her shoulders, no way Lillian would laugh and shout and scream for the horse to win. Belle knew already how Lillian would be. Stiff, unamused. Easy to ignore.

Belle smiled down at Sarah. "Well, I guess we're on our way to the trottin' park."

Sarah grinned back. "I wanna be at the very front!"

Belle shot a look at Lillian. "Well, maybe not the very front, Sarah. But near there, I promise." She reached down, taking Sarah's other hand. "I promise."

* * *

Rand leaned against the railpen and sighed with relief. Everything was done. Bertha was snoring in the corner of the pen, fed and bathed, exhausted from her ordeal this morning. There was clean straw, and the dirt had been swept. It had taken him more than two hours to do it, but finally she was as ready as he could make her for the judges. Now he could relax.

He glanced around the roofed, open-sided building. Earlier he'd been surrounded by people, but now there were only a few men left, and the barn was quiet except for the rustling of the animals, the now-and-again clank of feed buckets. He reached into his pocket and took out the plain gold watch that was another legacy from his father. It was nearly time for the races. No wonder everyone was gone.

He shoved the watch away. He hadn't been to the trotting park in two years. Lillian had always thought Sarah too young to go, and though he hadn't agreed, he didn't care enough about it to fight. Now, though, he was alone, and the morning had left him feeling restless.

And he'd run out of things to do to lose the image of Belle's smile.

The races might be just the thing to do it, and if nothing else, it was better than sitting around here. He'd just get Bertha a little more water and then head up to the park. He reached over the fence for the bucket.

"Rand! Rand Sault!" A high, feminine voice came from the far end of the barn.

Rand let the bucket fall. He straightened, turning to see the woman who called him.

Two women actually. They hurried across the floor toward him, their booted feet raising little clouds of dust. He recognized them immediately. Lydia Boston.

And Marie Scholl.

He swallowed, suddenly remembering his conversation with his stepmother—had it only been two nights ago?—and feeling the absurd urge to bolt. But then the two of them were smiling in front of him, and he had no choice but to say hello and smile back.

He made a small bow. "Ladies. How nice to see you."

"Randall Sault! You should be ashamed of yourself, stayin' away so long!" Lydia scolded prettily, shaking her dark head. "We missed you the other night at the singin' party. Paula was sure sorry you weren't there. We all were."

Singing party. His mind went blank for a moment, and then he remembered. "Too much to do," he said briefly. "I'm sorry I couldn't come."

"We missed you." Marie smiled. She was wearing blue today, a sprigged frock that made her look gentle and feminine, and for some reason it made him think of Belle and her yellow wool delaine. Which was absurd. Belle never looked feminine, nor gentle. Even in demure yellow she looked rebellious and startling, like a firebrand dropped in the middle of a hayfield. Marie would never look that way. She would never do anything shocking or unconventional.

The thought comforted him. He smiled back at her. "I'll try to make the next one," he promised.

Lydia smoothed back a dark brown curl. "I guess you've reason enough now that Belle's back in town. No one expects you to go out visitin' when your sister's just come home."

"Stepsister," he corrected.

She gave him a startled look. "Well, yes, that's what I meant. Anyway I figure it's been nearly a week now, and it's about time you were out doin' some socializin'. Paula said she wanted to have another singin' party next week and that you're to come. Bring Belle if you can. Goodness knows we'd all like to see her."

"I've heard so much about her," Marie said. "Lydia tells me she's just a character."

"Well, now, you know I only mean that in the kindest sense, Rand," Lydia gushed. She turned to Marie. "She was always doin' the craziest things, even when she was young. She was always in trouble. Wasn't she, Rand?"

The air around him suddenly seemed too thin. Rand took a deep breath. "Yeah. Yeah, she was."

"Once she even dared Rand to jump off the Rock Mill bridge. Remember that?"

He felt cold. "I remember."

"But he wouldn't do it. No one could blame him actually. No one even knows how deep that pool is. They say there's a team of horses and a wagon at the very bottom of it."

"Really?" Marie turned an interested gaze to him. "How ever did they get there?"

Rand's throat closed up.

Lydia answered for him. "No one knows. Some drunkard probably. I guess there's a hundred stories about it. Oh, goodness, there's Ben Groves!" She shot them an apologetic look as she went hurrying off. "I'll be right back. Ben! Ben!"

Rand stared after her, still reeling over her words. A hundred stories, she'd said. None of them true. Rand's stomach knotted, the memories of his mother's suicide crowded, dark and menacing, at the edge of his mind. Frantically he pushed them away.

"A hundred stories," Marie said softly, as though she'd read his mind. "Well, now, I never knew that. Can you imagine? I guess now I'll have to find someone who can tell me all those stories."

"Charlie knows them," he managed.

Marie's face fell. Rand thought he saw a swift flash of disappointment cross her pale brown eyes.

But then she smiled. Lightly. Softly. She glanced nervously toward Lydia and Ben Groves. They were too far away to hear, but still her voice was very soft, very shy. "I'd rather hear them from you."

"Oh?" Her comment took him by surprise, the last vestiges of memory drained away. She was disarmingly, naively honest. Rand ran his tongue over his teeth. "I'm not sure Charlie would like that."

She laughed lightly, nervously. "Oh, but Charlie—he's—we're not—it's not like that."

Suddenly Rand understood. He glanced at Marie, who was looking at him with those shy, honest eyes, and he knew that this had all been a plan, that Marie had deliberately sought him out. She wanted him, maybe even thought she loved him. Charlie had only been a substitute, and Rand realized that he had hurt her when he'd drawn away. He had treated her unfairly. Had thought for a few months that he might want a wife and then thought better of it, so he'd simply stopped seeing her.

But he wasn't sure how he felt now, and before he could decide, she looked at him nervously, licked her full lips, and something about the way she did it triggered a memory. He took in her slender curves, the way the blue-sprigged calico flared gently over her hips. He remembered a kiss he'd stolen from her last summer. Chaste, gentle, barely touching. Remembered the way her lips had felt under his.

He remembered Lillian's words of a few nights ago. *"You should be thinking of marriage, Rand. After all, you're nearly twenty-eight."*

Marie Scholl. *Maybe.*

He gave her his best smile. "So you and Charlie are just friends, huh?"

She flushed. "Yes."

"And you don't think he'd mind that we're standing here talking to each other, alone."

"N-no."

"Or that he'd mind if I asked you to come to the races with me this afternoon?"

She looked shocked, confused for just a moment, and then she lifted her eyes to his, smiling. "Well—he's in Cincinnati buying a new ram."

"Guess he can't mind, then."

"No." Her smile widened. "I guess he can't."

"Good. Then let's go." He offered his arm. Lydia was still talking to Ben Groves not far away, but he knew Marie had forgotten all about her friend. Rand was in no mood to have Charlie Boston's sister following behind them anyway. Being seen alone with him at the races would hardly tarnish Marie's reputation. There would be a hundred other people there, jostling and crowding for space. There wouldn't even be a chance for them to be alone.

And he didn't regret that. He didn't want to look into her soulful brown eyes and know she wanted him to kiss her. He didn't want to have to make that decision. For now all he wanted was to forget about everything, and Marie Scholl had always been the perfect way to do that.

She talked animatedly beside him as they made their way past the stands selling food and crafts, weaving their way through the crowd. Before they even reached the track, he heard the sounds of cheering, and he hastened his step, anxious to get there. He wanted to stand at the rail and watch the horses sweeping around the third-of-a-mile track, wanted to feel Marie's hand at his elbow and hear her voice cheering along with his. But he didn't want to make conversation.

When they came to the trotting park, he threaded his way through the people, pulling Marie behind him until they were near the front. The first race had already ended, but cheers still filled his ears. He couldn't hear the words Marie was shouting at him. Someone jostled them, and Marie reached up and grabbed at her hat, holding it in place and laughing as the second race began.

"Come on, Devil!" Someone beside him shouted. "Come on, now! Faster! Faster!"

"Go, Dan! Get that nag runnin'!"

"Holy hell, that mare's a doer!"

Rand laughed, for the first time in days feeling free and unencumbered. The excitement rushed through him, the blood in his fingers and cheeks tingled. The horses flew around the track, their hooves pounding the dirt, nostrils flaring. He glanced back at Marie. Her cheeks were flushed, her eyes glittered with excitement.

"Who do you want to win?" he shouted to her.

"The—!"

"The what?"

"The roan!"

"The roan it is." Rand pushed through the people until he was against the rail. He felt her behind him, at his back. He leaned forward. "Come on, boy, run! Run!"

The horses rounded the final curve. The roan strained to the front. Rand felt the blood rushing to his head, felt the pull of the muscles in his neck as he yelled along with the others.

"Rand!"

Marie's voice was like a gnat in his ear. He ignored it. "Come on! Come on!"

"Rand!" Her hand pulled at him, grabbing his elbow. "Rand!"

The horses pounded the short stretch. The crowd surged forward.

"Rand!"

He swung around, annoyed. "Just a minute!"

"But look!" She pointed into the crowd. "Isn't that your—?"

"My what?"

"Your daughter!"

He thought he heard the word wrong, but still he couldn't keep himself from following her finger. He stared into the crowd, searching, looking—

And then he saw her. Sarah. She was above the crowd, and her round face was lit with joy. She screamed with the others, pointing and laughing. He heard the echo of the horses, the drumlike sound of their hooves hammering the dirt, heard the cheers as the horses raced through the finish line.

"The roan! The roan won!"

But it all faded to the back of his mind, vague sounds and shapes that had nothing to do with anything. He felt Marie grabbing his arm, the bump and nudge of the people around him. And he saw Sarah clap her plump little hands and look down smiling.

Into Belle's face.

Belle's smiling face. The same face and the same smile that had burst through his consciousness this morning, that sent him reeling as if he'd never seen the sun before.

Rand's chest felt tight. His heart pounded. And he suddenly wished like hell he was alone with Marie so he could kiss her.

Chapter 13

The next day Belle waited outside the home exhibits listening to the hawk of the vendors, the *baa* of the sheep in the livestock ring a short distance away. The sun was hot, the afternoon felt more like an Indian summer than the start of fall, and she pushed at the brim of her large hat, forcing it back from her eyes.

Damn, where were they? She'd been standing here for the last hour waiting for Lillian and Sarah to make an appearance. They had disappeared this morning almost the moment they arrived back at the fair, hurrying off before Belle had a chance to react or protest. The thought filled her with frustration, a nagging ache. In the two days she'd been at the fair, she hadn't spent a single second alone with Sarah. Lillian was always there, grabbing hands and taking control with exasperating skill.

The way she always had.

Belle stared at the sheep in front of her unseeingly. Her mother was a master at making sure everything went the way she wanted it to, and Belle already saw the effect on Sarah: the resentment in the child's eyes, the too-obedient way she followed orders. Belle recognized it too well—that resentment had been in her own eyes once, along with a hundred plans to escape, a hundred places to hide. She wondered if Sarah had found those places yet, if she'd ever gone to the canal and sat on the banks just watching the packet boats, or pulled a few bass from the Hocking River. Had Sarah ever hidden in the loft of the barn and watched the world go by?

Or had no one shown her those things yet?

Belle sighed, wishing—again—that she knew where Lillian and Sarah had gone this morning. She was certain they would come back here. Lillian had a pie entered for judging, as well as a collection of preserves that Belle hadn't even bothered to look at. Eventually her mother would be back—with Sarah anchored to her side, no doubt.

Almost in response to her thought, Lillian and Sarah stepped from the building. Belle jerked away from the pole she was leaning against, meaning to hurry over. But then she paused. They were with someone else, a woman she'd never seen before. Another one of Lillian's friends probably. Belle steeled herself for the inevitable scrutiny and walked over.

"Hey there, Mama," she said, pasting a broad smile on her face. "I've been lookin' for you."

Lillian stiffened. Her smile was equally forced. "Why hello, Isabelle." She glanced at the woman standing beside her, "Marie, have you met my daughter, Isabelle?"

"I don't believe I have." The woman called Marie smiled and extended her hand. "Hi there, I'm Marie Scholl. It's so nice to meet you at last. After all the stories I've heard, I was beginning to think people were making you up."

Belle paused, taken aback for just a moment. The words were sincere, and she thought she saw real pleasure in Marie Scholl's face, pleasure without a hint of disapproval. It was so odd coming from one of her mother's friends that Belle wasn't sure she was really seeing it. She took Marie's hand warily. "Oh, I'm real all right," she said. "Much to Mama's dismay, I'm afraid."

She felt Lillian tense beside her, but Marie just took the words as a joke and laughed—a clear, trilling laugh that rang in the air. "From what I've heard, I imagine you were a handful when you were a child. I have a few children like that in my class."

"Marie is the teacher we brought in from Virginia last year—and a good friend of ours," Lillian explained.

Belle frowned at the strange emphasis in her mother's voice and then ignored it. "I see. So you've only been here a year?"

"Just one year." Marie nodded. Her eyes sparkled. "But I love it here already. Everyone's so friendly—especially your family."

Lillian smiled, and there was something in her eyes that made Belle feel vaguely uncomfortable. "It's our pleasure, Marie. Isabelle, did I tell you that Rand—"

"Grandma, can I have some cider now?" Sarah whined.

"In a minute, Sarah," Lillian's fingers tightened on Sarah's hand. She looked at Belle. "Marie is—"

"Grandma, I'm thirsty."

Lillian frowned. "In a minute. I'm talking to Belle right now. As I was saying," she went on, "Marie is a good frie—"

"I want some cider." Sarah twisted against Lillian's skirts, pulling at her hand. She sent a pleading glance to Belle. "I'm thirsty."

It was too good a chance to miss. Belle stepped forward. "I'll take her to get some cider, Mama."

Lillian's lips tightened. "It's quite all right, Isabelle. She can wait. You shouldn't spoil her."

"But I was heading over there anyway," Belle said, smiling. She held out her hand to take Sarah's. "And this way you can talk to Marie. I just know you have plenty to say to her."

The desperation in Lillian's face would have been funny if it wasn't so hurtful. Belle struggled to ignore it, to tell herself it didn't matter.

"It's all right, Mama," she said. "It'll only be a minute."

Marie nodded and smiled. "We'll wait right here for you."

Lillian was caught. They both knew it. Belle saw the flash of panic in her mother's eyes, the tight anger. Lillian couldn't refuse without it looking odd, and God knew she wouldn't do that. Slowly she released Sarah's hand. Almost before the child's fingers were loose, Belle grabbed them. Sarah's chubby hand felt warm and sweaty in hers, and when Belle looked down, Sarah's smile was wide and relieved.

"I want two cups of cider," she said.

Belle laughed. "Come on, then." She threw a smile at her mother and Marie. "See you in a few minutes."

Then she and Sarah were walking away, across the path to the open space where vendors hawked candies and cider. Away from Lillian. Belle suddenly felt light and carefree. The sun was warm, the air was clear and sweet, and she was alone with Sarah. Belle wanted to run for the sheer joy of it, but she walked slowly instead, knowing Lillian wouldn't take her eyes off them and wanting to prolong the few short steps to the vendor as long as she could, to treasure this time alone with her daughter.

Sarah tugged at Belle's hand. "We're walkin' too slow. I'm hot."

"That cider'll cool you right up," Belle assured her. "Too bad we've got to stay around for the fair, or we could go swimmin'."

"Swimmin'?" There was a touch of longing in Sarah's voice. "I'm not allowed to go swimmin'."

Belle jerked to a stop in the middle of the fairway, sure she hadn't heard right. "You're not allowed to go swimmin'?"

"Huh-uh." Sarah shook her head. "Papa says it's dang'rous."

"Dangerous?" Belle squatted down even to Sarah. "The river or the canal?"

"Both."

Belle frowned. When she was young, she and Rand had spent hours at the river, at the canal. Fishing, swimming, betting on who could skip rocks the farthest. Those were some of her most treasured memories. It was impossible to believe they weren't Rand's, too, impossible to think he would deny such pleasures to his daughter.

Well, maybe he would, but she wouldn't. Belle took a deep breath and got to her feet. "We'll see about that. I'll tell you what, you and me will take a trip down to the canal just as soon as we get home. How would you like that?"

Sarah looked at her warily. "I'm not s'posed to."

"It's all right. You'll be goin' with me." Belle started toward the cider vendor. "It's about time we had a little fun."

"Will we go swimmin'?"

"No." Belle shook her head. "I think it'll be too cold to go swimmin', Sarah. But we'll stick our feet in the water and watch the boats go by. How does that sound?"

Sarah tugged on her hand. "I wanna go there now."

"Not yet. But soon. As soon as we get home." Belle turned to Sarah with a smile. "And this will be our secret, Sarah, all right? Don't tell your papa or Grandma."

" 'Cause they won't let me go," Sarah said sagely.

Belle nodded. "That's right. They won't let us go."

"I won't tell," Sarah vowed.

"Neither will I," Belle said. "It's a promise."

Just saying the words made her feel better, just as Sarah's promise filled her with a warmth nothing could take away. Sarah needed her. She needed someone to let her swim in the canal and fish in the river. Someone to teach her about the places to run away to, the places to be free.

Belle wanted to be that someone. More than anything she wanted it.

So she would make it happen. Because once she'd been a girl who needed someone to show her the same things. Because the boy who'd discovered them with her was gone forever.

But Belle had not forgotten them, and neither would her daughter. She would make sure of it.

The ride home from the fair was silent, and for that Rand was grateful. In the back of the wagon Sarah played quietly while Lillian watched, and though Belle was perched on the seat beside him, she hadn't said a word. He told himself he was happy about that, and he held himself as stiffly as he could to keep from touching her, to keep from having to mutter a quick "sorry" or hear her indrawn breath. From the corner of his eye he saw the way she studiously surveyed the passing scenery, and a hundred questions spiraled through his mind. *"Where were you at the fair? What were you doing? Who were you doing it with?"*

It drove him crazy, and he hated that it did. He had deliberately stayed away from her during the last three days. He'd taken his meals with neighbors or bought something from a vendor, and he'd spent two nights huddled in the freezing cold in the back of the wagon, ostensibly watching over Bertha, but in reality shivering alone until dawn, thinking of the rest of them in bed at home, warm beneath heavy quilts. But he still couldn't get the memory of her smile out of his head. Nor could he forget the sight of Sarah laughing on her shoulders, and the way Belle's eyes had sparkled in return. It ate away at him until he couldn't sleep, or eat, and he dreaded the end of the fair, since it meant she would be around all the time. At home he couldn't avoid her, couldn't keep Sarah away from her.

Ah, Jesus, what was he going to do?

He tried to concentrate on Sarah's meaningless babble as she played with a pile of rocks in the wagon bed, but he couldn't completely force the questions from his mind, and he wondered what Belle was thinking.

"This is my fav'rite one," Sarah said. She leaned forward, extending a grubby hand with a gray stone clenched between her fingers. "See, Belle?"

Belle glanced down and smiled. "That's a fine rock, Sarah."

"You wanna know what I call it?"

"What's that?"

"It's name is Anna, 'cause it looks just like my friend Anna."

"Oh, really?" Belle turned in the seat, leaning over to scrutinize the stone more closely. The movement made her braid fall over her shoulder. It brushed Rand's arm. He jerked away, and her gaze came up slowly to meet his. He turned back to the horses.

She went on speaking as if nothing had happened. "Your friend Anna is round and gray?"

Sarah giggled. "No. It just looks like her some."

The giggle made Rand wince. He heard Sarah's wistfulness, the touch of hero worship, and he knew that she was doing her best to impress Belle.

It made his heart fall. Rand urged the horses to a faster pace. "Sit back, Sarah," he said sternly. "I don't want you falling down."

"But—"

"Listen to your father, Sarah," Lillian said.

The talk stopped. Belle moved back around to face the front. He felt her disapproval hovering between them like a fog, and he set his jaw and stared straight ahead, wishing he could make the miles between here and home disappear.

They did finally. It seemed to take forever, but at last they reached the wooded road just before the farm. Rand's relief was overwhelming as he pulled the wagon into the drive.

Belle was off the seat almost before he came to a stop. She reached for Sarah before he even knew what was happening.

"Let's find a good place for these in your room," Belle said, grinning. She scooped up the pile of rocks and tucked them into her skirt pocket.

Lillian made a move to stop them. "Supper will be ready soon," she protested.

"Just call us," Belle said. She threw them both a triumphant smile, and then she grabbed hold of Sarah's hand and the two were gone, into the house before he or Lillian had time to say a word.

Lillian stared at the open front door, her mouth open, and it occurred to Rand that he had never seen her look so flabbergasted.

In seconds she snapped her mouth shut again. "Well, I—" she took a deep breath and looked at him. "Something has to be done about this."

He ran his tongue over his teeth, turned the reins over his fingers. "I don't suppose you have any suggestions?"

"Talk to her."

"And say what?"

Lillian sighed. She touched her chignon, mechanically smoothing away a nonexistent stray hair. "I don't know. There must be something you can say. She listens to you."

Rand laughed shortly. "Not anymore."

"Obviously she doesn't realize how much this behavior hurts Sarah. When she leaves—"

"When she leaves, she'll try to take Sarah with her," Rand said slowly, staring out at the woods beyond the barn. "That's what worries me. I'd rather have Sarah hurt and here than gone."

Lillian said nothing. He turned to look at her. Her eyes were lowered, her slender fingers pulled at the fringes of her heavy black shawl. As if she felt his stare, she looked up. "Yes, I suppose she means to leave," she said, and he heard the relief in her tone, though she tried to hide it. "What do you suggest we do to keep her from taking Sarah?"

"I don't know," he said, wishing he could say otherwise, wishing he had any idea at all.

"Yes, that's what I thought." Lillian's sigh filled the air between them. She got to her feet. He felt the wagon move as she stepped over the side and jumped to the ground. It surprised him; he couldn't remember Lillian ever getting out of the wagon without help before. She pulled the edges of her shawl more firmly about her and glanced up at him.

"Oh, Randall," she said, and he got the impression that she was trying to explain something to him, that it was important he understand. "She was always such a stubborn child. I—I did my best to control her, but it wasn't until we came here that anyone could tell her what to do. That person was you." She waved away his protest. "Oh, I know things became—impossible. Life has a way of doing that with Belle. I just . . . well, I've given up. I suppose I have no choice but to trust you to do what's right."

He couldn't speak, didn't know what to say, and before he could even think of the right words, she gave a short, affirming nod. "Well, then, I suppose I should go inside and find them."

She turned and walked away. She was up the stairs and through the front door before he could even say a word.

He stared at the house, his mind a blank except for Lillian's punishing words. *"I trust you to do what's right."* He wasn't sure what she meant. The whole speech had been a confession of sorts, and it surprised him. He had never known what Lillian thought about his role in driving Belle away, was never sure how his stepmother felt. All he knew was that she shouldn't have forgiven his actions. Hell, he couldn't forgive them himself. But she'd made it clear she didn't blame him.

She blamed Belle.

The realization made him remember his first impression of Lillian. She'd arrived at the farm one June morning with his father, who had been in Columbus to see about shipping grain. It was an unlikely pairing, but one Rand understood. She was young and pretty, and his father had been alone a long time. But Rand had also thought her stiff and unyielding, and he had looked at twelve-year-old Belle and seen the rebellion in her eyes and known that Lillian couldn't control her daughter—and that she resented it.

No, Lillian had never expected anything good from Belle, and he wasn't sure why, but when it came to what happened six years ago, Lillian was wrong. She was wrong to trust him and wrong to blame Belle. He knew whose fault it was. At twenty-two he'd seen the innocent love in Belle's eyes and done his best to crush it. But not before he'd nearly gone mad with longing. And not before he'd taken her.

Belle had been fifteen.

He had been an animal.

The memories hammered at him, and angrily Rand fought to push them away. Lillian was leaving this mess in his hands, and he didn't want it. He'd spent the last three days doing his best to avoid Belle, and he knew he couldn't confront her, even though Lillian wanted him to. Even the thought of talking to Belle frightened him, because he no longer knew how she would react. Since the day on the stairs she seemed softer, more vulnerable, and that terrified him more than he wanted to admit.

No, he couldn't face her. The thought brought a lump into his throat, made him shake. He clung to the idea he'd had three days ago, that Belle would get tired of all this and leave. She would go eventually, he knew. All he had to do was make sure she didn't take Sarah with her.

He could do that without facing Belle, without even talking to her. It meant he had to work harder at keeping her and Sarah apart. He could be with Sarah most of the time. The corn would be ready to cut soon, and after that he would mostly be husking and threshing out in the barn. She could be with him then. He could keep Sarah so busy, she wouldn't have time for Belle. And if he had to put the fear of God into Sarah to force her to keep her distance, well, he could do that too.

The idea made him feel better. Rand tapped the reins, and the horses moved forward eagerly to the barn. Yes, it was a good plan. What was even better was that he could put it into effect without having anything to do with Belle.

And maybe—maybe he could even forget her smile.

Chapter 14

Belle spent a restless night waiting for dawn, lying in bed until she heard Lillian's soft step on the stair and Rand's sturdier one. She heard them talking in the kitchen, heard the clanking of pots and pans and smelled the rich scents of coffee and bacon.

Quietly Belle got out of bed, hastily washing in the basin on the washstand and brushing and rebraiding her hair. She grabbed her old, worn brown calico from the bag she still hadn't unpacked—not that there was that much to unpack anyway—and pushed it back under the bed. She stepped into the dress, shoved the floppy hat on her head. Then she sat impatiently on the edge of the mattress until she heard the slam of the back door, the crunching of her mother's steps on the road as she went to the springhouse.

Belle's heart pounded; excitement made her blood race. It felt familiar and good, welcome after the tension of last night, and she had to force herself to keep from laughing with pure joy as she crept from her room to Sarah's and carefully pushed open the door.

She stepped inside, closing the door softly behind her. Sarah was a lump in the bed, sound asleep. "Sarah?"

The little girl whimpered.

Belle went closer. She raised her voice. "Sarah, wake up."

Sarah's eyes opened. "Belle?" She blinked sleepily, groggily focusing on Belle's face.

"Come on." Belle looked around the room. Her eyes fell on the blue gingham Sarah wore yesterday, and she grabbed it from the chair. "Hurry up, now, we don't have all day."

Sarah rubbed her eyes and frowned. "Where're we goin'?"

"To the canal. Remember?"

"The canal?"

"Shhh—yes. Come *on.*" Belle let out a harsh breath of exasperation. She held out the dress, waiting. "Do you want to be doin' chores all day, or do you want to have fun with me?"

Sarah smiled, pushing back the covers and wiggling to the ground. Quickly she dressed, her little arms pushing through the sleeves impatiently.

"Where's your sunbonnet?"

"There." Sarah pointed to the hook by the door.

"All right, then." Belle lifted the bonnet and handed it to Sarah. "Let's go. Be real quiet now, Sarah. Real quiet."

She waited until Sarah nodded in understanding, then Belle eased open the door and peeked out. She heard nothing. Hopefully Lillian was still at the springhouse. Rand was certainly in the fields. All she had to do was get herself and Sarah down the stairs and out the front door. Once they reached the field on the other side of the road, they'd be safe.

Carefully, silently, she motioned to Sarah to follow her. The two of them ran on tiptoes down the hallway, down the stairs, pausing only for a split second when the third one creaked. Once they were on the front porch, Belle grabbed Sarah's pudgy hand, pulling the child with her as she ran across the front yard, across the road.

She didn't slow down until they were halfway into the field and the house was a good distance behind them. Sarah was breathing heavily, her round cheeks were flushed.

Belle smiled. "You all right?"

Sarah nodded, wide-eyed. "D'you think Grandma saw? She'll spank me if she sees."

"She won't spank you," Belle reassured her. "You're with me. It's all right."

"She don't like me goin' to the canal."

Belle's smile widened. "I know. Come on, now, you won't get in trouble."

"Promise?"

"I promise." Belle nodded. She started walking, and after a moment she heard Sarah's pigeon-toed steps behind her, crunching on the stubbly brown grass. The sound made Belle smile. She felt more free than she had in days—in years. The sun was growing warmer, but just now the morning air was cold, and it smelled of frost and grass and dirt.

"How far is it?" Sarah asked.

Belle stopped, squinting into the distance. "Just past those trees up there." She slowed her step until Sarah came up beside her. "D'you like muskmelon?"

Sarah tilted her head. "Yeah."

"Well, then, you're in for a treat. There's this man I know who runs a stand by the canal. He's got the best muskmelon you'll ever eat. . . ." Belle let her sentence trail off into nothing. It occurred to her suddenly that it had been six years since she'd even been to the canal. Shenky might not even be there; his stand might be long gone.

The canal might not even be the same.

The thought made her chest feel tight. She doubted it had changed; nothing else in Lancaster had. But the canal wasn't like everything else in Lancaster. Every day had been different there when she was young—it was why she'd loved it.

God, how she wanted it to be the same.

"Are we almost there?" Sarah's voice held a note of excitement.

"Almost."

They walked in silence. Sarah tugged at the ties of her sunbonnet. "It's chokin' me."

"Take it off."

Sarah stopped, looking up in confusion. "Take it off?"

"Yeah." Belle frowned. "What's wrong?"

"Grandma says never take it off."

"Grandma's not here."

"No-o-o." Sarah hesitated, and though Belle could see Sarah was tempted, she dropped her hand from the ties, leaving the bonnet firmly in place. Her eyes took on a new wariness.

Damn Mama anyway. It had been the same when Belle was a child. Tortuous bonnets and coats of itchy wool and starched cotton were somehow necessary to keep rebellious little girls sweet and ladylike. Belle turned away and kept walking. Then she reached up and took off her own hat.

The cool air felt good on her hair. Strands of it came loose and fell in her face, and she blew them aside. "Damn, that feels good." She didn't look at Sarah. "Did your papa ever tell you the story about the hoggee and his mule?"

"No." Sarah sounded uncertain. "What's a hoggee?"

"That's what they call the tow-mule drivers on the canal."

"Oh." Sarah pushed at the brim of her bonnet. "What about him?"

"Well, there was this one hoggee called Boggs. He had this mule—smart as a whip and everyone knew it. His name was Bandit, 'cause he would steal things when no one was lookin'. He'd steal the oats right out from Boggs's hand and he'd find the bag of sugar and eat it so the other mules couldn't. One time that mule even stole a watch from a passenger. When they found it on him, he had it tucked in his harness just like he could tell time. 'Course, he prob'ly could, that mule was so damned smart."

That brought a smile. Sarah studied her as if trying to figure out if Belle was teasing. "Mules can't tell time."

"That's what you think. Bandit could—or so they said. I never saw him do it myself."

"That's silly."

"I don't know about that. Boggs used to say that mule could count too. Damnedest thing. They'd stop at the warehouse for supplies, and Boggs would say, 'Count them bags for me, Bandit, so I know how much to credit.' And damned if Bandit wouldn't do it right ev'ry time." Belle laughed. "But then Boggs got married. His wife decided Bandit was too ugly, so she made him a hat—a straw one with big red flowers. Well, Bandit hated that hat. He'd do anythin' to get rid of it, and Boggs's wife just kept findin' it and puttin' it back on his head. So you know what that mule went and did?"

"What?"

"He shot a hole through it."

Sarah stared at her in silent disbelief. "But, Belle, mules can't shoot."

"Bandit could."

"You saw him?"

"Yep. He just put that gun on the ground and hit the trigger with his hoof. Shot it ev'ry time."

"Oh." Sarah said nothing more, just walked in silence as they moved through the field to the edge of the trees, but the next time Belle looked down, the sunbonnet was bouncing limply against Sarah's back.

Belle hid her grin.

They reached the canal a short time later, coming over the flat, pine-covered hill overlooking Hooker's Station. Even before they passed the drover's tavern, they heard the sound of water and the lap of boats along the waterway. Though the main business for the canal was done near town, there were still old warehouses lining the banks here, their stilted fronts jutting out over the water, their clapboards old and splintering. Shouts from two or three teamsters calling to an incoming barge carried over the water, along with the short, blaring bursts of a canalboat horn and the jangle of the mules' trace chains. The smell of oil and mule and grain filled Belle's nostrils, and she stopped and closed her eyes, inhaling deeply, contentedly. Oh, she had missed this.

She opened her eyes again, smiling. "See that bridge over there?" she asked Sarah, pointing. When Sarah nodded, she went on. "Your papa and me used to jump from it all the time. We'd get on a boat headin' to town and then jump off and walk on back. That was some of the best fun I ever had."

Sarah's eyes were wide. "Papa used to jump too?"

Belle nodded. "Yep."

"Where do them boats go?"

"Everywhere." Belle shrugged. "All down the river."

"Forever and ever down to China?"

"I don't know. Maybe some of them."

"I wanna jump. Can we?" Sarah's voice was sharp with excitement.

Belle laughed. "Sometime maybe. Not today."

Sarah's eyes were wide and wondering as she stared at the bridge—almost as if she'd never seen it before, though Belle knew that couldn't be true. Still, she imagined no one had ever told her the stories or shown her the excitement. Probably Lillian had always been along, or Rand, or someone to say, "Stay away from the edge, Sarah," or "Hold my hand and don't let go."

Well, she wouldn't do that. Belle moved purposefully toward the warehouses. "You hungry?"

Sarah nodded. Her booted feet pounded alongside Belle's as she hurried to catch up, but she didn't take her eyes from the bridge ahead. "Yeah."

"Then let's find that muskmelon."

There was a barge coming up the canal, moving slowly through the water, and Sarah stopped for a moment to watch. She pointed to the mules, whose heads were buried deep in their feedbags as they pulled the boat along. "Is that Bandit?"

Belle smiled. "Prob'ly not. You'd know if you saw Bandit—he'd be wearin' a hat with a hole in it. Unless of course he found a way to get rid of it again." She nodded toward the buildings lining the waterway in front of them. "Come on, now, there'll be plenty of time to watch for Bandit."

The warehouses were just as she remembered them: bustling in the front, where they faced the road, where wagons unloaded their wares and foremen shouted and haggled with each other, and lazy at the rear, where the overhanging building sheltered the platform below and teamsters waited for the next barge to come creeping around the bend.

They looked just as old too—she would have sworn

each peeling board was exactly as she'd left it, each rickety chair the same that had been there before. It made Belle feel as if time had stood still, as if she were young again and hurrying through each warehouse in search of Shenky.

"Kin I help ya, ma'am?" An older man rose from his chair as they approached one of the platforms. He shoved at the brim of his hat, tilting his head to see better. "Or are ya jest—Belle? Belle Sault?"

Belle smiled broadly. She slammed her hat on her head and held out her hand. "Hey there, Poke, how's things?"

"Why, now, I jest doan believe it, no sir, I doan." Poke grabbed her hand, pulling her forward into his arms so quickly, she stumbled on the short step to the dock. She was enveloped in his heavily muscled arms for a second, squeezed so hard she nearly lost her breath. "Where ya been, girl? Why, it's been 'bout—"

"Six years." Belle pulled away breathlessly. "I just got back a week or so ago, thought I'd come on down and say hey." She motioned to Sarah, who stood there uncertainly. "This is Sarah."

Poke smiled, squatting until he was nearly eye level with Sarah. "Hey there, honey. You're Rand's little girl. I think I seen ya around once or twice, ain't I?"

Sarah shook her head somberly and eased toward Belle.

Poke stood up. "Well, you're a right purty 'un, that's for sure."

Sarah reached up and grabbed Belle's hand. Belle smiled reassuringly, wrapping her fingers around Sarah's, reveling in the moist warmth of the child's hand. "Tell me, Poke, is Shenky still around?"

"Lookin' for melon, eh?"

Belle laughed. "We didn't have breakfast."

"Yeah, he's still here." Poke jerked his head. "Around the front of Clarke's there. Ya got back jest in time. Says this is his last year on the canal."

Belle glanced toward the barge, now moving to the coal warehouse at the end of the line. "Water looks low this year."

"It's been low most years." Poke sighed. "Took a loss for the first time two years ago and ain't made a profit since. The railroads . . ." He shrugged, letting his words trail off sadly, then he smiled as if the sadness had never existed. "Well, ya come on back soon, Belle, won't ya? We'll have a drink. And bring that little mite with ya."

"I will." Belle nodded a good-bye, and she and Sarah wound their way between the other buildings to the road in front. Poke's words left her feeling vaguely melancholy, and for the first time Belle noticed the changes. When she'd left, the stop at Hooker's Station was always moving, always bustling. Usually there were three or four barges pulled up to the platforms. The line of wagons delivering goods had reached far down the road, and peddlers hawked their wares on every corner.

But today there was only one barge, and the three wagons pulled in front of the warehouses were a sorry reminder of the days when there had been twenty. It made her feel unexpectedly sad, but only for a moment. The sight of Shenky's stand made her spirits rise again, and Belle forgot her conversation with Poke the minute she saw the bent old man puttering around the cabbages. She turned to Sarah, pressing her finger to her lips in a warning to be quiet, and the two of them tiptoed toward him, stopping only a few feet behind.

"Hey, Shenky," Belle said.

He jumped, whirling around so quickly his hat went flying off his head, clutching his chest. "Dammit, you near gave me—" his mouth dropped open in surprise. "Christ A'mighty, if it ain't Belle Sault back from the grave!"

She laughed. "Don't make me dead so damn quick, Shenky." She gave him a big hug and then bent for his hat, dusting it off and handing it back to him with a flourish. "Miss me?"

He snorted. "Like the corn misses a crow. Damn you, girl, where you been?"

"New York City."

"Hmmmph. I guess you're too big for your britches now—bein' a big-city girl and all."

"Yeah, I guess so." Belle's smile widened. " 'Fact I almost decided not to come around. After all that big-city food I figured you wouldn't have anythin' even worth lookin' at here today."

"Not worth lookin' at? Are you blind, girl? Did you just plumb leave your sight back there in goddamn New York City? You won't find cabbages this good anywhere—who's that trailin' behind you like a goddamn shadow?"

"Well, you just scared her away with your yellin' and carryin' on," Belle said. She turned around, motioning for Sarah to come up beside her. Sarah took a few tentative steps, her eyes never leaving Shenky's craggy face. "This is Sarah."

"Hmmph. She's a pretty thing."

"That's what Poke said."

"Poke?" Shenky's pale blue gaze shifted back to her face. He frowned and moved away, his stoop-shouldered gait staggering and uneven as he went to a bushel basket of melons. "That good-for-nothin'? He and I ain't never agreed on anythin', you know that. So I s'pose you two come in here for some muskmelon, and you're lucky, Miss goddamn New York City, 'cause I just happen to have a few." He stopped and turned around, shaking a gnarled finger. "And you won't find nothin' this good in that town."

Belle nodded. "I know it."

"Hmmmph. Just you remember it." He reached down, pulling up a round, webbed melon and thumping it with his finger. "I don't know why I'm even doin' this," he muttered. "They're all ripe as can be. Nobody's ever bought a sour melon from old Shenky. Nobody." He put the melon aside, picked up another one, thumped it, and then smelled the stem. He held it out to Belle. "I s'pose you want me to cut it for you."

"Please."

"Hmmmph. Well, then, come on over here, Miss City-girl-who-can't-cut-a-melon." He shuffled to the back of the stand, where the remains of several other melons were piled in a basket. The sweet, musky scent hovered in the air. With a single *whack* of a long, thick knife, the melon was split in two, the orange flesh glistening with juice, the white seeds a glob in the center.

"Here you go." Shenky's face was still stern as he handed Belle half and motioned to Sarah to come closer, but his blue eyes were shining. "Come on up here, little girl—or don't you want a piece of this prize-winnin' melon?"

Silently Sarah came forward. Shenky put the half melon in her pudgy little-girl hands, and she looked down at it, and then up again at him as if she was fascinated.

Belle grinned. "How much do I owe you, Shenky?"

"Owe me?" His frown deepened. "Don't insult me, girl—you don't have enough money to pay me what this melon's worth, so I don't want a thin'. You just go on off and enjoy it—and don't you come around botherin' me again, you hear?"

"Yes, sir." Belle saluted, fighting to keep from laughing. "Not again, I promise."

"Good." Shenky put his hands on his hips, watching them as they walked from the stand, and it wasn't until they were nearly to the street that he spoke again. "Welcome home, Belle. It's good to see you."

She turned and smiled. "You too, Shenky. You too."

Chapter 15

Rand bent, sluicing water from the back-porch cistern over his head and neck, not caring when the water splashed his shirt and shoulders. It felt good, cool and wet, and for a moment the headache he'd been nursing all morning disappeared.

But only for a moment. It slammed back, full force, when he glanced up the back stairs. For the most part he'd managed to avoid Belle last night and this morning, but now seeing her was unavoidable. He knew she'd be sitting at that table, waiting with Lillian and Sarah for him to come through the door for dinner. He would have to sit there and eat and somehow—somehow—keep from looking at her, from thinking about the past, from remembering her smile.

Christ, he wasn't sure if he could do it.

Anxiety was a hard lump in his stomach as he grabbed the rough huckaback from the rail and dried himself off, and it only grew as he trudged up the stairs to the kitchen. Taking a deep breath, he opened the door.

The kitchen was empty.

Rand stopped in the doorway, frowning. The table was set for dinner. The pitcher of buttermilk was frothy, as if it had just been poured, and the smell of green beans and ham filled the room. Two pies sat on opposite corners of the table, and apple butter and pickles glistened in their dishes.

But it was quiet except for the hissing of the coffeepot. Where the hell was everybody? He ran a hand through his damp hair, raking it back from his forehead, and went to the hallway. "Lil?" No answer. He tried again. "Lillian? Sarah?"

"I'm in here!" Lillian's breathless voice came from the hallway. She hurried into the kitchen, her arms full of dead and wilting mums from the vase in the hall. She swept past him, laying them on the porch to throw in the compost pile before she went to the stove. "Tell Sarah to come in, won't you? I called the two of you nearly ten minutes ago."

Rand went to the door. "Sarah!" he called. "Sarah, come in for dinner!" Then, when there was no answer, he turned back to Lillian. "Are you sure she's out here?"

Lillian pulled the pot of stew off the stove. "Wasn't she right behind you?"

He shook his head. "I haven't seen her all day."

Lillian's head jerked up. "You haven't seen her all day? I—I thought she was with you."

"With me?" Rand's heart slammed into his stomach. "What do you mean, with me? I assumed you were watching her."

Lillian blanched. She dropped the pot of stew to the table. "No. I thought she was out in the fields with you." Her voice rose slightly. "Oh, good Lord. I haven't seen Isabelle either."

"Belle?" *Jesus.* He felt strangled suddenly. Rand braced a shaking hand on the doorframe, trying to steady himself, to think. No one had seen Belle. Sarah was missing. *"I'm not leavin' and I'm not takin' Sarah away. I'm stayin' here, with her."* Belle's words came crashing back. *"I want to tell her the truth about me."* Sweet Christ, it couldn't be true. He wouldn't believe it. She'd *promised.* But the truth slammed into him, in spite of his reassurances. Belle was gone. Sarah was gone. And promises were just words. She'd taken his daughter, he knew it. She'd probably planned this from the beginning.

"I'll kill her," he muttered through clenched teeth. "I swear I'll kill her."

"Rand—"

He inhaled deeply, forcing a composure he didn't feel. "Keep looking," he ordered tersely. "Check their rooms, see if anything's missing. I'm going into town. If they took the train, someone's bound to have seen them."

Without waiting for Lillian's answer, Rand swept past her, racing to the barn. His hands shook as he saddled Duke. *Jesus, please let me be wrong. Please . . .* The words rang in his head, a useless litany. Useless because he knew he wasn't wrong. They were gone. His heart raced as he led Duke from the barn, and his mouth went dry when he saw Lillian rushing across the yard. She was pale; he saw the fear in her face. He didn't need to hear her speak to know what she was going to say.

"Sarah's things are still there," she said breathlessly as she approached him. "But I didn't see Belle's clothes, and she wouldn't think to take Sarah's. Oh, Randall, she's gone."

Rand mounted the horse quickly. "Check Alspaugh's," he said tersely. "Maybe they went over there. Or maybe Dorothy and Kenny saw something."

She nodded, but before she could say anything, he urged Duke into a run, past the house, onto the road.

Damn. Desperately he tried to think of where Belle would go this time. Back to Cincinnati? Or would she go north, to Sandusky? Or, Christ—there was Columbus . . . Cleveland . . . The possibilities sent his heart slamming into his throat. Belle was too damned clever; he had no idea what she would do next, or where she would go. She was just as likely to return to New York as leave it forever.

He should have watched Sarah more closely. He'd always known Belle would take the first opportunity to take her. Rand pushed the horse to a faster pace. Belle and Sarah could already be in town by now. If they'd started early, they could have made it even on foot. When the hell was the next train?

Rand couldn't remember, and the question sent panic racing through him again. If they'd gone already, his only hope was that someone had seen them. Surely someone would have. People *knew* Belle. They knew Sarah. The two of them together would have been noticed. . . .

Or maybe not. Maybe they hadn't even gone into town. Maybe they wouldn't even take the train. . . .

He refused to think of the possibility. Belle had to know he would come after them the moment he discovered them gone. Surely she would take the easiest, fastest way out of Lancaster. Wouldn't she?

He dug his heels into Duke's sides.

By the time he got to the train station, both he and Duke were sweaty and heaving. There was a train on the track, belching ash-filled smoke into the air. *Please,* he thought. *Please let them be on that train.* He dismounted and ran inside.

The room was crowded, and there was a line to the clerk. Desperately he scanned the room, a hard lump in his throat. But there was no Belle. No Sarah. His heart sank into his stomach. Christ, they weren't here. They weren't here. That meant only one thing: They were either gone or on that train.

He prayed it was the latter.

Rand pushed into the line, ignoring the shocked gasps and "Excuse me!'s" of the waiting passengers, and leaned into the window.

"Well, hello there, Mr. Sault." A freckle-faced boy, barely more than eighteen, greeted him, looking surprised. "If you could just wait your turn—"

"What trains have left this morning?"

The boy frowned in confusion. "What trains? Well—uh—only two so far."

"To where?"

"Uh—Sandusky left at—uh—early this mornin'. Cincinnati pulled out 'bout twenty minutes ago."

Rand felt a tap on his shoulder.

"Excuse me, mister, but we're waitin'."

Rand turned and glared. The woman clamped her mouth shut and shrank away. He jerked back to the boy at the window. "You know my daughter, Sarah?"

"Why, yes, Mr. Sault. Pretty as a pic—"

"Was she on either of those trains?"

"Uh—"

"A blond woman would have bought the ticket. My stepsister, Belle."

The boy shook his head. "No one like that today, Mr. Sault. And I didn't see Sarah, I know it."

"You're sure?"

"I—I think so."

Rand leaned forward, eyes narrowed. "You have to be sure."

"I'm sure." The boy swallowed nervously. "No one like that."

The woman tapped Rand's shoulder again. "Listen, mister—"

Rand stepped away from the window, exhaling deliberately, forcing himself to calm down. They hadn't taken the train. The idea wound its way through his mind slowly, and just as slowly he forced himself to believe it.

He tried to think, forced himself to consider the options. There was the National Road, of course, but he doubted Belle would have taken a stage. Too slow. He could catch up to them on horseback in no time. The canal would pose the same problem—especially now, when the water was so low that packet boats were forced to stop all along the route.

Which meant only one thing. Belle would have done what he least expected, the one thing he wouldn't think of until it was too late.

She would have hitched a ride.

The thought sent panic rushing through him. If she'd done that, it would take him days, even weeks, to hunt her down. Wagons passed this road every day. A wagon could go anywhere, take any route, go any direction. And once she got to a big city, she could simply disappear.

It had taken the detective he'd hired nearly four years to track her last time, and she'd only gone as far as Cincinnati. This time she was older, cleverer, and she had more to hide.

God. Dear God, please don't let it be true. Please, I can't take it again.

Someone jostled him, and Rand looked up, surprised to find he was still in the train station. People were staring at him, and he realized suddenly how strange he must look—hatless, sweating, his wet shirt clinging to his chest.

Slowly he left the station. Duke was waiting patiently,

but the bay's sides still heaved from exertion, and sweat was drying, foamy and white, on his sides.

"Sorry, boy," Rand murmured, running a hand over the gelding's muzzle. He should let the horse rest awhile, he knew, but he couldn't. Rand clenched his fist on Duke's mane and forced himself to uncurl his fingers, to step away. His gaze traveled down the busy Lancaster street, noting the people milling about, hearing the sounds of the wagons and horses and voices before he mounted the horse again and started down the road. He had to think, had to work out a plan. Something that would cover the most ground in the shortest time. Something that would find them before they had the chance to disappear. Maybe he should round up all the neighbors—tell them some suitable lie about how urgent it was to find Belle and Sarah. It would be hard to pull them away from work—they were all readying to cut corn, none of them could spare the time. But he could come up with some crisis, he was sure, some worry that would spur them all into action. . . .

He could get Kenny Alspaugh and Paul Miller to help, Rand was sure of it. Maybe even Jack Dumont. They could each head in a separate direction. Hell, by the end of the day surely one of them would find something.

Hopefully. Rand closed the distance to the house as quickly as he could. *Please let them be back,* he prayed as he approached it. *Please, God, I'll never ask you for anything again. Just let Sarah be here. Please, please let her be here.*

He was barely to the drive before he was off Duke, leaving the horse standing in the yard while he ran to the porch, up the stairs, and yanked open the door. "Lillian?"

She came running from the kitchen, Dorothy Alspaugh close behind. Lillian's face was pale with worry. "Did you find them?"

His hope died in his chest. "They aren't here."

"No." She shook her head, winding her hands in her skirt, and he saw her struggling for control. "You didn't find them."

"No." He glanced at Dorothy. The older woman was watching them with an expression too worried to be curious. "Hello, Dorothy."

"Rand." She nodded a greeting. "I just came over to help. We've looked all over." She flashed a concerned look at Lillian. "I've been tryin' to tell Lil not to worry —it's early yet."

Dorothy's words seemed to stiffen Lillian's spine. "I told Dorothy we were expecting Belle and Sarah back for dinner." Her eyes warned Rand to watch his tongue. "After all, Belle did say they would only be going for a short walk."

"I'm sure they'll be back soon," Dorothy said soothingly. "They probably just lost track of time."

Rand forced a smile. "You're probably right. Is Kenny home?"

"Y-yes." Dorothy frowned. "He's in the fields."

"I'll be right back, then. I thought I'd just go over there for a minute—just a minute." Rand threw as reassuring a glance to Lillian as he could muster, and then he was out the door, running for Duke.

Belle absently swatted away a horsefly and pulled her skirt up farther over her legs, kicking her bare feet in the cool, murky water. The day had turned warm in spite of the frost this morning, and she leaned back on her elbows, lifting her face to the sun, feeling good, too lazy to wipe away the sticky melon juice still staining her skin.

"Mmmmm," she murmured, closing her eyes. "This is the life."

She heard the splashing of little feet in the water, and Belle opened her eyes again to see Sarah scoot closer to the edge and lean over to watch the water churn around her toes.

"Careful," Belle said lightly. "It's deep."

"I'm lookin' for fishes." Sarah turned to look at her, the half-eaten melon still in her hands. Her face was shiny and orange with juice.

Belle laughed. "I don't think you'll find many fish here. Got to go to the river for that. We'll do that sometime."

Sarah turned back to the water. "I never been fishin' before."

"You've never been fishin'?"

"Nope." Sarah paused. "Papa said I couldn't by myself."

"Well, you wouldn't be by yourself. You'd be with me."

Sarah nodded, putting aside her melon to stare at another barge coming up the canal. "Is *that* Bandit?" she asked, pointing a chubby finger at the mules tugging on the long ropes.

Belle squinted into the sun, pretending to study the mule across the water. It was true there had been a Bandit, along with a Boggs, but the rest was pure fiction, a story she'd made up for Rand one day long ago when they were still friends and they'd been sitting by the canal just like this.

For a moment Belle heard his laughter again, just as it had been that day, loud and rumbling, filling the air until she had laughed right along with him.

Much too long ago. Belle frowned. It was another memory she'd tried hard to forget.

"What's wrong?" Sarah asked. "Are you mad?"

Belle shook her head, forced a smile. "No, just thinkin'."

" 'Bout Bandit?"

"Yeah."

"I wish I could see him." Sarah rested her chin in her hands and looked wistfully out onto the water. "D'you s'pose he'd do tricks for me?"

"He might."

"I wish we could jump from the bridge today." Sarah sighed.

The sound was strange coming from such a small child, and it pulled at Belle's heart. She reached out, tentatively pushing a short blond hair from where it stuck to Sarah's face, and Belle felt embarrassingly happy when Sarah didn't flinch at all.

"We will someday," Belle said, glancing at the bridge, though she knew neither she nor Sarah would be jumping anytime soon. The bridge, like many of the other things on the canal, showed signs of wear. Though it looked the same from a distance, there were boards missing from one side, and the wooden railing was rotting away. It would probably fall apart before they even got across it.

"Promise?"

Belle hesitated. "Oh, Sarah, I—"

"Please, Belle?" Sarah's brown eyes were wide and pleading.

Don't lie to her, said the voice in Belle's mind. *You hated lies when you were a child.* But Sarah was looking at her so hopefully, and Belle felt her conviction waver. Why ruin such a wonderful day? It couldn't hurt to tell Sarah what she wanted to hear. Just this once. After all, she was just a little girl. She would forget it soon enough.

Belle sighed. "All right," she said. "I promise."

Sarah's smile was worth the lie.

"There are six of us," Rand said, looking around the table. "That's enough to cover quite a piece. We should at least be able to find out if anyone's seen them."

Jack Dumont put down his cup of coffee and rubbed his eyes. "I'll go out toward the river. I gotta pay a visit to Jenkins out there anyhow."

"Fine. Kenny, you head to Green Castle, and Paul, you can go on out to Amanda. I'll head toward Carroll. That way, I can check the canal. . . ." He let his words trail off when he saw Lillian blanch. She set the coffee-pot on the stove with shaking hands. Rand finished lamely, "Then we'll all meet back here."

"We'll find 'em, Lil, don't you fret about it," Paul Miller rose and crammed his hat on his head. "They'll be safe and sound, you'll see. Prob'ly just lost."

Lillian nodded, but her slight smile was forced. "I'm sure you're right, Paul."

"Let's go." Rand couldn't keep the urgency from his voice. "We've only got a few hours till dark." Not that it mattered, he thought, but for Lillian's sake he had to pretend Sarah and Belle were in danger. It furthered his purpose anyway. He wanted to get going. Every hour they spent in planning gave Belle another hour to get farther away. Another hour to escape.

"All right, then." Kenny rose slowly. "We'll meet back in what—say, three hours?"

"Fine." Rand bit off the word. He got to his feet. "And then we'll—"

Laughter—light, childish laughter—floated from the yard, through the open back door. He froze, his order caught in his throat. *Sarah.* He was afraid to turn around and look, afraid to believe. *It's only your imagi-*

nation, he warned himself. *Only because you want so badly for it to be her. . . .*

"Yes, we did! We used to catch salamanders all the time down by the river." Belle's voice came from the back porch.

Rand spun around, his breathing suddenly tight and painful. He heard steps on the stair.

"I tried. I ain't never caught one."

"You aren't quick enough—" Belle said, stepping into the doorway. She looked up at the crowd gathered in the kitchen and stopped so quickly, Sarah bumped into the back of her legs.

"Belle, don't stop!" Sarah laughed.

"Sarah." Rand heard his voice, but it didn't sound like his. It sounded harsh and scared and unbelieving, and it was the only thing in this whole weird scene that didn't feel like a dream. "Christ, Sarah." He lunged forward, hearing Lillian's screech of relief behind him as he pushed past Belle and clutched at Sarah, holding her so tightly in his arms, she squealed.

He buried his face in her neck, pressed his cheek against her hair, smelling her little-girl scent: dirt and water and the musky-sweet odor of melon. He felt Lillian at his back, felt her hand on his arm, and he knew he should put Sarah down, knew he was embarrassing his neighbors, but he couldn't release her, could no more put her down than he could stop breathing, and he didn't care. Oh, God, he had truly believed he would never see her again, had believed it with every part of himself, and no one else in this room could understand what that meant.

"Papa. Put me down!" Sarah was squirming now, and reluctantly Rand lifted his head and bent until her little feet touched the floor and she scrambled away from him.

It was only then that he saw—really saw—Belle. It was only then that his worry and fear faded away, leaving in its place a suffocating, unbearable anger. He jerked up again. Belle was staring at him, and there was a look on her face he couldn't decipher, a dawning awareness that only made him angrier. "What the hell did you think you were doing?" He snapped. "Where the hell were you?"

She frowned, glanced at the men gathered around the table before she looked at him again. "We were at the canal," she said slowly, carefully.

"The canal."

"That's what I said." She licked her lips and glanced down at Sarah, who was gathered against Lillian's skirts. "We went to visit Shenky."

"Shenky."

"Yeah."

"I see." He struggled to maintain calm, acutely aware of the men standing silently behind him, of Lillian's censure. It took everything he had to keep from strangling Belle with his bare hands. "You didn't tell us where you were going."

Her chin jerked up then, her eyes flashed. "I didn't think you and Mama would approve." She looked past him to the men. "I guess I was right about that. Looks like you were gettin' a posse up. Hey there, boys."

He heard the murmur of nervous, uncertain hellos behind him.

Kenny Alspaugh cleared his throat. "Well, I guess ev'ryone's safe and sound, eh? Looks like we'll just be headin' on home, Rand."

Rand nodded. He didn't turn around, kept his eyes fastened on Belle's face. "Thanks. I appreciate the help."

"No problem at all."

"See you later."

He heard them shuffle out, heard the hasty steps down the hallway and the opening and closing of the front door. And then there was nothing but silence.

But before he could say anything, Belle lifted a brow, gave him that look he was beginning to hate—that infuriating mix of sarcasm and indifference. "Quite a search party you had goin' there," she said insolently. "I didn't know you cared so much."

"We didn't know what had happened," Lillian said softly. "Your clothes were gone."

"My clothes?" Belle said in surprise. "I didn't take them. They're upstairs, under the bed. I haven't unpacked yet, Mama."

"Well, you can imagine how worried we were."

Belle snorted in disbelief.

The sound shattered Rand's control. He slammed his hand against the door. It crashed to the wall, shivering on its hinges. Lillian and Sarah jumped, but Belle only flinched, and she didn't move away.

"Papa?" Sarah said in a small, frightened voice.

Frightened. Of him. The knowledge only made him angrier. Rand twisted around. "You listen to me, Sarah. You are not to go anywhere alone with Belle. I mean ever. Do you understand me? Nowhere."

He heard Belle's catch of breath behind him, Lillian's breathless *"Rand."* Rand ignored them both. He kept his eyes focused on his daughter. "Do you understand?"

Sarah frowned. She glanced at Belle and then back to Rand. "But, Papa—"

"Do you understand?"

She nodded, wide-eyed.

"Good." The sight of her wary expression made Rand hesitate, but only for a second. He thought of his promise to himself earlier, to put the fear of God into Sarah if he had to. Well, it was there now. He wondered why the thought didn't fill him with satisfaction, why it just seemed to sit there on top of his rage.

He jerked his head at Lillian. "Go on," he said tersely. "Get out of here."

"Rand—"

"Take Sarah and get out."

Lillian's mouth tightened, but she grabbed Sarah's hand and left the room. He waited until he heard them go upstairs, until he heard the quiet latching of a door, and then he spun around to face Belle.

"What the hell is wrong with you?" he exploded. "Christ, don't you ever consider other people? Are you that damned selfish? You disappear without a god-damned word to anyone—" He broke off, too angry to think, even to breathe. "What the hell were we supposed to think?"

He expected her to retreat, expected her to back down, but she didn't. Her brown eyes glittered as she faced him, and her expression was hard and angry. "How about that Sarah and I were havin' a good time?" she asked. "Hell, she was with me, Rand. It wasn't like she was goin' to get hurt."

He didn't bother to contradict her. "I went into town. I checked the train."

Her eyes widened; she stared at him in disbelief. "The train?" She crossed her arms over her chest, laughed bitterly. "You thought I was takin' her away."

"Weren't you?"

She looked away; he saw the working of her jaw, the clenching of her fingers on her arms. "I told you I wouldn't take her. I told you I was stayin'."

"And I was supposed to believe you?"

"Yeah," she said. "You were s'posed to believe me.

But I guess I should have known you wouldn't. I guess you've changed too much for that, haven't you?"

He glared at her, ignoring her comment—along with the urge to flinch at the truth in it. "Why the hell should I believe you?"

She looked surprised and—hurt. But only for a second, and then that sarcastic look was in her eyes again, and her words were quiet and condemning. "Why shouldn't you? When have I ever lied to you?"

They startled him, those words, shocked him into silence—an indictment he couldn't fight or deny. He told himself it didn't matter, that she had taught him not to believe her, but when he tried to remember how, he couldn't, and he was struck with the notion that he'd wronged her again, felt the nudge of guilt.

Don't let her do this to you. Don't let her change your mind. The voice rang in his head, and he tried to listen to it, tried to hold on to his anger, to tell her to pack her damn bags and leave.

He opened his mouth, meaning to say the words, wanting to, but before he could, Belle looked up at him, and that strange mix of things in her expression, that half-defiant, half-defenseless way she stood, made him think of the other day, when he'd asked her to keep their secret from Sarah, when he'd stumbled upon Belle standing at the top of the stairs. It made him think of a time six years ago, when he'd seen that same wounded look in her eyes, when he'd felt her pain and hadn't been able to stop himself from destroying what was left of their friendship.

It's your imagination, he told himself. But it wasn't, and he knew it. He knew that look in her face, had seen it a hundred times in his nightmares.

The last of his anger melted away, replaced by horrible, hot guilt that closed his throat, by voices screaming blame in his ear. He wanted to say he was sorry, wanted to do something—anything—to get rid of the memories. But when he opened his mouth to say the words, all he heard was, incredibly, "I—I was worried."

"You shouldn't have been," Belle said slowly. She took a deep breath, and suddenly that vulnerability he'd seen was gone, replaced by a gaze so measuring and cool, it made him feel instantly small. "She was with me."

Then she turned away from him, and when he thought she would walk out the door, she paused and looked over her shoulder at him, still with those cold, cold eyes. Eyes that showed him unexpectedly and completely that she was her mother's daughter, that perhaps she had inherited something from Lillian after all.

Her chilly voice only emphasized it. "I'm goin' back over to Hooker's Station," she said. "I guess I could use a smile tonight."

And before he could say anything more, she was gone.

Chapter 16

The evening air was cool. The setting sun had stolen the summerlike warmth of the day, but in return it drenched the sky in color: blood-red against the dark hills, then orange and yellow and green and violet, a rainbow rising to dark blue just overhead. The sight left Belle cold. There couldn't be a sky beautiful enough to make her feel welcome here, no rainbow of color could take away the harsh chill of Rand's words.

She squeezed her eyes shut, feeling hot despite the cold evening air. He thought she was a liar—the knowledge infuriated her. Even after she'd given her word, he hadn't believed her. She'd said she wasn't taking Sarah away, and yet he thought she had done just that. God, he'd even checked the train. Her hands clenched at her sides; she felt the harsh heat of anger in her cheeks. She was no liar, and Rand knew it; knew her word was good. Once, he never would have doubted that.

But it was obvious now that Rand preferred to be her enemy. She'd been wrong to think his smile of a few days ago meant anything at all. He'd been caught up in the moment, as she was, but it had only been a moment. Nothing more important than that. Knowing that made things easier again, black and white. She could hate Rand; God knew she'd been doing it the last six years. She had plenty of practice. And if hating him brought an uncomfortable stab of sadness, well, she was used to that too.

Belle took a deep breath; the cold air burned her throat, tingled in her nose. She didn't want to think about that now. What she wanted was a place where she could forget everything, where there were people who knew who she was and trusted her. People who knew the only lies she'd ever told were harmless stories and poker bluffs. A place where harsh words disappeared in smoke-filled rooms and laughter. She hoped—oh, God, she hoped—that the tavern at Hooker was as she remembered, because it was such a place. And she needed that tonight more than she could ever remember needing it before.

She walked faster. Before long the hill overlooking Hooker's Station stretched before her, with the tavern holding its lone sentry at the top. The old clapboard building was grayed and battered, the flat-topped pine that sheltered it as weathered as the tavern itself. A few wagons loaded with feed, potatoes, and melons were already out front despite the earliness of the hour.

Anticipation made Belle's step lighter as she hurried up the rise. As she approached the narrow porch, she heard the tinny music of a piano, the murmur of talking, and she smiled with relief as she pushed open the door and stepped inside.

The tavern was just as she remembered it. The short, scarred bar to the left and the rickety tables surrounded with benches hadn't changed; the same smoke hung heavy just below the rafters, giving the room a blue-gray cast, filling her nostrils with the acrid-sweet scent of tobacco. At the back of the bar someone was running his fingers across the untuned keys of the piano, plunking out a melody she didn't recognize.

The tension of the last weeks, the last hours, seemed

to ease a little bit; Belle closed her eyes and breathed in the smell of smoke and beer and sweat and loved it.

"Well, I'll be hanged, if it ain't Belle Sault!"

The familiar voice made her eyes snap open. She glanced toward the sound, at a tall, skinny man leaning over the bar. He had a huge smile on his face, his gold tooth winked in the lamplight.

"Bobby!" She smiled, hurrying over. "Why, Bad Bobby Barrows, I never once thought you might still be tendin' bar here."

"Ain't ever left," he said. "I've just been sittin' here waitin' for you to come back."

"Well, I'm here now." Belle plopped onto a stool. It rocked crookedly beneath her. "And I'd be much obliged if you'd hand me a beer."

Bobby nodded. His gaze swept past her shoulder. "Looks like there's a few more here who've missed you, girl."

Belle spun around on the stool to see another tall, lean man coming toward her. "Charlie Boston!" she laughed, warmed by the welcoming smile on his angular face. "I wondered if I'd see your skinny old self down here tonight."

She was instantly enveloped in his arms. Charlie squeezed her once and stepped away, holding her at arm's length while his gaze swept over her. "I can't hardly believe my eyes. Belle Sault. Why, you've grown into one fine-lookin' woman."

Belle flushed, pulling away. "Yeah, well, you look the same, Charlie. Just as ugly as ever."

"Ain't that the truth." He laughed. "I heard you was in town, but I didn't believe it. Figured you'd've shown up by now."

"Well, here I am." Belle grinned broadly, reaching back to take the beer Bobby slid across the counter, feeling more at home than she had in the last week and a half. This was what she'd wanted all night, this comfortable familiarity, the easy laughter. "And I dearly hope you haven't gotten any better at poker."

Behind her, Bobby snorted. "You're damn right about that."

Charlie looked pained. "Don't you go tellin' lies like that, Bobby Barrows. You know it ain't right to fool a lady."

"A lady?" Bobby teased. "I don't see one of those in here."

Belle laughed. "And you aren't goin' to either." She glanced over the crowd in the direction of Charlie's table. "Any of the others here?"

"Some of 'em." Charlie nodded. "John Dumont's waitin' for me to bring you on over. And I think you know Abe Shearer."

Belle took a sip of lukewarm beer. "Ben Drymon?"

"He's long gone. Went to California a good while back. Mike and Tom left too." Charlie broke into a grin. "But you got the best of 'em right here, little girl, just see if you don't."

"The best ones to beat at poker, anyhow," Belle teased.

Charlie shook back his dark, shaggy head in a sudden whoop. "Damn, if you ain't changed one bit, Belle," he said, taking her arm and leading her through the smoky room toward a table against the side wall. "You want to play a few hands—or are you too old now for that?"

Belle lifted a brow. "Too old to win a game of poker? Not hardly."

Charlie laughed. "Come on, then," he said, heading to where John Dumont and Abe Shearer sat talking. A deck of cards and a pile of coins lay abandoned in the center of the dark, pitted table. "Hey, boys, look what the cat dragged in!"

"Well, damn!" John slapped his heavy thigh and sat back in his chair, a huge smile on his face. "Where the hell you been, girl?"

"New York City."

"New York City?" Abe rubbed his long chin. "I guess we better count ourselves lucky, eh, boys? Ain't ev'ry day a New York City gal decides to grace us with her comp'ny."

"Don't I know it," Belle said good-naturedly, pulling out a chair and sitting down. "You boys better treat me right, too."

"Guess we could let her win a few hands," John offered.

She gave him her best challenging look. "If I remember right, Johnny-boy, you'll be lucky if I don't."

"Damn, Belle Sault, you got a mouth on you." John shook his head. "That big city ain't changed you, that's for sure."

Belle took a sip of her beer, then grabbed the cards, shuffling them with an ease born of years of practice. "I'll tell you one thing that hasn't changed," she said, winking at John. "I can still beat the pants off you boys."

"Don't be too damn sure." Abe grinned. "We've had plenty of time to practice."

"You'll need it." Belle leaned forward. "Now, boys, are you in or out?"

There was a chorus of "ins," and Belle dealt the cards, settling onto the hard wooden chair and putting her elbows on the table so that she could look at her own hand.

"So what you been doin' in New York?" John asked, studying his cards.

Belle shrugged. "A little of this, a little of that. Whatever I can find."

"Damn, would I hate to be your boss." Charlie chuckled. "With your sass, I'd have to fire you before the week was out."

She gave him a wry glance. "Then it's a good thing you aren't my boss, isn't it? Stop jawin' so much and tell me how many cards you want."

"Give me two." He slapped his cards on the table, and she dealt him two in return.

"You come back to stay?"

"Don't know." Belle shrugged with deliberate nonchalance. "Maybe."

"Your mama must be glad to see you." Abe took a sip of beer and traded three cards.

Belle snorted. "Oh, yeah, she's just overjoyed."

There was a considering look in John's dark eyes. "Imagine Rand's glad to have you around again."

At the sound of his name Belle stiffened. Slowly she willed herself to relax. Carefully she took two cards and tucked them into her hand. "I s'pose that's what he told you."

"Rand ain't told me a thing," John said. "He don't spend much time down here anymore."

Belle looked up. "No?"

John shook his head. "Too busy with the farm, I guess."

The knowledge made Belle strangely uncomfortable. She hadn't been the only one who loved this place. Before Cort died, he and Rand had spent nearly as much time here as she. Belle frowned. She remembered how the three of them used to play poker with Charlie and the others, how Rand had once belonged at this table, had joked and laughed with the rest of them while Cort flirted with the women. She could still picture the way it had been, could hear the coarse jokes and the irreverent talk, the playful insults like the ones they traded tonight.

It bothered her that she remembered it so well. It bothered her that Rand didn't spend much time here anymore.

But mostly it bothered her that she cared at all.

She took a deep breath, forced away thoughts of Rand and all those memories. It wasn't why she was here. She only wanted an easy game of poker, she reminded herself. A beer and the companionship of people who liked her. That was all she wanted, at least for tonight.

"Rand prob'ly has better things to do than hang around all day with you good-for-nothin's," she joked. "Now, ante up, boys, so I can take your money."

The only sound in the kitchen was that of Lillian washing the dishes. It was a familiar, comforting sound, a light splashing, a steady rhythm—plop the dish into the tub, then one swish, two, and another quick dunk to rinse. *Plop, swish, swish, splash.* Lillian had washed dishes this way since Rand had known her, probably long before that.

The noise was as soothing as ever, more so because tonight he needed that soft familiarity, the everyday habit. He wanted things to be the way they'd always been, to be able to sit here in the kitchen and read and think while silence accompanied him long into the night. He wanted the quiet, uneventful routine of waking up in the morning and working numbly through a day where nothing surprised. He'd managed to harden himself to life the last six years, and he wanted it to stay that way, wanted those elusive dreams, the disappointments, to keep their distance, to only come out on those nights when the moon was bright and the sky was cloudless. He could handle it that way, could easily live through those sleepless nights. Because then it was simply longing for things he would never have.

Not worry over the only things he did.

He sighed, leaning back in his chair, looking up at the planked ceiling, listening for some sign that Sarah was still awake. He heard nothing, and he hadn't really expected to. She'd gone to bed almost right after supper, too tired even to eat. He wondered what she was dreaming, if maybe she was reliving the day at the canal. Rand felt a shaft of jealousy at the thought. He should have been the one to take her there, and it annoyed him that Belle had thought of it first. And frightened him too. Today at supper he'd heard again the hero worship in Sarah's voice when she talked about Belle, and it filled him with a dread he couldn't erase.

"Well, then."

Lillian spoke quietly, but the words seemed to crash in on his thoughts, and they made him jump before he glanced up to see her drying the last dish and stacking it on the shelf above the sideboard. She turned to face him, wiping her hands on her coarse cotton apron. He knew the expression she wore, that tight, *this hurts me more than it hurts you* look, and he tensed and reached for his lukewarm coffee.

She pulled out a chair and sat at the table across from him. "Randall," she said, "we need to talk."

He took a sip of coffee.

She sighed. "I think we may have done the wrong thing today."

He raised an eyebrow. " 'We?' You mean me, don't you?"

She gave him a reproving glance. Her long, slender fingers played with the oilcloth covering the table. "I don't think losing your temper was the best way to handle it. You frightened Sarah. She's already forgotten it, but still . . ." She took a deep breath. "The worst thing, of course, is that you made Belle angry too."

He regarded her silently. God knew she couldn't berate him more than he already had himself. Over the last two hours he'd thought of nothing but how stupid he'd been. He should never have said those things to Belle, should never have lost his temper and told Sarah not to go anyplace alone with her. Belle had told him she wasn't going to take Sarah, and he should have at least given her the benefit of the doubt. But he hadn't even done that. He hadn't believed her, had preferred to think she was lying just to pacify him, and today he'd seen the hurt in her eyes and known she'd been telling the truth after all.

In the past he never would have made the mistake of doubting her. Once, he would have believed anything she said, would have trusted her implicitly. Belle lived by her own rules and always had, but she could be a steadfast, trustworthy friend when she chose to be, and she had always had a generous heart.

With the thought came a memory—one so old he thought he'd forgotten it—an image of Belle, thirteen years old, facing his father in the kitchen. Rand remembered the way she stood, long-legged and gawky, her face expressionless while Henry quizzed her about where Rand had been the night before. It had been over something stupid, a silly race between him and Charlie Boston on the Rock Mill Road. It was forbidden, and Rand had done it anyway, and enlisted Belle's help to "borrow" the matched bays that were Henry's pride and joy. Rand remembered his father's anger when she refused to tell. Henry punished her by demanding she clean the pigpens, a chore they all hated more than anything.

But she wouldn't say a word, and there had been no resentment in her face—and no anger. Not once during the six hours it had taken her to clean those damn pens did she blame Rand with a look or a word. Not even when Henry forbade him to help her. And as far as he knew, she never held it against him.

Rand took a deep breath. *Some reward you gave her,* the voice inside him accused. He swallowed through a tight throat, steeling himself against the onslaught of guilt, refusing to feel it. *It was a long time ago. Things have changed.* Yes, they'd changed. That mindless loyalty she'd given him was gone, and he told himself he didn't care, that the price he'd paid for it had been too high.

And he didn't want mindless loyalty any longer. All he wanted was to keep Sarah with him. No matter how hard he tried, he couldn't forget the way he'd felt standing on the street in Lancaster, knowing Belle and Sarah hadn't taken the train. Knowing it might take him years to find them.

He didn't ever want to have to go through that again. He would do whatever it took to keep it from happening, and if that meant he had to enlist Belle's help, if that meant he had somehow to swallow his pride and tell her how truly sorry he was for not believing her, then he would do it.

He told himself an apology was all it would take. A nice "I'm sorry" all wrapped up in pretty words and a smile. She was good at accepting apologies, he remembered. Quick to nod and laugh. Quick to forget. The thought of it made him feel more relieved than he expected; suddenly he was burning with the need to do it, restless with the desire to see a forgiving smile in her eyes instead of that damned vulnerability, that burning anger.

Rand rose from the chair so quickly, it rocked.

Lillian started. "Rand?" She frowned as he went to grab his coat and hat from the peg by the door. "Rand, where are you going?"

"To find Belle," he said roughly.

"Why? What will you do?"

"Apologize," he said, and then smiled at the bewilderment on her face. "Isn't that what you wanted?"

"Well, I—"

He didn't stop to hear the rest. He was out the door in seconds, shrugging into his coat as he hurried across the yard to the barn. All he wanted was for this to be over, and the sooner the better. If he was lucky, he could find her tonight. She said she'd be in that old tavern overlooking Hooker's Station, and he hoped she was still there. In his mind he imagined it. She'd be sitting at the table playing cards, drinking a beer, laughing with the boys as if it didn't matter that she was a woman, as if the conventions that kept good women out of taverns somehow didn't apply to her. He knew exactly how she would look, with her elbows on the table, sleeves pushed back, leaning forward to tease one of the men who watched her. *"Now's your chance, boys. Are you in or out?"*

Yes, he knew just how she'd look. It would be the perfect place to apologize, the perfect time. She would be relaxed and happy. He would take her outside and give her an engaging grin of his own. *"I'm sorry,"* he would say. *"Please forgive me for doubting you."*

The vision was so strong, he almost felt her breath, heard the little catch in her voice, and Rand took the last few steps to the barn at a run. Within moments he had Duke saddled, and he led the gelding out of the barn into the brittle night air.

The moon was round and full; wisps of fog hung low

over the dips and valleys of the road, misted the trees. He smelled the frost in the air; it burned his lungs, made his eyes sting. It was a beautiful night, but Rand didn't have the time to appreciate it. He urged Duke to a faster pace, wanting already to be there, feeling a sense of urgency that he didn't stop to analyze.

From the outside the tavern looked just the same, just a tumbling-down old building with light slanting through the windows and the low sound of music and talk vibrating from its walls. The sight of it reassured him somehow.

He smiled and pushed open the door.

The smell of smoke and beer immediately assailed him. The odor put him at ease, even though he hadn't been inside since he'd brought Sarah home two years ago—before that even. The place looked just the same. Clouds of smoke hung gray and heavy, illuminated by the oil lamps set into the walls. The floor was sticky from spilled beer, and the straw strewn upon it stuck to the soles of his boots. It was crowded, more so than he'd expected, packed with men lining up at the bar, gathered at the rickety tables.

He peered through the gloom, trying to see her, hear her. Then suddenly he did.

"All right, boys, give me all your money."

Her voice carried through the room, husky with laughter and smoke, heavy with that giddy edge he remembered. Rand followed the sound with his gaze, and he spotted her just where he should have expected to see her.

He felt immediately swept back in time. They sat at the same old table: Charlie Boston, Abe Shearer, John Dumont, and Belle. The only person missing was Cort, and Rand felt a familiar pang of sadness, a grief that he quickly pushed away. The same table, the same chairs.

They were waiting for him, he thought, just as they'd waited for him this same way six years ago. But of course they weren't, and just as he realized it, he saw Belle lean forward and spread her cards on the table.

The motion was so familiar, it sent a shiver of shocked recognition running through him. He saw her look up and laugh, and the sound of it from across the room jarred him, as did Charlie's answering laughter.

For the first time since he'd decided to apologize to her, Rand hesitated. She didn't seem upset at all. Quite the opposite, and the knowledge brought a tremor of unease. *Go home,* a small voice told him. *Leave her alone, walk away.* But his boots felt glued to the floor, and his mouth was dry, and Rand knew he couldn't leave. Not yet. Not until he at least had the chance to ease his conscience, to appease the guilt he felt over today. Before he knew it, he was crossing the room, heading toward that table, every step heavy, as if it were taking him closer and closer to some inescapable doom.

He was almost to the table when he caught Charlie's gaze. Charlie started and frowned, and then he said something to the others. Immediately they looked up. Except for Belle. Her back was to Rand, and he saw her stiffen, saw her head come up and the tensing of her shoulders.

Turn around. Get the hell out of here. But it was too late to stop now. Rand took the last few steps to the table, halting just behind her.

"Rand Sault." John Dumont grinned in surprise. "What the hell are you doin' here? Somethin' on fire?"

Rand smiled slightly. "Nothing that drastic. I just dropped by to pick up Belle. It's getting late."

She didn't look at him, but he felt her surprise. "You shouldn't have bothered," she murmured, bending her head to look more closely at her cards. "I can get home on my own."

"I know, but we were getting worried." The lie fell from his lips easily. "Your mama sent me to come get you."

Across the table Charlie lifted a curious eyebrow. "Things *have* changed," he said, and there was a needling sharpness in his voice that made Rand uncomfortable. "I remember days when Mama didn't send anyone till two or three—if then."

"We have a busy day tomorrow," Rand said stiffly.

Charlie gave him a skeptical smile. "I see."

"Surely you can stay for a minute or two," John said, sliding over on the bench and patting it with his hand. "Sit a spell, play a hand or two. Belle's winnin' all our money."

"So I heard."

Abe grinned. "So you'll join us? Have a beer? It's been a while since we've seen your face 'round these parts, Rand."

Rand shook his head reluctantly. "I'd like to, boys, but I can't. Maybe some other time." He put his hand on the back of Belle's chair, gave it a little shake. "Come on, Belle. Let's go before it gets too late."

This time she twisted to look at him, her cards held tightly between white fingers, her chin raised. Her eyes were dark and unfathomable in the dim light, but he felt her anger.

"I'm not goin' anywhere," she said tightly.

He smiled—at her, at the rest of the table. "Come on, Belle," he said as calmly as he could, adding a bit of pleading to his voice just for show.

She made a sound of disgust and turned around again. "Later. I'm in the middle of a game."

The vision was fading before his eyes, the whole reason he was here suddenly falling out of reach. Desperation made him unscrupulous, lent an edge to his voice. "Sarah's waiting to say good night."

It was a terrible lie, but it worked, just as he knew it would. Belle stilled. "Sarah's waitin'?" There was a hint of hope in her voice, a carefully optimistic note that made Rand feel mean.

But not mean enough to stop. "Yes," he said.

"Well, then." She put her cards on the table and pushed back her chair. "Guess I've got to go, then, boys."

Charlie nodded. "Tomorrow night? We need a chance to win back all our money."

"If I can." She smiled at him and then at the others, and then she turned to Rand, and the smile died. "All right," she said, and there was no forgiveness in her voice, no compromise at all. "Let's go."

Chapter 17

The muffled sounds of the tavern filled the silence between them as they stepped outside, a low hum of noise that was somehow reassuring in the quiet darkness. Rand watched as she moved ahead of him to the edge of the porch. She hugged herself as if she were cold. Her breath came in frosty clouds of air.

She stopped at the step. "Where's the wagon?"

He licked his lips, feeling oddly nervous. "I didn't bring the wagon. Just Duke."

"Just Duke?" She turned, frowning, and then abruptly she put it together. He knew the exact moment she realized he'd lied to her. Her expression froze, and her eyes immediately shuttered. "You didn't come to take me home."

"No."

"Sarah's not waitin'."

"No."

She swallowed. She looked at him for a moment, and he saw her struggle to keep her expression even, saw the way she pressed her lips together as if the motion would keep her from saying something she didn't want to say. She hugged herself tighter and turned to look at the canal winding below the hill, a black satin ribbon in the moonlight. "Then why are you here?" she asked, her voice hard and too loud. "If you came to yell at me again, you can just turn around and head back home. I'm not listenin' to it anymore."

He took a deep breath. "That's not why I'm here."

She stiffened. "No? Then why?"

"I came to tell you I'm sorry." The words were out before he had time to think about them, and Rand cursed himself, furious at their starkness. He'd wanted to wrap them up in pretty sentiment, in properly chastened phrases. But now they stood between him and Belle, and he knew he had no choice but to continue. "I didn't mean what I told Sarah—about not being alone with you. I was—wrong. I should have trusted you. I should have believed you. I'm sorry now I didn't."

She snorted in disbelief. "And you think that makes it better, Rand? You think just sayin' you're sorry makes everythin' all right?"

Rand frowned. A twinge of dread crept through him. He wished like hell she would turn around and look at him. "I don't know. Doesn't it?"

"No." As if she'd heard his unspoken wish, she turned slowly to face him. "I don't want your apologies. They don't mean anythin' to me." She took a step backward, tilted her face to look at him, and the moonlight fell across her cheekbone and her jaw, glinted on her hair, and sent her eyes into shadow. But still he saw her expression. It was tight and angry. "Don't tell me your lies, Rand, I don't want to hear them tonight. I know you don't believe a word I say. I know you wish to hell I was a thousand miles from here. Don't lie to me and tell me it's not true. Just don't lie."

Then before he knew it, she was stepping from the porch and hurrying down the rise, stumbling away from him. He stared after her, stunned. This was not the Belle he knew, not the vision he'd expected. What happened to the soft smile, the warm brown eyes? Where the hell was her quick forgiveness? She was walking away, just walking away. . . . His panic rose, but for what he didn't know; why, he couldn't tell. All he knew was that he couldn't let her go. Not yet.

He raced after her, catching up to her halfway down the hill.

"Belle." He breathed. "Belle, wait."

She kept walking.

"Belle." He stepped in front of her, forcing her either to stop or to walk over him.

She stopped. Looked up at him without even a hint of emotion on her face. He'd never seen her this way. Never so remote, so—so untouchable. As if she might break if he touched her. He hated it. He hated the look of it, the shutters in her expressive brown eyes and the stiff way she held her soft mouth. Hated the way it made him feel. Lost, as if there was something he expected to find in her face, something he wanted—needed—to see.

But it wasn't there. It wasn't there at all.

"You hate me, don't you?" he asked quietly. The words surprised him. He had no idea where they came from or even why he said them.

But Belle didn't seem surprised. She only took a deep breath and looked away. "Yeah."

Her voice was flat, but he heard the feeling beneath it, the pain she tried to hide. And suddenly he remembered. That voice, that familiar monotone, slid over him, plunged him back into a memory, into another night, another time. That summer night when it all began. The taste, the smells, the sounds—they were all around him: the lightning bugs flashing across the wheat fields like tiny stars, the midsummer air warm and balmy on his skin. The rhythms of a fiddle and an old guitar blended with laughter and voices, and the scent of spicy ginger beer and roasted corn was heavy in his nostrils.

She was just fifteen. And beautiful. The most beautiful thing he had ever seen. Blond and vivacious, always laughing, beguilingly honest. She had blossomed during the spring he'd spent in Cleveland with his uncle. He saw the way she laughed and talked with the boys, who hovered constantly around her, and he told himself he shouldn't care, though he did. Sitting there across the fire from her, watching her talk and laugh with Charlie Boston while some of the others danced, he cared. He watched the way firelight danced along her hair, her face, watched the golden dappling of it on her skin, and the hunger, the longing, was so great he couldn't stand it.

But it was wrong to feel that way about her. She was too young. She was his responsibility. Hell, there were a hundred reasons why he shouldn't want her, and so he fought it, and searched out Elizabeth Thornton and asked her to dance. Spun her around the fire to the strains of the guitar until they were both dizzy. Looked into her pale blue eyes and saw brown ones. Touched the softness of her red hair and pretended it was blond. And then, after the dance, he'd pulled her, laughing and protesting, to the fire. He kissed her, slowly, lingeringly, and pulled away to find Belle watching him from across the flames.

Her face was white, her eyes overly bright. She caught his glance and jerked to her feet, hastily stumbling away as if something were after her, running until her sprigged gingham dress was a pale shadow in the darkness. And despite every ounce of sense he had, despite the voice inside telling him, ordering him, to leave her be, Rand lurched away from Elizabeth Thornton, leaving her sitting alone by the fire as he raced after Belle.

He found her in the shadows a short distance away, behind a haystack. She was crying.

That was enough to stun him into silence. He'd never seen her tears before, and they rocked him to his core, brought a realization he didn't want to acknowledge, hoped he could ignore. But they also worked magic on her face, made her skin luminous, brought reflections of moonlight glittering across her cheeks, and he got lost in that and forgot the rest.

"Belle," he said, but when he tried to touch her, she flinched away. "What is it? What's wrong? Did Charlie say something—Jesus, please—don't cry. Don't cry. Ah, God." He pulled her into his arms, cradling her against his chest. Slowly, slowly she melted into him, and he felt her mouth against his shoulder, felt the wetness of tears on his throat. "Shhh, little girl, it's all right," he murmured into her ear over and over. "It's all right."

She tried to draw away, but he kept her there, anchored to his chest, letting her pull back just enough so that he could see her face. She wouldn't look at him. The tears were running down her cheeks, and she wiped at them angrily, looking away from him. Her voice was a strange, flat monotone: "I'm sorry. I'm just a fool, that's all. I thought—" She licked her lips, took a deep breath. "I didn't know you cared for Elizabeth."

"I don't."

She laughed—a wavering, nervous sound. "You have a funny way of showin' it. You kissed her."

Because I wanted to kiss you. *The words caught in his throat. He tried to swallow around them. "That doesn't always—it doesn't always mean anything, little girl."*

She nodded shortly, and they stood there in silence for a few minutes. She wanted to say something; he saw the movement of her mouth as she struggled with the words, and he waited, because he wanted nothing so much as to just stand there and watch her, just smell the clean, soapy scent of her skin, the smoke of fire in her hair. Then she pulled away from him. Reluctantly he let her go.

"Rand, I've been thinkin' maybe we shouldn't spend so much time together. I've been watchin' you since you came back from Cleveland, and I know—" She paused, he thought he heard a break in her voice, and she looked away for a moment. "I know there are—other people you want to spend time with. Maybe you should. Maybe I just get in the way."

Her words stabbed into his heart, and the hell of it was that he knew she was right. Not for the reasons she gave him but because of other reasons, because he wanted her so badly, he could scarcely think. He knew he should agree with her, should tell her it was what he wanted too, and he opened his mouth to say the words.

But then she looked at him again, and he saw the fierce longing in her gaze.

It was then he knew.

She was sweet on him.

She was sweet on him. The realization made cold sweat break out on his skin. He'd been blind. Fiercely, horribly blind. They had always been good friends—even more than that, best friends—but now he saw the last month had been different. There had been an intensity about her, a yearning he'd mistaken for friendly affection. He'd seen the tears in her eyes tonight and assumed they were because of Charlie or something else, but they weren't. They were because she was sweet on him and he had hurt her by kissing Elizabeth.

Oh, God, how had he not known?

The thought sent him into a new kind of hell. Because he had counted on Belle to keep him at bay, and he knew now that she wouldn't, and he wanted her so badly, he was willing to take her even this way, knowing she was too young—God, only fifteen—too young to know her own mind, too young to really be in love, though she probably thought she was. He knew all that, and he didn't care, and he hated himself for it.

Sweet Jesus, what was he going to do?

Run away, *the voice inside him said.* Run now, while you still can, while you still have the strength. *But he didn't. He looked down into those eyes, at her wary, uncertain expression, and he suddenly didn't have the strength at all. Maybe he'd never had it. He smiled at her, and the darkness he was so afraid of hovered on the other side of that smile, waiting to pounce.*

Run away. Run away. *But instead he stepped closer, and the words he'd been wanting to say for so long came out in a rush, falling over his tongue before he could stop them, control them. "I want to kiss you, little girl," he whispered, and with the words came a surge of desire so strong, it terrified him. But then he heard her soft gasp of surprise. He saw the hesitation in her eyes, the pleasure threatening to curve the corners of her mouth, and he forgot everything.*

"I'm sorry I hurt you," he said slowly. "I didn't know."

She moved back to him then. Wrapped her arms around him and leaned into him until he felt her breasts pressing against his chest, felt the softness of her hair. "It's all right," she said, smiling a quick pardon. "I'll forgive you. But only if you stop callin' me little girl. And only if you kiss me."

". . . only if you kiss me. . . ."

"Rand? Rand, are you all right?"

The sound of her voice—real now, not memory—jerked him back from the visions. He stared at her, unseeing for a moment, still reeling from the force of the emotions that had shaken him in the past. But then he looked at her. Really looked at her, as he'd tried not to since she returned two weeks ago. Looked at those vulnerable brown eyes and the brave way she held herself, as if daring the whole world to hurt her.

And he knew in that moment that he'd been lying to himself. He hadn't followed her here to apologize for not believing her. Hadn't followed her to tell her he trusted her. He hadn't wanted forgiveness for today.

He wanted it for a cold November night six years ago.

"Oh, Jesus." He raked his hand through his hair and stepped back, suddenly trembling.

She lifted a brow. Her voice was heavy with sarcasm. "Somethin' wrong?"

"No. No." He shook his head. "I—" he took a deep breath, forcing his voice steady. Sweet Jesus, he had to get away from her, had to lose those memories, the singing of those words in his mind. "*. . . only if you kiss me, only if you kiss me, only if you kiss . . .*" He stepped back again. "Listen, why don't you take Duke and go on home? I'll walk." He heard the panic in his voice and knew that she did too, but he didn't care. Not about anything but getting away from her. "Take the horse. Go home. I need the walk." Then, when she didn't move, he said brokenly, "Please, Belle, just get the hell away from me."

She shrugged, and there was a wealth of meaning in the gesture, an angry indifference that wounded him. "Fine," she said shortly, turning away, and he wanted to call her back, to make her stay.

But he didn't know what he would say. There was nothing to say except *I'm sorry,* and he was already too sorry for too many other things. So he just watched her leave, watched her take the horse and ride away down the rise, her hair glimmering in the moonlight, all soft gold and yellow and brass.

It was then the images came drifting back, along with the sound of her voice, roughly sweet: "*. . . only if you kiss me . . .*" This time he didn't have the strength to fight it, and he let it come, washing over him in waves of bittersweet memory: the way she'd felt against him, soft and warm, and the taste of her mouth, and all the things he'd tried to forget about her, all the things he wanted to stay forgotten.

And he wondered if he would ever be able to forget them again.

"The potatoes need to be brought up," Lillian said matter-of-factly, turning from the stove. "I've put it off far too long."

Belle looked up groggily from her oatmeal. She'd had a sleepless night, had laid awake thinking about Rand's apology, wondering what the hell he wanted from her. She'd hoped to gain some peace this morning, but from the look on her mother's face, that was impossible. Lillian was standing there, her hands planted firmly on her hips, watching as if she expected a reply.

Belle tried to remember what her mother said. Potatoes. Something about potatoes. She looked down at the lumpy gray oatmeal and gave it an idle stir. "That's nice," she said, hoping it would be enough to make Lillian go away.

"Are you listening to me, Isabelle?"

"No."

Lillian gave an exasperated sigh, one Belle recognized all too well from her childhood. "Then hurry up with your oatmeal. We've got work to do."

Belle's head jerked up. *"We?"* she asked incredulously. "You want *me* to help you with somethin'?"

Lillian nodded. "You and Sarah. The two of you have been running around this farm like children. It's about time you did some work."

"Sarah *is* a child."

"One is never too young to be useful."

The words had the unwelcome ring of familiarity, and Belle winced. "Oh, yeah."

Lillian threw her a disapproving glance. "Isabelle."

"There's nothin' wrong with havin' a good time, Mama. Maybe you should learn *that* instead of all these lessons you're constantly preachin' on."

"Finish your breakfast." Lillian untied her apron and hung it on a peg near the door. She pulled another from the peg, an older, coarser one, and put it on with crisp efficiency, tying it with a flourish. She pulled open the door, and a draft of cold morning air streamed into the kitchen. "Sarah!" she called. "Sarah, get in here now!"

"Oh, for God's sake, Mama." Belle pushed back her bowl and got to her feet. "I'll help you if it'll make you feel better, but let Sarah go on and play."

"Sarah played yesterday."

It was an obvious reprimand for the trip to the canal, and Belle took a deep breath and bit back the retort that sprang to her lips. She was too damned tired today to go toe-to-toe with her mother, and it didn't matter anyway. She already knew Lillian would get her way, and Belle and Sarah would be pulling potatoes all day, and that was just the way things were going to be. There was no point in fighting it, and Belle wasn't sure she wanted to anyway. At least she and Sarah would be together, and Belle was fairly certain she could think of some way to make pulling potatoes fun.

Sarah came bursting in the back door. "Here I am!" She threw a big smile at Belle. "Belle, c'n we go back to the canal today? I bet Bandit's there, and we can jump off—"

"Later, Sarah," Lillian said firmly. "We have work to do today."

Belle made a face. "I hope you like pullin' potatoes."

"Pullin' taters?" Sarah frowned. She looked at Lillian. "But, Grandma, I want Belle and me to go to the canal!"

"The canal will still be there tomorrow." Lillian handed Belle an old brown apron and motioned to the door. "Come along, now, both of you. It's already almost noon."

"It's already almost noon." God, how often she'd heard those words when she was a girl. The sound of them now sent annoyance racing through her. Lillian grabbed Sarah's hand, and the two of them went out the back door. Belle gulped the last few sips of her coffee so quickly, she nearly burned her throat, then she put on the apron and followed her mother and Sarah out the back door and to the side of the house. The day was sunny, but there was a chill in the air along with the lingering dampness from last night's frost. It would be winter soon. Winter, when there was nothing to do but stay cooped up inside, when the morning was as dark as the night before.

It made Belle tired to think of it. Not because she didn't like winter but because being imprisoned by snow and ice meant there was no place to go, no place to escape to. And after last night she was beginning to realize just how much she needed such a place.

Despite herself she thought of Rand again. Of the way he'd come into the tavern and lied to her, of the way he said *"I'm sorry"*—all that sincerity, all that hope tied up in two words. The two words she'd waited six years to hear. *"I'm sorry."*

She'd pictured them a hundred times in her mind, imagined him on his knees in front of her, begging for pardon. There were times when she thought the only thing in the world she wanted was to hear him say, "I'm sorry. Please forgive me."

So that she could laugh in his face and walk away.

She'd nearly done that yesterday. Had refused to accept his apology, had left him standing there alone in the moonlight. But somehow it didn't fill her with the satisfaction she'd expected. Instead she felt—empty. Disappointed.

Belle told herself it was because he'd apologized for the wrong thing. He'd apologized for thinking she took Sarah, for not trusting her. But not for treating Belle so badly six years ago. Not for any of that.

She should have accepted his apology, she knew. But something had burrowed inside her, a burning resentment that made her want to reject him, to hurt him. She wanted him on edge, nervous and uncomfortable. She wanted to punish him.

"Belle! Don't dawdle."

Her mother's voice broke into her thoughts, and Belle looked up to see Lillian and Sarah already in the garden. Lillian held a beat-up bushel basket, and Sarah was looking at a trowel as if it were some sort of weird monster. For the first time since her mother suggested it, Belle found herself not minding the thought of pulling potatoes. If nothing else, it would take her mind off last night. It would keep her from searching the fields, looking for some sign of Rand. It would keep her from wondering what she would see when she looked into his face today. And what she would do about it.

She hurried over to the garden.

"There's another trowel over there," Lillian said,

pointing. "Isabelle, why don't you start at that end? Sarah, you come and work with me."

"But I wanna work with Belle."

Lillian frowned. "Belle's got her own work—"

"It's all right, Mama." Belle smiled. "Come on, Sarah. You and me can pretend we're huntin' for buried treasure."

"Yeah!" Sarah beamed. She came hurrying over. "I'll be Pirate Kate, 'n you can be my slave."

Belle raised an eyebrow at Lillian. "Pirate Kate?"

Her mother's frown deepened. "Rand reads her those terrible things, not I."

Belle knelt until she was even with Sarah. "Don't listen to her," she said in a loud whisper. "I saw her read 'Bandits of the Osage' once."

Sarah frowned. "What's an Oh-sawge?"

"It's a place. But they've got Indians there."

"I heard stories 'bout Indians. Mean ones that scalp people. I had a bad dream 'bout 'em once."

Belle smiled reassuringly. "Well, they're mostly gone from here. But out west there are plenty of—"

"That's enough, Belle." Lillian came marching over, taking Sarah firmly by the hand. "Go on into the kitchen and get a rag," she instructed Sarah. She waited until the child had gone a few yards before she turned again to Belle. "You'll give her nightmares."

Belle sighed and got to her feet. "I'm just tellin' stories, Mama."

"They aren't fit for a child's ears." Lillian made a sound of exasperation. "Pirates, Indians—the next thing I know, you'll be telling her stories about outlaws and criminals."

"Only if I can think of one with plenty of blood in it," Belle joked. "Really, Mama, you're gettin' upset over nothin'. They're just stories, just a little fun, that's all."

Lillian's face tightened. "Oh, for heaven's sake, Isabelle, you haven't changed at all." Angrily she turned away.

Belle felt the heat of a flush on her cheeks. Her mother's words sounded strangely familiar, and she remembered last night, when John and Charlie had told her she hadn't changed at all and she'd thought it a compliment. Had laughed and smiled and agreed that no, she hadn't changed. The echo of those words rang in her mother's voice, only now they were touched with scorn.

And Belle suddenly realized they weren't a compliment at all. They were more like a curse.

She watched Lillian grab the bushel basket and move with small, weary steps to the other end of the garden, bending at the waist as if she were an old woman carrying a burden too heavy to bear. Belle knew without asking what that burden was.

It had always been the same. It had always been her.

The knowledge made her chest tight, and that, too, was familiar. She'd felt that particular ache since she was a child. For a lifetime she'd seen the disappointment and bitterness in her mother's face, had known that somehow she wasn't the daughter Lillian wanted. In her mother's eyes she had never been good enough. Never gracious enough, or sweet enough, or proper enough. But Belle thought she'd learned to live with that. In the last six years she thought she'd made peace with it, had learned to make a place for herself.

It was a shock to realize it wasn't true. A shock to realize her mother could still reduce her to nothing. *"You haven't changed at all."* The words whittled away at her, banging against her defenses, and along with them came the urge to believe them.

Even though they weren't true. She *had* changed.

She'd had no choice but to change. The impetuous, carefree girl she'd been was gone; that girl had disappeared one freezing November, had shattered beneath the onslaught of Rand's betrayal and her mother's angry words. *"You're a disgrace to this family, a disgrace, do you understand me?"*

Belle swallowed through the lump of tears in her throat, forced herself to take a deep breath and look away. She was done with those memories, done with the restless nights spent hoping her mother hadn't meant the words, wishing somehow that they were a lie. Knowing they weren't. In all those nights Belle had made herself one promise: Her mother would never, never make her cry again. She could live with the fact that Lillian didn't love her. She could live with knowing she would never be the daughter her mother wanted. But she would never let Lillian see how much that hurt.

That's what Belle told herself, anyway. And if deep inside was the hope that maybe someday—someday she would wake up and it wouldn't hurt anymore, then it was only a trivial wish, a passing fancy. A dream that didn't matter now and never had.

But she knew that was the biggest lie of all.

Chapter 18

He waited outside the schoolhouse until the bell rang. The front door opened, and the children came streaming out, talking in high-pitched, excited tones, swinging empty lunch pails and carrying McGuffey's Readers close to their chests. He stood there by the stump in the schoolyard, nodding hellos to the children as they passed, hearing their "Hey, Mr. Sault"s with half an ear. His eyes were trained on the old clapboard schoolhouse, on that open door, and his mouth was dry. He should not be here, he knew that.

But he had no choice. The images from last night still danced in his head, haunted his dreams. Over and over he saw Belle's golden hair, saw the shadowed wariness in her eyes and the defensive way she held her chin. And over and over again he heard the words from their past: ". . . *Only if you kiss me. . . .*"

No, he had no choice at all.

Rand waited until the last child had left the schoolyard, until their voices echoed back to him from the road, and he straightened and looked at the open door.

He swallowed and went inside.

Marie was near the far wall, writing something on the big blackboard. Her handwriting was neat and even, every letter perfectly rounded, perfectly spaced. She reached up to push away a stray hair from her face, and the motion was graceful and delicate even though she didn't know anyone was watching.

Rand leaned against the doorjamb and crossed his arms over his chest, striving for nonchalance even though he felt stiff and vaguely guilty. " 'The fat hen is on the box,' " he read. "Exciting reading."

She jumped; one hand fluttered to her chest and she spun around, her eyes wide and startled. "Oh—Rand—" She breathed, blushing. "I—I didn't hear you there."

"Sorry," he said. He stepped closer. The room smelled like chalk dust and woodsmoke from the stove in the corner. "I didn't mean to scare you."

"Why you—you didn't. That is, you did, but it's fine."

Rand's smile widened. She was prettily flustered, the knowledge made him feel more confident, even a little cocky. "I just came by to see if I could carry your books home."

"My books?" She glanced at the pile on her desk involuntarily. "Well, I—I'm not sure I should let you."

"Why not?" Rand moved closer. "How can I get to be teacher's pet if I can't spoil the teacher?"

She flushed again. God, she was so easily discomfited—nothing like Belle, who was always so quick to spit out a teasing retort.

He told himself it was refreshing, told himself it was what he wanted. He gave Marie his best smile. "I promise I won't bite."

She looked at him, and he saw the measuring expression in her eyes, knew she was wondering what he was doing and whether she should go along with it. Knew also that she would. So he waited patiently, working to keep his guilt at bay, trying to concentrate on the softness of her face and the way the serviceable gray dress clung to her curves, trying to imagine how that brown hair would look coming loose over her shoulders. Brown hair, not blond. He stepped closer. "Come for a walk with me, Marie."

She sighed, a giving-in sigh, a soft surrender. He tried to remember if she'd made that sound before he kissed her last summer, and couldn't. "All right," she said, smiling. "Just let me get my cloak."

He followed her to the back of the schoolroom, waited while she clasped her cloak about her shoulders. She moved quickly, a little nervously, as they went outside and she latched the door behind them.

"I didn't get the chance to congratulate you for taking second prize at the fair," she said as they started down the path. "Bertha was lovely."

"As lovely as a pig can be." He chuckled.

"I—I watched with your mama," she said.

"Did you?"

"I meant to come down afterward, but then Lydia came over, and—"

"And you didn't think she would approve."

She threw him a look. "That wasn't it at all," she said, and there was a heat in her voice he found interesting. "You know how she can be—she just pulled me away to something. But that's all."

"You weren't worried she'd tell her brother?"

"Tell him what? I told you Charlie and I are just friends."

"I see." He nodded thoughtfully. "I'm not sure he'd say that."

He heard the slight catch of her breath. "Why would you think so? Have you talked to him?"

"I saw him last night down at the tavern."

Her face went rigid. "And you talked about me?"

"No." He shook his head with a smile. "No, he was

playing poker with—Belle. I got the impression he wasn't happy to see me."

"Oh. I can't imagine why." She was quiet for a moment. They walked slowly, their footsteps sounding a crunching rhythm on the leaf-strewn road. "Does Belle often go to a—a tavern?"

Rand shrugged. "She used to spend a lot of time down there when she was younger. I guess she never grew out of it."

"Doesn't your stepmother care?"

"She doesn't have much to say about it." He stopped just under a huge oak tree at the edge of the road. The leaves nestled around his feet, fluttered from the mostly bare branches overhead. "I didn't come here to talk about Belle." He paused, measuring the words. "Does Charlie know you and he are 'just friends'?"

Her eyes widened, and there was a touch of annoyance in her voice. "I don't know what he thinks. And I'm not sure I know what you mean. Are you—"

He barely heard her words, but her face filled his vision: the big eyes, the rosy fairness of her skin, her full mouth. He felt the books pressing against his stomach, and he wanted to drop them, to pull her close until he felt her breasts and her hips against his body, until he buried all those visions of Belle in Marie's form and flavor.

But the books were in the way, so he merely stepped closer and bent until her mouth was inches from his and he heard the words stop in her throat, heard her startled breath and the soft "oh my," before he kissed her.

She didn't back away, didn't move. Her lips were soft and heated beneath his, parting slightly—ever so slightly—until he took advantage and forced them open so that he could taste her, so that he could run his tongue along her lips and dip inside. She tasted of peppermint and smelled of roses, and she was so damned feminine and pretty and gentle that he wanted somehow to destroy it. Wanted to grab her roughly and jerk her against him, to see if she would gasp in surprise at the touch of his body or melt into him.

But mostly—oh, God, mostly—what he wanted was a different taste, a different scent. What he wanted was bourbon and sweet coffee, soap and water and sunshine. Sweet Jesus, what he wanted. . . .

Rand jerked away, stepped away, putting feet between them now instead of inches, feeling the rush of blood into his chest, his fingers. He squeezed his eyes shut and tried to calm down.

But when he opened his eyes again, Marie was staring at him, and her lips were pink and slightly swollen from his kiss, her eyes almost black with emotion.

"Rand," she said—the word was a rush of sound, a drawn-out breath—"Oh, Rand."

He swallowed. This was what he'd come here for, that look of wonder. This was what he needed. There was innocent passion in her eyes, he'd seen it enough not to mistake it, and he knew he could make it less innocent, knew he could turn it into lust and desire, knew he could make her hunger for him.

It would be enough. He could make it enough.

He forced a smile. "So," he said, and the word felt tight, leaden on his tongue. "What about Charlie?"

She licked her lips. "Don't worry about Charlie."

He nodded and started walking again. He heard her light, quick steps behind him as she hurried to catch up, and then she was beside him and she laid her hand possessively on his arm. He let it stay there as they walked for a while in silence.

Finally she broke the quiet. "I know you've been busy," she began. He heard the hesitation in her voice, the slight plea. "What with the corn needing to be cut and all, but I thought—I hoped—well, will you come to Paula's singing party tomorrow night?"

He wanted to say no, but he knew he couldn't. He'd made a declaration of sorts and he couldn't back down. Couldn't kiss her and ask her—however tacitly—not to see Charlie and then ignore her. He knew she wanted to be cosseted and displayed. Probably she had some new dress she wanted him to see. And if he planned to make her his wife, he needed to show a real interest in her. The townspeople expected it. She expected it.

The idea only made him tired. But Rand smiled down at her and tried to look happy. "Yeah," he said. "I'll come."

Her face shone. "Oh, good. I've a new gown—it's the prettiest shade of green."

"I'm sure it's pretty on you."

She flushed. Her fingers tightened on his arm. "Oh, I almost forgot. Paula wanted me to ask you to bring Belle too. Everyone's looking forward to seeing her."

He felt the slow tightening of his gut, a pounding in his head, and he hesitated. "I don't know—"

Marie looked at him beseechingly. "Please."

She smiled that pretty, feminine smile, and his stomach knotted, his heart sank in his chest. "I'll ask her," he said faintly.

"Promise?"

"I promise." He said the words and saw the brightening of her face and tried to tell himself it didn't matter. He could spend the evening playing games and laughing with Marie; he could even forget Belle was there. He could ignore that shining golden hair and that warm laughter, he knew he could.

He told himself that as he walked Marie home and

listened to her light chatter. Kept telling himself as he left her at the door and smiled a good-bye.

But it was a lie, and he knew it—and knew there was no way out. He would bring Belle to that party. He would bring her there and pretend he was happy to be doing it. He would watch her laugh and joke until he couldn't bear it anymore.

And then he would try to bury his dread.

In the touch of Marie's skin and the smell of her hair.

Belle opened her eyes, blinking at the sunlight streaming through the big doors of the loft, wondering how long she'd been asleep. From the color of the sunlight she guessed it was probably only late afternoon. She stretched, leaning her head back against the rough wall of the barn, breathing in the musty scent of hay. She wished she could stay here all day and all night—God knew she'd slept better the last two hours than she had since she'd arrived home.

But then, the loft had always been an escape. She glanced around at the huge hayforks hanging from the walls, the hay stored for the winter. She'd needed this today, this time away from everything and everyone. A time just to sit here in the straw and think and sleep without the fear that she would be found. The moment they finished pulling potatoes this morning, she ran to the barn, and the peace of the loft was a balm to her battered spirit, a place where the disturbing memories of last night and the pain of this morning couldn't touch her.

When she was young, she'd come here often to hide in the corners. Sometimes she had lain on her stomach to stare out the huge window overlooking the barnyard, gazing at the rustling fields of corn and wheat and the hills stretching as far as the eye could see. When she was young, she had never even imagined there was a world past those hills.

Now she knew there was. But as bustling and exciting and frightening as that world could be, she had never loved it as much as the one she watched from this loft. She wanted to stay here forever, to let Rand and her mother just fade away, to grow old sitting in this barn telling stories to Sarah.

Belle smiled at the thought. In spite of what she'd told her mother, her favorite stories had never had much to do with bloodthirsty pirates and scalping Indians. Instead they were about adventures on the canal and talking mules and pretending she could fly when she jumped from the apple tree in the orchard beyond.

They were stories she'd made up on her own because no one else was there to make them up with her. No mother to play games with. No father to get down on his hands and knees and pretend he was a horse for her to ride. Belle closed her eyes again, remembering how much she had wanted that as a child, wondering if Sarah felt that way too. Maybe not. After all, Sarah had a father who was more than a pious portrait on the wall. Sarah had Rand.

And now she had a mother too.

Belle took a deep breath and got to her feet, brushing loose strands of hay from her skirt. She'd been away too long, escaping when she should have been spending time with Sarah. Maybe they could go out to the pond and hunt for frogs, or even go out to the old orchard and lie in the sun and eat apples that had fallen from the trees. Or the canal—Sarah had said this morning she wanted to go back to the canal. Maybe they could saddle up Duke and head on over there for an hour or two. Maybe she could even get some hoggee to put a straw hat on a mule and pretend it was Bandit.

The idea was compelling. Quickly Belle hurried out the big doors to the road, nearly running down the drive to the house. Bushels of potatoes were gathered at the base of the back steps, but Lillian was nowhere in sight, nor was Sarah. Belle went up the stairs, pulling open the door so hard, it slammed against the wall.

At the stove Lillian jumped. "For goodness' sakes, Isabelle, slow down." She turned back to stir the fragrant pot of stew simmering on the stove. "Tell Sarah to grab a couple of those potatoes when she comes in, won't you?"

Belle looked around. "Where is she?"

"I assume she's right behind you. Isn't she?"

"No."

Lillian looked over her shoulder, a frown on her perfect features. "Isn't she with you?"

"No." Belle shook her head. "I thought she was in here."

"Oh, Lord, not again." Lillian dropped the spoon, her face paled. "She said she was going to the barn to find you. Didn't she show up?"

A twinge of worry nudged at Belle. "No," she said. "No, I was alone. But she prob'ly just got interested in somethin' else. I'm sure she's around here somewhere, Mama."

"There's no need to panic," Lillian said calmly, though it was clear she was starting to. "She's probably outside in the yard." She swung open the door and leaned outside. "Sarah! Sarah! Come here this instant!"

"If I was playin' and havin' a good time, I'd never come to that voice," Belle said. She went to the door and stepped past her mother. "Sarah!" she called. "Sarah, come on back and we'll go down to the canal!"

There was no answer.

"Oh, good Lord," Lillian whispered.

"I'm sure she's fine," Belle said, trying to ignore her mother's anxiety. There was no call to be worried, not yet. "Where's Rand? Maybe she's with him."

"He went into town early this morning," Lillian said. She started down the steps, her fingers gripping her apron. "She was here after he left—Sarah! Sarah! Young lady, don't you play games with me! Come here!"

Her mother's voice shattered Belle's nerves. She heard the panic in them, the fear, but she knew that high, punishing tone much too well. "Mama," she said, grabbing Lillian's arm and pulling her to a stop. "Mama, don't call her that way. She won't come—"

Lillian yanked away. "Sarah!"

"Mama, listen to me—"

"Don't you tell me what to do!" Lillian turned on her, eyes blazing. "You haven't spent more than a few days with this child. I've been with her the last two years. She is nothing like you—do you hear me? Nothing! She's a good girl."

Belle jerked back. The words hit her with the force of a blow, the bitterness in her mother's gaze, in her mother's words, ripped into her, bringing back all the old feelings. She tried desperately to keep them at bay. *She doesn't mean it. She doesn't mean it*—the litany rang in her head, and Belle struggled to believe it.

"Mama," she tried, but the word came out broken and hesitant, and Lillian wasn't listening anyway.

She had already turned away. "I want you to go up to the springhouse," she ordered. "And then to the orchard, wherever you think she might be. I'll try the cellar and the yard. Now, hurry." She looked over her shoulder, her face icy cold. "And Isabelle, you bring her right back if you find her, do you understand me?"

Belle nodded. "Yeah, Mama," she said dully. "I understand."

And she did. She understood better than she wanted to. The emotions were there, on Lillian's face, in Lillian's eyes, and Belle knew that to her mother Sarah was more than a granddaughter.

She was the daughter she'd never had.

Belle watched as Lillian hurried away across the yard calling Sarah's name, and an unexpected, unwelcome pang of jealousy surged through her. She wondered if Lillian had ever been this worried for her. Wondered if all those times she'd sat in the hayloft ignoring her mother's calls to come home, there had even once been a touch of panic in Lillian's voice.

Somehow she doubted it.

It bothered her that the thought hurt, made her uncomfortable that she was jealous of her own daughter. *You should be glad she loves Sarah so much,* she thought. Except that she knew what love meant to Lillian, knew it meant stifling rules and overprotective demands. *Or maybe that was just for you.*

Belle swallowed, pushing away the thoughts. It wasn't important now what Lillian thought of her. What was important was finding Sarah—and finding her first so that she could protect the child from Lillian's anger. Because Belle knew Sarah was probably just hiding, just as Belle had done a hundred times. She was almost certain that somewhere Sarah was listening to Lillian's panicked voice and giggling as if it were all a game.

But by the time Belle had checked the springhouse, the barn, and the orchard, she wasn't so convinced. She told herself she was only starting to get worried because she heard Lillian's call in the distance, and it sounded more panicked than ever. There was an edge of hysteria to it that was high and biting, lingering long after her voice died. It shivered up Belle's spine, prickled against her skin. It was all right, she told herself. Sarah was just playing. Just having a good time. Of course she was. She had to be.

"Sarah!" Belle called. "Sarah, come on home now! I promise you won't get in trouble!"

Where the hell was she?

"Sarah! Sarah, if you come out now, I'll give you a big surprise!"

Her voice vibrated in the air. The only answer was the nickering of a horse in the pasture.

Sarah was all right.

She was only hiding.

She was just playing a game.

But the reassurances felt hollow. Belle hurried to the smokehouse. Sarah would be there, she knew it. Probably playing in the ash pile. She would be covered in gray and streaked with soot, oblivious to the calls. . . . Belle tore open the door.

There was no one there. Nothing but blackened hooks and dust that rose in the draft. No little girl playing in the ashes, waiting to be found.

Oh, God. Oh, God, where is she? The panic Belle had not allowed herself to feel suddenly flashed through her blood, making her heart pound and her knees weak. *Where is she? Where is she?*

"Sarah!" she called, and she no longer even made the attempt to soften her words, or even to offer bribes. All she wanted was an answer, and it could be anything. Laughter, tears, anything. Just as long as it was an answer. She understood now the stark relief on her mother's and Rand's faces when she and Sarah came back from the canal. For the first time she understood what she'd done to them, how worried they must have been, how frightened. The thought made her sick with shame.

God, where is *she?*

"Sarah! Sarah!" Belle heard her mother's voice blending with hers, a singsong echo in the hills. *"Saaaaaarah!"* "Sarah!" *"Saaaaaarah!"* "Sarah!" It almost made her crazy, the rhythm of that sound.

But Sarah was nowhere. Not in the pasture, not in the smokehouse or the privy. And Belle knew from her mother's cries that she wasn't anywhere else either. God, where could she be? Where the hell could she be? Belle tented her hand over her eyes, staring into the sun, hoping to see her—a speck against the hills, a spot of movement. Why the hell hadn't she just taken Sarah with her to the barn today—or even to the canal, like Sarah wanted? Why hadn't—

The canal.

The thought plunged into her mind, sent her heart falling.

Not the canal.

But she knew suddenly that it was exactly where Sarah had gone. She heard the little girl's voice in her mind, heard all the things Sarah had ever said about the canal. *"Can we go to the canal today and jump off the bridge?" "You mean the boats go forever and ever down to China?" "Papa used to jump too?" "I wanna jump. Can we?"*

Belle felt sick with fear, and she realized with a nauseating sense of guilt that this was what she'd been hoping for from Sarah, this independence, this sense of adventure. She'd spent the last two weeks doing her best to inspire it. *"Your papa and me used to jump from that bridge all the time. We'd get on a boat headin' to town and then jump off and walk on back. That was some of the best fun I ever had."* She'd told all those stories,

stories about going alone to the canal, and fishing in the river, and running barefoot in the grass.

But there was one thing she'd forgotten. One thing she hadn't thought about at all. She'd been twelve years old when she'd done those things, not five.

And she had never been alone. There had always been Rand, or sometimes Cort.

The panic surged through her now, making her blood race, filling her mind with images: Sarah walking along the bridge, scurrying to jump on one of those boats, dodging the tow chains—the heavy, clumsy tow chains . . .

Belle ran. Her feet pounded the ground so hard, her teeth banged together. God, how could she have been so stupid? Why hadn't she thought? She should never have said those things to Sarah, should never have tried so hard to be a friend that she'd forgotten she was an adult and Sarah was just a little girl. Such a little girl.

Please, God, let her be all right. Belle pulled her skirt over her knees and ran faster. There were so many things to be careful of—had she even mentioned them? The deep, murky water, the slippery decks of the barges. And those missing boards at one end of the bridge—the rotten rail. *Oh, God . . .*

"Mama!" she screamed, sliding down the path from the springhouse to the yard. "Mama!"

Lillian came racing around the corner of the house, breathless and pale. "Where is she? Did you find her?"

"She's at the canal." Belle gasped. "I know it. I told—her. Dammit, I told her—what to—do—"

Lillian blanched. From the front drive came the sound of a wagon, the crunch of gravel beneath heavy wheels, the steady, hollow clop of horses' hooves. She gripped her apron. "Rand," she said. "Thank God."

Belle didn't wait. She went dashing around the corner of the house, racing in front of the wagon.

Rand jerked up on the reins. "What the he—"

"It's Sarah." Belle breathed. She felt Lillian behind her, heard her mother's breath, harsh and ragged as her own. "She's at the canal. She's gone to the canal by herself. To jump off the bridge."

"Christ." Rand's face went white. He jerked his head toward the seat. "Get on," he ordered. Then, while she scrambled to get aboard, he said to Lillian, "Stay here. Get hot water ready. And blankets. Lots of blankets."

Then he hit the reins, and they were off.

Chapter 19

"What the hell's going on?" Rand shouted over the noise of the wagon, but he didn't slow, didn't take his eyes from the road.

Belle grabbed onto the edge of the seat, trying to keep her balance as they hurtled down the road. "Sarah disappeared this afternoon. She's been talkin' about the canal, so I figured—"

"Who was watching her?" The question was bitten off and angry.

Belle flinched. "No one."

Rand's face hardened. She saw his anger, knew that he had already assigned blame—and she also knew that she deserved his contempt this time. Guilt swelled in her chest, a deep, throbbing ache that made her sick with worry and self-recrimination. She was to blame, after all. She should have been watching Sarah. She should never have taken her to the canal the first time, or told her stories. Should never have urged Sarah to take the same meaningless, stupid risks Belle had been safe taking at twelve.

What kind of a mother was she anyway?

No kind of mother at all.

The thought brought a lump into her throat, sent a wave of hopelessness crashing over her. But it was true, and she knew it. She hadn't acted anything like Sarah's mother. She'd been too busy being Sarah's friend. She wanted Sarah to like her, and Sarah did. But liking was different from loving or respecting. Yes, she was Sarah's friend. Sarah's ally. But she wasn't Sarah's mother. Being a mother meant keeping a child safe, taking responsibility.

And you've never taken responsibility for anything.

Belle squeezed her eyes shut. *"Don't go to the canal alone," "Stay away from the well," "Don't climb on those fences."* The rules she'd always hated mocked her now. For the first time Belle realized what they really meant. They meant the difference between life and death. They meant safety, they taught caution.

And she had deliberately taught Sarah to disobey them.

Belle felt faint at the thought. *You're to blame if something happens to her. You're to blame.* She remembered all the times she'd ignored the rules, thought of all the things she'd done, and with a flash of insight she realized just how much danger she'd been in. Hell, Rand and her mother had been right not to trust her. She couldn't even take care of herself. How the hell could she take care of a little girl?

She thought of that day she and Sarah spent at the canal. The way the sun glinted off the water, hiding the lethal murkiness below. She thought of Sarah's rapt gaze as she looked at the bridge. God, why hadn't Belle seen it then? Why hadn't she realized that the idea of jumping off that bridge onto the boats below would take hold in Sarah's imagination? Why hadn't she remembered what it felt like to have that same thought eight years ago, when she was still a child—the challenge, the exciting question of what it would feel like to have the wind whoosh by you, to feel the rough deck beneath your feet and know you'd done it?

Why hadn't she remembered?

"Can't you go any faster?" she yelled.

Rand shot her a quick, contemptuous look. "We're going as fast as we can." He stared back at the road, and his expression was grim, his jaw set. Belle thought of Sarah's melon-stained face and the gurgle of her laugh, thought of her wobbling, deliberate walk, the way her bare feet pattered on the floor. *Please, oh please . . .*

As if Rand heard her plea, he slapped the reins against the horses, yanked them into a sharp turn that sent Belle slamming into him, sent the wagon careening around the corner and onto the road leading to Hooker's Station. Belle almost wept with relief when Rand slowed the wagon in front of the warehouses. She was off before it even stopped, was running past Shenky's stand and down the boardwalk. There was a break between the warehouses, a space the width of one person, maybe two, and she tore through it, skirting the rotting harnesses and crates littering the ground, scraping her hands against the splintery sides of the building when she lost her balance. She heard Rand's footsteps just behind her, heard the harsh gasp of his breathing joining hers. The blood pounded in her ears; she tasted the bitter salt of panic on her tongue. *Please, God, let her be all right. Let her be all right and I'll never break another rule again. I promise. Please—please, I promise. . . .*

"Sarah!" Her voice bounced off the walls, an eerie, hollow sound. "Sarah!" She pushed through the last few feet, burst out onto the loading platform, skidding to a stop just before the canal dipped away below her. Involuntarily she glanced toward the bridge.

Her heart stopped.

Sarah was there. Sitting on the edge of the bridge, in a space where the railing had broken away, her little feet dangling bare in the chilly breeze, her hair shimmering in the sunlight. Waiting for a barge to make its way down.

Belle surged forward. "Sarah!" she called, and was stunned to see Sarah look up and wave and struggle to get to her feet—

"Christ!" Rand lurched past her, pounding down the length of the loading platforms toward the bridge. "Sarah, sit down!" But Sarah only looked confused at his shout, and she stumbled.

Belle gasped. She felt suddenly faint. "Sarah!"

Sarah regained her balance and smiled. "Belle! Papa! Look what I can do!" She held her hands out and took a step along the edge.

Belle's stomach fell. "Sarah, no!" Her feet seemed to move without her, her body felt heavy and leaden as she ran down the loading docks after Rand, dread and fear hammering in her head. Rand wasn't going fast enough. Oh, God, he wasn't going fast enough.

Then everything seemed to happen in slow motion. She and Rand reached the bridge at the same moment Sarah took another step. Belle saw the wavering of her daughter's body, the swift look of panic as she lurched to the right—

Belle lunged toward Sarah, but Rand was already there, grabbing at her, pulling her back from the edge, grasping her with desperate strength. Belle didn't think. Desperately she ran to them, and suddenly she was enveloped in Rand's arms, too, her face pressed against Sarah's back—smelling her skin, her hair.

For a moment—just a moment—Belle was overwhelmed with a sense of security, of warmth, of belonging. The feeling was so strong, it made her weak, and she clutched at Sarah, wanting things to stay just this way for only a few seconds longer. But then Sarah struggled in their arms, and Rand was stepping away, Sarah was sliding out of his grasp. The moment she hit the ground, she turned and smiled up at Belle. "Did you see me?" she asked. "I was doin' it real good before then. I been practicin'."

Something inside Belle snapped. Before she knew what she was doing, she grabbed hold of Sarah's arms. The relief, the fear, the guilt all welled up inside her, crashed around her, a mix of feelings that put an edge to her voice and made her feel out of control and strange.

"Don't you ever, ever do that again," she said, giving her daughter a little shake. "Do you hear me? Not ever again."

And then, to her horror, she started to cry.

Rand stared at her in shocked surprise. He felt out of place as he watched her cry, watched her gather Sarah up in her arms and pull the child to her, and he knew he had looked just that way a few days ago, when Belle brought Sarah back from the canal the first time. He saw himself in Belle's movements, knew how relief and fear and panic forced every other emotion away, how it took refuge in anger. He saw himself in the way she shook Sarah and in her desperate scold, and it surprised him.

He had not thought her capable of it. He had not expected her even to realize the danger, thought she would simply shrug it away—or worse yet, be proud of Sarah for trying such a daring thing. That she wasn't surprised him. Puzzled him. He'd told himself she was still the girl she'd been six years ago—reckless and impatient, irresponsible. The things about her that *were* different—that fierceness in her manner, the vulnerability she worked so hard to hide—were only little changes, unimportant ones that had more to do with independence than with growing up. He told himself Belle hadn't really changed.

But now he wondered if maybe he was wrong. If maybe he only saw what he wanted to. If maybe he was so afraid she would crawl back inside him that he had deliberately refused to look at who Belle was, who she had become.

Because the woman kneeling on the dock, crying through her fear, the woman who had sounded for a moment like all the mothers he'd ever known, was not a woman he knew.

And he couldn't look at her now and believe she was the same girl of six years ago.

The realization sent a trickle of fear sneaking through him. He wanted to tell himself he was wrong—that she was still the Belle he'd always known—but then he heard her whispering to Sarah, and he knew she wasn't.

"I'm sorry," she was saying. "I didn't mean to yell at you. But you scared me, Sarah. That water's deep, and when I was tellin' you about the bridge, I forgot to tell you how scary it was. The only reason I could even jump at all was because your papa was there holdin' my hand."

Rand tried to swallow.

Sarah smiled warily. "It *was* scary. And real high."

"I know. It's pretty high." Belle sat back on her heels, wiped at her face with her sleeve. "I think you're too little to do it all by yourself. I was fourteen before I could."

"I'll be fourteen soon," Sarah said hopefully. "C'n I do it then?"

Belle's smile wavered. "I guess so. But until then I want you to promise me you won't come back to the canal by yourself. You take me or your papa with you."

"All right."

"You promise?"

"Uh-huh."

Rand nudged her with his knee. "Say it, Little Bit."

"I promise." Sarah looked at Belle. "I'm sorry I made you cry."

For a second Belle looked embarrassed. But then she got to her feet and wiped again at her face with her hand. Her eyes were still huge and glistening, her cheeks were pink from rubbing, and tears left dirty tracks through the dust on her skin. She looked unsteady and breathless and disheveled.

And Rand thought, *This is the mother of my child.*

He caught his breath in surprise. The mother of his child. He'd never had the thought before, and now Rand found he couldn't stop it, couldn't prevent the idea from taking hold. He imagined what she must have looked like, her body softly swollen and rounded, her movements graceful and seductive in spite of the clumsiness of pregnancy. He imagined her skin, translucent with life, her brown eyes lit with that soft tranquillity that infused expectant mothers, the wisdom that spoke of things men only dream about.

In that moment he knew that he *had* been wrong about her, that she *had* changed, and he'd just refused to see it. He thought of last night and the memory of that long-ago summer evening when she'd said ". . . *only if you kiss me* . . ." and suddenly the memory lost its power, was supplanted by a much more evocative picture—that of Belle heavy with his child. Why had he never thought of her that way before?

Rand swallowed. His gut clenched, his heart pounded so hard he thought he might pass out. *Because it was easier to think of Sarah separate from Belle, not a part of her at all. It was easier to think of Sarah as belonging only to him.* . . . And in a hot, aching flash of awareness Rand knew why he'd tried so hard to suppress the image.

It was the most erotic one he'd ever known.

Far more erotic than a green girl trying her first kiss. It was the image of a woman, with all that meant—wisdom and serenity and secrets, rounded softness and knowing smiles, desire and need and forgiveness . . . things a girl hadn't learned yet. Secrets a girl didn't know.

Sweet Jesus . . .

"What do you say we go on home and have a piece of pie?"

Belle's voice broke into his thoughts. Rand stared at her, unable to take his eyes away as he watched her take Sarah's hand.

"Pie?" Sarah asked hopefully.

"I thought I saw your grandma makin' pumpkin." Belle's smile was soft and watery. "It's about my favorite kind."

"Mine too," Sarah said.

"All right, then. Let's go."

She and Sarah started off, talking animatedly and moving down the dock hand in hand, with the sunlight glinting off their hair. Blond and blond. *His daughter. The mother of his child.*

Rand tried to push the words away, but they lingered there, raising questions he didn't want to think about, feelings he refused to look at. He saw the way Belle's hips moved beneath that old wool skirt, the strong and graceful sway, and he wondered how maturity had changed the body he remembered, if her breasts were fuller, or her skin warmer, smoother. . . .

He swallowed, struggled to think of Marie Scholl, to think of the scent of roses and the warm, tingling softness of her lips. But the images felt cold and distant, and he could no longer remember what Marie felt like, even though he'd kissed her only a few hours ago. He couldn't take his eyes off the woman walking in front of him, her fingers tight around a little girl's hand. Woman. Not a young girl anymore. *When did that happen? Why didn't you see it before now?*

Slowly, feeling disconcerted and strange and frightened, he followed them back to the wagon. But he kept his distance, though he saw the way Belle kept looking back to make sure he was there. Even that was frightening, a memory of other days, when the habit of keeping each other in sight had been strong and unbreakable. *Don't let her get to you. Don't think of it. Don't think of her,* he told himself. It was too dangerous.

But it was impossible not to think of her. He didn't look at her when he got to the wagon, kept his distance as he lifted Sarah into the back and took his own seat beside Belle. He felt weak and unsettled, and he took pains not to brush against her. But he was aware of her anyway. He felt her heat, smelled the scent of sunshine and dirt on her skin. Rand forced his eyes forward, tapped the reins, jerking back from the touch of her arm as the horses started. *Think of Marie,* he told himself. *Think of dark hair and roses. Think of—*

"I'm sorry." Belle's voice was low and soft, so soft he could barely hear it above the noise of the wagon. "I know you're mad, and I guess you have a right to be. I'm sorry."

He swallowed, kept his eyes fastened on the road. "I'm not mad."

He felt her gaze darting to him, felt her disbelief in the air.

"You're not?" she asked.

He heard the stark amazement in her tone, and it, too, had the feel of danger. Rand's fingers tightened on the reins. *Lie to her,* he told himself. *Be mad, if that's what she expects.*

But he couldn't. "No," he said softly.

"Why not? It was my fault. I should never have told her we used to jump off the bridge. But I didn't think she would . . . I didn't think."

"You couldn't know," he said, searching for something—anything—to say, something besides the questions dancing in his mind. *How did it feel to know my baby was inside you? Did you think of me at all?* But she was waiting, and so he forced out words. Any words. "When you spend more time with her, you won't make those mistakes."

She twisted on the seat. He felt her staring at him. *Don't look at her. Don't say a word.* And he didn't. Not for minutes. He felt her settle back, felt the silence stretch taut between them, let it grow until he couldn't stand it anymore. Even then he didn't want to speak, was afraid of what he might say. But he heard his voice anyway, heard what he said with a vague sense of detachment, as if it wasn't him at all but some disembodied voice. "Paula Rice is having a singing party tomorrow night. She wants you to come."

Belle made a soft sound of disbelief.

His jaw tightened.

"Are you all right?" she asked slowly. "I mean, Sarah almost jumps off a bridge, and it's my fault, and you're actin' like it doesn't even matter—"

"It does matter."

"Then I don't understand."

He was so tense, he felt as if he might explode. It took everything he had to keep the images of her at bay, to concentrate on the conversation and keep from asking the question burning in his mind. Desperately he searched for words. "There's nothing to understand," he said finally. "Sarah's all right. Nothing happened."

He felt her confusion, and something else, something that felt suspiciously like fear. It startled him, enough so that he turned to look at her.

It was the biggest mistake he could have made.

She was staring at him. Her brown eyes were large in a face still pale from panic. But there was no panic in her expression now. There was only wariness, a caution that squeezed his heart and made his fingers clench. Christ, he hated that look, hated the way it made him feel. Lost and wanting. Lonely. Like last night and the night before and every hour since she'd walked into the kitchen and said *"Hey, Rand"* a week and a half ago.

Had it really only been that long?

You're losing control. The voice rang in his head, heavy with warning. He knew he should get away from her now, yet he couldn't. He felt suspended, lost in eyes that were shuttered against him, eyes that held secrets he was suddenly longing to know, and the urge to lean forward and kiss her was so overwhelming, he felt nauseated with it.

He turned away, stared sightlessly at the horses.

"Never mind," he said hoarsely. His heart was pounding in his ears. "I promised I would invite you."

"I can't believe Paula wants me there."

He kept his eyes forward. "I guess she does."

"Why?"

He shrugged. "I suppose she probably wants to see you again, but I don't know for sure. She didn't ask me directly."

"Who did, then? Lydia?"

He thought of Marie and felt a twinge of uneasiness. "Someone you don't know. Marie Scholl."

"Oh. Marie."

Rand frowned, surprised. His uneasiness increased. "You know Marie?"

"I met her at the fair." Belle shrugged. "Mama introduced us."

Lillian introduced them. Rand wished suddenly that he had never mentioned Marie's name. He felt the warning of disaster, the fine edge of fear, and he thought, *Take it back. Tell her it doesn't matter if she goes or not. Tell her if she wants to stay home, it would be better.* But he said none of those things. He said nothing at all. Just waited for her to say no. Prayed she would say no—and prayed he would let her when she did.

She hesitated a minute, maybe more, and then she took a deep breath. "All right," she said slowly. "I'll go."

He felt no surprise at her words, and in the quiet, shivery aftermath of her answer he felt something else entirely, something he didn't want to look at too closely or think about at all.

Because in spite of everything, he knew he had wanted her to say yes.

And it scared the hell out of him.

Chapter 20

The moon was too bright, it shone through the thin muslin curtains, painting the room in dark and light, in cold blue shadows. Belle watched it move across the floor, watched its slow rise and slower descent, and it felt as if she were witness to every crawling second of the night.

Over and over she relived the day in sharp, painful clarity, from the second Sarah disappeared until the moment they found her. Belle could not lose the image of Sarah perched precariously on that bridge, and she knew that if Rand had hesitated even one minute longer, they would have been trying to drag Sarah from the murky waters of the canal instead of holding her warm, vibrant body in their arms.

It was that thought that haunted Belle, that thought that kept her from falling asleep and sent a shudder racing up her spine. She died a little every time she remembered it. It was funny, but in all those years she'd spent away from Sarah, Belle had never once thought about losing her daughter. Not once had she thought about all the terrible things that could happen to a little girl.

And now she couldn't forget them.

Just as she couldn't forget the feelings that had rushed over her as the three of them stood on the bridge with

Rand's arms tightly around her and Sarah. Relief. Joy. Belonging. In that moment Belle realized that she'd never known what it meant to really belong, to be part of something bigger than herself. In that moment she had been, and the feeling was so huge and warm and sweet that everything else paled in comparison. It embraced everything: fear and relief, love and loss.

It was such a pure, all-encompassing emotion that she knew she would never truly understand it, not in ten years, not in a hundred. Belle had always thought she loved her daughter, but now she knew just how little she'd understood love. In the last two weeks Sarah had sneaked inside her, had stolen a piece of Belle's heart—a piece she hadn't even known existed. And now she couldn't imagine a life without her daughter, couldn't remember the life she'd led before she came back home, before she'd seen Sarah chasing the cat off the porch.

And Belle knew she didn't want to live a life without Sarah again.

It was a sobering thought, one that grew in her mind until dawn colored the sky and she heard Lillian moving around downstairs. Quickly Belle washed and dressed and hurried to the kitchen.

Rand looked up when she came into the room. He stopped in the middle of pouring coffee. "Good morning," he said in surprise. "You're up early."

Sarah twisted around in her chair. "Mornin', Belle. Will you go to the pond with me today? There's a big ole frog out there, 'n we can throw rocks at it 'n see if it'll sing. Papa says it will."

Belle smiled. Her heart swelled at the sight of Sarah's puffy morning face, the sleep-rumpled hair. "Oh, it will," she said. "We'll go out there in a little while."

"*After* we pickle onions," Lillian interjected. "I'll need your help this morning, Belle. Rand was just telling me the corn's ready. The cutters will be here Monday. We've plenty to do before then."

"All right," Belle said distractedly. She took a seat.

"Coffee?" Rand asked.

She nodded. "I need it this mornin'." She poured a cup and liberally laced it with sugar and cream.

"I know what you mean."

Rand's voice was low, a little harsh, and for the first time Belle noticed that he looked as tired as she felt. There were deep shadows beneath his eyes, and his mouth was pinched and tight.

A twinge of guilt shot through her. She took a sip of coffee, swallowed quickly. "One of those nights again?" she asked.

His eyes widened—again in surprise, as if he thought she would have forgotten his bouts with sleeplessness. "Yeah."

"Still drinkin' warm milk?"

He looked at her quizzically. "It never helped much."

"It didn't taste good either."

His eyes didn't leave her face. "No."

Belle looked down, disconcerted by his gaze, feeling the blood rise in her cheeks. Something about his look disturbed her, the same way his words had yesterday when he'd asked her to the party, when his quiet invitation made her feel weak and strange, made her say yes despite her best intentions. That moment standing on the bridge had changed something between them; she felt the shift in the air, in the shape and tenor of his glance. Something was different, something that made her feel uncomfortable and exhilarated and nervous, something that took her anger and urged her to move carefully, cautiously.

Sarah climbed down from her chair. "Come on, Belle," she said. "Hurry 'n eat so we can go play."

Lillian looked over her shoulder. "Not until the onions are done. Dorothy'll be here shortly."

Sarah pouted. "But, Grandma, we gotta go see the frog."

"The frog will still be there later."

Belle pushed aside her coffee and got to her feet. "Come on, Sarah. Let's go on outside for a minute. I want to tell you somethin'."

Lillian frowned. "Isabelle—" she said sternly.

"Just for a minute, Mama," Belle said. She grabbed Sarah's hand.

"But—"

"It's all right," Rand said slowly. "Let her go."

His gaze was slow and scrutinizing; it made Belle feel strangely light-headed. Discomfited, she turned away, ushering Sarah to the door.

"Where're we goin'?" Sarah asked as they stepped outside into the frosty morning air. "Can we go to the pond—"

"Not now," Belle said firmly. She closed the door behind them and sat on the step, pulling Sarah down beside her. "We're goin' to help Grandma with the onions first, because she asked us so nice, and then we'll go out to the pond when we're done."

"But the frog might be gone by then."

"He won't be gone." Belle smiled as reassuringly as she could, resisting the urge to pull Sarah into her arms and squeeze her tightly. "Besides, I know a special way to get frogs to come out, and if you're real good today, I'll show you how."

Sarah looked at her with wide eyes. "Really?"

"Uh-huh." Belle glanced out at the yard, white with frost that was rapidly melting in the sunlight. She heard the cows lowing in the pasture. It was so peaceful now, it was hard to believe there was anything dangerous in the world at all. Belle licked her lips. "I want to tell you somethin', Sarah. Can you listen real carefully? This is important."

Sarah nodded. "All right."

"Good." Belle searched for the right words. Though she'd spent all night rehearsing them in her head, now she felt tongue-tied and oddly nervous. She took a deep breath and twisted to look into Sarah's face. "Yesterday, when you went to the canal by yourself—that was a very bad thing to do."

"But you said we could jump—"

Belle winced. "I was wrong, Sarah. Your papa told you not to go down to the canal, and he was right. I was a big girl when I did all those things. You're not a big girl."

"I will be soon."

Belle nodded. "Someday. But not yet. D'you remember why you can't go down there by yourself?"

" 'Cause it's dang'rous."

"That's right. It's dangerous." Belle squeezed her hand. "Lots of things are dangerous, Sarah. That's why we tell you no sometimes, so you won't get hurt. That's why your grandma and your papa make rules."

Sarah's face scrunched up in thought.

Belle squeezed her hand. "We can play together and have a good time, but we have to follow the rules so we don't get hurt."

"But can we—can we still go to the pond?"

Belle smiled. "Well, I don't know. Is there a rule?"

"Papa says I ain't s'posed to go by myself."

"That's good. But I don't guess you'd be by yourself if I came along, would you?" Belle got to her feet, and when Sarah held out her hand, Belle pulled her up too. "Anytime you want to go to the pond, or the orchard, or anywhere else, you just ask me. I'll go with you if I can."

"Anywhere?"

Belle grinned. "Just about."

"Will you come to the pond 'n show me the frog secret?"

"Yeah, I'll show you the frog secret."

Sarah tugged on her hand. "Let's go now."

Belle knelt until she was even with Sarah. She put a finger to her lips and grinned. "There's another rule, Sarah, but this one'll be our secret, okay?" She waited for Sarah's nod before she went on. "You've always got to help your grandma when she asks you."

"She yells at me when I don't," Sarah said.

"That's right." Belle tried not to laugh at Sarah's glum face. "But good girls help their grandmas, and right now Grandma needs us to help pickle some onions for the cutters." She threw Sarah a conspiratorial wink. "But I'll tell you what: I know your grandma pretty well, and I'll bet if we're real nice, she'll let us go early so we can find that frog of yours."

Sarah's eyes lit. "Really?"

Belle squeezed her hand and smiled. "Really."

The wagon jounced and rattled on the pockmarked road. Every jerk sent pain into Belle's already clenched jaw, made her curl her freezing fingers more deeply into the laprobe tucked around her legs. Her whole body was tight, both from cold and tension, and she was glad the moon hadn't risen quite yet, glad for the dark that wrapped her in soothing, shadowed blindness. It made sitting next to Rand easier somehow, as if by not seeing anything but his shadow, she could pretend he wasn't there, pretend the two of them weren't on their way to a party she'd forgotten all about until this afternoon, when he'd come into the kitchen while they were pickling onions. Until he'd looked at her with that searching, puzzled glance and said in an oddly soft voice, *"We'll leave after supper."*

That voice reminded her again of her thought that things had somehow changed between them, even though the only solid evidence of a change was when he'd taken her side against Lillian at breakfast. Even that felt elusive and not quite real.

And it could be nothing, she told herself. *It could just be your imagination.* Maybe.

Maybe not.

Belle swallowed. She glanced at the darkened forest along the road, wishing suddenly that she'd never said she'd go to Paula's party. There was a strange sense of inevitability about it that reminded her of that cold autumn night six years ago, when everything had fallen apart around her.

She told herself she was wrong, that tonight was nothing like that time, that it was just a harmless party, a chance to have a little fun and nothing more. But she didn't really believe it. Things were too different, and she was too aware of him beside her, too aware of his watchful quiet, of his strange tension. When they finally pulled up in front of Paula's house, Belle waited as patiently as she could as Rand maneuvered the buckboard into place along the front of the huge white house, next to a wagon whose canvas top sported the words *Thaddeus Horner, Music Master.* But the moment they stopped, she pushed the lap blankets aside and shoved them under the seat, jumping to the ground and moving to the house before he had the chance to touch her or say anything.

He tied the horses quickly. When she reached the leveled sandstone steps to the house, he was already beside her. The parlor curtains were drawn, but light glowed through them, sending silhouettes dancing against the fabric. Belle heard laughter and talking, a rumble of sound in the quiet night. Rand knocked on the door. Almost immediately it was flung open.

"Rand!" Paula Rice swept into the doorway, a rustling, shimmering streak of bronze silk and ruching and strawberry-blond hair. "Marie told me you were comin', but I didn't believe her. And you've brought Belle too!" Belle found herself suddenly enveloped in Paula's arms, overwhelmed with the scent of violet water. "I'm so glad you came." Paula stepped back, holding Belle at arm's length. "Oh, you look just wonderful—doesn't she look wonderful, Lydia?"

Lydia Boston moved into the doorway, genteel and polished in a gown of dark green silk, her gaze scrutinizing as Belle took off her too-big man's coat. Belle ignored it. She and Lydia had never really been good friends anyway; all those years ago Lydia had been, if not the source of the lies that fed the gossip mill, then at least an eager contributor. She had been in love with Rand then herself, and he had rejected her, and Belle had long since realized that Lydia had only acted out of jealousy and anger.

But just the same, Lydia had never liked her, and tonight, seeing Lydia's hard smile of greeting, Belle knew things hadn't changed. Not that she gave a damn. Charlie's sister had lost the power to hurt her years ago.

Belle forced a hello.

Lydia's smile didn't quite reach her eyes. "Hey there, Belle, it's so nice to see you. And you, too, of course, Rand." Her voice was cloying—so sweet and insincere, Belle's teeth ached.

Rand didn't seem to notice. "Good to see you, Lydia." he said, sweeping off his hat. His hair shone dull gold in the lamplight. He glanced into the open parlor. "Who's here?"

"Why, everybody," Paula gushed, taking Belle's coat. "Tim and David Parker—you remember them—and Sally and Paul. Sophie Lang, of course, and Tom Webster, and . . ." She chattered on, and Belle listened with half an ear. She was too busy looking into the crowded parlor, trying not to catch anyone's eye as she took in the rows of mismatched chairs and the people milling around the refreshment table at the back of the room. There was no one here she remembered, or even wanted to remember, except for Lydia and Paula. And Lydia sure wasn't worth getting reacquainted with.

". . . and Marie of course," Paula finished, taking Rand's coat and hooking it beside Belle's on the pegs by the door. "I know you're anxious to see her, Rand, so go on in. Help yourself to gingerbread and cider."

Belle felt him pause. Studiously she avoided his glance, felt a wave of relief when he finally turned and went into the parlor, disappearing among the others. She forced a smile and looked at Lydia. "Well, how have you been, Lydia? I saw your brother the other night. He seems happy as ever."

Lydia's smile looked stretched. "He's been just fine," she said, throwing a glance into the parlor as if she were searching for something. "Until lately of course."

"Until lately?"

Lydia swung her head back around. "Oh—well—he said he lost some money to you last night."

"Are you still playin' cards, Belle?" Paula laughed. Her hand fluttered to the onyx broach on her breast. "I thought sure you'd outgrown that by now."

Belle raised a wry brow. "No point in outgrowin' it when there are people like Charlie just achin' to lose their money."

"I suppose not." Paula said. She put her arm around

Belle's shoulder, pulled her close. "Now, Mr. Horner only just arrived, so we have a few minutes. You just have to tell me where you've been all this time. There's a rumor goin' around that you were in New York City."

"Well, that's a true one," Belle said.

"Good heavens, such a big city! I was tellin' Lydia I couldn't even imagine a city like that. Why, I'd get lost in minutes. Didn't I say that, Lydia?"

Lydia nodded distractedly, still scanning the parlor. "You surely did."

"How ever did you survive there?"

Belle shrugged. It was hard to do, wedged as she was against Paula's shoulder. "Dumb luck, I guess."

"Tilly Bronson's cousin, Tom, lives in New York City. She told me he got pickpocketed just last month."

"That'll happen," Belle said. She frowned at Lydia, who wasn't paying any attention at all. Charlie's sister was practically goose-necked near the parlor door.

"Thank goodness it doesn't happen here." Paula released Belle finally, stepping away in a whoosh of violet-scented air. "I'm happy enough to be—really, Lydia, what *are* you lookin' for?"

"Well, nothin' really—ah!" Lydia turned back to them with a smug smile. Belle felt a twinge of discomfort. It only got worse when Lydia walked over to take her arm. "Why don't you come on in the parlor with me, Belle? I'll bet you're thirsty after that trip, and Paula has the best cider."

Belle studied Lydia suspiciously, trying to decide whether to go with her or not. There was a glint in Lydia's eyes that didn't bode well at all.

She hesitated and looked at Paula, thinking to mutter some excuse about wanting to talk to their hostess a bit longer. But just then there was a knock on the door, and

Paula rushed to answer it. "Oh, please go in," she threw over her shoulder. "Help yourself, Belle."

The chance was gone. Belle couldn't think of a single excuse not to go with Lydia. Her feeling of dread grew stronger. She tried to ignore it as she turned back to Lydia. "You don't have to watch after me, Lydia. I'm sure you've got—"

"Oh, but I insist." Lydia pulled her toward the crowded parlor.

There was no escaping; Belle felt uncomfortably closed in as they stepped into the room. In the far corner the music master was running his fingers over the keys of the piano, checking the tuning. It was too loud, and the air was too hot, and the musty smell of a room closed up for too long was only barely covered by the nauseating scent of burning oil and orrisroot potpourri. There were people everywhere—sitting, laughing, talking.

She glanced at Lydia, who had dropped her talonlike grip to survey the room again. There was a predatory look on her face that reminded Belle—too much—of the women at church two Sundays ago. Lydia patted her dark hair self-consciously. "Why, it seems as if everyone's here, doesn't it? Now, where did that handsome stepbrother of yours get to?"

The question sounded odd, forced. Belle tensed. The piano pounded in her ears. "He's around somewhere, I guess. Where's—"

"Oh, there he is!" Lydia's voice was high with satisfaction, so much so that Belle turned again to look at her. Charlie's sister was staring toward the piano, and her gray eyes were sharp, her features tight. Feeling again that strange sense of dread, Belle followed her gaze.

And knew instantly what Lydia Boston wanted from her.

Rand stood on the other side of the piano. He looked relaxed, happy as Belle hadn't seen him in—in so long, she couldn't remember. He held a cup of cider in his long fingers, and he was laughing. Laughing while he bent over a songbook spread open on the piano. Laughing while the lamplight shone down on his hair, gilding the tawny, sun-streaked strands with light.

Laughing while he looked into Marie Scholl's smiling face.

Belle's breath stopped. Her chest felt tight, and there was a fierce, burning pain somewhere in the region of her heart. Marie Scholl. Suddenly everything fell into place: the way her mother had introduced Marie at the fair, the subtle smile on Lillian's lips, the way she emphasized the word *friend.* And Rand's invitation of yesterday. *"Marie told me to ask you."*

Belle felt the color drain from her face. God, she was going to be sick. Right here, in front of everyone. The realization plunged through her, along with a wave of such intense jealousy and pain, it made her dizzy.

Oh, God. Oh, God, please don't let me care about this. But she did care. She cared with every part of herself, so much, it made her shake, and before she had a chance to fight it, to shove it back into that dark place in her heart, that place where she was safe, he did the one thing that stripped her defenses clean.

He looked at her.

It was as if the years fell away, as if she were flung back in time to that first night so long ago, when she'd watched him kiss Elizabeth Thornton from across the fire. Belle saw him stiffen, saw the dawning realization in his eyes, and she felt caught in time, trapped in a memory from which there was only pain and no escape.

She felt the warm air on her skin; the odor of potpourri faded beneath the scent of firesmoke and Charlie Boston's bay rum. And Belle suddenly knew she'd been lying to herself all these years, that she'd told herself she could harden her heart, make her feelings for Rand disappear in anger, fade away. But they hadn't faded at all.

She was still in love with him.

Panic crashed over her, caught in her throat, made her knees weak. She felt Lydia's hand on her arm, saw Rand lean down and murmur something to Marie, and then he was leaving the piano, moving through the crowd, and Belle knew why she'd felt that sense of inevitability, of fate. Because just as he had that night so long ago, he was coming to her now.

She jerked away from Lydia. Distractedly she heard Lydia's shocked gasp, but Belle didn't stay to listen, and she didn't give a damn if the others saw or what the hell they thought. All she cared about was getting away. She couldn't bear it if he saw how she felt—it would destroy her to listen to his explanations or his pity. She pushed through the people, desperate to get to the door, to disappear in the darkness where she could gather her strength. All she needed was a minute—just a minute. Enough time to remember who she was and what she wanted. She could face him then, she knew it, when her walls were back in place, when she'd had time to really remember how it was.

Paula was just coming through the parlor. "Belle, where are you going? Mr. Horner is just about to start—"

Belle didn't even listen. She flew past Paula and her violet-water scent, was across the hall before anyone could say a word or even come after her. But by the time she reached the front door, she heard the voices. The murmurs of concern, the hushed, gossipy whispers that fell into the silence left by the piano.

All so familiar. All so painful.

She wrenched open the door and plunged into the night.

Chapter 21

He told himself not to go to her. He told himself it would be madness. But the words were rote and meaningless now. The last few days had been building to this moment, the longing he'd been fighting for days—years—exploded within him. He felt the warmth of Marie's hand beneath his, and knew that he should try to lose himself in her. He also knew he wouldn't.

"I'll be right back," he whispered—a whisper because it took all his strength to do even that. Before she had the chance to answer, he moved away from her.

He told himself he would only talk to Belle. Here in this room he could handle anything. With all these people standing around, he could control himself. But then she bolted, rushing outside, and Rand hesitated, knowing that out there the darkness and the moonlight and the cold would conspire against him.

He should not go after her.

Christ, don't go.

But then he had the other thought, the most powerful one of all.

She is the mother of your child.

Before he knew it, he was hurrying across the parlor, into the front hall, wrenching open the door. The freezing air hit him with the force of a blow, burning through his lungs, shivering across his skin, and he had the brief thought that it was a good thing Lillian had taken up the potatoes yesterday. Tonight was the killing frost, he knew the smell in the air, the taste. He stood on the porch, searching the yard, the shadows, trying to find Belle, wondering if she'd even bothered to take her coat.

From inside the house the piano sounded. They were starting. He heard the harsh tones of Mr. Horner, heard the rise of voices. They rumbled, muffled, in his ears: "Me, May, Ma, Mo, Moo"—the practice scales. A horse whinnied from the row of wagons. Rand followed the sound with his gaze.

He saw her then. She was leaning against the wagon. The moonlight stole the color from her, she was nothing but a spot of pale in the darkness, a movement of shadow and light. She had forgotten her coat, and she hugged herself against the cold, her head tilted to look at the sky. She hadn't seen him yet, he realized, and for a moment he had the strange, disconcerting thought that she was waiting for him.

But she wouldn't be of course. The only question was why she hadn't run off for home without him. Almost as if she'd heard his thought, her chin came down, and she stepped away from the wagon and toward the horses.

Then she saw him and stopped, and the look she gave him was colder than any killing frost.

But he stepped down the stairs anyway and walked across the yard, past the other wagons, until he was only a few feet away from her. She didn't budge. Didn't even flinch.

"The party's inside," she said.

"Are you all right?" he asked quietly.

She laughed bitterly, softly. "I'm fine."

"Are you sure?"

Her mouth tightened, she gave him a quick glance,

and then looked away, focusing her gaze on the porch beyond. "Go away, Rand," she said. "Leave me alone."

He hesitated. "Belle—"

She jerked back to look at him. "Things are fine just the way they are," she said, and there was a desperation in her voice that tugged at his heart, made him feel inexplicably sad. "I only came back for Sarah—just Sarah. I hoped . . . you'd be gone. I didn't come back to start things again."

He nodded. "I know."

She went on as if she hadn't even heard him. "I figured—I don't know, I thought—you'd be married by now."

"Is that what you wanted? For me to be married?" he asked even though he thought—knew—he didn't want to know the answer.

She licked her lips. "Yeah," she said, but there was a touch of hesitation in her voice, as if she were trying to convince herself she believed it. She swallowed; her mouth moved as if she were trying to fight back tears. "But I see I was just a few months too early."

He didn't pretend to misunderstand. "You mean Marie."

"She's the one, isn't she? She's who you're goin' to marry?"

No. I don't know. "Yes."

She laughed slightly, looked up at the sky. The movement sent her profile into relief, he saw the shadows from the house play across her features, the short, straight nose, the slight overbite, the angle of her cheekbone. The moonlight reflected off the wetness in her eyes. "Well, that's good," she said. "She seems nice. You'll be happy with her."

"I hope so."

"Mama must be overjoyed."

"She likes Marie."

"I guess everybody does." She looked at him and—incredibly—she smiled. It was weak, he saw it tremble even in the moonlight, and it surprised him. But not as much as what she said next. "I'd like to get to know her better. If we're goin' to be . . . related, I s'pose I should."

Her words took his breath and twisted his heart, and he looked at her and saw again the change. He'd expected defiance and anger. What he got was acceptance—and the strange, foreign sense that she wanted him to be happy, that it didn't matter to her with whom he made a life so long as he was content.

It shocked him even more than what she'd said, and once again he remembered that first kiss six years ago, the way she'd curled her arms around his neck and urged him closer, the way she touched her lips to his, and he knew that girl would never have let him go like this—not ever so easily. The girl she'd been would have tried to hold on to him, would have seduced him because he was so easily seduced, would have smiled at him and cajoled him with a word, would have made him forget Marie even existed.

It was that girl he'd expected tonight.

Instead he had the woman of yesterday.

And she was more compelling than ever.

Run away. Run. Run. But he couldn't. God help him, he couldn't run away. Couldn't look away. Because Belle was again that woman, and she was both familiar and strange—a woman he wanted—needed—to know. The realization brought his fear into sharp, bitter focus. It hovered between them; he saw it in the shadows on her face, in the intensity of her eyes. It crept into her stance and her mouth and shimmered on her skin.

His control was slipping away, falling from his grasp.

He thought of all the things he didn't know about her, all the things she'd been and done and seen the last six years, all the ways she'd looked.

And then he thought of the things he did know about her: the way she felt, soft and hard, yielding and solid. He thought of the clean, astringent scent of soap. He thought of the heated wetness of her mouth and the heavy satin of her hair.

He thought of how much she'd loved him once.

It broke him.

Before he could think, before she could react, Rand surged forward. He took her face in his hands, ran his fingers over her jaw, touched his thumbs to her mouth. He heard her gasp of shock with some part of him, felt her shudder—with pain or fear or passion, he didn't know, didn't care. He held her tightly, so tightly, he knew she couldn't move or protest, molding his hands to her face, plunging his fingers into her hair, lifting her chin. He felt her breath against his skin, heated, moist, and it pulled at the desire he'd kept buried for six long years, the desire that had haunted his dreams and had him waking, wet and hard, in the middle of the night, wanting and knowing he shouldn't want, needing and knowing he couldn't have.

She made a sound, and he bent and took it from her. Brushed his lips across hers, feeling the softness of her mouth, a softness that tingled on his, that made him want to force her lips open to find the sweetness he knew was there. He wondered what she would taste like tonight—apple cider and gingerbread or sweet coffee—and found that he wanted none of those. He wanted just the taste of her alone. Just that heady, humid taste he'd kept in his memory all these years.

The thought made him almost insane with longing.

Rand deepened the kiss, pressed her mouth open, touched his tongue to hers—

She jerked away. He heard the sharp, desperate sound she made in her throat, and with a start Rand realized she was shoving at him, pounding her palms against his chest. He dropped his hands, sluggish and dazed from the force of his desire. She scrambled away from him; he caught a whiff of soap just before she slipped beneath his arms, and he grabbed for her, suddenly panicked that she would run, needing her to stay.

"Belle," he gasped, but she was already beyond his reach. Blindly, his heart pounding in his ears, he spun around. "Belle—please. Please. Don't go."

She stopped, twisted to look at him, and her eyes were dark and fathomless in the shadows, her expression bleak. He felt her fear; it shivered between them, stabbed him with unrelenting shards of memory. It had all ended on a night like this, after all. A night with a killing frost.

"I'm sorry," he said hoarsely. "God, Belle—"

She stepped back as if his words frightened her. "No," she said slowly, her voice a mere whisper. "Don't do this to me again. I can't . . . I don't want to care about you, don't you understand? I don't want to care."

Then, before he could answer her, before he could do anything, she turned and ran away from him, stumbling, to the house without once looking back. He heard the sudden tones of the piano crash into the darkness as she opened the door, and then he heard it slam shut behind her, leaving him standing alone, in cold silence.

The darkness reached for him, and he recoiled from it, told himself she was right, that it was better this way, that he should never have kissed her, or reached for her, or wanted her. It would be better for them both if he kept his distance, if he didn't remember the way things had been before. If he didn't remember the sheer brilliance of her smile, or the way she made him laugh, or the love she had for life that always made his dream of leaving Lancaster seem somehow—unnecessary, unimportant.

He should not remember those things.

No, he should not.

But he did.

And God help him, he missed them.

She felt shattered. As if someone had sent her heart and soul flying into a thousand pieces and left her there, just an empty shell in the bright gaiety of a room she didn't want to be in, the center of laughter she wanted no part of. She heard the whispers around her, knew the others were retelling the old gossip—the scandal of the sinful love between Belle Sault and her stepbrothers. She could almost hear the hushed murmurs—*"She had an affair, first with Cort and then with Rand. Why, it was immoral"*—and she knew they were wondering why she'd raced out just now and why Rand had followed her and not returned. She wanted to go home, she wanted to run away, but she couldn't. Not because she gave a damn what they all thought of her but because leaving like that would only be admitting that she cared, that the stories they told were true.

She would never give them the satisfaction. Never.

So she sat there, studying black notes that jumped all over the page, feeling the bruising of her mouth and the grip of his fingers on her face. She sang along, trying to remember words that kept flitting out of reach, tasting the sweetness of apple cider from his lips and the heated salt of his skin.

She felt cold and hot and unsteady; it was all she could do to focus on Mr. Horner and pretend she understood what he was saying. And when they took a break for apple cider and gingerbread, she saw Lydia bend to Paula and smile, and Belle knew the rumors would be flying again, even though Rand's name was already linked with Marie's.

You don't care. You don't care. And it was true it didn't bother her when they talked about how careless she was; she didn't give a damn if they spoke in scandalized tones about how she spent every night playing cards in a tavern or drank like a man. She didn't even care if they spent hours speculating on where she'd been for six years and what she'd had to do. Those things couldn't hurt her.

But the rest—the rest could. She remembered the rumors from before, the stories that both Cort and Rand had been in love with her, that they'd fought each other for the chance to have her. The rumors had only grown worse when Cort died that summer. It had been a tragedy; Cort died only two months after his father, after Rand came home from Cleveland for Henry's funeral. They'd been grieving anyway, and Cort's death had . . . Well, it was a terrible time, and the gossip had only made it unbearable, had turned the innocent race that killed him—a fun, spontaneous game between brothers—into an old-fashioned duel for her hand. A duel Rand had won.

She'd been called many things then. Cort was reckless and volatile, quick to fight over any slight, real or imagined, but everyone liked him, and in their search for someone to blame, she was an easy scapegoat.

And though the lies that she was responsible for her stepbrother's death had hurt, what hurt worse were the words they'd used to describe her relationship with Rand. The most precious thing in her life, the thing she treasured above all else, had been turned into something twisted and sordid.

And it hadn't helped that Rand believed it too.

Belle swallowed, tried to push the thought out of her mind, along with the memory of the night it had all disappeared. She tried not to hear the words that came echoing back from that time, but they were there anyway, tormenting her, hurting all over again. *"I don't want you, don't you understand? I don't want you."*

That night, too, had only started with a kiss. A kiss that held—despite its roughness—something more, a sweetness just beyond her grasp, a joy she knew she could find if she only reached for it.

That was what scared her now. Because reaching for that sweetness had ruined her life six years ago. Loving him, trusting him, had brought disaster.

Belle's heart raced, her throat grew tight. Too well she remembered that November night, the cold look in his eyes, the revulsion in his face, the way he'd turned from her. It was as she'd told him, she couldn't live through that again.

It frightened her that even those memories hadn't killed the love she felt for him. She hadn't managed to destroy that feeling in all the lonely nights she'd been without him, all those dark days she'd spent nursing the memory of his betrayal, the way he'd rejected their friendship as if it were nothing, the way he'd rejected her. He had taught her not to trust him, and she had learned the lesson well.

She had not forgotten that. She might still love him—she couldn't seem to help herself—but even love wasn't enough to make her trust him again.

The thought gave her strength, the words became her litany. Belle recited them over and over in her mind, letting them grow stronger as the singing died and the others began milling around. And as the minutes passed, she felt calmer, more in control.

Then she saw Marie Scholl coming toward her through the crowd, and the fear came back, along with a hopelessness she couldn't shake, a fierce stab of jealousy over the fact that Marie was the one he'd chosen, and not her.

Belle forced herself to look up at Marie and smile as the schoolteacher came closer.

Marie motioned to the empty chair beside Belle, an anxious, concerned look on her face. "Do you mind . . . ?"

Belle's stomach flipped. She swallowed and shook her head. "Sit down."

"I'd been hoping to have the chance to talk with you." Marie sat in a swoosh of pale green silk, a drifting cloud of rosewater. She leaned forward, lightly touching Belle's arm. "I was worried when you went rushing out. Is everything—"

"Everythin's fine," Belle said stiffly. "It was just a little—hot—in here. I needed some fresh air."

Marie looked sympathetic. "I've always found orris-root a bit too strong for potpourri, but Paula claims it's her favorite." She smiled, she squeezed Belle's arm tightly and then released it. "But I'm glad to see you here now. I was so looking forward to having the chance to get to know you."

"Really?" Belle couldn't help the sarcasm in her voice. She gestured at the crowded room. "Why? I figured they'd have filled you in already."

Marie looked taken aback, but only for a moment, and then she recovered with a smile. "Well, Rand was right about you. You *are* rather honest."

Belle bit back a sarcastic laugh. Honest, hell. If she were truly honest, she would tell Marie that just looking at her dark prettiness set her teeth on edge. Belle glanced away, toward the piano, where Mr. Horner was busy gathering the leather-bound songbooks into a neat stack. "You'd better watch yourself," she said blandly. "They're all wonderin' why the hell you're talkin' with me. 'Specially since you know the stories."

"Oh, the stories." Marie leaned closer, close enough that the scent of roses lingered in Belle's nostrils. "Well, I try not to mind Lydia much. She's a nice girl, but she has a terrible tendency to gossip."

Belle looked at her in surprise.

Marie smiled. "I think she's always been a little in love with Rand, don't you? She's just looking for a way to hurt him. Those stories"—she made a dismissive gesture—"why, they're ridiculous. I'm only sorry she involves you as well."

"You don't believe them?"

"Of course not." Marie shrugged. "I can't imagine Rand would ever want to hurt his own brother—and the notion that you're the cause"—Marie's eyes twinkled—"well, Belle, you don't really seem like the kind of girl who trifles with men's hearts."

Belle stared at her. She couldn't help it; Marie's comments surprised her, confused her. They seemed out of place coming from Marie, in contrast with her soft, womanly prettiness. Belle would have thought Marie would be shocked by the stories, that they would offend her prim sensibilities. But Belle had not expected that Marie Scholl would have a strength of character that went deeper than her reserve. Or even that her primness hid such a nonjudgmental mind.

It must be what Rand saw in her. For a moment Belle was overwhelmed by Marie's complexity—by her scent and pretty face and the reassuring smile that so readily dismissed the gossip—and she knew it would be easy to like Marie. Easy to be her friend even in spite of Rand and the fact that he planned to marry her.

Marie laughed. "You look so shocked, Belle. Don't tell me I'm wrong. The stories aren't true, are they?"

"No." Belle shook her head. "No, they're not true." *Not mostly, anyway.* "It's nice to know someone in this town doesn't believe everythin' they hear."

"It's the same everywhere," Marie said. "There are plenty of Christians who don't act much like Christians. Sometimes I think there's no charity in the world anymore."

"Sometimes," Belle grinned, "I think there never was. And if you ever saw Reverend Snopes at Sunday dinner, you'd know what I mean."

Marie laughed. It was a high, pleasant sound that carried through the room, above the talk. It made Belle want to laugh along, but then she saw Rand come in the doorway, and the smile and the laughter died right out of her.

He looked disheveled, windblown, and there was a tension in his movements that filled Belle with a sinking feeling. Especially when he looked up and caught her gaze. Because the look in his eyes held more than desire, or anger, or any of the things she had expected to see.

They held despair.

It made the joy she'd taken in Marie's words shrivel to nothing. His look cut through her, tore at her heart, made her feel lonely again, and afraid. It made her remember the feel of his mouth on hers, the way he'd held her head so tightly she couldn't escape, and she knew that even if that alone hadn't frightened her, the sight of his despair would have. It was too much like before.

But she didn't move when he crossed the room. She heard Marie's laughter and talk with one part of her mind, but the rest of her—the heart of her—was focused on Rand moving through that crowd, on his long, loose-hipped stride. He was in front of them in seconds, a taut, palpable presence. His face was hard, his eyes burning. "Belle, let's go."

"There you are!" Marie looked up at him with a smile. "I thought you'd left for good, and I'd been counting on you to give me a ride ho—is something wrong?"

He looked at Marie as if he hadn't realized she was there. "No. Nothing's wrong." He hesitated. "You need a ride?"

"If you don't mind. Tim Parker was supposed to take me back with him, but then Sophie felt ill, and I wanted to wait for you. . . . Rand, you look pale."

"I'm fine," he said tightly. His gaze went back to Belle, and it was as uncomfortable as before. "Are you ready to go?"

Belle faced him evenly, though her heart was pounding. The thought of riding back with him, even with Marie in the wagon—especially with Marie—made her mouth dry, her palms sweat. She swallowed. "You go on ahead and take Marie home," she said. "I'll get someone else to give me a ride. I heard Lydia say Charlie was comin' to get her. I'll just go back with him."

"Don't do that on account of me, Belle," Marie said softly.

Belle threw her a reassuring smile. "It's all right, Marie," she said carefully. "Besides, I might be able to get Charlie to go on over to Hooker's Station later."

"Are you sure?"

Belle glanced at Rand. He was silent, watching her, and his hazel gaze seemed to sear right through her; it stopped the words in her throat. He didn't want her to go with Charlie—or he didn't want to be alone with Marie, Belle didn't know which. But he didn't say anything, and she realized he wasn't going to argue, wasn't going to insist she come along with them. He was going to let her go with Charlie, and he was going to take Marie home, and he would probably kiss her in the moonlight. The thought made Belle feel sick.

"I'm sure. You two go on." She nodded and got to her feet, anxious to get across the room, to escape. She felt jealous and aching and embarrassingly foolish for feeling anything at all, and the feelings only grew when Rand looked at her with that searching, puzzled stare. He opened his mouth, and she knew he was going to say something—and also knew she didn't want to hear it. Desperately she stepped away.

"I think I'll just go find Lydia and make sure they don't forget me," she said, pasting a smile on her lips.

"Good night, Belle," Marie said.

Rand stepped forward. "Belle—"

She jerked back. "Don't wait up for me," she said. And then she turned and plunged into the crowd, trying not to feel the heat of his gaze. Or the sinking of her heart.

Chapter 22

The morning sun was bright in the sky when Belle finally pushed back the covers and got out of bed. Her head was pounding, and she told herself it was because of the beer she'd drunk with Charlie Boston last night after they dropped off a disapproving Lydia. But she knew that wasn't it. She'd gone to the tavern and tried to get her mind off Rand, and his kiss, and Marie, but she couldn't. She couldn't forget the touch of his hands on her face or the desperation in his grip—as if he were afraid to let go of her, afraid she would run. And even through the strong, malty beer she tasted the lingering sweetness of apple cider—and wondered if Marie Scholl was tasting it too.

It drove her crazy, that one thought, and Belle wished now that she hadn't talked to Marie, that Rand's intended hadn't searched her out or said she didn't believe the rumors. Belle wished she'd found soft, pretty Marie insipid and boring, wished she didn't care for the woman at all. But the hell of it was none of that was true. Belle liked Marie Scholl. She was the kind of woman Belle would like being related to, the kind of woman she would have picked for Cort, or for a real brother if she'd had one.

But not for Rand.

God, why had he kissed her? Why had he even touched her?

The question tormented her as she washed, circled in her mind when she reached for the wool challis skirt and basque she'd left hanging over Jesus John's portrait. She winced as her father's disapproving face reappeared, silent and condemning, and for just a moment she wondered what he would say if he knew of Rand's kiss. The thought depressed her. Even though she couldn't remember her father, she felt she knew him. She knew from the portrait how important and distinguished he was, how pious. It was almost as if Lillian had hung the painting in Belle's room in the hopes that John Calhoun's respectability would rub off on his wayward daughter.

Belle snorted at the thought. If anything, it had exactly the opposite effect. That sanctimonious portrait told her as much about her father as she ever wanted to know, told her exactly what he would have said about Rand's kiss—the same thing her mother had said once before: *"You're a disgrace to this family, do you hear me? A disgrace."*

But this time Belle knew that her mother was right. Kissing Rand could only lead to trouble, and Belle didn't need her mother—or her father—to tell her that. But she found herself wishing for her stepfather's kind and attentive words, or for someone on this damn farm to talk to. Someone who would really listen.

The kind of someone Rand had been once.

Belle swallowed. He wasn't that way anymore, and she had to remember it. She tried to tell herself he had no power over her at all. Last night she'd been vulnerable and hurt; it was the only reason she'd let him get close enough to kiss her. But it wouldn't happen again. All she had to do was remember the way he'd treated her before, how easily he ruined her life. She couldn't trust him not to do the same thing again. She would make herself stop loving him. The past could stay the past.

In spite of the words Belle's stomach was tight as she went down the stairs. It was all she could do to keep her breathing steady, and her heart was in her throat when she went down the hallway and stepped into the kitchen, ready to face him.

It was empty.

The relief that surged through her was so overwhelming, she sagged against the doorframe. Thank God she'd slept in. Rand had probably already gone to the fields. With any luck she wouldn't see him until dinner.

She felt a little light-headed at the thought. She poured some coffee and added a healthy dose of sugar and cream before she sat down at the table and took a sip. It was hard to swallow, her stomach rebelled at the taste—just as it rebelled at the thought of breakfast. Belle glanced at the plates still sitting on the table. They were brown and sticky with maple syrup and bits of scrapple, and though usually it was one of her favorite foods, today the heavy smell of the fried pork and cornmeal slices nauseated her.

She gagged, squeezing her eyes shut against the sickness. She tensed as she heard steps on the back stair, felt a moment of anxious fear when the back door opened. A quick gust of bitter morning air swished past her before the door closed again.

"There you are," Lillian said. "I wondered if you were ever going to get out of bed."

Belle opened her eyes, relieved it wasn't Rand. "I was tired."

"I can see that." Lillian was breathless. She held a crock of cream that still dripped from the springhouse.

She nodded toward the oven. "There's scrapple for breakfast."

Belle's stomach knotted. She shook her head. "No thanks."

Something passed through Lillian's eyes—Belle had the strange notion that it was disappointment—and her mother hurried to the dry sink. She set down the crock of cream with a heavy clank. "Oh. It used to be your favorite."

"It still is. I'm just not hungry."

"I see." Lillian's tone was slightly sharp, almost—hurt.

Belle dismissed the notion quickly. It couldn't be, not from her mother. Still, Belle felt a twinge of guilt, and she glanced again at the table, wondering if she could get down a bite or so. But the sight of the dirty plates still turned her stomach, and reluctantly she looked back to her mother. "I'm sorry, Mama," she said. "Maybe tomorrow. Where's Sarah?"

"She took some eggs over to Dorothy's," Lillian said. "She'll be back soon." Carefully she poured the cream into the butter churn. "I thought we'd pick apples to-day."

"That sounds fine."

"I thought perhaps a few pies for the cutters would be a good idea."

Belle nodded. "I'm sure they'd like that. They've al-ways raved about your apple pie."

"First prize at the fair two years ago," Lillian said proudly. She set the crock aside and shoved the warped lid onto the churn. "There are some bushel baskets out in the barn. When you're finished there, would you get them for me, please? Rand said he'd bring them in last night, but . . ." she waved dismissively.

"All right." Belle put down her coffee with relief. "I'll go on out and get them now."

Lillian threw her a glance, a frown wrinkled her smooth forehead. "Are you feeling all right, Isabelle?"

"Fit as a fiddle," Belle said wryly.

"You didn't tell me how the party was last night." Lillian straightened. She pushed back a few loose strands of hair, tucked them deftly into the tight bun at the nape of her neck. "Did things go—well?"

Her mother's look was anxious and concerned. It brought instant anger; Belle knew exactly what Lillian was getting at, knew she was wondering if the rumors had started again. The reminder that her mother still cared so much sent resentment surging through Belle.

She threw her mother a sarcastic look. "Why, everythin' was wonderful, Mama," she said as sweetly as she could. "I managed to get through the whole night without disgracin' myself one time."

Lillian had the grace to flush. "That's not what I meant," she said quietly.

"Wasn't it?" Belle cocked a brow. "Then maybe it was Marie you were worried about. Well, just so you know, Lydia Boston already told her all the gossip about us, but it doesn't seem to matter to her. She still likes Rand. A miracle, isn't it? I guess you must feel much better knowin' that."

Lillian's hands tightened on the butter paddle. Her knuckles were almost white. "Marie's a good Christian girl. I'm sure she feels she's in no place to judge."

"Not like everybody else." Belle snorted.

"Belle, please." Lillian's voice was so soft, it was almost inaudible. "You seem unhappy. I only wondered if maybe something happened at the party to upset you."

The gentleness of Lillian's statement took Belle by surprise. She felt oddly transparent, as if her mother had somehow seen right through her. It made her nervous, even more uncomfortable than she'd been before, and Belle hurried to the back door, needing suddenly to escape the warm, stifling kitchen. "I'm just fine," she said tightly. "Nothin' happened." She pulled open the door, took a deep breath of freezing air. "I think I'll go on out and get those baskets now."

Lillian nodded.

Belle swept out the door, shutting it firmly behind her, shutting her mother and her strange questions away, along with the memory of last night. The cold morning air was brittle and refreshing against her skin, and Belle closed her eyes and took a deep breath, letting it burn her throat, her lungs, inhaling the crisp autumn scents of frost and must and apples, the sharp odor of chickens and manure. The chill eased the headache pounding behind her eyes, and with a sense of relief Belle stepped down the stairs and started out to the barn. She was halfway across the yard when she heard Sarah's voice calling behind her.

"Belle! Belle! Wait for me!"

Belle turned. Sarah ran across the yard, her dress flying behind her, her steps uneven on the tangled grass. She came to a staggering, breathless halt.

"Where're you goin'?" she asked.

"Just to the barn to get some bushels. Your grandma wants to pick apples today."

Sarah twisted her chubby hands in her skirt. "I'm good at pickin' apples."

"Oh, yeah?" Belle smiled. "You mean to tell me you'd rather do that than play?"

Sarah looked at her consideringly. "Are you goin' to pick?"

"I s'pose I'm goin' to have to."

"Then I will too."

Sarah's declaration swept through Belle; she felt warm and tingly and suddenly good. She smiled and offered her hand. "Well, come on, then," she said. "Let's get those baskets, and then we'll go out to the orchard and have some fun."

Sarah skipped beside her as they walked, every jerking movement tugging a little on Belle's arm. "Can we jump—"

"No jumping for a while," Belle said firmly. Involuntarily she thought of Sarah on the edge of the canal bridge. Her fingers tightened around the little girl's hand. "We'll do somethin' else instead."

"Like what?"

Belle shrugged. "I'll think of somethin'."

"A game?"

"Yeah. A game." They stepped through the barnyard, past the pigpens to the huge open doors of the barn. She peered into the dimness. "I wonder where those bushels are?"

"They're down here." Sarah pulled her past the stables at the far end of the barn.

The round, slatted baskets were there, just as Sarah said, carefully stacked. Belle let go of Sarah's hand and grabbed two by their handles. "Now, how many of these d'you think you can carry?"

"Five," Sarah said. "As old as me."

"Five," Belle said thoughtfully. "Why don't we start with one and see how that goes?"

Obediently Sarah held out her hands. Belle settled a bushel into her arms, smiling when the little girl scrunched up her face.

"Is it too heavy?" she asked.

Sarah shook her head. "Huh-uh. I can carry lots more." She watched while Belle pulled two more baskets loose. "When we're done pickin' apples, c'n we have a social like the one you and Papa went to?"

Belle frowned. "A social?"

"Yeah—c'n we have one? Grandma says it's like a party—with dancin' 'n' everythin'. Ain't it?"

Belle shook a bit of straw from a basket onto the floor. "Sometimes there's dancin'," she said, shoving it onto her stack.

"Like last night?"

Memories flashed through Belle's head. She pushed them away. "No," she said, hearing the slight edge to her voice. "There was no dancin' last night. Just singin'."

"I like to dance," Sarah said. "Papa dances with me sometimes. Only he ain't done it for a long time."

She sounded so wistful that Belle paused and looked over. "I'll bet that's fun," she said, uncertain what else to say.

But Sarah brightened as if they were the perfect words. "You c'n dance with me instead."

Belle shook her head with a smile. "Oh, Sarah, I can't dance."

"Yes, you can. Please? It's easy." Sarah looked up at her hopefully, the big basket clutched awkwardly to her chest. "I'll show you."

The pleading in Sarah's voice grabbed at Belle's heart. It was easy to give in. "All right," she said. "But just for a minute."

Sarah smiled. She let the bushel fall from her arms and stepped around it. "First we bow," she instructed somberly. She grabbed hold of her skirt and watched Belle expectantly. "You first."

Belle bowed with a flourish. "Now what?"

Sarah dipped in an awkward curtsy. "Now you hold out your hands."

"Like this?" Belle asked, spreading her arms.

"Uh-huh—but you have to hold me." Sarah stepped closer and grabbed Belle's hands, holding them tightly between her chubby fingers. " 'N' you put your feet out so's I c'n step on 'em."

Belle laughed. "I thought you were supposed to teach me how to dance. I can step on feet just fine without your help."

"I step on *yours,*" Sarah said, frowning. " 'N' then we dance."

Obediently Belle stuck out her feet, wincing as Sarah stomped down on her toes. Sarah's fingers tightened around hers as she tried to catch her balance.

"You got to hold me closer," she instructed.

Belle pulled her tight against her legs. "Like this?"

Sarah nodded. "Now you sing a song and we dance."

"We dance." Belle glanced down at her daughter. "You mean like this?" She picked up her foot. Sarah lurched to the right with the movement, slipping off.

"You're not doin' it right," Sarah scolded.

"That's because I'm not sure how to do it."

"You gotta do it like Papa does." Sarah pulled away, pouting.

"Like Papa does what?"

It was Rand's voice. Belle froze, she felt the blood drain from her face. His voice came from the stable behind her, and she had the quick thought that he must have been there the whole time. Watching them the whole time. Her mouth went dry.

Sarah dodged around her, hurrying toward him. "Papa!" she said happily.

"Hey there, Little Bit," he said.

Belle heard him come out of the stable, the swish of straw, the whisk of movement. Heard him pick up Sarah, imagined his quick hug.

"C'n you show Belle how to dance?" Sarah asked. "I was tryin' to, but I can't."

"You were, huh?" He moved into Belle's line of vision. She heard the rustle of his footsteps, saw the walk that was still smooth and swivel-hipped even with Sarah held tightly against him. The very grace of it made her stomach flip. She thought of last night and the way his mouth felt against hers, the rough heat of his callused hands against her face.

Don't let him do this to you. But then she looked up at him, and it felt as if her heart went slamming through her body, as if God were deliberately trying to make sure she lost this battle.

Sunlight filtered through the cracks in the walls, gilding his hair and his skin, touching the shadows in his face. He stood there, holding Sarah in his arms, looking for all the world like a loving, doting father, like a good friend. Nothing at all like the man who kissed her last night.

But then he bent to let Sarah down. When he straightened, Belle saw that his expression was carefully neutral. Anger stabbed through her, a quick, piercing pain. He had sent her world into turmoil last night, and now he was looking at her as if he didn't even remember, as if none of it mattered.

Because it doesn't. You knew that.

"Belle can't do *our* kind a' dancin'," Sarah said. "We hafta teach her."

He looked down at Sarah. "Maybe she doesn't want to learn how."

"But she does. She said she did." Sarah sent Belle a pleading look. "Didn't you?"

Belle had to force the words from her throat. "I don't know, Sarah. My feet might not be big enough for you to stand on."

"Yeah, they are. Come on, Papa, show her!"

He sighed. "Little Bit—"

"Please!"

He took a deep breath, ran a hand through his hair. "All right, but just for a minute. I've got things to do." He reached down, grabbing Sarah's hands. "Step up on my shoes—"

Sarah tugged away. "Not *me,*" she said impatiently. "I know how. Show Belle."

Rand's head jerked up; Belle saw the shock register in his eyes—the same shock she knew showed in hers. Her stomach twisted, she felt the heat of embarrassment work its way over her cheeks. "Sarah, we don't have time," she heard herself say. She stepped back, out of reach of Rand's hands. "Come on, let's get these baskets back to Grandma—"

"But I want Papa to show you how to dance." Sarah whined.

"He's got other things to do."

Sarah ignored her. "Papa, you said you would."

Belle saw him hesitate, saw the way he ran his tongue over his teeth, as if he were considering Sarah's order, and desperation surged through her. *No. No, please don't . . .* But her prayers failed her; she knew the moment he looked up at her, with that careful blankness in his eyes, that he was going to do as their daughter asked. He was going to teach her to dance.

She felt light-headed; all the blood rushed to her fingers, pounded in her heart. She licked her lips, but there was no wetness in her mouth at all, nothing but a tight dryness.

"Rand," she said, but her voice sounded low and raspy, not like her at all. "This isn't—"

He glanced at Sarah. "We need some music," he said.

"I c'n sing," she said brightly. She stepped back,

plopped down on an upended bushel, and began clapping her hands. "All right. Ready, set, go!"

Belle's palms grew clammy. Her pulse raced in her ears; it was louder than Sarah's off-tune humming, louder even than the sound of her own breathing. She wiped her hands on her skirt, struggling to control her nervousness, to face him as he stepped toward her—one step, two—and then he was in front of her, and in spite of herself she noticed the way his collar hung open, noticed the wiry curls of hair on his chest.

Remembered what it felt like.

Belle licked her lips again, forcing the thought away, forcing her gaze to his face. For once it was reassuring to see that neutral expression, not to know what he was feeling or thinking. It made it easier somehow. Easier not to feel anything when he took her hand. He cupped it in his palm, tugged her toward him—just a little, but unexpectedly, so Belle stumbled forward. His hand stiffened, supporting her before she fell into him, stopping her only inches away. And then she felt his other hand moving to her waist, felt his fingers sliding into position, molding to her.

It took her breath away. The heat of his hand seemed to sear her. She could feel his skin against hers as if the layers of clothing protecting her had simply melted away, and she felt his fingers spasm against her, heard his quick, bitten-off breath.

"All right," he whispered, his voice hoarse and raw. "Ready? One-two-three, one-two-three . . ."

She couldn't look at him. Every inch of her was aware of him as he led her into the first steps of the dance. She felt the brush of her skirts against his legs, the press of his hips against hers. His scent was all around her, the clean tang of verbena shaving soap and the musk of leather, and Belle was hot and breathless, the collar of her dress too tight, choking her. She tried to focus on the steps, on the steady *one-two-three, one-two-three* of his motions, tried to concentrate on Sarah's humming, but Belle felt stiff and clumsy, and the low timbre of Sarah's tune was meandering and odd.

Rand's hand tightened around hers. "You're shaking," he said in a low voice.

"I'm not." Belle swallowed, directing her gaze to a spot of oil on his shirt, just below his collarbone.

"Yes, you are."

She felt the heat of his breath on the tender skin just below her ear, felt the tiny curls there shiver in response. It sent chills up her spine, goose bumps over her arms. Belle tried to draw away, but he held her fast, kept her moving in that never-ending rhythm, *one-two-three, one-two-three. . . .* And he was right, she *was* shaking. She felt overwhelmed and strange. The smell of him, the feel of him—it was as if all the dreams she'd had in her life had come down to this moment, when she was as close as she could be to him without feeling pain, when there was no roughness and no anger. . . .

Only fear. Fear that hovered inside her, made her draw back when he drew closer, made her afraid to look in his eyes, afraid to see—anything. Anything would frighten her, she knew. Even that careful bland look. Especially that, because it hid so much, because when he looked like that, she could tell herself it was because he cared, because deep inside he regretted their past.

But that was just a lie, she knew. It was only her imagination, only because she wanted so badly to see it in his eyes. Fear rushed through her at the thought. She stopped so abruptly, he stepped on her feet.

"That's enough," she said, pulling away, disentangling herself from his hands, his arms, keeping her gaze carefully averted.

"Not yet!" Sarah protested. She snapped to her feet, her round face turned down in disappointment. "You didn't even dance my way yet."

"That's right, we haven't," Rand said slowly. He offered his hand again. "Well?"

Belle looked at him then, despite herself, despite every warning ringing in her head, and she knew in that moment that she was right to be afraid. Because she saw the burning in his gaze, and it seemed to be all over her, inside her, around her, to touch her in deep, wet places that no one but he knew existed. Places that ached for him even after all these years.

Places that would always ache.

Belle stepped away, tore her gaze from his. "Not now," she said abruptly, and her voice sounded weak and far away. She grabbed a basket from the floor, held it against her as if it could protect her. As if anything could protect her. "Sarah, we've got to get these bushels back to your grandma. She's waitin'."

"But, Belle, you said—"

"She's right, Sarah," Rand said quietly. "Go on, now. I guess you've got apples to pick."

Relief made Belle weak. Her fingers tightened on the basket. She bent to grab another one.

"But will you show her sometime?" Sarah said plaintively.

"Maybe sometime."

Sometime.

The word plunged into her, a quiet threat, a lingering promise.

No, she thought. *Not sometime.*

Not ever.

Chapter 23

That evening Belle slumped into the chair, burying her face in her hands. The hard work of the day had left her tired and aching, but in spite of that her mind was wide awake and restless.

And it was his fault. All his fault. Belle had tried to bury the feel of him, had done her best to concentrate on picking apples and lugging the full bushels to the back stairs. But all that work had only exhausted her, made her feel more tired and vulnerable than ever.

Even helping her mother make four apple pies hadn't taken Belle's mind off the dance in the barn or her uncomfortable reaction to it, and now she was beginning to wonder if anything would, or if she was just destined to relive it in her mind for the rest of eternity. The thought made her heart clench in her chest. God, she hoped not. All she wanted to do was forget it, to go up to her room and sleep blissfully for days. But it was early yet; supper was only just over, and though it was rapidly getting dark outside, there was still an hour before Sarah went to bed.

An hour to sit here in the kitchen and wait. An hour to dread Rand's return from the barn. She'd been lucky so far. He hadn't bothered even to come in for supper tonight. She'd hoped it was because he was too busy, and she hoped it lasted. Another hour was all she wanted. One more hour.

Lillian pushed back her chair and got to her feet. "Sarah, would you help me clear, please?"

Sarah looked up from swirling her fork through the rest of her pie. "I can't."

"Why not, young lady?"

" 'Cause I'm pretendin' I ain't got no hands."

"Well, pretend later." Lillian reached for Sarah's plate. "Tonight's bath night, and I'd like your help while I heat the water."

"But I—"

Wearily Belle looked up. "I'll help, Mama."

"Isabelle, I think—"

"Let Sarah be." Belle got to her feet and grabbed two plates from the table, bringing them to the dry sink. "She's just a little girl. She can go play before bed."

She looked up to see her mother staring at her. It sent an instant stab of irritation through her. "What is it?" she asked, unable to keep the sarcasm from her voice. "Afraid I'll break somethin'?"

"No. No, not at all. It's just—well—never mind." Lillian frowned as if she were trying to understand something, and then she shook her head and looked back at the dishes.

"I was thinkin' I can take my bath tommorra," Sarah said from the table.

"Why's that?" Belle asked.

"Weeellll." Sarah hesitated. Belle could almost see her searching for a reason. " 'Cause I'm not dirty now."

Belle's weariness seemed to evaporate. It was all she could do not to smile. Sarah looked almost comical staring up at her, with her short hair standing in little cowlicks all over her head and her brown eyes big and solemn. "And you'll be dirty tomorrow?"

"Uh-huh."

Belle leaned down until she was face-to-face with Sarah. "I think you're dirty now," she teased. "And if you won't take a bath, how'm I goin' to teach you a new game?"

Sarah looked skeptical. "A bath game?"

"Well, I was goin' to teach you one, but now I don't know. If you won't take a bath . . ."

"I might take a little one." Then, when Belle frowned, Sarah said, "It can only be a little one, or my skin'll get all wrinkly."

From the sink Lillian made a sound that was suspiciously like strangled laughter.

Belle straightened. "All right, then, it'll be a little one. But you have to promise to do what I say."

"And you'll teach me a game?"

"Yep." Belle got to her feet and grabbed the few remaining dishes from the table.

Lillian took them from her and plunked them into the washtub. She ran her hand across her forehead. "Would you put more hot water on for me, please, Isabelle? There's an extra pan there. I'll go on out and get the tub—"

"I'll do it, Mama. You go on upstairs and get some rest. I'll give Sarah a bath." Her own words surprised Belle, but suddenly she realized it was exactly what she wanted. It was the one thing that could put the memory of today and last night out of her mind. A night alone with Sarah, doing what mothers did everywhere. A night washing Sarah's hair in the quiet lamplight, teasing a smile from her.

Belle wanted it so badly, it was almost painful.

Lillian looked at her in surprise. "But—"

"Please, Mama." Belle reached for the heavy pan beside the stove, struggling to keep from revealing just how important this was to her. "Just trust me for once. I'll take care of it. I can. Really."

Lillian looked away, into the washtub. "Of course you can," she said slowly.

"Then, you'll let me?"

Lillian took a deep breath. "I suppose I don't have much of a choice. You are—" *her mother.* The words fell unspoken between them; the anticipation of them lingered in the air.

But Lillian didn't say them. She kept her gaze on the dish in her hand. She swirled the washrag over it carefully, slowly. "When you were young," she said, her voice so soft Belle had to strain to hear it, "you were just the same. I used to have to beg you to take a bath. There was this—this wooden doll one of the hired hands made you, and we would fight over whether you could take it in the water." Lillian lifted her hand as if to explain, and then she let it fall again, limply, uselessly. "I was always so afraid . . . it would fall apart."

An odd sadness came over Belle at her mother's words. She looked away, looked at Sarah, who was grabbing knives and forks off the table. "Maybe," she said, equally quiet, "you should have let it."

Lillian shrugged. She glanced up, smiled weakly. "I think I could use some rest after all. We've plenty to do tomorrow."

Belle nodded. The sadness drifted away as if it had never been, but she remembered it, and as she listened to Sarah play, the memories flitted through her mind, snatches of a life so long ago that they felt vague and not quite hers. Her aunt's house in Columbus. Cold parlors and slippery chairs and stiff-necked nightgowns that were torture to wear. Aunt Clara's high, shrill voice screeching at her to come in from the yard, and a house that was so quiet, even the slightest noise sounded like thunder.

Those years before Lillian married Henry Sault seemed like someone else's life now, and though Belle didn't doubt her mother's story, she also didn't remember it. In some strange way she regretted that. Regretted not remembering the touch of her mother's hands, the roughness of a huckaback towel against her skin. She wondered if Lillian had ever told her stories while she sat in the bath, or if that Saturday-night ritual had held as much cold withdrawal as all the others.

She wished she remembered. Belle thought of it as she lugged in buckets of rainwater from the cistern to heat on the stove and dragged the tub across the floor to sit on a square of oilcloth. She thought of it the way she wanted it to be, with a gentle fire roaring in the background and the touch of scented water on her skin. Thought of her mother's hands, soapy and soft, moving in her hair. The images filled her mind, making Belle feel warm and safe and—oddly—sad when Lillian murmured a good night and disappeared, and Belle heard her mother's footsteps creaking quietly on the stairs.

The hushed evening felt suddenly as if it had a hole in it, as if it weren't quite complete, and Belle knew it wasn't just because of Lillian. She tried to ignore the feeling as she grabbed an apron from the peg on the wall and tied it around her neck and waist.

"Come on, now, Sarah," she said, smiling. "It's time for your bath."

Sarah looked up from the table. "Already?"

"It'll be over before you know it." Belle patted the side of the tub. "Hurry, now, before the water gets cold."

Reluctantly Sarah came over to her. She eyed the tub warily. "Grandma gets soap in my eyes sometimes."

"Well, I'll try not to," Belle said as she unfastened Sarah's many buttons. She lifted the striped calico over Sarah's head, and then she unfastened shoes and pantalettes and stockings until Sarah stood chubby and naked before her. "All right, now, into the water."

Belle lifted Sarah into the tub, waiting until the little girl settled in. "Is it too hot?" she asked, watching Sarah sit gingerly, almost as if she were afraid the water would touch her.

Sarah shook her head. "Huh-uh. Can we play the game now?"

Belle laughed. She grabbed the bar of soft yellow soap and a cotton washrag. "All right." She held up the soap. "Now, don't get scared, but Grandma told me there's a troll in this soap, and his favorite thing to do is tickle little girls."

Sarah's eyes grew round. "It is?"

"Uh-huh." Belle nodded. "I'll try to keep hold of him, but he's real slippery, and if he escapes . . ." She shrugged. "Well, you know what'll happen."

"I'll hafta get away."

"You try your best." Belle nodded somberly. She dipped her hand in the water. "Now, give me your foot fir—oh, no! He's escaped! He's comin' after you. . . ." Her hand surged through the water, toward Sarah, who squealed in delight and scrambled back. Water went sloshing all over, splashing onto the oilcloth-covered floor, over Belle's arms, soaking her dress. Belle didn't care. She was too wrapped up in trying to catch Sarah.

And in the laughter on her daughter's face.

He stayed in the barn as long as he could, waiting there until long after he had anything left to do, fiddling with a harness he'd fixed yesterday. He twisted it over and over again in his hands, testing its strength, wondering if it needed another stitch here or maybe one there, and knowing it didn't need anything at all.

Still he worked it, because the barn was quiet and safe, the dimness heavy with the rustling of animals and the soft swishing of his own movements. The sounds, the smells—hay and manure, musk and leather—were comforting, a balm to his spirit, and he wished he could stay out here forever, where there was nothing to tempt him, nothing to fill him with a wanting that seared his soul and made him weak with dread.

You should never have danced with her. No, he should not have. He'd known it even as Sarah asked him, known it when he looked at Belle and saw her wordless protest. But still he'd felt himself reach out for her, heard himself say, *"We need some music,"* before he was even aware of wanting to speak. He'd told himself not to touch her, but he couldn't help touching her. The way her lips felt, the smell of her hair, the feel of her. . . . Those things had tormented him since last night, when he'd kissed her. She had tasted the same—yet not the same. There was a different scent to her hair than he remembered. And the feel of her—*Sweet Christ, the feel* . . .

The temptation of her was more than he could bear—or maybe it was just the wary way she looked at him that did it. Maybe it was just the vulnerability he saw in her eyes that made him ache to touch her. To erase it, or ease it, or even just because he hated that look, hated the way it made his heart lonely.

It frightened him, how much that look affected him. How needy it made him. It dissolved all the promises he'd made to himself over the years, scattered them like dust at his feet and left him with nothing but memories of soft, throaty laughter and eyes that lit up when he walked into the room. Nothing but images that shifted before his eyes, just out of reach, too vague and shapeless to grab. Memories, that was all. Memories he'd tried hard to forget.

He felt as if he were on the edge of a bottomless pit, looking down into vast, hollow darkness, and there was nothing there to save him this time if he fell, and he wondered if it was the same kind of darkness his mother had seen before she drove that wagon off the bridge at Rock Mill all those years ago, the same kind of desperate obsession she'd felt for his father, that had sent her into insanity.

He'd always thought it was the same. When he was twenty-two, and possessed by Belle, he'd believed he was looking into the same darkness his mother had. Believed his obsession with Belle was as destructive, as dangerous. He remembered the way his mother had been before she killed herself. The love between her and his father had been a great, enduring one, but in those last years that love had corrupted itself, had become predatory and cruel, had etched itself in her sharp features. Rand had seen the way it suffocated and exhausted his father. Her constant, obsessive watching pushed Henry away; her jealous rages and bitter accusations destroyed them.

Finally it had become uncontrollable. Rand remembered the days he and Cort stayed out in the fields until dark, hoping she would be asleep when they came home so that they wouldn't have to watch the way she tortured their father with her endless questions, her cloying tears. But those days came more and more often until they were all like that, until even the nights screamed with the sound of her angry suspicions and the gloom of her depressions filled the air clear into town, scented the kitchen with the sour odor of sauerkraut.

Rand was ten years old the day she drove away for the

last time, and the sky was so gray, it was as if it mirrored her sadness. She left the wash boiling in a kettle in the yard and harnessed the team and left without a backward glance, and the miller said she didn't hesitate when she drove off Rock Mill Road into the millpond below. He said she slapped the reins and forced the horses to go so fast, they couldn't stop. And it was only because there were witnesses that anyone knew what happened to her at all, because they'd never found her body. They'd never found a single thing that told them there was anything but water in that millpond.

She'd been gone eighteen years, but she haunted Rand. She haunted him because her darkness was inside him, because he understood the kind of obsessive emotion that held on so hard, it was impossible to fight or resist. Because there was a time when he felt he would die if he didn't have Belle beside him every moment of every hour, and he knew that was how his mother had felt about his father, knew he was just like her.

He thought he'd destroyed it. During the last six years it had disappeared—or if not that, had at least burrowed deep inside him. But now he was on that precipice again, and it was more dangerous than before. More dangerous because Belle was not the girl he remembered, and he could not get the woman she was out of his mind. More dangerous because it felt as if there had always been an emptiness inside him, and she had filled it just by walking into his arms. Just by being in the room.

Ah, Christ . . .

Rand glanced down at the harness in his hands. His fingers were trembling; his fear was a throbbing, palpable shadow in the pale lamplight. He forced himself to think of tomorrow, of going to church and listening to Reverend Snopes's rhythmic, lulling sermon. He thought of meeting Marie in the churchyard afterward, of her warm smile and pretty face. She could make his fear go away, he told himself, though he knew she couldn't. Last night, driving her home after the singing party, had taught him that. Even now, less than a day later, he couldn't remember what she'd said, couldn't say if he kissed her good night or not.

No, he didn't remember Marie. But he remembered the long, cold drive home alone, climbing the stairs to his room, pulling back the heavy quilt on his bed and sliding naked between the sheets. He remembered hearing the clattering of Charlie Boston's wagon coming up the drive, Belle's laughing good-bye, and her step on the stairs. He heard the closing of her bedroom door, and he'd laid there, stiff, muscles clenched, with darkness all around him, inside him. In his heart and in his mind. It had taken every ounce of his control not to follow her into her room, and it was only fear that held him back, fear that drenched him in sweat when he imagined her movements—imagined her nimble fingers on the buttons of that yellow gown, imagined her stepping out of it, imagined the way her cornsilk hair would cling to the brush when she combed it out, how it would crackle and fall to her face, her shoulders, her breasts. . . .

He'd wanted to bury himself in her, to touch her in places he'd only dreamed about, to make love to her the way he hadn't six years ago. He wanted her wet and pulsing and hot around him, wanted her covered with his scent, branded by his body. He wanted all of it. As much as he had wanted it six years ago. More than that.

And no thought of Marie could make that go away. He wondered if it ever would.

But he tried again anyway. He put aside the harness and closed his eyes and thought of her. Tried to smell the scent of roses and imagine what Marie would feel like in his arms, wondered if she could dance. Probably she could. Probably she was good at it. Not like Belle, who stumbled over his feet nervously, clumsily, who bit her bottom lip when she concentrated, who trembled against his hands. No, Marie would be easy to dance with, smooth and practiced and warm.

He got to his feet, holding on to the image, and went to the barn door. The night was quiet; the house quieter still. There was one light glowing in the kitchen. Lillian, no doubt, reading as she sometimes did after Sarah had her bath. The thought made him tired, and Rand suddenly longed for bed, for sleep too deep for dreams. Carefully he blew out the lamp, sending the barn into darkness, and stepped out into the night, closing the door behind him.

He walked slowly across the yard, keeping his eye on the kitchen, hoping Lillian wouldn't be offended when he didn't sit down to talk with her. He was so damned tired, it was all he could do to drag himself up the back stairs. Maybe she'd be so engrossed in the "Ladies' Department" of *The Ohio Cultivator* that she wouldn't care if he walked straight through. He pulled open the back door, hoping. Maybe a simple good night would be enough—

He stopped short.

It wasn't Lillian in the kitchen.

It was Belle.

She was on her knees, behind the half bath, mopping up spilled water with a towel. Her sleeves were pushed up over her elbows, her back was to him, and her long braid trailed, loose and straggling, over her shoulder, nearly touching the floor. The room was warm and humid, fragrant with the scent of lavender-softened lye soap and water-soaked oilcloth.

The door clicked shut behind him. She glanced over

her shoulder at the sound, and when she saw it was him, she jerked up, cracking her shoulder on the rim of the tub.

"Damn." It was a breathless sound, almost inaudible. She scrambled to her feet and turned to face him. "I—I didn't hear you come in," she said, rubbing her shoulder.

He wanted to say something, knew he should say something, but he couldn't. All he could do was stare. The bodice of her dress was dark with water, a stain that trailed down to her waist, fanned over her skirt. Her collar was open, revealing her throat, a pale triangle of flesh, and the striped wool challis of her dress clung to her everywhere else, forming to the soft swell of her breasts, clinging so closely, he could have sworn he saw the beating of her heart. Her skin was rosy from heat, and tendrils of hair curled over her forehead, against her cheeks, dangled to her shoulders. She looked at him uncertainly, with a startled surprise that brought back his hot, dark dreams, and he thought of the press of bodies and the slick heat of skin, thought of her laughing as she wrapped those slender arms around his neck and pulled him close.

She swallowed, gestured limply to the tub. "I was givin' Sarah a bath," she said. She fumbled with the towel, laid it over the edge of the tub, and then she crossed her arms over her chest. "I just put her to bed."

"I see." It was all he could say. Even that seemed weak and strained.

"I'd move the tub back, but—"

"I'll do it."

She nodded. "Well, then," she said, motioning to the stove. "Mama left some stew warm for you if you're hungry." She moved around the far side of the bath, toward the doorway, and he realized with a start that she was moving away, heading for bed. "I guess I'll see you in the—"

"Don't go." The words fell from his mouth, unexpected, unwanted, but once they were said, he realized he couldn't take them back, that he didn't want her to retreat tonight, to run away to separate bedrooms and darkness. His earlier thoughts came rushing back: She was dangerous; he should run away from her. But suddenly the thought of sitting here with her, eating supper, was more seductive than his warnings, and much too tempting to resist.

He spoke before his courage died. "Keep me company while I eat."

She stopped; the uncertainty on her face grew stronger, brighter, touched with wary fear. She gripped the back of a chair; her knuckles were white. "I don't think—"

"I'm not asking you to think," he said slowly. "I just want some company, that's all."

Her indecision was almost painful to watch. But then she swallowed, nodded slightly, and let go of the chair. "All right." She said the words, though her tone told him it was anything but all right. Rand didn't give a damn. He didn't care what made her stay, just that something did, and when she glanced at the stove and said, "I'll get you some supper," he felt such a clean, hot stab of relief, it made him weak.

Rand pulled out a chair and sat down, waiting while she dished stew into a bowl and cut a thick slice of bread for him. It was strange watching her. He couldn't remember that she had ever served him before, and it was such a womanly, wifely thing to do, it made his throat tight. But he said nothing as she set the food before him, along with the pot of coffee.

"D'you want some?" he asked, motioning to the pot.

She sat gingerly across from him. "All right." She scooted her chair back, just an inch or so, but it was enough to show him how nervous she was, and when he poured her coffee, she drew it toward her, stirring in sugar with careful, stiff movements.

He nudged the pitcher of cream with his fingertip. "Cream?"

"All right."

"Do you think you could say something besides 'all right'?"

"All—" She caught herself and glanced up at him, and a smile touched her lips; sheepish laughter flashed through her eyes before it vanished in caution. She glanced away. "Yeah. Please pass the cream."

"That's better." He pushed the cream toward her, watched as she poured it, so much, it nearly turned her coffee white. He watched her take a sip, watched her short, slender fingers as she set the cup down again. She sat back in her chair, turned so that she was looking at the tub in the middle of the floor but not at him, and he tried to think of something else to say to ease the tense silence, wondered what had happened to all those conversations they used to have. Had they just disappeared? Or did they linger somewhere, whispering in the air, in the weedy scent of the canal, in the sunlight?

He hated that he missed them so much. So much, it ached inside him. "Did you get all the apples picked?"

She nodded shortly. "Yeah. Mama made pie." She started to rise. "I'll get you—"

Rand surged forward, catching her wrist before she could go. Her gaze shot to her hand, to him, and it was so full of apprehension that he released his hold instantly. She jerked her hand back—too fast—and looked away, and he saw that she was trembling, just as she had this afternoon, in the barn.

His breath was a tight knot in his lungs. "I don't want any pie," he said.

She sat back again, but her body was stiff. She looked like a nervous colt ready to bolt at the slightest movement. She kept her hands in her lap, took a deep breath. "All right, then. No pie."

Silence again. Rand took a bite of stew. It was heavy in his mouth, and it took all his effort to chew and swallow. He grabbed the thick slice of bread, tore a piece off, and tried to think of something else to say, something even more innocuous than before. Finally he blurted the first thing that came into his head. "You were back late last night."

He cursed himself the moment he said the words, knew they were stupid, that they would bring up things he didn't want to talk about, shouldn't talk about. But despite that, he couldn't dismiss them, couldn't tell himself he didn't want to know. He did. He was burning to know.

Her head jerked up, defiance flashed in her eyes. "Charlie and I went over to Hooker."

He tried to keep his voice casual even though the words sent jealousy surging through him. "Did you win any money?"

"We didn't play poker."

"You just talked."

"And drank." Her jaw tightened, her expression was faintly hostile. "Why d'you care? I figured you'd be so busy with Marie—"

"I was." He looked down at his plate, noting with surprise that he'd shredded the piece of bread into tiny pieces. "We talked. About . . . things."

"Things?" She raised a sarcastic brow. "What kind of things? Lydia maybe? Or Cort?"

Her words froze inside him. When he spoke, his voice sounded harsh. "No, nothing like that."

"She didn't tell you Lydia told her all the gossip?"

His heart twisted. "No."

Belle made a sound of disbelief. She stared into her coffee. "Well, she did. But I don't guess you need to worry. Marie doesn't believe anythin'."

"She doesn't." He knew he should feel relief at Belle's words, but he didn't. He didn't feel anything at all.

"No." She kept her gaze focused on the cup in her hands. "I guess you prob'ly haven't told her the truth."

"No."

"Are you goin' to?" She asked in that flat monotone, that voice he hated. It wrapped around his heart, his throat.

"I don't know," he said slowly. "Should I?"

Her gaze snapped to his; her brown eyes were full of surprise and uncertainty and something else. Something that looked suspiciously like pain. "I don't know," she said quietly. "I don't know what kind of marriage you want, Rand. If I was her, I think I'd want you to tell me." She looked away again. "But I'm not her. And I—I know you're . . . ashamed . . . of me anyway. You've got this whole town believin' a lie, and I guess—I guess there's no reason to change." She shrugged. "I s'pose Marie'll be happier that way."

Her words were like blows, pounding against him, knocking away his breath. He heard the pain in her voice, the way she struggled to hide it, and he felt guilty and contemptible. He remembered Sunday dinner at the Millers' two weeks ago, when he'd told her he was ashamed of her and meant it. When he'd hurt her with words because it was easier than hurting himself. And now he knew it wasn't easier. That hurting her tore him apart inside, that what he'd told her had all been a lie.

He wasn't ashamed of her. He had never been ashamed of her. He was ashamed of himself. Now more than ever. He closed his eyes, and when he opened them again, it was to find her staring at her hands.

"Belle," he said. "Look at me."

She did. Cautiously. Guardedly.

He swallowed. "I'm not ashamed of you. I—I was never ashamed of you."

She frowned. Something—hope maybe?—flashed through her eyes, disappeared quickly. "But you said—"

"I was angry when I said those things." He laughed self-deprecatingly, looked down at his hands because it was safer than looking in her eyes, than imagining hope and wishing he could bring it to her again, wishing she would look at him with trust, the way she used to. He took a deep breath, and his words fell out before he could stop or think about them at all. "You know, the other day, I was . . . remembering that time down at the river, when we were fishing with Cort, and he was teasing you about—about something."

Her voice was soft. "About how stupid I looked fishin' with a bunch of boys. He said the whole town was laughin' at me."

"Yeah." Rand nodded. He remembered the scene as if it were yesterday, remembered the soft gurgle of the river, the way the sun fell through the leaves to dapple the ground. He remembered her standing on the bank, barefoot, her skirt hiked up around her knees while she tied a cork to her line. "I remembered thinking then how . . . special . . . you were. Like God had given me this gift. . . ." He shook his head, trying to find the right words, feeling suddenly as if the rest of his life depended on them, as if they were the most important thing he would ever say. He looked up at her. "You were the best friend I ever had. I was never ashamed of you."

He saw the soft flush creep up her throat, over her cheeks. She glanced down, and he knew by the way she bit her lip, by her tiny smile, that he had embarrassed her, and he knew that he should feel embarrassed himself. He'd revealed too much, much more than he wanted, and he already felt the change between them, the softening, the comfortable familiarity growing in the wake of his words. But though he knew he should feel afraid, knew that he shouldn't have said anything to bring her closer, he didn't care. Suddenly all he wanted was the Belle he used to know, the friend who shared his secrets, his hopes, his dreams.

He wanted it more than anything. The urge to touch her, to make her smile, was so strong, he leaned forward, reached across the table until he could lift her chin to look directly into her eyes. His heart clenched; he waited for her to flinch, to move away.

She didn't. She was very still, barely breathing, and he saw the searching look in her eyes, knew she was testing him. He wished he knew what to do, what to say, but he couldn't think of anything, and he felt tongue-tied and desperate, sure she would pull away and leave him, afraid that she would.

"Belle—" he said. "I'm sorry."

She didn't say anything for a moment, and he saw the uncertainty in her deep brown eyes, the hesitation. And then, just when he knew she would never forgive him, just when he was ready to drop his fingers and retreat to his room, to silence and loneliness and shame, she smiled.

Incredibly she smiled.

It was soft, barely there, but it was a smile nonetheless, and it was so startling, he dropped his fingers from her face and stared at her, uncertain whether to trust it, wondering what it meant. He took a deep breath, and then, with infinite care, he said, "So you . . . forgive me?"

She tilted her head, looked at him quizzically, with that enigmatic smile still on her lips. "I guess I do," she said quietly. And then, suddenly, the smile broadened, suddenly it was shy and irresistible and genuine, and so warm, Rand felt dizzy in the heat of it. "Yeah, I guess I do."

Chapter 24

She was alone in the house. Lillian and Rand had gone to church, and in spite of the fact that Sarah had gone, too, Belle was not tempted to join them. She could count on one hand the times in her life when she'd stepped into a church, and each time had left her with a bad taste in her mouth. Even being with Sarah couldn't soften the hypocrisy Belle felt in the air, the sanctimonious attitudes of their neighbors.

And more than that, she wanted to be alone. To walk through the house without having to think or react or protect herself. She wanted to just be—just for a few hours—to do nothing but sit in the kitchen and smell the aroma of stewing chicken, to walk in the yard and feel the breeze blowing in her hair.

She wanted to just be home.

Home. It was a funny thought, unfamiliar and new, but true nonetheless. In the last few days she'd begun to think of this house as home again, to feel comfortable walking the halls and coming down for breakfast, to feel like she belonged when she walked through the barnyard. It had sneaked up on her slowly, but now she realized that she felt, if not exactly whole again, then at least close to that, at least more herself than she'd felt at any time in the last six years.

It was a good feeling, and a little bit frightening too.

Frightening because being herself meant doing the one thing she had made a vow never to do.

It meant forgiving Rand.

She had not intended to do it of course. She had wanted to be strong, to keep him firmly away from her, to hold the sword of her anger between them. It was what protected her, what kept her from caring too deeply or wanting too much. But last night, when she'd looked into his eyes and seen not passion there, or lust, but simply regret, her hostility had fallen away from her. She'd forgotten that this was the man who hurt her so badly in the past, forgotten that she was afraid of him still. All she saw was the friend she'd missed so badly all these years, the friend who was dearer to her than herself.

And after last night Belle knew she'd been lying to herself about not wanting to trust Rand again. The truth was she did want to trust him. She wanted to confide in him and talk to him. She wanted his keen understanding and that lightning-sudden smile that crinkled his whole face, the smile that had drawn her to him when she was twelve years old and new to Lancaster and needing a friend.

And love had nothing to do with that.

Belle sat on the porch railing, leaning against a pillar, and stared out at the road, at the fields beyond it. No, love had nothing to do with being friends with Rand again. She could learn not to love him. She could learn not to care that he didn't love her.

But despite herself the images from yesterday, from the night before, plunged into her mind. The feel of his body close to hers, the touch of his lips. She tried to ignore them, tried to remember what those things had brought her before—the revulsion in his eyes, the way he'd pushed her away—but the memory seemed blurry and vague, and it shifted out of reach, leaving her only with last night, with the gentle warmth of his fingers against her jaw.

Friends. Just friends, that was all.

She could do that, she knew she could, she wanted to. Talking to him would be enough. Laughing with him would be enough. She would be happy knowing he confided in her, knowing that he came to her when he was worried or upset, when he wanted to celebrate or have fun. She could bear the fact that he was married, knowing she was the one he'd go fishing with, that she was the one he would sit and talk to on a hot summer day.

While Marie was the one he was kissing.

The image of the singing party swept into Belle's mind, the image of Rand laughing down at Marie, covering her hand with his, and with it came the sick feeling again, plunging through her stomach, into her heart. Belle squeezed her eyes shut. She could bear even that, she told herself. It was a little enough thing—a touch, a kiss. It was little enough to give up for the sake of their friendship. It meant nothing. He'd told her that himself, a long time ago. *"I didn't know you cared for Elizabeth."*

"I don't."

"You have a funny way of showin' it. You kissed her."

"That doesn't always mean anything, little girl."

Little girl.

She'd forgotten that. The nickname squeezed her heart; she remembered it along with all the other ones he used to call her: *sweet girl, honey girl, my girl.* Casual endearments, words that wrapped around her soul, made her feel like she belonged to him, made her feel special and cherished, and . . . and young.

Little girl.

It made her think of all the things they used to do when they were friends: fishing in the river, jumping off canal bridges, playing poker, and racing horses, and it occurred to her suddenly that they were all childish things. All things people did until they were adults, until they had responsibilities such as children and wives and farms. Things men like Charlie Boston still did because they were waiting for something better, waiting for a future. Things she'd always done because there was nothing else to do.

But now there was Sarah. And Rand had the farm, would have Marie. Those carefree days of fishing and wasting time were gone forever.

Belle glanced out at the fields beyond the pasture, at the brown stalks of corn. There was no time to waste on a farm. The cutters would be here Monday, then there would be husking, then milling. After that they would thresh the already cut wheat during the dark months of winter, and after that there was plowing and sowing in the spring, harvesting oats and wheat and hay, and then the corn again. . . . It was an endless cycle. Belle remembered how Henry spent every day in the fields or in the barn, how work had taken from sunup to sundown. She remembered thinking once it was a good thing he was married, because he had so little time that he needed someone who would always be there, to fit into the few free moments he had.

There had been little time for anyone else. Only family. Henry saw his friends on Sunday, and that was all. Just Sundays.

And Belle suddenly realized that Marie wouldn't be just the one Rand was kissing. She would be the one he was talking to as well.

Just friends.

It didn't seem like very much anymore. And not enough.

But it was the only choice she had. She would not stand in the way of Rand's happiness, and she knew he was happy with Marie. Belle had seen the laughter on his face as he talked to the schoolteacher at Paula's party—a carefree laughter Belle hadn't seen in years. Yes, he was happy, and she loved him enough to give him that happiness. She loved him enough to learn how to be "just friends" again.

No matter what it took.

The sermon was long. Rand shifted in his seat, arching slightly to ease the hard press of the pew from his spine, and tried to concentrate on what Reverend Snopes was saying. It was hard to do, especially because his mind hadn't been on the sermon since it started. Rand couldn't even remember what the theme for this Sunday was. Redemption probably. Hell, it was always redemption, and though usually that particular sermon left him feeling uncomfortable and vaguely guilty, today it didn't. Today he already felt redeemed. Forgiven.

He thought of last night, of the way Belle had smiled at him, her soft words. It filled his heart like nothing he could have imagined, made him feel whole again, somehow complete, as if her smile had been the one thing missing all these years. They were friends again, or well on their way to becoming that, and the knowledge made him feel relieved and slightly drunk, sent a frisson of excitement tingling through his blood that had nothing to do with fear or desperation or darkness.

He felt so good, he even smiled when Snopes embarked on another long-winded prayer, and when the sermon was finally over, and the congregation was rising to leave, he threw the reverend a quick, irreverent grin. Snopes only looked confused.

Rand laughed lightly to himself and started for the aisle.

"What is it?" Lillian asked, putting her hand on his arm. "Did I miss something funny?"

He shook his head. "Not really."

"You were smiling."

"I just feel good today."

Lillian looked at him quizzically. "Oh? Why is that?"

"No reason." He shrugged.

"I see." Lillian sounded puzzled. "I just wondered—oh, look, there's Marie."

Rand stumbled. His heart stopped. Marie. He looked up, following Lillian's gaze. Marie was just outside the door, standing demurely next to the steps, her hands clasped in front of her, the breeze blowing the ribbons on her straw bonnet, snapping the hem of her pale green dress. The same dress she'd worn to the singing party the other night, he remembered, and the thought made him stiff with tension.

He'd forgotten about her, and now the reminder took away his contentment, sent guilt rushing through him. Of course, Marie. His mind sped back to the other night, to the long ride home, and he wished again that he remembered what the hell he'd said to her. And then he remembered Belle's words last night. *"She didn't tell you Lydia told her all the gossip?"* Christ, he'd forgotten that. He'd been so wrapped up in Belle's forgiveness, he'd forgotten all about Marie.

Lillian patted his arm. "I see Stella over by the tree. I'll get Sarah. We'll be there when you're ready to go home." She moved off, leaving him alone in a crowd that surged around him as he stood motionless by the doorway.

Then Marie looked up. She saw him, and her eyes lit. The smile on her face was wide and warm and pleased. Like Belle's smile. Not like Belle's.

He moved toward her, feeling the guilt roil in his stomach with every step he took. It made his throat so tight that he could barely say hello when he got close to her, so he offered her a smile instead.

"Rand, there you are!" she said, and then she blushed prettily. "I've been waiting for you."

He sighed. "Hello, Marie."

"I've been hoping to see you here," she said, frowning slightly. "I was worried about you the other night. You seemed so—so preoccupied driving home."

Christ, he wished he could remember anything she'd said. Anything at all. Rand raked his fingers through his hair. "We're cutting the corn tomorrow," he said, as if that explained everything.

She nodded as if it did. "I see. How's Belle?"

"She's—she's fine."

"I was looking forward to seeing her today." She glanced around, surveying the people moving past them. "Is she still inside?"

"No. She didn't come. She doesn't—like church."

"Oh." Marie's eyes darkened in sympathy. "I guess I understand why. It must be hard to face gossip all the time."

He felt supremely uncomfortable. He wanted to ignore her statement, to pretend she hadn't said it. But he couldn't. She was watching him as if she expected a reaction, and he knew he had to say something, to try to explain something he should have told her from the start. Christ, it was so much easier before she knew the rumors, before she knew anything about him but his present life. He wished it could have stayed that way.

Rand took a deep breath, plunged in. "Belle said Lydia told you the gossip about—about her. About me."

"Yes, she did." Marie shook her head regretfully. "I've told her not to repeat those things to me again. People can be so contemptible."

The words surprised him, though he knew they shouldn't. Belle had already told him Marie cared nothing for the gossip. But somehow, hearing the words come from her mouth, seeing the compassion on her face, disturbed him, annoyed him, and he wasn't sure why.

He couldn't keep irritation from his voice. "What did Lydia say?"

Marie looked taken aback. "Well, I—I don't like repeating this."

"Tell me anyway."

She hesitated, and her gaze was measuring, considering before she looked away, obviously uncomfortable, and took a deep breath. Her voice was steady and emotionless, as if she were reciting an oration she didn't particularly like. "She says that you and your brother were in love with Belle. That you raced each other to see who could have her. That your brother . . . died in that race."

It surprised him that the words still had the power to hurt, but they did. They seared through him, slammed against his heart, made him feel angry and ashamed and aching. But still he wanted to know more, felt an insane urge to know more, to torture himself with the stories that had been spoken behind his back for six years. "What else?" he asked in a hoarse whisper. "What else did she say?"

Marie looked nervous. "Rand, it's obvious this hurts you—"

"What else did she say?"

"Well." Marie squirmed. She licked her lips anxiously. "They say that—oh, Rand, this is so absurd—"

He felt a quick surge of anger. "Tell me."

She looked at him uncertainly. "Lydia says that after your brother died, you and Belle, well, you . . . you were . . . together." She took a deep breath. "But then Belle ran off somewhere. No one knows why. Lydia thinks—some of them think—maybe she was a . . . a fallen . . . woman in New York, but not everyone believes that."

He worked to keep his tone even. "She was no whore."

Marie stood her ground. "I didn't think she was."

They stood there in silence. He heard the murmur of people around him, the quick bursts of laughter that punctuated the low and earnest voices, and Rand struggled to remember Lillian's lessons, to keep his anger and his pain under control, to keep them hidden. But he didn't succeed, he knew it the second Marie touched his arm, the moment he saw the deep, genuine compassion in her eyes.

"I certainly don't believe them, Rand," she said softly.

Her steady conviction annoyed him. He wanted to hurt her somehow, to crack her faith in him, misplaced as it was, and because of that, his words were harsh and rough. "What if the stories are true?"

She looked confused. "I don't understand."

"What if they're true?" he asked, unable to help himself, wanting to see the same contempt in her eyes that he felt for himself. "What if I told you they weren't lies? Would you still be standing here talking to me? Or would you be running back to Lydia and your safe little friends?"

"Rand." She stepped away, her brow wrinkled in bewilderment. "I'm not sure what you want me to say—"

"Just answer me. What if those stories are true?"

"Are they?"

"Parts of them," he admitted, and then abruptly wished he hadn't when he saw how still she went.

But her voice was very calm. "Which parts?"

He hesitated. Christ, what was he doing? Why the hell tell her anything at all? She would believe anything he said; she'd told him that. He could tell her the safe lies he and Lillian had concocted. Lies that would restore her confidence in him, would make their life together safe and easy.

But then he saw her pressed lips, the way she watched him, waiting, and Belle's words from last night floated through his mind. *"If I was her, I'd want you to tell me the truth,"* and he knew then he would tell Marie the whole story, because he respected her enough to do it. Because Belle was right.

"Cort died in a race with me," he said. He focused his gaze on Lillian and Sarah in the near distance, on the huge, shedding maple tree. "That much is true. But it wasn't over Belle. It was a game, an accident, that's all." He paused. "And Cort—he took care of her. They were like a real brother and sister. He wasn't in love with her."

"But you were."

Her voice was soft, so quiet, it sent his guilt plunging back, crashing through him, a relentless rhythm that left him lonely and aching. "Yeah," he said slowly. "I was."

She was silent for a moment, and he didn't look at her, instead imagining her face, the expression he knew he would see in her eyes. Contempt and anger, revulsion even—all those things he'd felt himself, all the emotions he knew he deserved. Even Belle's forgiveness didn't ease those things in him, and he wondered if anything ever would.

"And now?" Marie's voice startled him. Her face was carefully blank, her eyes guarded, but he heard the edge in her voice, recognized the need for reassurance.

And he wanted to give it to her. Wanted to say, *"It's been over a long time. I'd like to marry you. Would you marry me?"* Wanted the safety of being with her, of burying his needs and his desires in her body, of the comfortable harmony of liking instead of loving. He wanted all those things, and so he opened his mouth to tell her the lie, to drown himself in caution and security.

But then he saw her face, saw the careful way she stood, as if bracing herself for pain, and he knew that lying to her would only hurt her more, that she already knew what he'd been hiding from himself all this time.

He was still in love with Belle.

He'd never stopped loving her.

The realization startled him, brought his fear crashing back. Christ, he was so damn afraid. He felt the darkness move over him, felt the inexorable stealth of it sliding through his blood, and he knew that even Marie couldn't save him from this, that eventually the madness would catch up with him. He could not stop it. He had never been able to stop it. Slow it, yes; control it, for a while; but the darkness would always be there, as long as he was alive. It was a part of him he could never escape.

Like Belle was.

Sweet Christ, like Belle . . .

"You still love her, don't you?" It was as if Marie read his mind, and though she spoke in a hushed voice, it seemed too loud, seemed to pierce his head and the air around him. "It's not over."

Rand swallowed. "No," he said. "It's not over." The

admission hung in the air between them, the unsaid spoken now, and because of that the words seemed to take on weight and size, permanent, unerasable. Inescapable. "I still . . . love her. I'm sorry." Inadequate words. Silly words.

She flinched. "I think I've . . . I think I've always known that, really." She laughed slightly, sadly. "Last summer I hoped . . . and now . . . But I guess I always knew I wasn't really the one you wanted."

"Marie, I—"

She held up a hand to forestall him. "It's all right, Rand. We can't always help who we love." She offered him a wavering smile. "But I wish it could have been me."

Chapter 25

Belle stood in the kitchen, pulling the lid off a crock of pickles, listening idly to her mother, Dorothy, and Stella chatter as they prepared dinner for the men cutting corn in the fields. Paul Miller, Jack Dumont, and Kenny, along with two men Rand had hired in Lancaster, had been out there since before dawn—before Belle had even stirred from sleep.

In a way it was a relief that they had gone out so early, that she hadn't been faced with seeing Rand in the morning, that she hadn't had to smile and be the friend she'd vowed to be yesterday. In a way she liked avoiding him, because as long as she avoided him, she didn't have to think about the things she was giving up, not about the kisses or the touches. Not about Marie.

But then again, there was something inside her that wished she had said good morning to him, that yearned to see him. A part of her that hungered for the sound of his voice, for the time when just the sight of him lifted her spirits and sent joy racing into her heart.

Things have changed, she reminded herself. *You can be his friend, but nothing more.* Belle sighed and looked at the pickles shimmering in brine. It had only been a day since she'd made the decision, but it was already becoming hard to remember.

"Damask napkins." Dorothy Alspaugh's voice cut

into Belle's thoughts. With a sense of relief she glanced up to see Dorothy shaking her head. "Have you ever heard anything so ridiculous? I told her I thought hand-made ones would do just fine, but she insisted. Said she thought it made the doctor look better. I said there was such a thing as looking *too* much better."

"Folks gettin' above themselves." Stella whisked the cover off an apple pie. "She was in Millers' the other day buyin' a length of velvet. Velvet, can you imagine? And green at that. Why, it'll make her look sallow is all."

Belle spooned the pickles onto a plate. "Maybe it's not for her. Maybe it's for her daughter."

Stella sniffed. "What daughter?"

"Or her cousin." Belle shrugged. "Who cares what she's buyin'? It's not your money."

Dorothy turned from the sink and stared. *Like a frog who just swallowed somethin' too big for its own throat,* Belle thought, smiling to herself as she looked down at the plate.

Stella harrumphed. "It don't matter if that's so or not. I'm just sayin' she's gettin' above herself."

"You had store-bought napkins when we were at your house for dinner," Belle pointed out.

"Those were a *gift—*"

"Isabelle," Lillian said. Her voice was soft, but there was a warning in her tone, one that Belle had heard too often to miss. "Dinner's just about ready. Why don't you call for the men?"

"I'll go too." Sarah spoke from the corner of the kitchen, where she was playing quietly with a jar of buttons. "Then c'n we go dig up Janey? I wanna play with her again."

"Goodness," Stella said quietly.

Belle looked at her, staring until Stella flushed and

glanced away, and then she turned to Sarah. "We'll dig up Janey tomorrow, Sarah," she said. She set aside the jar of pickles and wiped her hands on the apron Lillian had insisted she wear. "Come on, now, let's go call your papa."

"Make sure Kenny hears you," Dorothy said over her shoulder. "That old man's getting deaf as a house, but don't you know he won't admit it. I don't wanna have to go out and fetch him in."

Belle stifled a laugh. "I'll call loud," she promised. She went to the door, waiting until Sarah got to her feet and hurried after her before she opened it and stepped out onto the stoop. She looked at Sarah. "All right, you goin' to help?"

Sarah nodded.

"On the count of three—ready? One, two, three . . . Dinner!" Belle put her hands to her mouth, yelled the word as loudly as she could. She heard Sarah beside her, calling in a high, little-girl tone. Their voices blended, carried off into the breeze, disappearing over the hills.

"Let's do it again," Sarah said. She mimicked Belle, putting chubby hands around her mouth. "One, two, three—"

They both shouted: "Dinner!"

The sound vibrated around them, and Belle stood there, listening, feeling a flutter of anticipation when she heard the shouts of answer from the field, bouncing through the corn. Sarah grabbed onto her skirt, curling her fingers into the material, leaning against Belle's legs.

Belle closed her eyes. It felt so good, the feel of Sarah's body next to hers, the sound of voices in the air. It touched the loneliness that started deep inside her, the loneliness that had been there for a very long time. She heard the movement of the women in the kitchen, the murmured, discordant tones of their squabbling and gossip, and even that she didn't mind. Even that made her feel a part of things, and she knew that she had missed this, too, this busy socializing, this gossipy bickering. The things she'd thought she always hated.

Well, she didn't hate them anymore. She wasn't sure she ever had. Being away from it, being just one other person in a city where nobody meant anything, had shown her that. There was something to be said for women bustling together in a kitchen and men joining to work the fields. There was something to be said for being part of a town where everyone knew your business.

She opened her eyes and pulled Sarah closer, running her fingers through the little girl's short hair. Belle thought about Rand cutting it, and the thought made her laugh; she couldn't believe she'd ever been angry about it, or upset. She understood now, knew that Rand was just being a father, just trying to make Sarah happy. And hair grew back so quickly. By the end of the winter it would be long again, blond and heavy. Like Belle's. She would make sure Rand didn't cut it again, at least not until Sarah was old enough to know her own mind—

Belle stopped mid-thought.

She was thinking of the future.

It startled her. She stared at the fields unseeingly. The future. She had never thought of it before, not really. Had never wondered where she might be next year or the year after that, next week, or even tomorrow. One day at a time, hour by hour, minute by minute. She planned her life that way—or actually she never planned it at all, just let it happen without thinking about where it might go. It had never mattered to her before. She had never let it matter.

But now, suddenly, it did. Now she found herself thinking about the things she would do with Sarah in the winter, in the spring, in the heady, grassy days of summer. Found herself wondering if she would still be here, and what would change. Rand was getting married; there would be no place for her, not really. She was Sarah's mother, but she wasn't Rand's wife, and Marie wouldn't want her around, whether she knew the truth or not. Marie would want to make her own life with Rand.

And Sarah.

The thought squeezed Belle's heart. She looked down at the top of Sarah's head, stroked her hair. She realized now why Rand had never wanted her to tell Sarah the truth, why he'd fought her wish to tell.

Because telling Sarah the truth would only hurt and confuse her if Belle left. And Rand thought she would leave.

Maybe she would have done that once. But not now, not anymore. Now she wanted to see her daughter grow up, to play a part in Sarah's life. Belle wanted to see Sarah at ten, and twelve, wanted to see her playing in the fields and wearing her first grown-up dress and pinning up her hair. But mostly—oh God, mostly—what she wanted was for Sarah to call her Mama.

But Sarah would be calling Marie that.

The pain welled inside Belle, making it hard to breathe, bringing tears to her eyes that she blinked away. She didn't know what to do about that, didn't know how she could change things. She couldn't stand in the way of Rand marrying Marie, regardless of whether she loved him, or Sarah. But she knew she couldn't leave either. Even if Rand married Marie, even if she had to watch her daughter call another woman Mama, Belle knew she would never leave this town, not as long as Sarah and Rand were in it. She would be his friend, and Sarah's aunt, and she would watch them change and grow around her, and take what joy in it she could. Because she knew now it was all she was ever meant to have.

And maybe it would be enough.

Maybe.

"Here they come," Sarah said. Just as she spoke, Belle heard the men as they broke from the fields and walked across the pasture. They looked tired, their skin and clothes and hair covered with corn dust and pollen, their faces striped with sweat.

Belle swiped at her face with the back of her hand, wiping away the last vestiges of tears, and tightened her hold on Sarah, watching the men come toward them. She raised her chin, tried to smile. "I hope you boys are hungry," she said. "We've got enough food for the whole town."

"What'd you say, girl?" Kenny Alspaugh asked, rubbing his face.

Paul Miller grinned. "Well, now, I hope that's true, 'cos I'm hungry enough to eat most of it myself."

They each went to the cistern, sluicing off their faces, their necks, washing their hands in the bucket left off to the side. Paul and Jack and Kenny. Belle looked out, toward the field, just as the others stepped beyond the fence. The two hired cutters and Rand. He was talking to them, gesturing slowly, not looking toward the house. His clothes were dusty like the others, sticking to his back in dark, sweaty places, and his hair looked pale from pollen. Belle's fingers tightened on Sarah's shoulders, her heart flopped into her stomach. She struggled to keep her smile. *Friends,* she reminded herself. *Just friends.*

Then he looked up and caught sight of her.

He stopped dead.

The two cutters stopped along with him, pausing mid-speech, following his gaze, and Belle felt the blood rush to her face, felt her heart pound in her chest. He was staring at her as if he'd never seen her before, a stare that seemed to dance along her skin, made her fingers tingle. But before she had time to really understand what was in his eyes, he straightened and tore his gaze away and continued his conversation.

She felt vaguely, embarrassingly disappointed. But then he washed and followed the others up the stairs, stopping for a moment beside her.

"Hey there," he said softly, and the quiet hush of his voice shivered over her skin, sank into her stomach. Then, before she could answer, he leaned down to tweak Sarah's nose. "What're you up to, Little Bit?" he asked.

"Nothin'," Sarah said.

"Nothing?" Rand chuckled. "Well, then, I guess you've been a good girl." He stepped into the kitchen, and Sarah followed, babbling happily, leaving Belle alone on the stoop.

She listened to the talk and laughter in the kitchen, heard the men tease their wives as they loaded up their plates with chicken and ham, potatoes and biscuits and applesauce. And even though she'd felt like she belonged just minutes before, now Belle only felt isolated and lonely.

And it was all because of that look, that strange look that made her think of kisses and dancing and hungry words. That look that reminded her she was not Marie.

Belle swallowed. No, she was not Marie. It was time she started remembering that. She glanced at the door, moved toward it purposefully, and then she went inside.

They were all talking, even Lillian was smiling as she

dished up mounds of boiled potatoes and sauerkraut. The men ate as if they hadn't seen a meal for days, shoving food onto their forks and into their mouths, swallowing almost before they could chew, and following it up with long, loud gulps of buttermilk and coffee.

"It looks good this year, Rand," Jack Dumont was saying. "Those ears is just startin' to glaze."

"A fine crop," Paul agreed, spreading apple butter thickly on a biscuit. "Should get a helluva price for it, but you might have to ship it farther out. I'm thinkin' of doin' that myself."

"Always thinkin', never doin'." Stella laughed, slapping at his hand. "Don't you listen to him, Rand, he ain't seen a train pract'ly since they laid the track."

Belle made her way slowly around the table, looking for a place to stand. Dorothy and Stella stood beside their husbands, ladling food on their plates as fast as it was eaten. Sarah was at the far end of the table, squished against the wall, dragging her fork through a pile of cooked dried corn while Lillian juggled dishes behind her. And Rand—Rand was hunched over his meal, nodding as the others spoke.

Belle took a deep breath. She didn't want to be here suddenly, didn't want to watch him and think of him, didn't want to have to pretend she didn't care. Quietly she left the kitchen and went down the hallway. She stepped out on the front porch, closing the door behind her, along with all the noise, all the laughter. It was quiet here; there was nothing but the sound of the oaks blowing in the heavy breeze, the scatter of leaves on the ground and the calls of the birds who still lingered in the last days of fall.

Quiet. Belle sighed. She settled herself on the rail and leaned back, closing her eyes, listening to the sounds and letting them calm her, feeling the breeze blow through her hair, across her skin. Gradually she felt better. Gradually thoughts of Marie and the future faded away. She felt calmer, stronger, able to go back inside and face Rand and know that things would be all right. Yes, things would be fine. She would make them—

The front door squeaked open.

"Mind if I join you?"

Belle's eyes snapped open. Rand was standing in the doorway, a plate in one hand, a fork in the other.

"You didn't eat anything," he said.

Her throat tightened. She straightened against the pillar, feeling nervous and uncomfortable, even though there was no reason to be. No reason except for her own thoughts. "I wasn't very hungry."

He motioned to the plate. "Want some pie?"

"No."

He hesitated for a moment, and then he took a deep breath, gestured to the rail. "Can I . . . ?"

"Oh—yeah." She moved over, swinging her legs over the rail so that he could sit. "Have a seat."

He sat beside her, not close, but close enough for her to see the trailing spores of pollen and dust on his shoulders and his neck. The heavy canvas cutting sleeve still covered his left arm, stiff and unyielding, dark with dust and fraying at the edges.

She gestured to it. "You'll need a new one of those soon," she said.

He glanced at the sleeve. "Lillian'll make a new one." He shrugged. He looked at her. "Or maybe you could do it."

A shiver went through her, a longing that froze her heart. She looked away. "You wouldn't be able to get your hand in it if I made one," she said. "The last thing I ever sewed was a sampler."

He chuckled softly. "And you did a damn poor job of that, if I recall."

Belle made a face. "I think Mama gave up on the idea that I'd ever be a seamstress, that's for sure."

He shrugged. "You can always hire someone to sew."

"Yeah." Belle sighed. She heard him chewing, heard the scrape of his fork along the plate. She stared straight ahead, out at the road, watching the grass blow in the Alspaughs' field, thinking about the day she and Sarah had run across it on their way to the canal. It seemed a long time ago now, though it wasn't really, only a few days. It felt like weeks.

It was a moment before she realized he'd set aside his plate.

She turned to look at him and found that he was staring at her, the same way he had earlier, when he'd come in for dinner. That same scrutinizing, curious stare that made her heart jump into her throat, made her feel strangely weak.

"What is it?" she said, and her voice came out too high, squeaky with nerves. "What's wrong?"

He swallowed. "Nothing," he said, but she heard the lie behind it. "I was just—just wondering what you were thinking about."

Belle shrugged in surprise. "I don't know. Nothin' really. Just that day me and Sarah went to the canal."

"Oh." He ran his hand through his hair, corn dust sprinkled his shoulders at the movement. Then he looked away from her, glanced down at his hands. "I always wanted to take her there, you know. To show it to her for the first time. I thought she'd like it."

"She did." Belle smiled, remembering. "We went to Shenky's and had some melon, and she got it all over her face. We put our feet in the water, and I told her stories. I told her about Bandit."

"Bandit." He said the word wonderingly, as if it were a memory he couldn't quite grasp. Then he smiled. "Oh, the mule."

She nodded. "Yeah. She liked that story."

"I'll bet she did." He laughed slightly. "She probably can't wait to see him."

"She'll drive us crazy till summer with it," Belle said.

His laughter died abruptly, along with the smile. He still didn't look at her. Still kept his gaze fastened on his hands, rubbing his fingers with his thumb. "Till summer," he repeated softly. And then, "Tell me something, will you?"

There was a soft hesitation in his tone, a caution that crept inside her. "What's that?" she asked quietly.

"All that time you were gone, when you were in New York, what did you do?"

"Do?" She shrugged. "I don't know. A little of this, a little of—"

"No." He looked up suddenly, and the look in his eyes forestalled her, cut her words dead. "Not that answer. I don't want the answer you give everyone else. Tell me. Tell me what you really did."

Belle swallowed. His eyes were nearly burning in their intensity. He was looking at her as if he could find the answer just from her expression, as if he could somehow read her mind. She looked away, unable to bear it, not wanting to be affected by it, unwilling to let him see so far inside her. But the words fell out anyway. Honest words. Words she'd barely even admitted to herself. "I worked in boardinghouses," she said. "But I was cold mostly. Hungry sometimes. Always lonely." She looked up, at the trees in front of her, at the huge limbs shadowed against the sky. "I wasn't like you, Rand. I never wanted adventure. I remember when you used to ask the canal-boat captains if they would take us all the way to China." She paused for a moment, thinking. "I never wanted that. I would've been happy here."

"Then why did you go?"

The soft question cut into her like a knife. It brought back all the memories, all the little things she'd tortured herself with over the years, the things she was afraid to think about again. She remembered his harsh voice, and her mother's. Remembered the fear and confusion and pain. It festered inside her, a dark place in her soul, a pain so bad she couldn't look at it for more than a moment, couldn't face it.

She didn't know what to say, how to answer him, so she said the only thing she could, the only answer there was.

"Because," she said quietly, looking at him. "Because you wanted me to."

She saw the way her words hit him. He looked stunned for a moment, and then he closed his eyes, squeezed them shut as if he couldn't bear to look at her. She couldn't tear her eyes away, not when he opened them again and looked at her, not when she saw the anguish in their hazel depths, and the regret.

And not when she saw the longing.

"Christ." The word sounded torn from him, raw and aching.

Fear shot through Belle. *Look away,* the voice inside her warned. *Back away.* But she couldn't move, couldn't speak as he leaned toward her. He was going to kiss her, she knew it, and part of her knew she shouldn't let him. Part of her knew she would only be hurt if she let him. But the other part—oh, the other part longed for it so much. The other part wanted this kiss, since she could have nothing else, wanted the heat of his lips on hers and the erotic tease of his tongue.

And it was that part that won. That part that reveled

in the soft brush of his lips against hers and heard the sharp rasp of his breath with a shiver of anticipation. And when he pressed into her, and Belle felt his hands at her waist, felt his fingers tighten, that part of her was swept with longing so intense, she put her arms around his neck, pulling him closer, tangling her fingers in the heavy, dusty weight of his hair.

Oh, God, she had dreamed of this. For years she had dreamed of this kiss, of this moment. She felt the gentle pressure of his mouth, and her lips parted beneath it, and then he was dipping inside, touching her tongue with his, filling her senses with the flavor of apple pie, sweet and rich and cinnamony, along with the taste of him, a taste she remembered even though she couldn't put a name to it, a taste that set her skin on fire, made her entire soul cry out with yearning.

She heard him moan deep in his throat, felt the urgency in his movements as he pressed closer, the same urgency she was feeling, the same, intense sensation of soft, wet heat and flaming touch, and she knew that this —*this*—was what she wanted. This heady excitement, this touching that led to other touching, this yearning that went beyond the memory of pain.

Not just friendship. Love.

She wanted love.

And it was the one thing she could not have.

Sickness swept through her. Sickness and a fierce, unrelenting pain. Belle jerked her head back, banging it on the pillar, twisting away, fighting his arms, his hands, his mouth. "Rand," she whispered and she heard the desperation in her voice, the pain. "Please—"

And then she heard the front door open.

Belle froze. She glanced toward it, and with a shock she saw her mother standing there, saw the color drain from Lillian's face, the slow realization. "Mama," she said. Rand jerked away, twisted to look at the door.

"Jesus." It was more a sound than a curse. He dropped his hands from her, struggled to his feet. "Lillian . . ."

But Lillian didn't look at him. It was almost as if he didn't exist. She stared at Belle, and Belle had the sudden feeling that the world had faded away. All that was left was this—this porch, and this moment, and she and Lillian staring at each other. Everything focused down to this, to the hatred in her mother's eyes, the condemnation.

And then Lillian backed inside and closed the door behind her.

Chapter 26

"Mama—" Belle tore away from Rand, lunging to the door. She heard his protest behind her, saw him reach for her, but the image of her mother's hatred glowed in her mind, unrelenting and too strong to ignore. It was time to face her now, Belle knew that, and in the light of it nothing mattered, not Rand's kiss, not anything. Belle yanked open the door. It slammed shut behind her.

Voices floated from the kitchen. Stella, Dorothy, Kenny . . . talking away as if nothing had happened, as if it were just an ordinary day cutting corn, and the mundaneness of it seemed suddenly not quite real, took on the twisting, fanciful quality of a nightmare. Belle stood there for a moment, listening for Lillian's voice, not hearing it, and then she heard the steps upstairs, the sharp clap of boot heels.

Belle hurried up the stairs. "Mama!" she called. "Mama!"

There was no answer, but it didn't matter. Belle knew exactly where her mother was. She hurried down the hallway, stopping just before the last door, the door farthest away from her own.

It was cracked open, as if Lillian had rushed inside and forgotten to close it. Belle nudged it with her hand, pushing it open until she could see her mother on the far side of the room.

Lillian was standing by the window, staring outside, at the fields the window overlooked. She was just standing there, arms crossed, spine ramrod-straight, but the chignon at the back of her neck had loosened, and strands of pale blond hair escaped to curl against her face. It made her look softer somehow, in spite of her rigid posture, more approachable.

Though Belle knew that was just an illusion.

She stepped inside the door, shut it softly behind her. "Mama," she said quietly.

Lillian didn't turn around. "How long has that been going on?" she asked, and though her voice was calm, Belle heard the faint edge of tension beneath it. "How long?"

Belle pressed her palms against the door, taking strength from the hard, smooth feel of wood. "Mama, it's not what you—"

"How long? A week? Longer?"

Belle swallowed. She shook her head. "No. Not that long."

"I see." Lillian's fingers tightened on her arms, her gaze stayed focused outside. "You know he's going to marry Marie Scholl."

The words sent a shaft of pain stabbing into Belle. "Yeah. I know. She's a nice girl."

"Yes, she is." Lillian took a deep breath; it echoed in the room, in the muslin curtains edged with crocheted lace, in the eaves. It bounced against the huge wardrobe and fell over the wedding-ring quilt on the bed. "Then I don't understand why you won't leave him alone."

The accusation was like a slap. Belle felt the heat racing into her face; anger made her voice tight and harsh. "What makes you think it's my fault?"

"Isn't it?" Lillian turned then, and her pale eyes were blazing. "Everything has been—fine since you've been gone. Rand has been fine. He's been seeing Marie, we've had no trouble at all. But since you've returned . . ." The anger in Lillian's eyes faded, replaced by a bleakness that was somehow even more hurtful, a hopelessness that made Belle feel guilty and sad. "What else can I think but that you're tempting him?"

"Mama, you're wrong." Belle could barely say the words. "You're . . . wrong."

"Am I?" Lillian's mouth tightened, her fingers were white where she clenched her arms. "Then perhaps you should explain it to me."

Belle stared at her mother. *Explain it to me.* As if it were that simple, as if she could explain it in a word or a sentence or even a lifetime. Hell, she couldn't even explain it to herself. "I—I don't—"

"I thought it was over. I . . . hoped . . ." Lillian closed her eyes, shook her head. "I hoped we could all live together peaceably. But it's obvious we can't. With you and Rand . . ." Her voice trailed off; her face was tight with what looked like revulsion. "Good Lord, Belle, have you even thought of what people will say?"

"I don't give a damn what people say," Belle said, and though she tried to control her feelings, her voice was sharp with anger and pain. "They've always talked about me. It doesn't matter. And it's not like that—"

"Then how is it?" Lillian glared at her, her words were razor sharp, each one honed, each one stabbing. "Explain it to me, then. Tell me why I am continually having to protect this family from you."

"Mama, why do you hate me so much?" The words slipped out before Belle could stop them, and she heard the hurt in her voice, a hurt she no longer had the strength to fight.

The words shivered between them; the outside sounds seemed suddenly loud. Lillian stared at her in shock, and then she sagged, crumpling to the edge of the bed, her face buried in her hands, her fingers trembling.

Belle stared at her, unable to move. She had never seen her mother lose control before, and it was frightening, confusing—somehow reassuring. It made Lillian seem more human somehow, vulnerable as she'd never been. Belle had the unexpected urge to comfort, to soothe her mother as Lillian had never soothed her.

"Mama," she whispered, afraid to touch her, afraid not to. She dropped onto the bed beside her mother, laid a cautious hand on her arm. "Mama—"

Lillian's hands dropped away from her face. She looked up, and Belle saw the wetness of tears glimmering in her mother's eyes, a pain she'd never seen before, never even imagined.

"I don't know what else to do," Lillian said, her voice broken and harsh and completely unfamiliar. "You are so much . . . like him."

Belle frowned. "Like who?"

"Your father." Lillian sighed. She looked out the window, her hands convulsively crumpling the material of her apron.

"My father?" Belle could not help her surprise. She would never have thought she was anything like the man in the portrait upstairs.

But Lillian nodded. "He was the most irresponsible man I ever knew. But he could talk—oh, the man had the prettiest words. I was . . . overwhelmed by him."

"I—I didn't know that about him. He seems so—pious."

Lillian glanced at her, frowning in confusion. "Who?"

"My father," Belle said. "His portrait isn't—"

"The portrait," Lillian repeated slowly. "I see." She took a deep breath, looked down at her hands. "Isabelle, the man in the portrait is not your father."

Belle stared at her mother, sure she'd misheard, sure she didn't understand. But before she could ask, before she could make sense of it, Lillian looked up and straightened her shoulders.

"The man is John Calhoun, that's true. And I was married to him. He was my father's assistant, a brilliant politician. Everyone said it was a wonderful match." She paused. "You know all this, I realize. But what you didn't know was that I was very young—just sixteen. And John"—she looked away—"Well, John was much like his portrait. He was a very serious, very important man. A little self-important." A soft smile touched her lips. "But we suited each other very well."

She stared out the window again, and Belle waited, unmoving and listening, feeling oddly as if the world was about to open up beneath her and unsure whether or not she wanted it to. Unsure if she wanted this level of trust, or wanted to hear her mother's secrets. Part of her wanted to stop Lillian right now, to refuse to hear the rest, to let the future go on without knowing what her mother was about to tell her. And the other part was afraid to say a word, afraid that if she did, Lillian *would* stop, and she would never know the truth.

So she waited, torn, almost dreading the words when they finally came.

Lillian's voice was soft with memory. "It was the summer they started work on the canal. John took me to see them dig. It was a—a present to me, I think, a sop he threw me because he was gone so much and I was so often home alone. The foreman was Jack Murphey. He was . . . very handsome, very charming. I'm afraid I fell a little in love with him then. It was a—a foolish thing to do. But I was lonely, and Jack was lively and entertaining. I believed he loved me too."

Lillian fell silent.

"Jack Murphey was my father," Belle said quietly.

Lillian nodded. "John never . . . he never knew. I was ready to leave him, to run off with Jack, but"—she closed her eyes as if it still pained her—"but Jack left first. I don't think he ever . . . meant to stay."

Belle heard the sadness in her mother's voice, an ache she recognized. She knew exactly how it felt to love someone who hurt you, knew the desperation and panic of being pregnant and alone, the feeling that your life was moving out of control. She knew how it felt to be lonely and afraid and hungry for something—anything—to call your own.

She knew all that, and so when Lillian looked at her and Belle saw the hesitation in her mother's eyes, she took Lillian's hand. "I know, Mama," she said. "I know."

Lillian made a sound, a small, breathless laugh. "You are so like him. I always thought John would look at you and know—you were so very different from either of us." She shook her head, and then she looked up, and there was a bright intensity in her eyes. "I have always wanted the best for you, Isabelle."

Belle sighed and looked away. "Maybe that's true."

"It *is* true." Lillian gripped Belle's hand, squeezed hard. "I have not loved you as much as I should, I know that. I have been so . . . afraid. You are so much like him, I—I saw trouble wherever you went. Every time I look at you, I see him, I see the terrible mistake I made." She took a deep breath. "But I do love you, in my way. And I have always wanted the best for you."

Belle winced. "The best, Mama? Is that why you

threw me out six years ago? Is that why you called me a disgrace to the family?"

Lillian closed her eyes, swallowed hard. "I'm sorry for that," she said softly. "You'll never know how sorry."

Belle had not expected that. Not the apology, nor her mother's obvious regret, and it threw her for a moment, took away her sarcasm, cut through the pain still remaining from that time. She did not want to feel for her mother, did not want to forgive her, but she found herself thinking she should. Found herself looking at Lillian and wanting to reassure her, to tell her that it was all right, to say things were better even though they weren't, even though there was a piece of her that wanted to keep a firm hold on her resentment, a part she wasn't sure she wanted to heal.

"I was afraid," Lillian said, continuing on in the face of Belle's silence. "Everything was—it was so much like before. So much like—like it was with Jack . . ."

"But I'm not my father," Belle said quietly.

"No."

"And I—I'm not sure I can just forget what you did, Mama. I'm not sure I can forgive."

Lillian nodded slowly. "It is your decision of course."

The silence fell between them. Lillian sat there, staring at her hands, and Belle felt her mother's sad acceptance, felt the memories between them, along with the heaviness of regret.

And she knew then that she didn't want to live in the past. Not anymore. She'd been there for such a long time already.

She took a deep breath. "I'm not sure I can forgive," she repeated. "But I—I'd like to try."

Lillian looked up, and smiled—a small, tender smile that made Belle feel sad for all the time they'd lost, all the things there would never be between them. But her mother's next words made the ache disappear, filled her with a hope she'd never felt before, never known she wanted.

"Oh, so would I," Lillian said quietly. "So would I."

Rand threw himself into cutting corn, relishing the hard, backbreaking labor. He ignored the sharp-edged leaves that sawed gently and persistently at his back and neck, and grabbed the stalks in the crook of his left arm, whacking them off with the machetelike corn knife—a single stroke that had taken him years to perfect—dropping the butts to the ground to drag behind him until he had all he could carry. Then he lugged the bundle to the shock one of the hired cutters had started and went back for another load.

The *swish, thwack, swish, thwack* of the blade and the rustling of the stalks were a constant rhythm in his ears, the soreness of his hand and arm a welcome relief to his thoughts, and he concentrated on it and not on the endless rows of corn that allowed no breeze in, or the pollen from dry tassels that dribbled into his collar, itched where it clung to his sweaty face. The pattern was all, the *swish, thwack, swish, thwack* filled his ears, forced his numb arms to move, his fingers to grasp the wooden handle of the knife. He could think about that, and not about anything else. Not about the fact that he'd followed Belle and kissed her, not about the fact that he was burning for her and he didn't know what to do about it.

He'd dreamed about her last night; the vision was still so vivid in his mind. She was at the end of the yard, smiling at him, calling to him, and the sun was falling across her hair, the breeze molding her dress to her body. Seductively she gestured for him to come closer, and when he did, when he reached for her and tried to pull her close, she stepped away from him before he could touch her, stayed out of reach, and her laughter was warm and lilting and infinitely beguiling.

He woke up drenched in sweat and painfully aroused. Had fallen asleep only to dream the same thing again, only this time he caught her. This time he ran his hands over her body and felt her heat against him. This time he kissed her—a hot, wet kiss that pulled him in, sucked at his soul until he couldn't escape, couldn't breathe, and suddenly she was gone and there was darkness all around him. Frightening, horrible darkness that made his heart race and his breath harsh and rasping.

Darkness that reminded him of his mother, and that bottomless pool at Rock Mill, the pool where they'd never found her body—

He squeezed his eyes shut, trying to block the image from his mind, trying to forget it and the words that echoed in his head, circled over and over and over. *You love her, you love her, you love her.*

Christ, yes, he loved her. But he'd loved her once before, and had destroyed them both with it. He'd loved her with the blinding, inescapable hunger of obsession, and all it had got him was a life full of lies and obligations, six years of darkness and frustration.

Six years without her.

He saw again that cold November night in his mind. The night everything changed. It was a husking bee, and he remembered her pulling the husk away from an ear to reveal ruddy kernels. The red ear. She had looked up at him then, and the flush that stained her cheeks, her sudden shyness, made him almost dizzy with need. He had wanted her for weeks, and she had kissed him and teased him and pulled away as if that were all there was, and he knew that for her there was nothing more. He knew she was too young to know better.

He wanted to kiss her then, but it was Charlie Boston who stood up and took the forfeit, Charlie Boston who swept the red ear away from her and made a great show of kissing her forehead, because she was too young even to be there with them and they all knew it. But still Rand remembered how inflamed he'd been, how Charlie's kiss only made him think of all the things he wanted from her, all the things he could never have.

His control slipped away from him then, and when they'd arrived home and he'd pulled the wagon into the barn, he'd swung her down from the seat and taken the kiss he wanted. She had laughed and kissed him back, had tangled her hands in his hair and looked into his face and pressed her body against his. And then, when the kiss was over, she started to pull away.

He had not let her go.

Rand swallowed, thinking back, wishing he didn't remember it, wishing he could erase the image from his mind and tell himself it hadn't happened that way. But he knew it had, and he couldn't keep it from torturing him, couldn't blind himself to the truth or block the memory. He saw it all again, and it seemed far away and hazy, an experience too colored with emotion to remember properly, a vague and fuzzy dream.

But it was no dream. It was no dream when he pushed her up against the barn wall, feeling desperate and frustrated and overcome with longing. It was no dream when he pulled at her clothes, yanking up her skirts and pushing down her bodice to reveal her breasts, when he pressed against her and heard the sounds she made against his mouth. He had wanted to pleasure her too, but he was too aroused, and she was too young, and he was inside her before he knew it, thrusting against her, in her, knowing he was being too rough and hating himself for it, hating himself for taking it this far, but unable to stop. Christ, unable even to slow down.

It was over quickly. A minute, maybe two, and he was left with guilt and horror to stay with him for a lifetime. Left with that expression on her face, the confused fear, the bewildered hurt. Left with the cold darkness that had descended within him, the horrible, terrible guilt that made him jerk away from her, made him say the words that had haunted his nightmares ever since. *"Get away from me. Christ, get away. I don't want you, don't you understand? I don't want you."*

Words that had been more for himself than for her. Lies to convince himself that he wasn't the monster he knew he was. Christ, lies. So many goddamned lies. His whole life had been full of them, and now he wanted them all to fade away, wanted to tell himself the truth for once.

And the truth was that he would destroy her again if he loved her. He knew he would.

But God, he wanted to love her.

Ah, Christ, why the hell had he followed her?

Because even his fear wasn't strong enough to resist the temptation she offered. Because he'd come in from the fields and seen her standing on the back porch, Sarah pressed against her legs, and she was such a perfect vision of home and family that it stopped him dead, brought his heart pounding into his throat.

He had never thought he wanted that before, but seeing her there, with loose tendrils of hair blowing against her cheeks and her fingers tight around Sarah's hand, he wanted it with an intensity that frightened him. In that moment all of his dreams disappeared, all those vague and elusive yearnings that had haunted him since he was a boy melted away as if they were unimportant and foolish—the dreams of a boy who didn't know what life meant, the hopes of someone who'd never touched a child or held a woman in his arms.

Yes, that was why he'd followed her. That, and the vulnerability he'd seen in her face when she was in the kitchen, the way she hung back and watched them all as if she didn't belong, the uncertainty in her eyes. When he heard her go onto the front porch, it was all he could do not to rush after her, all he could do to sit calmly and wait a few minutes longer. In the end he hadn't waited long at all. He'd bolted his food and reached for a piece of pie and gone to her, telling himself he only wanted to talk to her, telling himself he just wanted to see her smile the way she had a few nights ago. Just a smile. Just some idle conversation.

But then she'd said the words that took his breath away. *"She'll drive us crazy till summer with it."* A simple comment, but it had startled him just the same. Not because of the words themselves but because of their implication. Till summer.

She was staying till summer.

Sweet Jesus. Somewhere in the back of his mind had been the thought that this was only temporary, that someday she would leave and take his madness with her and things would return to normal. Things would just go on. Deep inside he'd thought that if he could just control himself a little longer, it would be enough. He could survive this if he just waited it out.

But she wasn't going. She was staying.

And he wondered why the thought didn't fill him with cold, stark terror. Why he didn't run from her as fast as he could, why he didn't beg her to leave. Instead he found himself asking her about her life the last six years, and feeling an absurd, overpowering urge to somehow protect her from that, to somehow take away the pain he saw in her eyes and the loneliness he heard in her voice. To somehow ease the anguish he knew she felt over his betrayal.

In that moment nothing else had mattered, not his own desperation, not the darkness, not his fear. He'd heard that pain in her voice, and it made his heart ache, and all he wanted was to make it go away, for himself and for her, all he wanted was to bury himself so deeply inside her that they both forgot the past.

Christ, all he wanted . . .

Rand squeezed his eyes shut, forcing the images from his mind, forcing himself to listen to the corn, to the soft rustle. Feeling his entire body protest, he swung the corn knife into the stalks, concentrating until the corn was all he thought about, the dusty, brittle stalks, the leaves, the dry husks. He heard the men calling to each other, but other than that there were no sounds but the ones he made.

Swish, thwack, swish, thwack.

But those sounds didn't take away the darkness.

And nothing touched the fear.

Chapter 27

For some reason she had not expected him to come in for supper. She had counted on that, had hoped he would stay out in the barn the way he'd been doing lately. She already felt too vulnerable.

But when Sarah came through the door, leading Rand by the hand, Belle realized that she was lying to herself. She *did* want to see him, she was hungry to see him. She found herself devouring him with her eyes, taking in his thick, tousled hair and the drops of water clinging to his throat from washing. She found herself following one with her gaze, watching it trickle down the strong, tanned flesh of his neck to disappear in the curls revealed by the open collar of his shirt, and she felt dizzy and breathless and a little shaky.

He glanced up at her. "Hey there," he said, looking quickly away. His voice sounded thin and strained. He released Sarah's hand, gave her a little push. "Go on and sit down, Little Bit."

Lillian set a platter of cold sliced ham on the table beside a bowl of hard-boiled eggs. "Kenny said you finished the west field today," she said quickly, as if trying to fill the tense silence. Her movements were tight, jerky with what looked like anxiety. Belle knew her mother was probably nervous. In spite of their conversation this afternoon, Lillian wanted Rand to settle down and marry Marie. Though Belle and her mother had reached a kind of understanding, nothing they'd said changed that wish, and Belle knew nothing ever would. It was just the way things were.

"It's just about done," Rand said, taking his seat. He kept his eyes carefully averted, looking at his plate, the food, Sarah—anything but Belle.

"Just remember there's the Alspaughs' husking bee tomorrow." Lillian set the pot of coffee on the table and settled in her chair, rearranging her skirts around her. "Dorothy's counting on us being there."

Belle suddenly felt cold all over; she heard Rand's bitten-off curse.

"I don't have time," he said curtly.

"Of course you do." Lillian's voice was smooth, unflustered. She handed him the plate of ham. "I've already said we'll be there."

"C'n I go too?" Sarah asked.

"Of course," Lillian said. "We'll all go."

Belle swallowed. Her throat felt tight, and when Lillian handed her the ham, she forked a slice onto her plate and stared at it, wondering how the hell she was going to get it down. "Maybe I should stay home," she said slowly. "It might be better if I did."

Lillian looked at her sharply, but her voice was quiet and gentle. "Don't be absurd. You're part of the family."

Rand's head jerked up. Belle saw his surprised glance at Lillian, and then he looked at her, and his intense, hazel-bright gaze took her breath away. She wanted to look down, to break the connection, but she couldn't. In his eyes was the reminder of this afternoon, and in her mind she felt the touch of his lips, the wet heat of his tongue.

She licked her dry lips, forced herself to look away, to

focus on her plate. "All right," she said, and her voice sounded strange to her own ears, quiet and weak and oddly hoarse. "If you say so."

"I do." Lillian sliced into her meat. "Marie will be there, Rand. I'm sure you'd like to see her."

"Marie." His voice was flat. "I don't think—"

"And John Dumont of course. He was a good friend of yours once, I remember . . ."

Her mother's words faded to a low hum in Belle's mind. Marie would be there. Belle's heart sank; her hands trembled as she cut into her ham. She didn't dare look at Rand. His emotionless reply told her better than anything that he was feeling guilty. Probably he was regretting their kiss, vowing to himself it would never happen again.

That would be best, she knew. It should never happen again. They should never kiss, never even touch. They should be friends, but that was all. Just two people who talked together on Sundays, two people who enjoyed each other's company.

But not two people who longed for each other.

No, not that. Caring for him in that way had ruined her life once before; the way he treated her then nearly destroyed her. She could not take the risk it would happen again, didn't want to.

Still she couldn't keep herself from looking up, from watching him while he ate. Couldn't help looking at his long, agile fingers and thinking about how they felt against her skin. She watched the movement of his full lips and imagined the press of them against her own; she saw the gleam of lamplight on his chest and wished she could remember how the curls there felt against her hands, her breasts.

You can't have him. You want his friendship more. But the reminder was only a weak voice in her head, and she had to force herself to remember there was no other choice. Rand didn't love her. He might want her, but he loved Marie—Belle had not imagined the happiness in his smile when he was with the schoolteacher. She couldn't fight that, and she didn't want to.

She thought again of how things would be when he was married to Marie, thought of Marie standing at Rand's elbow on harvest days, waiting to load his plate as soon as he emptied it.

Belle swallowed hard, trying to remember that night six years ago, the night of the husking bee. Trying to remember the roughness of his kiss, the revulsion in his eyes when he'd pushed her away.

But the memory seemed hazy now. Instead of the rough touch, she remembered a gentle one. Instead of revulsion, she saw the yearning that had been in his eyes this afternoon, felt the gentle touch of his kiss. It was like those first kisses, when she was just a girl and infatuated with him. Those soft, pleasurable touches, lips and tongues and shivers that left her weak and aching. It made her remember other things about that long-ago night in the barn. Made her remember the way she'd wanted him then. The way she'd pushed against him with her hips and moaned against his mouth and longed for something she didn't know how to ask for.

And she knew she wanted that again. Wanted the pure feeling of needing him, desiring him. She wanted that elusive something she couldn't name, the sweetness that she knew was somehow just beyond her reach.

Yes, she wanted it. She wanted to experience that one more time before she gave him up forever.

The thought startled her into stillness, her fork felt suddenly heavy and clumsy in her hand. She heard her mother droning on without hearing the words, and Belle glanced up at Rand, catching her breath when their gazes caught, and she saw something flash through his eyes, something that sank into her heart, her soul. A longing that matched her own. She saw his eyes fall to her lips, felt the caress of his gaze on her skin.

She took a deep breath. "Are you—are you goin' to the barn tonight?" she asked, and then realized that she'd just interrupted her mother.

Lillian stared at her in disbelief. "Isabelle, please—"

Rand nodded. "For a while," he said. He pushed aside his plate, still piled with ham and a half-eaten egg. "I think I'll go out there now in fact. There's plenty to do."

"You haven't eaten much, Randall," Lillian noted.

He glanced at his plate as if he'd forgotten it. "Oh. Well, I—I'm not hungry really."

"C'n I come out with you, Papa?" Sarah slid from her chair.

He hesitated and then he nodded, and Belle knew he was doing his best to keep from looking at her. "Just for a little while," he said. "It's close to bedtime."

"I'll call in an hour," Lillian said.

Sarah looked at Belle. "You come too."

Rand inhaled sharply. The sound made Belle's stomach tight, and she shook her head slowly. "Not tonight, Sarah," she said. "Some other time maybe. I'm pretty tired. I think I'll go on up to bed."

He grabbed Sarah's hand, and the two of them went to the door. "See you in the morning, then," he said, opening it.

Belle nodded slowly. "In the mornin'," she agreed, gripping her fork with tense fingers. "Sleep well."

It was late, and though his body was tired and his muscles burned with exhaustion, he was still wide awake.

He was so sore from cutting corn that the sheets hurt his naked skin, the blankets felt too heavy and too hot.

But it wasn't that discomfort that kept him from falling asleep. It was something else, the fierce, burning heat of longing, the pain of constant arousal. He closed his eyes and he saw her. He fell asleep and he dreamed of her. The vision of her was like a demon before him, tempting and alluring, a siren song he couldn't stop, a need he couldn't ease.

He should never have come in for supper. He hadn't been able to eat, or think. He found himself watching her when she wasn't looking, found his gaze traveling up the graceful curve of her neck, wondered what the skin there would feel like against his mouth, what it would taste like. He watched the way she ate, the slow, deliberate chewing, the touch of her tongue to her lips when she drank, and he wondered how it would feel to have her mouth pressed to his throat, his chest.

For a while, an hour, Sarah had distracted him, but then she was gone, and he'd stayed alone in the barn until all the lights were out in the house, until he was sure Belle was in bed. He didn't know if he could control himself if she wasn't, didn't know if he could keep from pressing her against a wall and just taking her. It had been hard enough to walk past her room, to look at the door and know she was behind it. He had to remind himself that he had hurt her the last time he couldn't control himself, that he'd humiliated her, and he didn't want to do it again, didn't know if he could keep from doing it. But even with that reminder it had taken every ounce of strength he possessed to keep from joining her, to keep himself walking to his own room, his bed, to stay there.

And now he wondered how he would bear it past tonight. How he would go on tomorrow night and the next and the one after that, how he would keep himself from wanting her, from touching her.

Ah, Christ, how?

He heard the creak of the floorboard in the hallway. Rand stiffened, waiting for the sound of a step. In seconds he heard what he was waiting for, a soft footfall, a quiet tread. Lillian probably, he thought, holding his breath as if afraid she could somehow sense the state he was in.

He laid there, listening, hearing it come closer and closer, waiting for it to pass his door and fade away, his whole being focused on the sound. One step, two, and he waited for the three, waited for the pass.

It stopped.

He heard the quiet click of his door.

His heart stopped in his chest, his breath caught. Carefully, Rand rose to one elbow. The door creaked open. Beyond it he could see nothing but dark hallway, nothing but shadow. "Who's there?" he asked harshly. "Sarah?"

"No." The voice was a whisper, but with a shock he recognized it, and cold sweat broke over his skin, sent his heart racing. He watched wordlessly as she slipped inside, closing the door tightly behind her, and he thought, *This is a dream. This has to be a dream.* It could be nothing else. She stood there, just as he'd always imagined her, palms pressed against the door, the white lawn of her nightclothes glowing in the darkness. A spirit, a formless dream.

But even as he thought it, the moon came out from behind a cloud, drenching his room in moonlight, dancing over her hair, her form, casting her face in shadow, and he knew it was no dream. Her arms were bare, and her hair was loose and waving over her shoulders, down her back. The white lawn caressed her body, falling against wide hips and small breasts, molding to the line of her leg.

"Christ." He heard his own voice, and it sounded hoarse and far away, not like his at all. "What are you doing here?"

It was so quiet, he heard her swallow. She made a sound, a nervous laugh that died away in the darkness, leaving nothing but silence. Silence so deep that even the quiet of her voice echoed in his mind.

"Don't make me go," she said, and he heard the defenseless plea in her voice, the vulnerability that had haunted him since her return. "Please."

He fisted his hands, forcibly kept himself from going to her. "Belle—"

"Don't." She shook her head and took a step toward him. "Don't say anythin'. I know this doesn't mean anything'." She touched the top fastening of her nightgown, loosing it so that the fabric fell open, and then she unfastened the next one, and the one after that. "But I thought . . . I mean, I want . . ." She took a deep breath, as if marshaling her courage, and then she spoke quickly, the words falling over themselves, a rumble of sound where every word was crystal clear and startling. "I want you just for tonight. Then I promise I won't bother you again."

Christ. Oh, God. Sweet Jesus. The imprecations flowed through his head, a litany of denial, a rush of protest. But they faded away, fell away from him and left him dry-mouthed and aching, left him with a vision who was slowly unfastening her gown, revealing herself to him button by button, and suddenly nothing else mattered. Not the fact that he shouldn't touch her, not the lies between them, nothing. He had wished for this, had wanted a memory to erase the past, and now suddenly it was here, and he didn't want to wonder why, didn't want to analyze the reasons she was here or what she thought she was doing. He wanted her. Had wanted her as long as he could remember, and before he could stop to think about it, he pushed back the coverlet and went to her.

He heard her gasp, small and quiet, and he realized that he was naked, and aroused, and that she had never seen him this way, not completely unclothed. He stopped, just a foot away from her, close enough to touch. *Don't run.* The thought brought a surge of desperation, an ache that sent a lump into his stomach and made him strangely weak. He wanted to grab her—sweet Christ, he wanted to grab her—but he didn't.

"Run away from me," he said slowly, hoping she wouldn't do it, praying she would. "Do us both a favor and run away."

She shook her head, looked at the floor. "I . . . can't," she said, and then she looked back and met his gaze, and her expression was so starkly revealing, it took his breath. She reached out, he felt her slender hand on his chest, the heat of her fingers against his skin. Her eyes were huge and luminous in the moonlight. "I can't."

It stole the last of his control, those words. They plunged through him, an admission and a curse, a fantasy he'd longed for. He saw her fingers trailing through the hair on his chest, felt the gentle tug, the seductive tease, and he couldn't resist any longer, didn't want to. With a groan he pulled her to him, burying his hands in her hair, holding her still for his kiss. He forgot that he would destroy her, that he would destroy himself. He felt the heat of her body through the thin white lawn, felt it against his chest and his hips, against the painful rigidity of his arousal. She was burning him, consuming him, and he plunged his tongue into her mouth, no longer wanting gentleness or sweetness but only the taste of her. Only the touch.

She moaned, twining her arms around his neck, pressing closer. He was drowning in her, drowning in the sweet, humid heat of her mouth. He grabbed her hips, bringing her as close as he could without being inside her, and he knew she was wearing nothing beneath the nightgown. He was so sensitive, he felt the soft, wiry touch of the curls between her thighs even through the lawn. *Slower,* he thought. *Go slower, don't hurt her.* But he couldn't stop, and he couldn't slow down, and the wanting crashed through him, made him nearly insane with need.

He ground himself against her, dragged his hands up her body, to her waist, her breasts, tangled his fingers in her hair to hold her prisoner. He felt her hands against his shoulders, gripping him, and he pulled her head back, angling it so that he could explore her more deeply, more intimately with his tongue, wanting all of her, wanting somehow to breathe her inside of him. He knew he was being too rough, but he was unable to help himself, knew he was bruising her, but was afraid to ease his hold on her, afraid she would run if he did.

But her hold on him didn't ease, and she kissed him back, touched him with her tongue and lips and teeth. He felt the urgency in her kiss, felt it in the clutching of her fingers against his skin. *Slow down, slow down, slow down.* But the need for her was like a madness in him, and before he knew it, he had backed her tight against the wall, had her pinned so that she couldn't move, and he grabbed the sleeves of her gown, jerking it over her shoulders so roughly, he heard it tear, yanking it to her waist, her hips.

He heard her whimper with some part of his mind, heard the urgent rasp of her breathing. He felt the press of her breasts against his chest, small and soft, her nipples peaked and hard, and he took them into his hands, heard the moan in her throat when he touched her. This was what he'd dreamed of, touching her this way, feeling the mature heaviness of her breasts, the curve of her hip. It nearly brought him to climax, just touching her. That, and the press of her hips against his, the way she answered his rhythm with innocent, primitive movements, jerking against him, making him so insane with desire, he grabbed her gown, balling it in his fists, lifting the hem.

Christ, he was drowning, bursting. He wanted her now, this way, wanted to thrust into her standing, feel her legs curl around his hips, take her weight and slam against her.

He was spiraling out of control. He devoured her with his mouth, heard her soft whimper and pressed into her, uncaring, led only by the promise of fulfillment, the groaning release.

God, he was dying. *You'll destroy her.* The voice rang inside his head. *You'll destroy her like you did before.* But even the words couldn't make him stop. The harsh darkness descended upon him; he felt the fear, the madness spreading though him, taking over. One more moment and it would win, he knew. One more moment . . .

He tore his mouth away and grabbed her tightly, held her still against him. She struggled a little, tried to move, but he wouldn't let her. His breathing was harsh and rasping. "Christ." He struggled to gain control, fought for sanity.

"Rand?" She looked up at him, and he saw the uncertainty on her face, the fear, and it was too much like before, too much like that night six years ago, when he had thrust inside her before she was ready, had taken her virginity without gentleness or care. *Sweet Jesus, not again. Don't let me do it again.*

She tried to press against him. Her hand tightened on his chest. "Rand?"

He took a deep breath, leaned his forehead against hers. "Don't," he said, covering her hand with his, stilling it against his skin. "This . . . is too fast."

"Too fast?" She sounded honestly confused, and in a moment of cruel insight Rand realized that she had been with no one but him. She knew nothing but this, nothing but this coarse, brutal assault on her senses, the rush of madness. No one had ever made love to her tenderly, or slowly. No one had shown her what it could be like. He was the only lover she'd ever had, and he had taught her only desperation and fear. Only painful coupling that had nothing to do with care and less with love.

And he wanted to show her something different. Wanted to make love to her with kisses and caresses, wanted to see her cry out in climax beneath him. He wanted all those things, and he knew he was too out of control to show her, too aroused to make it last.

So carefully, slowly, he pulled back from her, disentangled her other hand from around his neck and placed it at her side. And when she looked up at him in wary bewilderment, he leaned down and kissed her softly, brushed his lips across hers in the barest of touches.

"Too fast," he whispered. "Sweet girl, give me just a minute, and I can make it last for both of us." And then he closed his fingers around himself and began to stroke.

Belle watched him. She could not move, was too dazed by the sight of him, by the sheer strength of the emotions coursing through her. *"Too fast,"* he'd said, and she thought she understood him, thought there must be something more than this mindless, heedless need that blazed within her, that made her want to be inside him, to touch him with every part of her body. She had known, somehow, that there must be more than this, but she didn't know what, had nothing to base it on but the last time she and Rand had been together.

But this was nothing like that time.

She felt his other hand on her hip, holding her in place against the door. Just that simple touch made her weak; that and the way he shook, the trembling of his body as he slid his hand to the base of his arousal and then back again. She couldn't tear her eyes away, felt the heat start in her face and move through her loins and into her heart, felt it rush through her blood. She was hot and dizzy and shaking, and she knew if he took his hand from her, she would crumple to the floor, but he didn't move his hand. His fingers only tightened, she felt the press of them in her skin, knew there would be a bruise there in the morning, and she didn't care. Her nightgown was down around her hips; she was exposed to his gaze, but it didn't matter. Nothing mattered but the longing that sped through her, the yearning that made her tremble and try to pull him closer.

He stopped her with a look. "Not yet," he gasped, and his eyes seared through her, pinned her in place, the intensity in his gaze taking her thoughts, her breath. "Just—one minute. Just . . . one—"

He threw his head back, stiffening, grabbing her to him so that she felt him throbbing against her belly, felt hot wetness on her skin, slick and burning.

"Christ." It was a whisper spoken against her hair, a heated rush of breath. "Oh, Christ." Seconds passed, minutes, and then he pulled away from her, and Belle felt his fingers beneath her chin, forcing her to look at him, to look into eyes that were so intense with desire and tenderness that she couldn't speak, couldn't move.

"You should not have come here," he said slowly. "You know that, don't you?"

It was not a plea to go, she knew. Belle licked her lips. "I know," she said, and then, because she couldn't help asking, because she needed the reassurance, she asked, "D'you want me to leave?"

He smiled wryly, a little self-deprecatingly. "I think I promised you something first," he said.

She frowned. "You did?"

He bent and kissed her. A soft kiss, a touch that spun through her, a gentle heat. And when she tried to put her arms around him, to pull him closer, he wouldn't let her. He twined his fingers with hers and kept her hands at her sides, standing far enough away so she felt just the heat of his skin without feeling it, so she felt only the tease of his chest hair against her nipples.

His tongue traced the corners of her mouth, her lips, and Belle's stomach fell, her heart raced as he parted her lips with his tongue; slowly, tenderly dipping inside, touching her tongue with his, exploring her with deep, caressing strokes, consuming her. It was different from any of the kisses he'd given her before, so different that she didn't know what to do, how to kiss him back. But he urged her into it, teased her until she found herself responding to him, until she leaned into him and teased him in return with quick, light touches, caresses that made her feel somehow powerful and seductive, bold and irresistibly wanton.

And then, before she knew it, he was pulling away, kissing her jaw, moving his lips over her throat, touching the sensitive place behind her ear with his tongue. Shivers raced through her, hot and cold, soft and thrilling. She'd never felt like this before, never felt such powerful, overwhelming longing, never felt so cherished. She couldn't think, could only feel as he moved lower, kissed the hollow of her throat and her collarbone, dipped lower still until she felt the heated wetness of his tongue against her breast, teasing first one nipple and then the other, laving and nipping, teasing until Belle felt she would cry out with the pleasure of it. God, she'd never known, never even imagined. She felt his fingers tighten on hers, and then he was kneeling in front of her, his face pressed against her belly, his lips moving on her flesh.

She felt a rush of embarrassment, tried desperately to splay her hands across her stomach. But he wouldn't let her move. "No," she whispered. "Not there. There are . . . marks . . . from the baby."

He didn't move. She felt the soft caress of his sigh.

"Ah, Belle," he murmured against her. "Come to bed with me, sweetheart. Let me love you."

They were words, she told herself. Just words. Meaningless endearments. But they swelled inside her, infinitely sweet. Even if he had not said them, she would have followed him anywhere, but the words made her melt, dissolved any hesitation she still had, took away all regret.

He rose and pulled her with him to the bed, and she followed him willingly, stumbling over the nightgown that still dragged from her hips, tripping until he turned and smiled and eased it to her ankles so that she could step out of it, so that she was completely naked in front of him, with the cold air against her skin, colder on the still-moist places where he'd kissed her with his tongue.

He pulled her around, easing her backward until the bed was against the back of her thighs, gently pushing her until she laid back. She heard the quiet rustle of straw and the creak of ropes beneath his weight as he came down beside her. And then he was leaning over her again, kissing her with that same gentleness, the relentless heat that left her panting and longing, weak and desperate.

She ran her hand over his chest, feeling the soft, wiry curls over heated skin, the flex of muscles. She felt his fingers in her hair, tugging gently, fanning it over her shoulders, touching it with reverent, lingering strokes. His hand moved over her breasts, formed to her waist, her hips. And still he kissed her, kissed her until she was breathless, until her entire body cried out for him, for something, and she moved restlessly against him, unable to keep still, wanting something—something—she didn't know what.

And then he touched her. Touched the hot, wet center of her, slipped his fingers inside her. She stiffened, and he whispered against her lips, "This is what I promised, little girl. Let me. Don't fight it."

She didn't. She felt his hand against her, his fingers stroking her, circling her, touching her, moving until it felt as if every nerve was centered on his hand, on the sensations he created. The pressure grew, throbbing inside her, burning and climbing and growing—Oh, God, growing into a feeling she couldn't name, didn't know. She arched against his hand, twisted beneath his fingers, heard herself murmuring words she didn't understand, words begging for release, for something—

"Don't fight it," he said again, his breath hot against her ear. "Sweet, sweet girl, let go."

She surrendered. Release crashed over her, hard and intense and aching, a shattering bliss that flung her outward and then down, dropping inside her, pulsing through her, falling and falling until she convulsed against his hand. It left her weak and trembling, throbbing even after he took his hand away, even when he looked at her with eyes that left her shaken and bruised.

"There's more," he promised softly, rolling on top of her. She felt his heated weight, felt him nudge her legs apart with his knee, and then he was inside her, one long thrust, filling her, stretching her, hurting her. She cried out, and he silenced the cry with a kiss, was taut and motionless against her. "It's all right, little girl," he murmured against her mouth. "It's all right."

Then he began to move. Slowly, so slowly. Sinking inside her, and easing back, rocking against her hips until she relaxed, until her body accommodated him easily. She heard herself groan—it sounded so far away—and a tremor raced through her, she felt him everywhere, inside her, around her. Felt his hands on her body, and in her hair. It was nothing like that time so long ago, nothing like the hurried fumblings in the cold barn, there was nothing like the pain. She looked up to find him staring at her, his eyes dark and unreadable in the night, and heat enveloped her, a yearning so intense, she wrapped her arms around his shoulders and pulled him closer, wanting him deeper inside her, so deep he couldn't ever escape, so close no one could ever tear them apart. The throbbing began again, deep and sweet, hot and slick, and Belle closed her eyes and arched against him, felt his fingers close around her hips, holding her tightly as he stroked, long, hard thrusts that rocked them both, that brought the pressure building again, building until Belle thought she would go mad with it, until she dug her fingers into his shoulders and gasped his name and knew—*knew*—there would never be anything like this again for her.

And when release burst over her again and she felt him stiffen, heard his hoarse, strangled cry and felt the hot, wet flood inside her, she knew something else, too, something that sent despair crashing through her, sent desperation creeping into her soul.

One night would never be enough.

Chapter 28

She was gone in the morning. He would have thought last night was all a dream, except she'd left behind her fragrance, an elusive scent that clung to his sheets, his skin: soft musk and lavender-scented lye. Just that and a long blond hair that trailed across his pillow, a strand that shone in the morning light.

He wondered when she'd left his bed. He hadn't felt her go, had fallen into a deep, relaxing sleep the likes of which he hadn't had for years. Maybe never. But he wished she'd stayed, wished he was waking up to look into her face, to see her hair, rumpled and tangled from their lovemaking. He wanted to see her smile down at him, wanted to feel her warm fingers against his chest, in his hair. He wanted to bury himself inside her again, to love her with the slow, languid touches of morning.

But he knew it was probably best that she'd gone. It was probably better that no one saw her leave his room in the early morning hours. At least for now. He thought of yesterday, of Lillian's shock over their kiss, and he wondered again what she and Belle had talked about, if they'd discussed him at all, if they'd come to any understanding. He tried to remember supper last night, the change he'd noticed between them, but he couldn't concentrate on it. All he could remember was the touch of

Belle's eyes, the hunger for her that had driven away his appetite and his peace of mind.

That hunger was still there. Last night hadn't appeased it at all, but only honed it to a razor-sharp edge that had him hard and wanting again this morning. He thought of how she'd looked standing at the door, with the white lawn floating around her body. He thought of how her breasts had felt heavier, more rounded, how the curve of her hips had a maturity he'd only dreamed about. And then he thought of the way she'd tried to hide the marks on her skin from him, her uncomfortable embarrassment, and it made him weak, made him want to kiss every scar, to show her how much they meant to him, to make her understand how much he wished he had been with her when she was carrying Sarah.

He wished he had done that last night, but he had been too consumed with desire, too ruled by his need. But the next time he would. The next time he would go more slowly, would calm the beast inside him long enough to show her what she meant to him.

Yes, the next time.

Rand swallowed and sat up, rubbing his face with his hands. He remembered how she'd cried out beneath his hands last night, how her body had arched against his. Remembered how it had felt to be inside her, how she'd pulsed around him, and he remembered how he slammed himself against her, how he hadn't been able to get enough of her, not the taste or the feel of her. He'd driven himself in deeper and deeper, and when his release crashed over him, when he finally surrendered, it was to a sweetness so overwhelming and complete that he was stunned at the intensity of it.

And suddenly Rand knew that he'd loved her with his soul last night—that he'd done more than that. He'd given her his heart.

He wanted her for an eternity.

For six years he'd felt only half alive. He'd thought it was because of the dreams he'd given up, the things he'd put aside to take care of his responsibilities, his obligations.

But he knew now it wasn't that. Now he knew what he had yearned for all those sleepless nights. He'd wanted her. Wanted her smile and her laughter, wanted those days spent in the sun by the canal. He wanted to talk to her, to hear her ridiculous stories and the honest way she spoke, to see her in the morning and know she was his forever.

He'd thought she was his obsession, and maybe she was. Maybe he was destined to turn into his mother, to destroy them both with that darkness he was so afraid of. But after last night he began to believe maybe he wouldn't. Last night the madness had finally fallen away in the touch of her skin, the smell of her. It had disappeared, leaving behind gentleness and care, leaving behind a reverence for every inch of her. And he wondered suddenly if maybe it was only the denial that had blinded him, if maybe he was trying so hard not to want her that he'd forgotten there were no longer any reasons to deny himself. She was no longer fifteen. She was no longer his responsibility.

And this was no longer obsession.

There was no darkness in how he felt for Belle, and no danger. There was only need, and heated desire. He should have seen it long ago, should have recognized it when he saw her walking hand in hand with their daughter that day on the canal. The day he'd realized she was a woman, the mother of his child. The day he told himself all he wanted back was their friendship.

Yes, he wanted to be friends with her again. Friends who laughed and joked together. Friends who talked through the days. Friends who told secrets far into the night, and made tender, passionate love until morning. That was all he'd ever wanted. Not adventure, not faraway places. Just Belle. In his bed and in his heart.

Sweet Christ, he loved her.

It was that he'd been so afraid of.

But now the fear was gone.

The orchard was quiet. The sun had only just broken over the horizon, and the birds were starting to sing, but there was a stillness about the trees, a strange, seductive tranquillity that filled Belle's mind, her heart.

She should leave, she knew. It had been a mistake to go to him last night, a mistake to think she could give him up after one night, that after it she could go back to just being his stepsister, a casual friend. She had not thought it through, and now she wished she had. Wished for once that she wasn't so impulsive, that she had more of Rand's thoughtful steadiness. She would never have gone to him if she'd been more honest with herself.

She loved him, and love didn't go away after a night like that. It only grew stronger.

What a fool she'd been to think anything else.

Belle leaned her head back against the trunk of an apple tree, looking up through the nearly bare branches to the sky. Her body ached, not just because of the way he'd played her last night, but because she wanted him still. Just the thought of the way he touched her made her stomach flip, sent erotic shivers racing through her. It was nothing like six years ago, nothing like anything she could ever have imagined. She still felt the wonder of it, the sensations that crashed over her, the tender seduction of his kiss. She had not known it could be like that, and she wished now she had known, wished she'd had some idea. Oh, God, if she'd known, she never would have gone to him.

Because now she didn't know how she could bear to be without him, how she could be around him without remembering, without wanting. She didn't know how she could watch him marry Marie and know he was taking the pretty schoolteacher to his bed each night, and not hate him for it.

How the hell could she do that?

Leave, a small voice told her, but it was no longer so easy, and she knew it. If it had only been Rand, then maybe she could leave. Maybe she could get on the next train and run fast and far away. But it wasn't just Rand. There was Sarah too, and Belle knew that she couldn't leave Sarah behind. She couldn't wave good-bye to that little girl and go away. Not for a year. Not even for a week. Not ever.

But she couldn't take Sarah either. She'd abandoned that plan the day she'd seen those marks on the door and realized how much Sarah belonged here, how much Rand loved her. This was Sarah's home, this was her family.

And Belle could either be part of that family or leave it behind forever—alone.

There was no choice, and she knew it. She was bound here, as tied to the land and its rhythms as she was to Sarah. New York City had never been home, Cincinnati had never been home. Home was right here, in the gentle sway of the oak trees circling the house, in the cool dark of the canal. She belonged here in Lancaster. Even the gossip that surrounded her was as much a part of the ebb and flow of life as the corn; it linked her forever to the people she'd grown up with.

No, she could not leave.

She did not want to leave.

But she didn't know how to stay either.

Staying meant watching life go on around her; it meant watching things change, watching Rand's family grow up, being an aunt but never a mother. A few days ago she had thought it would be enough. She thought she could bear being a part of their lives without being necessary, to be the spinster aunt, the best friend, the wayward daughter. They were all roles she knew she could play, roles that required nothing but her presence. But after making love with Rand, she knew she wanted to really belong, to be an important part of their lives, to be as necessary as breathing. She could never be that for Rand. His life was planned already, and it included Marie, not Belle. He might want her, but he didn't love her, and she had no choice but to live with that.

Though there would never be anyone else for her. Since the day she and her mother had arrived, and Belle had seen him watching from the porch—a long, lanky eighteen year-old with hazel eyes full of dreams—she had loved him. First with the innocent love of a child, then with the curious infatuation of a girl, and now, finally, with the kind of lasting, soul-deep love that would be with her forever.

Belle sighed, closing her eyes against the rosy haze filling the sky, against the steady ache of tears. She didn't know how to live with that kind of love, but there was no other choice, not really. She would stay because she couldn't go. She would stay and try to make her life as complete as she could, try to take her joy from Sarah and the farm—and hell, even from her mother. All she could do was try.

She had disappeared. No one knew where she was. Not Lillian, not Sarah. Rand was so afraid she'd left for good that he checked her room, rifled through her things until he reassured himself that wherever she'd gone, it wasn't for long. Her coat and hat were still on the peg by the door, and the meager collection of dresses she owned still hung in the wardrobe. But it wasn't until he saw the small pile of coins on her bedstand that he felt relieved enough to go back to the fields and cut corn. She wasn't going anywhere without money, and he suspected that pile was all she had. But even then he watched the road all day, searching every wagon for a sign of her.

He tried to work through his worry, put his body and his mind into cutting corn, but he couldn't ignore the nagging sense that something was wrong, and when Lillian called him in the late afternoon to come get ready for the Alspaughs' husking bee, he dropped the corn knife and went inside eagerly, anxious to see Belle again, determined to talk to her.

She wasn't there. The house was empty except for Lillian, who was busy wrapping a buttermilk pie to take over to the party. She glanced up when he came through the door, watched him quizzically as he raced to the hallway and called upstairs for Belle.

"She's not here," Lillian said. "She and Sarah went over already. They took the baked beans."

The relief that raced through him at her words nearly left him faint. "So she was here, then."

Lillian frowned. "Of course she was here. Where else would she be?"

Where else? Cincinnati or Cleveland or even Columbus. Anyplace else. But he didn't bother to answer. He felt a sudden, desperate need to get dressed and get to a party he'd been dreading until this moment. He started for the stairs.

"Rand?" Lillian called him back. She looked up at

him, her smooth forehead wrinkled with worry. "Rand, is something wrong?"

He shook his head. "Nothing's wrong," he lied.

Her eyes were sharp. "I don't believe you," she said slowly. "Just as I didn't believe Isabelle when she came in today after being gone all morning." Her fingers tightened on the edge of the pie plate. "Please do me the courtesy of telling me what's going on in this house, Randall. Did something happen between the two of you? Did you have a fight?"

He swallowed. "No. There was no fight."

Lillian's gaze seemed to cut through him; he had the strange feeling that she could see what he was thinking, that she could look at him and know he and Belle had spent the night wrapped in each other's arms.

Lillian took a deep breath and looked down, and when he saw the flush moving over her cheeks, he knew he was right. She was aware of everything, there could be no more illusions between them.

"I see," she said slowly. "What about Marie?"

Rand didn't hesitate. "I broke it off with Marie on Sunday," he said. He smiled slightly, self-deprecatingly. "Or rather, she broke it off with me."

Lillian glanced up. "She knew?"

"Yes. She knew." Rand raked his fingers through his hair. He looked away, at an iron pudding mold hanging on the wall. "I don't think I hid it very well."

"No, I don't imagine you did."

He glanced at her. She was staring at him, and he had the feeling that she was waiting for him to say something, waiting for some declaration, or an excuse. Waiting for him to say he was sorry, that he would end it between himself and Belle. The same way she'd watched him six years ago, with that patient waiting, the same look that begged for an explanation.

And this time there was only one.

"I love her," he said. "I don't want to be without her."

He expected Lillian to wince, to try to dissuade him, but she did neither of those things. She looked at him steadily, and her voice was calm and even. "I know," she said quietly. "I suppose I've always known."

He frowned, perplexed. "And you won't—stop it?"

She smiled slightly. "Could I?"

"No."

"Oh, Randall." She sighed. She shook her head slowly, looking down at the pie on the table. "When I first married your father, I so wanted us all to be a family. A real family; brothers and sisters, a wife, a husband. . . . I wanted to believe you and Isabelle were really brother and sister. I wanted everything to be perfect." She touched the edge of the golden piecrust, crimping it between her fingers as if she could somehow change the shape. "But that was absurd, I know. We were all just strangers really." She smiled wistfully. "Not a real family at all."

"I don't know what a real family is, then," he said slowly. "What does it have to be, Lil, if not people who care about each other?"

She didn't look up. "I just can't help thinking sometimes, if I had done something different . . ."

"You couldn't have predicted what happened between Belle and me," he said slowly. "No one could. There was a time when I would have prevented it if I could, but now . . . now I'm glad I didn't."

"All I've ever really wanted is for her to be happy, though she won't believe it." Lillian's voice was soft and low, but he heard the pain in it, and the resignation. "And you of course."

"I know that."

"And this"—she looked up at him—"this will make you both happy?"

He inhaled slowly. "Yes."

She motioned to the doorway, and the smile on her face was small and yielding and a little bit sad. "Then I suppose that's all I can ask. Now, go get dressed. We don't want to be late."

By the time he and Lillian arrived, the Alspaughs' barn was full of people. The huge doors were opened into the yard, and outside there was a bonfire. The smell of smoke and burning leaves floated on the air, blending with the rich scent of baked beans and the sugary sweetness of doughnuts.

The husking was well under way. Stalks of corn were piled on the floor, and the older men were working steadily, with clean, economical movements, bending over the stalk and grabbing an ear, shearing the husk from one side with the flat, pointed husking peg before they yanked away the remaining husk and broke the ear from the stalk.

Rand looked past them, into the barn, his gut clenching anxiously when he didn't see Belle.

He glanced at Dorothy, who was setting Lillian's pie carefully on the long table in the yard. "Have you seen Belle? Or Sarah?"

"They were over there, last I saw." She motioned to the barn. "I know Belle was talking to Lydia's brother."

Charlie Boston. Rand turned away, scanning the yard for Charlie's tall, lanky form. It looked as if the whole town had come to the bee. There was no sign of her. No sign of her, or Sarah, and Rand had the quick, ridiculous thought that she might have taken this chance to leave, that maybe she was back at the house now, packing her bags.

But then he heard the cheering from the barn and saw the older men rise stiffly from their stools, drifting out to the table where their wives waited with full plates and coffee. It was time for the rest of them to take a turn. Rand looked up to see Lydia Boston gesturing to him.

"Rand, come on over!" she called. She came running up to him, a huge smile on her face. She looped her arm through his and pulled him toward the barn. "I thought you'd never show up, and here you live just next door."

"I shouldn't even be here," he explained. "There's our own corn to cut."

"Well, it'll be dark soon, and you can't cut it in the dark," she said. "It's time for some fun now. Come on and sit beside me."

Together they went into the barn. Lydia was chattering beside him, and Rand listened with half an ear, watching the people laughing and talking, scanning the barn for any sign of Belle. He saw Charlie Boston finally, but no Belle. And as Rand took his seat and grabbed his husking peg, he saw Marie across the barn. She glanced up and caught his gaze, and her smile was warm and welcoming, though a little wary too. And he noticed that when her gaze slipped from his to Charlie's, her smile grew even warmer.

Christ, where was Belle?

The others filed in, and Rand's panic grew. Especially when Kenny and the older men brought in another shock and spilled it onto the floor, and everyone dove in, both men and women, grabbing for ears, laughing and joking at who was husking the fastest, the slowest. He heard the jibes with part of his mind, and Rand grabbed a stalk himself and started to work, trying to listen and smile. But he couldn't concentrate. All he could do was wonder where she was.

It nearly drove him crazy; his fears nagged at him until he was ready to throw down the stalk, to leave the damn bee behind to go home and find her, reason with her. He was a half second away from doing it.

Then she walked in.

He had just grabbed an ear, was splitting the husk with the peg when he looked up and saw her. She was standing at the edge of the crowd, and when Charlie Boston called something to her, she smiled and came forward, breaking through the others until she was in plain view. She was wearing the wool challis gown she'd worn the night she gave Sarah a bath, and the colors in it—brown, green, rust—lent color to her skin, complemented the different golds in her hair. She had braided it simply, the way she always did, but when Rand looked at it, he saw instead the way it had been last night, crackling and wild around him, like heavy satin in his hands.

She was so damned beautiful. For a moment he couldn't move, just stood there, poised over the corn, watching her as she went over to Marie and leaned back against the corncrib. Someone threw her a husking peg, and she looped the leather straps over her fingers and laughed at something Marie said, and then she stepped forward to grab a stalk.

And saw him.

Their gazes met. She stiffened, and he saw her brown eyes widen, saw a flash of expression. But then it was gone, and the shutters were over her eyes again, the careful guard against feeling, and Rand knew that he'd been right to be afraid. He grew even more certain when she tore her gaze away and stepped back to Marie without looking at him again. As if she hadn't seen him. As if he didn't exist.

His chest tightened. His plans for a future with her

wavered in front of him, mocking him, a useless dream that had little meaning and less possibility. Last night had obviously meant nothing to her, and he wished he knew what she was thinking, what she expected, whether she intended that they spend the rest of their lives this way, looking at each other from across a room, wanting without speaking, burying the past and the present between them, denying a future.

The thought made him weak; he faltered when he picked up another stalk, rammed the husking peg into his hand. With a curse he dropped the corn, grabbing his fingers.

"What's wrong, Rand?" Lydia asked solicitously. "Did you hurt yourself? Can I help?" She leaned forward, reaching for him.

He shook his head, stepped away at the same moment he heard the raucous shouts around him.

"There it is!"

"Who's it gonna be?"

"Rand, you'd better take the forfeit now, 'fore someone beats you to it!"

He heard his name and glanced up. Marie had stepped forward, and she was laughing and blushing, holding a partly husked ear of corn in her hands.

A red ear.

She looked at him, their eyes met. For just a second, maybe two, and he saw in her eyes what they both knew —that everyone here expected him to kiss her, and that he wouldn't. He was not going to take the forfeit, and in the same split second he thought it, he glanced at Belle, and the look in her eyes sent his heart plummeting to his feet.

That desperate vulnerability was there again, along with a pain he didn't understand, and with a shock he suddenly realized that he had never told her he was no longer seeing Marie. Her words from the night of Paula's party came rushing back, along with his answer. *"She's the one you're goin' to marry?" "Yes."*

His heart fell. He knew she had seen him look to Marie just now, and she had misinterpreted it, thought he was going to kiss Marie, to declare himself. *Sweet Christ.*

Just as he thought it, Belle turned away, and Rand watched in stunned dismay as she pushed through the others and disappeared.

She was running away.

Sweet Jesus, running away.

He heard the others shout, saw Charlie Boston swoop toward a blushing Marie.

Rand dropped his peg and plunged into the crowd.

Chapter 29

She ran as fast as she could, pushing through the people, grabbing her skirt when she cleared them and tearing across the fields separating their farm from the Alspaughs'. She wanted to get lost, to disappear, to go someplace where no one could find her, where no one could look at her and see the pain she couldn't hide any longer.

She had not expected it to hurt this bad, not really. It had hurt before, when she first saw Rand with Marie, but not like this, not like this awful, blinding ache that made her feel as if she were falling apart inside, as if her heart and soul were shattering into a thousand pieces. Her heart had stopped beating when Marie got the red ear, it had simply frozen in her chest, and Belle hadn't been able to breathe, had felt faint and sick when she saw Rand glance up, saw his eyes meet Marie's.

Belle had known then that she would never survive this. She would never survive a future of watching that, of knowing he was going to kiss Marie and feeling such overwhelming, debilitating pain. Oh, God, she couldn't do it, couldn't—

"Belle!"

She heard the voice behind her and faltered. It sounded like Rand. It couldn't be Rand. He was in the barn, kissing Marie.

"Damn it, Belle, stop!" It was Rand. She heard his footsteps behind her, pounding the ground. "Belle!"

Belle didn't stop. She ran faster. The house was in front of her, and she raced up the back stairs, through the door. She didn't want him to see her like this, with tears streaming down her face and her courage in tatters. She did not want his pity, or his kind words. God, she couldn't bear it.

"Christ, Belle!"

She heard the door crash behind him, and then, suddenly, he was so close, she heard his breathing. She would never make the stairs before he caught her. The thought slowed her, had her stumbling to a stop just at the base of the stairs. She swiped a hand across her eyes and turned to confront him.

He nearly fell into her, but he didn't. He stopped inches away from her, and his eyes were burning, but whether it was with anger or pain she couldn't tell, didn't want to know.

"Belle." His hands flexed at his sides; she saw him struggle to catch his breath. "Jesus, what the hell are you doing?"

She lifted her chin and swallowed. "Nothin'," she said as steadily as she could. She motioned limply to the stairs. "I—I just thought I'd . . . go to bed, is all. I'm —all right. You go on back. I'm sure . . . Marie's waitin' for you."

He shook his head. "She's not waiting for me," he said slowly. "She's kissing Charlie Boston."

Belle frowned in confusion. His words made no sense, she didn't believe them. "Kissin' Charlie? I—I don't understand. I thought—"

"Marie and I ended things Sunday." He grabbed the banister, blocking her from moving, his fingers tightening as if he thought she would run and was bracing for it. His gaze seared through her. "When I realized I was still in love with you."

Belle winced. The words mocked her, taunted her, and she tried to step back, but the railing stopped her, kept her only inches from him. She laughed nervously, trying to still the disbelief and pain racing through her, knowing he was mocking her. "You—you . . . love . . . me." She looked away. "Yeah. And I s'pose you want to get married and live happ'ly ever after."

"Yes."

She looked at him, feeling the tears well in her eyes and not caring. "You don't have to do this, Rand. I mean, I know you feel some . . . some sense of duty . . . after last night." She swallowed, tried to force out the words sticking in her throat. "But I never meant for it to be anythin' but just . . . one time. That's all. Just once."

He stepped toward her. "What if I want it to be more?"

She stared at him in confusion. "It—it can't be."

"Why not?"

"I—I don't . . . believe you. Before, you—"

"Before," he repeated quietly. He reached out and took her hand, wrapping his warm fingers around her cold ones, pulling her against his body, whispering against her hair. "Ah, little girl, I was such a fool before. I was so afraid. You were so young, and I was so afraid of how much I loved you. I didn't want to hurt you. Christ, I didn't want to hurt you, and instead I ended up hurting you too much." He licked his lips, took a deep breath. "And if I have to, I'll spend the rest of my life apologizing for it. If you'll let me. Please. Please say you'll let me."

His hand tightened on hers, but he didn't pull her

closer, and she knew he wouldn't. Knew she could say, "No, I don't forgive you," and he would walk away. Knew she could say, "I don't love you," and he would never touch her again. And for a split second she wanted to say those things, wanted to end whatever it was between them, to completely destroy it the way it hadn't been destroyed six years ago. There was too much pain between them, too much anger, too much . . . joy.

Too much joy.

Belle closed her eyes. The emotion shuddered through her, and suddenly she realized that she didn't have the power to destroy what was between them. Nothing did. She could walk away, she could pretend to hate him, but the truth was that she never would. The truth was that Rand was part of her soul, part of her heart, and she could not turn away from him without losing a piece of herself.

And she had already spent too much time incomplete.

She looked up into his face, laid her hand against his jaw. "There's nothin' to be sorry for," she whispered. "I've never stopped loving you."

He closed his eyes. She felt the relief coursing through him, and it matched hers, a relief so profound, it made her smile, made her laugh—nervously, breathlessly. She dropped her hand, tried to pull away, but he held her tight, and then he opened his eyes and looked down at her, and the desire in his gaze slammed through her, made her weak and shaky.

"Show me," he demanded in a whisper. "Kiss me, Belle, and make it last forever. Because I will never, ever let you go again."

His words sent shivers through her, sent the blood pounding in her veins. Belle felt his hands on hers, the gentle strength of him, and she stood on her toes and lifted her face, brushing his lips with hers slowly, gently, the way he'd taught her last night, hungrily pressing against him, wanting the sweet solace of loving him.

He gave it to her. Released her hands and brought her to him so that she was hard against his body, so that she felt his heated arousal. Undid her hair and spread it over her shoulders, twined it in his fingers. He pulled her head back and she let him, parting her lips willingly beneath his onslaught, surrendering to him the way she had always surrendered to him, body and soul, heart and mind. He tasted of doughnuts and apple cider, and though she knew he had tasted of this once before, the memory was gone, that cold autumn night chased from her mind by this kiss and the ones before, by the deep, intimate strokes of his tongue. She was drowning in him, splintering inside, and when he pulled away and took her hand, taking her with him up the stairs, down the hall to his room, she didn't protest. Not when he closed the door behind them and led her to the bed, not when he pressed her into the mattress.

"Christ, I love you," he whispered against her mouth, and then again at her throat, at every place his kiss touched as he unbuttoned her dress and slid it away, as he peeled her chemise from her shoulders to reveal her breasts. "I love you," at the valley between her breasts; "I love you," at her nipples, her navel. A soft row of kisses and sweet words, lulling her, caressing her, making her forget there had ever been anything but this between them, this sweet, forgiving fire, this fierce yearning.

She felt him ease her dress, her pantalettes over her hips, heard his quiet laugh as he undid her boots and pulled them off, and she couldn't move, couldn't speak, was helpless as the cold air swept over her skin. And then she felt his kiss again, on her stomach, and instinctively she reached down to cover herself, to hide the marks that made her feel ugly.

But he grabbed her hands, moved them away, and she felt him trace the faint scars with his mouth, his tongue, heard his words against her skin. "You are so beautiful, little girl. You are so beautiful." Over and over again, until she began to believe them, until she did believe them. She believed him when he dipped lower still, parted her legs to nuzzle the curls between her thighs; she believed him when his hands tightened on hers, squeezing her fingers reassuringly just before she felt his deep, intimate kiss at the very heart of her.

And then, oh God, she had no choice but to believe him as he dipped his tongue inside her. She jerked, made a silent sound of protest, but his hands only tightened on hers, and he didn't stop, just kept stroking and circling, caressing her with his tongue until her breathing came fast and uneven, until she trembled against his mouth. He stroked deeply and slowly, and the sensations raced through her, along with that pressure again, the relentless press she remembered from last night, the helpless, feverish spiral of feeling, and she pressed against his mouth, wanting him deeper still, needing him at the very center of her. She gripped his hands, digging her nails into his fingers, losing control of her body and her mind as he pleasured her.

And then, when release finally came, when it broke over her in panting, relentless waves, she pulled him to her, gasping as he entered her in one deep thrust, raising her hips to meet his and twining her fingers in his hair. She felt the rock of his body against hers, the fullness of him inside her, and she thought, *This is how it feels to love him. This is how it feels . . .* just before all thoughts left her mind, leaving her with nothing but the touch and the heat and the taste of him, nothing but the mindless, ceaseless ache of pleasure as he sank into her over and over again, taking them both to an almost painful crest of need and surcease, to a climax where the words "I love you, I love you," swirled about them in the air, and she was never sure afterward who said them as she clutched him, feeling the hot, wet throbbing of him inside her even as she twisted beneath him in her own shattering, blinding surrender.

For a moment they didn't move. The heaviness of his body on hers filled her with contentment, with a repleteness that made her sigh when she felt his mouth move against her throat, his gentle kiss. She wanted this to go on forever, this dim, quiet world where there was nothing but the two of them, nothing but the shivering air around them and the musky-soft scent of their bodies. She wanted to touch him, and smile at him, and let his caresses make her feel warm and cherished. She wanted this forever. It was amazing to her that she had it, that he'd promised it to her.

He moved against her, eased off her in spite of her wordless protest. He took her hand and laid it gently on her stomach, raising to one elbow beside her so that he was looking down into her face, cradling her body against his.

"Did I hurt you?" he asked slowly, quietly.

"No." She shook her head. "No."

His hand fell to her hair, his fingers stroked through it, a lulling, mesmerizing touch, a soothing rhythm. In the dim light of evening his eyes were strangely hesitant, his expression uncertain.

He sighed. It was loud in the quiet, a sound full of relief and longing, and Belle smiled and touched his face, ran her hand over his jaw, hard and rough with stubble. He cupped her hand in his, held it to his lips, kissed her palm—a wet, open-mouthed kiss that sent shivers through her.

"After you left," he said slowly, whispering against her hand, "when I found out you were pregnant, I searched all over for you. I told myself it was because you'd lied to me. Because you ran off without telling me about the baby. I told myself that once I found you, I would take the child and let you walk out of my life, forget you." He paused, curling her fingers into his palm, kissing her knuckles with a gentle, spidery touch. "But I couldn't forget. You were in . . . everything. Everything I looked at reminded me of you."

His words pounded against her heart. "I know just what you mean."

He continued as if she hadn't spoken. "And the other day I was . . . looking at you. With Sarah. And I wondered—I wondered"—he took a deep breath, as if the words were hard to say—"how it felt to have my baby inside you. If you thought about me at all."

His admission curled inside her, a heavy, warm weight, a contentment that spilled through her heart, into her soul.

"I was . . . scared," she said honestly. "There were times I couldn't sleep because I was so afraid. I would lie there in the dark and wish for things to be different. I wished I wasn't pregnant, I wished I was home. I wished nothin' had changed."

He closed his eyes, and she felt his pain hovering between them in the early-evening light.

"But then," she went on slowly, "then one night I felt her movin' inside me, this—this flutterin' feelin', and I got out of bed and went runnin' to find you, to tell you. But then—then I remembered you weren't there." She uncurled her fingers, laid her hand against his face until his eyes opened, until his gaze was locked with hers.

"And after that I only wished you were with me," she whispered. "I never stopped wantin' you there."

"I love you, little girl," he said, and his voice was hoarse and raw. "Christ, I love you."

She smiled up at him. "Then stop callin' me little girl," she said, curling her arms around his neck. "And kiss me."

The morning sun shone brightly through the curtains when Rand opened his eyes. He blinked sleepily, groggily, and it took him just a moment to remember last night, to remember that she was here beside him, that he would wake up to her face every day for the rest of his life, make love to her every night. He rolled over, thinking to kiss her awake, to make love to her once more before he went out to the fields.

She was gone.

He laid there in shocked disbelief, wondering where she was, when she'd left, trying to remember if she'd said something last night, if maybe he'd misunderstood her, if perhaps she hadn't said she loved him after all. Maybe it was all a dream—the thought brought the dark desperation rolling over him again, filling him.

And then he heard the noise on the stairs.

It stunned him into stillness. He heard the hasty rush of footsteps, a loud "shhh!" the clack of something against the walls. She was leaving. Oh, Christ, she was leaving. He grabbed at the blankets, started to push out of bed—

The bedroom door opened.

"He's awake already!" Sarah's voice was high, squeaky with disappointment. "Oh, Papa, we was goin' to surprise you."

He twisted to look at the door. It was cracked open,

and Sarah was peering in, a frown on her round face. "You was s'posed to be sleepin!"

"I *was* sleeping, Little Bit," he said. The door opened all the way, and Sarah came bouncing in. He saw Belle behind her. She leaned against the doorjamb, a smile on her face and in her eyes, and as Sarah jumped on his bed and threw her arms around his neck, he felt such profound relief, it nearly made him weak. Belle hadn't gone. She hadn't gone. He wondered when he would start to believe she was going to stay.

" 'Mornin'," she said. She reached around the door and came inside, three fishing poles clasped in her hand. Her smile widened. "I thought maybe we'd go fishin' today."

"Fishing?" He looked at her over Sarah's head. "But the corn—"

She raised her eyebrows, and her grin was wide and infectious; it lit her entire face. "Thing's are goin' to have to change if I'm goin' to marry you, Rand Sault," she said. She walked to the edge of the bed and leaned over it, teasing him. "I expect to go fishin' at least once a week. I won't have Sarah growin' up without knowin' the finer points of catchin' a fat old bass."

"Oh, really?" He grinned back at her. "And just how do you expect to live if I can't do some farming once in a while?"

"Well, I don't know," she said. She leaned forward, brushing her lips against his. "I guess we'll just have to live on love."

"She kissed you!" Sarah squealed in surprise. "Does that mean Belle's goin' to be my mama?"

Rand laughed. He pulled Sarah to him with one arm and grabbed Belle's wrist with the other, sending the fishing poles clattering to the floor, suddenly realizing that he would never completely be sure of Belle, and that he wanted it that way. He wanted her vibrance, her impulsiveness. Wanted the unexpected twists she put into his life, the way nothing was ever dull around her. With Belle he never knew what to expect—except that things would never be the same. Thank God, they would never be the same.

"I guess that's what it means," he said, grinning. He gave Sarah a quick squeeze before he let her go. "Now, come on, Little Bit, and let's go fishin'—with your mama." He looked up into Belle's eyes.

His whole life brightened in the light of her smile.